KU-326-500

DEVIL IN THE DETAIL

A.J. Cross

PROPERTY OF MERTHYR
TYDFIL PUBLIC LIBRARIES

SEVERN
HOUSE

First world edition published in Great Britain and the USA in 2021
by Severn House, an imprint of Canongate Books Ltd,
14 High Street, Edinburgh EH1 1TE.

Trade paperback edition first published in Great Britain and the USA in 2021
by Severn House, an imprint of Canongate Books Ltd.

severnhouse.com

Copyright © A.J. Cross, 2021

All rights reserved including the right of
reproduction in whole or in part in any form.
The right of A.J. Cross to be identified
as the author of this work has been asserted
in accordance with the Copyright,
Designs & Patents Act 1988.

British Library Cataloguing-in-Publication Data
A CIP catalogue record for this title is available from the British Library.

ISBN-13: 978-0-7278-9037-5 (cased)
ISBN-13: 978-1-78029-768-2 (trade paper)
ISBN-13: 978-1-4483-0506-3 (e-book)

This is a work of fiction. Names, characters, places and incidents are either the
product of the author's imagination or are used fictitiously. Except where actual
historical events and characters are being described for the storyline of this novel,
all situations in this publication are fictitious and any resemblance to actual
persons, living or dead, business establishments, events or locales is purely
coincidental.

Typeset by Palimpsest Book Production Ltd.,
Falkirk, Stirlingshire, Scotland.

MERTHYR TYDFIL LIBRARIES	
0474814 X	
Askews & Holts	09-Nov-2021
	£12.99

ONE

Friday 30 November. 4.30 p.m.

L ugging her stuffed briefcase, the blonde woman emerged from her office building and headed across the darkened car park, head lowered against misting rain. Raising her key fob, she hurried across pooled tarmac to the grey Mercedes. Recalling that the boot was filled with boxes of books her mother had asked her to drop off at a charity shop, she diverted to the passenger door, opened it, dumped the heavy briefcase on the seat and paused, unsure now whether to go back inside to check her desk. Norm, her boss, was still there. If he saw her, he would probably give her something else to do. Or, worse, invite her for an after-work drink. She went quickly around the car, got inside. Wiping rain from her face with gloved hands, she backed out of her space and headed across the half-empty car park to the exit.

A sudden gap in traffic along the dual carriageway towards her, a flash of headlights, a quick handwave and she joined the steady flow of vehicles heading for the traffic island, where she became part of the downward surge past the mosque on the right. Continuing steadily on to the large intersection some way ahead, she saw the lights change to red, slowed and came to a stop. Tired, irritated by the incessant *whup-whup* of the windscreen wipers, she flicked them off and glanced at the bulging designer briefcase on the passenger seat. If she didn't have all she needed, next week was shaping up to be a total dis—

The passenger window exploded. Glass fragments, rain and wind struck her face, her hair. Two gloved hands appeared. One grasped the briefcase, the other holding something black, metallic. On autopilot, she reached for the briefcase, recoiled at an agonizing blow to her left hand. Someone was shouting at her through the window. The lights changed to green. A car hooted somewhere behind her. Those in front were already crossing the interchange. Getting into gear on the second attempt and releasing the handbrake, she drove, wind and rain hitting her face and a sensation of something oozing inside her glove each time she moved the steering wheel.

Reaching her house, she got out of the car, walked to her front door, unlocked it, went inside and stood. The silence was deafening. Letting her coat fall from her shoulders, she brushed rain from her face with her gloved hands, picked up the house phone, stared at the numbers on the keypad and looked up at her reflection in the mirror, a swathe of something dark across her face. The three numbers came to her. Feeling more oozing as she removed the glove from her right hand, she tapped the numbers. Her call was picked up.

'I-I want to report an-an attack. On my car. I'm bleeding.'

TWO

Monday 3 December. 6.30 p.m.

Detective Inspector Bernard Watts had on his listening face. Behind it, he was wondering why it was that every time he was inside this office, the tone of the man behind the desk conveyed that he, Watts, was personally responsible for whatever crime or misdemeanour was under discussion. He flexed his shoulders, shifted on his chair. He hadn't yet spoken so it was hardly a discussion. Brophy, elevated to superintendent, now a fixture at headquarters, was staring at him.

'Six attacks on stationary cars. *All* in November. *All* in the same area and *zero* investigative progress on any of them.'

Brophy's lips compressed. His eyes fixed on Watts' face. 'I know what you're thinking.'

Watts started a slow count. Brophy's mind-reading tendencies made him more wearing than usual.

'You're thinking I should be saying this to officers local to that inner-city area.' He reached for several very slim files. 'Think again. As of ten minutes ago, all six are ours, specifically *yours*, and the chief constable wants a quick resolution.' He jabbed the files. 'This kind of street crime flourishes in Birmingham and I can tell you why. This city has a big problem.'

As far as Watts was concerned, Birmingham didn't any more than any other big city, but Brophy was now on a roll. 'I'll tell you exactly what that problem is: years of urban planning, which has made it the city of the car. How did they do it? Buildings pulled down. A snake's nest of new roads laid. Pedestrians pushed underground. All of it intended to accommodate massive volumes of traffic entering and leaving the city.' Brophy took a breath. 'Which these days is mostly at a standstill, creating exactly the conditions for this type of crime, and don't get me started on Spaghetti Junction. An *abomination* is what that is.'

Brophy wasn't entirely wrong. Back in the sixties and seventies the car was king here. Knowing that Brophy wasn't about to come up with a solution to the problem he'd just outlined, a picture formed in Watts' head: Brophy, red-faced, vest-clad, single-handedly digging up a major dual carriageway, planting bulbs . . .

'You appear to be taking this very casually, but I can tell you, the chief constable isn't and neither am I.'

'No, sir.'

Brophy gave the files a push. 'These are your starting point. They follow a pattern.'

'They usually do and this type of carjacking is the least violent. More your grab-it-and-run style.'

'Really? Well, there's something I don't regard as "usual". The latest victim in this series says she saw a gun.' That single detail got Watts' full attention. 'Each vehicle attacked while stationary at traffic lights, passenger windows smashed, belongings pulled through and away. Targets all lone females, except for one.'

'That's how carjackers generally work within high-volume traffic,' said Watts. Except that in his experience a gun had never featured in this type of offence.

Brophy sent him a sharp look. 'I don't hold with that kind of laissez-faire attitude. I want quick progress.'

Watts averted his gaze from Brophy's index finger jabbing the files yet again.

'Have Jones and Kumar work the investigation with you.'

Watts was on his feet. 'I'll get started. What about Judd?'

'What about her? She's still on her training course at Tally Ho. Back on Wednesday.'

'Judd's familiar with inner-city car crime which could make her an asset.'

'I'll think about it.'

'She did a good job on the murder inquiry last summer,' prompted Watts.

Brophy glared across at him. 'What I remember is her breaking rules, going off on her own and getting herself knocked unconscious.' He pointed again. 'If I do assign her, you'll need to get a grip where she's concerned. Keep her in place.'

'Will do, sir.' He reached for the files.

Outside the office, following some deep breathing, he headed to the squad room and went inside. With a glance at the clock, he asked the two officers still there, 'What time are you off duty?'

Jones and Kumar exchanged glances. Jones answered. 'Ten minutes ago, Sarge.'

'Best get started, then.'

They came to the table, took seats, their eyes on the files Watts had placed there. 'You've heard about the spate of carjackings around the Bristol Road interchange?'

They nodded.

'Good, because they've been taken off the local lads, dropped in Brophy's lap and he wants them sorted, as of yesterday. Six in all, starting in early November, the last one on Friday, the thirtieth. All occurred in fading light in the late afternoon. If either of you can tell me why people have valuables in full view inside their vehicles while driving, I'd be interested to hear it.'

'Could have been worse, Sarge.' Kumar looked from him to Jones. 'Remember that one in the Lifford area? They weren't bothered about nicking stuff from inside the car. They were after the Beemer and beat the paste out of the driver to get it. Left him sprawled on the road outside his house and drove off in it.'

Watts opened the files, slid them across. 'These are more your inner-city "smash-n-grab" type.' He looked up at them. 'Except for one detail. The last witness says her attacker had a gun.'

'Blimey,' said Jones. 'From what you'd said, I was thinking that some low-life chancer was hanging around with a rock in his pocket, waiting for the traffic to slow, and took his chances.' With a glance at the two smooth young faces, Watts stood and hooked a finger. They followed him to a large wall map next to the whiteboard.

'Location says this was no chancer. See this?' He pointed. 'The Bristol Road interchange.' He ran his thick index finger upwards. 'It's fed by traffic going up this dual carriageway here, where a lot of it turns right.' He looked at both of them. 'And what's at the top of that carriageway?'

'A massive island,' said Kumar.

'Exactly. This wasn't any low life just "hanging around". He had a confederate there, watching the traffic as it moved around that island and heading down that dual carriageway to the lights.'

Jones eyed the map, then Watts. 'And the confederate is on his phone to his mate, telling him that nice wheels are on their way, woman driver, belongings on seat. Smooth.'

Watts was back at the table, reading a printed overview of the cases. 'Items stolen: handbags, laptops, a briefcase and the toolkit from a single male driver. Either of you care to bet he had long hair?' He opened the topmost file. 'The victim of the Friday the thirtieth incident described her attacker as young and athletic.' They stood either side of him, reading.

Kumar shook his head. 'If it's the same attacker for all six, he's a right cheeky bastard. That's not a bad description: tall, dark clothing, a hoodie and a padded jacket.'

Watts shrugged. 'Everybody looks tall if you're sitting in your car, shocked out of your bloody wits, covered in glass, watching your property disappear, and that description could fit any number of young inner-city types. He got phones, cash, credit cards and God knows what else from the handbags and the briefcase.' He pulled the files together. 'All six drivers felt safe, secure inside their vehicles. Now, they know different.' They watched as he headed for the door.

'Judd will be part of the investigation.'

'When's she back, Sarge?'

Watts glanced back at Jones. 'That a professional or a personal inquiry?'

He shrugged, grinned. 'A bit of both?'

'Wednesday. We start these cases tomorrow, nine a.m.'

10.50 p.m.

Alone in his office in a small pool of light, Watts was absorbing the details from the six files. It needed doing and there was nothing and nobody to get home to, except the cat. He made quick, neat notes, seeing the varying gaps between the attacks. The desk phone rang. He reached for it.

'DI Watts.'

'Message from emergency services, Sarge. Call received by them at ten thirty-five p.m. An attack on a vehicle in the inner-city area. Two occupants. One of them phoned it in – name, Molly Lawrence. She couldn't identify their location but they traced it via her mobile phone. Paramedics are on their way.'

Watts' head came up. 'Paramedics?'

'Repeating what I've been told. Can you respond?'

Watts wrote down the details. 'On my way.'

He got out his phone, sent a text, then followed it with a call. 'Jones, pick up Kumar and get yourself to the location I've sent you. It sounds like it might be another carjacking. I'll see you both there. *Move* it.'

THREE

Watts' phone rang as he left headquarters en route to his vehicle. It was Brophy, music in the background. He sounded stressed. Watts held the phone away from his ear. 'Yes, I heard. I'm on my way there now.'

Ending the call, he got into the BMW X3 SAV and gunned it out of the car park. Reaching Five Ways, he joined a queue of vehicles waiting as others surged towards it without let-up. Activating the blue light, he moved between slowed vehicles and around the island, then checked the dash clock. He was making good time, given the volume of traffic. He followed the on-screen route into the inner city, looking for an alternative route. Within minutes, vehicles immediately ahead of him slowed to a crawl. Way ahead, he saw more tail lights flaring. Road works. Single-file traffic. He swore. Within a minute he was barely moving, hemmed in by continuous cones. He killed the blue light. There was nowhere for anybody to go.

He inched along for a while, stationary traffic ahead as far as he could see. Then it started to move. He picked up speed as the road widened. Without warning, it narrowed again, then almost immediately split into two. He frowned, peering through the rain now hitting the windscreen, seeing vehicles quickly diverge left and right.

Getting no help from the satnav, he made an instant decision to pull to the left. The satnav demanded an immediate right turn. He swore again. 'You're more lost than I am!' Flashing lights in his rear-view mirror were followed by a quick blast of siren.

'You are joking.'

Another blast of siren. Watts inched forward, vehicles ahead pulling over as the road widened. As soon as he could, he did the same. The ambulance screamed past, its rear lights glowing as it slowed at another diversion sign ahead.

After several more minutes, which felt like forever, Watts took a sudden left exit and found himself in a dark, deserted and increasingly rundown area. A native of the city for all of his fifty-one years, he recognized nothing he was seeing. The road he was following led him into another, his headlights sliding over holes in tarmac, chunks of broken brick. Ahead of him the ambulance was now parked, its lights flashing over weeds. Forge Street, according to the broken street sign he'd just passed. A relic of old Birmingham's industry. Civic pride wasn't stopping him from seeing the area for what it was. Old. Neglected. Hopeless.

He pulled over and got out into buffeting wind and rain, his eyes narrowing on a car parked a few metres away. A dark-coloured saloon. One rear passenger door open. Two paramedics, each lugging hefty packs, were rushing towards it. He sped to them, got only swift nods at his ID. Whoever was inside that car was the priority.

Frustrated, he looked around at further urban desolation, ambulance lights illuminating oily water inside potholes, an abandoned petrol station beyond and several commercial buildings on the other side. All empty at this time of night. Probably empty, full stop, if the smashed windows were anything to go by. A sign on one wall read: *To Let. Prime light industrial property.* Some joker had inserted an 'i' between 'To' and 'Let'. He looked back to the scene. Both front doors of the saloon were now open, the paramedics leaning inside.

Seeing the squad car approaching at speed, he headed for it. Jones and Kumar got out. Both sound lads if you didn't let Jones get started on his favourite topics, one being the infiltration of the force by Freemasons. He was still getting to know Kumar. They were coming towards him.

'What we got, Sarge?' asked Jones.

'I haven't had a chance to establish any detail.' He pointed to one of the paramedics emerging from inside the car and started towards him. 'He might tell us.'

Watts halted a small distance away. Holding up his ID, head lowered, he peered inside the car. Male figure in driving seat. Upright. Unmoving. Eyes closed. Watts moved quickly to the car's passenger side. A female. Slumped to one side. Head towards the passenger door. Dark hair lying across face. He straightened, his eyes lingering on them. Both very still. Too still.

He looked at the two young officers. 'Gloves and shoe-covers, now. Keep out of the paramedics' way. Be ready to secure the scene as soon as they leave.' With a brief nod towards the petrol station, he added, 'When you do, make it a big area, including that forecourt over there. SOCOs and forensics are on their way.' The two officers headed back to the squad car.

Watts took a second look inside the car. One of the paramedics was shining a small, intense light on to the female's face. Watts' eyes drifted over it. She looked bad. He started at the paramedic's sudden, insistent voice.

'*Hello?* Molly Lawrence? *Molly*, can you speak? Can you move your hand?'

No response.

On the driver's side of the car, his colleague straightened. 'This one has to come out. He needs to go. *Now.*'

Watts looked from one to the other. 'Give me the general picture.'

'Not yet established but the driver looks like he's sustained a serious head injury. We could use some help here.'

Watts raised his hand to Jones and Kumar who came at full speed and helped to bring stretchers from the ambulance to the car. The unconscious male was carefully lifted on to one and moved quickly to the ambulance. In the light pooling from the ambulance's head-lamps, Watts was staring at the vacated driver's seat, the leather slick and wet, more wetness pooled on the seat. His attention moved to the female being brought out of the car. He looked down at her. Her hair fell away from her face as she was laid on a stretcher, her skin pallid, clammy looking. He looked at her hands, coated with thick, congealing matter. A blanket appeared and was placed around her. He watched as she was taken to the ambulance. Its doors secured, it moved away, lights flashing. He pulled out his phone, rang headquarters.

'I'm at Forge Street. Can you confirm that forensics are on their

way?' He glanced at his two officers. 'Yeah, we'll secure it till then.'
He cut the call. 'They'll be a few more minutes getting here.'

'What do you think, Sarge?' asked Jones.

'Possibly a carjacking which turned really bad, unless we learn otherwise.' He headed for his vehicle, got inside, rang the emergency services and asked to be put through to the ambulance call-takers.

'This is DI Watts, headquarters, Rose Road. I'm at an incident I responded to forty-five minutes ago at Forge Street in the inner city. One of the victims, a female, made an emergency call.' He picked up the rapid click-clack of computer keys followed by the call-taker's voice as she read details from a screen. Watts nodded. 'That's the one. The two victims are now on their way to hospital. Tell me about her call.'

'According to what I'm reading, she was in a really bad situation. Unable to give specific details as to her exact location, which was identified via her mobile service provider, along with her name: Molly Lawrence.'

'You've got a recording of the conversation.'

'As always.'

'Send it to me at headquarters as a matter of urgency. Mark it for DI Watts' attention. Thanks.'

Tuesday 4 December. 2.45 a.m.

The crime scene and surrounding area was flooded with intense white light which was doing nothing to improve the look of it. Watts headed to two SOCOs suiting up beside their van. 'What do you know about what's occurred here?'

'Only that there was an emergency call from one of two victims,' said one. 'We'll do a scene walk-through. Adam's on his way. He should be here soon, roadworks permitting. What can you tell us?'

'As you said, two victims, one male, one female. The woman's name is Molly Lawrence. She made the ambulance call.' He pointed at the Toyota now encircled by bobbing blue-white tape, more tape demarcating an extended area. 'Both attacked inside that vehicle. Both unconscious. Significant blood loss. Paramedics referred to a serious head injury to the male.'

Watts watched as they headed for the tape carrying lights, went under it, under more tape and on to the immediate area around the Toyota, closely followed by two more officers. One raised a still camera which began emitting whines and clicks, the other slowly, methodically videoing the ground around the car. After a couple of minutes, she stopped, raised her arm, then finger-pointed downwards to an area below and slightly beneath the car. Pulling on shoe covers, Watts headed for the white-lit area of ground and watched the forensic officer's gloved hand reach for something, her colleague producing a plastic evidence bag. She held up the item and placed it carefully inside. Watts looked at it through the plastic. A watch.

A forensic officer came towards Watts, pulling on a white scene suit. He pointed to the car. 'I want a closer look.' Another joined him, a small, high-spec video camera in one hand, in the other a high-intensity UV light source, protective goggles pushed high on his forehead. He looked inside the car. 'There's massive blood loss in here. I'll start by recording its location. With a bit of luck, there might be some which later proves not to belong to either victim.'

Watts pointed into the interior. 'The male was the driver.'

The officer lowered his goggles and activated the light source inside the car. It threw blue on to every surface, tracked by the video camera. Watts watched as it moved over the driver's seat, seeing again what was pooled there, this time in sharp relief, and whispered, 'Jesus, Mary, mother of . . .'

He walked around the car to a SOCO placing a yellow marker next to a patch of ground below the front passenger door. 'Got something?'

Following a finger-point, Watts crouched and looked at sparkles on the ground. Glass. In the dark and rush he hadn't noticed that one of the car's windows was shattered. He directed his question to the SOCO.

'Broken from outside?'

'Hard to say, given how auto-glass reacts to breakage. I'm taking a sample.' The fine tweezers in his hand released a glass fragment into a clear plastic tube. It was followed by two more. 'If we get a suspect within the next few hours, we'll compare these with any still caught in his hair or clothing.'

'Stick with the optimism,' murmured Watts.

He straightened, then turned to Jones and Kumar approaching. 'There's a lot of blood, plus broken glass from the front passenger window.'

They went to the car and peered inside it. 'This has to be a carjacking gone mega-bad,' said Jones.

'That's my thinking, until something says it isn't.'

Watts' eyes tracked the movements of SOCOs taking multiple pictures of the interior and exterior of the car, recalling Brophy's rattled tone as he himself left headquarters. Now, he had something to be rattled about.

Getting a hand-raise from one of the SOCOs, he looked to where she was pointing.

'See that?'

Watts lowered his head, following the finger-point to the driver's pale sun visor, a round, powder-edged hole in it, the surrounding area splashed red.

'Bullet hole,' said the SOCO.

Watts stared at it. He hadn't needed telling. She beckoned again. He followed her to the left-hand rear passenger door, looked inside and down to the carpeted floor, to where she pointed again at a small, shiny, metal object. Watts straightened, signalling to Jones and Kumar. They sped to him.

'A bullet casing,' she said, moving her finger upwards. 'Looks like it was fired from the rear of the vehicle towards the driver, possibly missed him and struck the sun visor.'

Applying a fluorescent marker pen to the carpet, she created a bright yellow circle around the casing. A forensic officer arrived to photograph it in situ as she moved to the visor, examined the hole. 'We'll leave the bullet where it is until the vehicle is back at headquarters.'

Watts turned to his two officers. 'Stay here. Write down everything you're told.'

He headed for the manager of headquarters' forensics department who had arrived a couple of minutes ago, now intent on an initial examination of the scene. 'Got any insights, Adam?'

'Probably none you haven't thought of.' He pointed at mounting cloud. 'This rain is in for the night. The photographic team has got full coverage of this whole area, and a detailed crime scene sketch. The trailer is on its way for the car. You've looked inside it?'

'Yes. A right mess.'

'When it arrives at headquarters, it'll be tested for fingerprints. I'll get the victims' prints for elimination. Your two officers staying?'

Watts nodded. 'There could be evidence here that we can't see. They'll guard the scene till others arrive to take over.'

'I'll leave one of mine in case anything does turn up. I'll be back here at around seven a.m. with at least six more for a daylight search.'

Watts gestured to Jones and Kumar, tapped his phone, spoke into it, kept it brief. In Watts' experience, the less detail Brophy was given, the better. 'Sir, an update on the Forge Street scene. The car is privately owned, reg number . . .' He gave it and clicked his fingers to Kumar, who passed him more details. 'Owner's name, Michael Lawrence, an address in the Moseley area. Two occupants inside the car, the second a female, identified as Molly Lawrence. That's about all we know so far.'

Hearing a shout of Adam's name from one of the forensic team, he cut the call and followed him to the Toyota. One of the forensic officers was holding up an evidence bag, the inside smeared. 'I've done a preliminary examination of the watch found on the ground next to the vehicle. It's covered in blood so we might get a print from it. I've been over the outside of the car, but it looks too wet for any meaningful prints.'

Adam glanced at Watts, 'Cheer up, Bernard. We'll examine the whole vehicle, plus watch, and test for DNA.'

They moved away, leaving Watts to his thoughts, such as they were. The bullet hole and casing he'd seen were signalling a possible scenario: a young idiot on the rob, puffed up with the sham power of a gun, possibly on drugs, getting inside the Toyota, losing control of the situation, turning it to carnage. Whoever he was, he needed finding, and soon.

He turned to Jones and Kumar. 'You two, plus one of Adam's officers, will stay here till seven a.m.'

'Sarge,' said Kumar. Neither looked thrilled at the prospect.

Watts left them and walked away to his vehicle. Inside, chilled to his bones, he reached for an old scarf and blotted rain from his hair and face, aware of a knot inside his chest. It looked to him like somewhere out here among the million-plus population was a youngster, a thief with a gun who didn't give a damn about anybody and had demonstrated it big time. He took out his phone and checked the time. Four a.m. A swift calculation produced an answer that suited his purpose. He tapped a number and heard Dr Connie Chong's voice, so clear across six thousand miles she might have been next to him. The clamour inside his head eased.

'Just ringing to ask how you're doing, how your mother is.'

'I'm fine. She's making good progress. We're expecting my

brother to arrive later today to stay with her so I can leave as planned. I'm due back at headquarters on Monday.'

He said nothing.

Her voice came again. 'What are you doing, Bernard?'

His eyes drifted over the scene beyond the misted windscreen. 'Looking at the end of the world.'

There was a brief pause. 'I see.' He heard her quiet laugh. 'So, here's the thing. Don't step off because I would *really* miss you and I couldn't come looking for you, could I?'

He rubbed his eyes, blinked. 'I'll be at the airport whenever you get in. Just let me know a time.'

'That's what I like about you, you know. Dependability. See you soon.'

'Yeah.'

Call ended, he started the engine, wondering if dependability was as boring to her as it sounded to him.

FOUR

Tuesday 4 December. 7.15 a.m.

Chloe Judd lifted the porridge-loaded spoon, her eyes fixed on footage recommended to her by Jonesy now playing itself out on her iPad screen. 'Watch the *flag,* Chlo,' he'd instructed. 'Keep your eyes on that flag.' Jonesy was a massive conspiracy theorist. According to him, what she was watching was a forty-nine-year-old con trick. Jonesy was also a known cynic. Her eyes widened. Enthralled, she watched, listened.

'One small step for . . .'

The scene moved on, switched to a ticker-tape parade for the years-ago spacemen waving and grinning.

'Jeez,' she whispered. 'How cool, how *fantastic* is that?'

Seeing the time, she leapt up, dumped her bowl in the sink, went inside the tiny bathroom to brush her teeth. Following a quick rinse-and-spit, she studied her reflection in the small mirror, ran her fingers through her hair and grinned.

'*This* is Chloe Judd, ace detective, taking one small step for womankind, and a massive leap as a police officer who doesn't give a—'

'Chloe!' A heavy hammering started up on her door, followed by Reynolds' voice. 'Chlo? Come *on*!'

Grabbing her coat and bag she left her flat, followed him to his car and got inside. He was now staring at her, open-mouthed.

'Say nothing,' she advised.

He pointed at the radio. 'There's some breaking news involving DI Watts. He's your boss, right?'

She listened, absorbed the newsreader's words, her eyes widening. 'Holy *sh*—!'

Inside his office, Watts re-started the emergency recording, ignoring Brophy's mutterings as the two voices drifted around the low-lit room a third time: *'Go ahead, caller. What's your emergency? . . . Caller? Hello?'*

Another voice, also female, this one resonating with fear and pain, her words punctuated by sobs.

'I . . . I can't . . . Oh . . . somebody, please help us . . .'

'Caller, can you hear me?' A brief pause. *'What's the nature of your emergency?'* The silence built. The operator's voice came again, insistent now. *'Which emergency service do you need?'*

'Ambulance . . .'

The ambulance call-taker spoke next. *'Hello, ambulance, is the patient breathing?'*

'I . . . I don't know.'

'Tell me what's happened.'

'. . . I feel . . . it hurts.'

'Can you tell me exactly what's happened?'

'. . . I'm . . . don't know . . . There's . . . blood.' A shaky intake of breath. *'. . . Blood all over my . . . hands.'* Her voice trailed off again.

'Can you give me your location?' Another pause, this one of several seconds. *'Where are you?'*

'. . . Don't know . . . He took our . . .' Her voice faded, came again, fearful, gasping. *'He might come back . . . A . . . man. Please. You have to help . . . please . . .'* Her last word trailed off to a whimper.

'Stay on your phone. What's your name?'

'Molly.'

'Can you describe your location, Molly?'

Watts listened to the operator inform a colleague that the caller is on a mobile phone. A deep groan brought her back on to the line.

'Molly? Who is there with you?'

'. . . Lost . . . an . . . awful place.'

The words were followed by the sound of weeping. Watts stared at the floor, waiting for the distraught voice to come again. It didn't.

'Stay with me, Molly. Molly, are you there? We have your location. Help is on its way.'

The recording ran on, the call-taker continuing to offer reassurance, followed by the first sound of approaching help.

'Molly? Molly! The ambulance is almost with you. Molly . . .?'

The room fell silent. Watts took his first full breath in the last two minutes. Brophy looked across at him. 'This is bad.'

'It is.'

'You were at the scene. What do you think?'

'Probable double shooting in the commission of theft.'

Brophy was at the window, his back to Watts. 'I'll tell you what this is. Anarchy of a degree that wouldn't be tolerated at Thames.'

Watts had heard more than enough about Thames Valley since Brophy's arrival here. More than enough of his view that in comparison, Birmingham was a lawless zoo. Brophy turned to him.

'As and when the press gets wind of this, you'll give the official line: *zero* tolerance of any offence involving a firearm. Got it?' He headed for the door. 'And you and I need to have a clear understanding about this investigation, given that it has all the features of inner-city auto-crime. As I said, the investigative approach is zero tolerance of firearms. *Clear?*'

Watts tracked him, thinking that Brophy had probably never delivered an original line in his entire career. Reaching the door, Brophy turned. 'But, there's still a need for caution.' Aware of the potential contradictions among Brophy's words, Watts got to his feet.

'I've seen what was done to the Lawrences. We need to find this shooter as a matter of urgency.'

'That requires discussion, tight planning. My office in one hour.'

Watts watched the door close on him, knowing that Brophy was hotfooting to confer by phone with the chief constable. He resumed writing his notes on what he had seen of the aftermath of the attack, adding the warning he'd just given to Brophy about dangerousness.

After a minute or so, he heard the door open, anticipating it was Brophy, back with more conflicting instructions.

'Hey, Sarge!'

'Morning, Judd.' Looking up at her, he half-rose. 'What the *bloody* hell is *that*?'

Judd ran her hand through spikey, blonde hair, several of its spikes tipped dark blue, others eye-searing pink. 'Like it? . . . Yeah, right, you don't like it.' She sat opposite him. 'The Bro ordered me back today, and am I glad! We had three brilliant days on interview techniques, plus role play and then it was hashtag *terminal* boredom. I was ready to slit a wrist or acquire a disease!'

'Has Brophy seen it?'

She ran a hand through her hair again. 'This? Yep, just now. He went on about my "responsibility to the job". Surprised you didn't hear him. He went ape—'

'You choose your moments!'

'Take it easy, Sarge. It's temporary.' She watched him head for the refreshment centre. 'Great, I'm gasping. Three sugars for me.'

He turned to her, coffee jar in hand. 'I've got enough on, without you turning up looking like your head's exploding.'

'I heard it on the radio.' She waited. 'Can I be on it?'

Bringing coffee to the table, he put one in front of her, sat opposite, keeping his voice low. 'You and me need to get some basics re-established. It's *Superintendent* Brophy. I'm your senior officer, I'm knackered after working most of the night and I can do without your *rattle*.' He watched her dig around in her bag, 'Just . . . dial down the volume. Better still, stop with the gabbing altogether while I get my head straight for a meeting with him.'

She put a finger to her lips, the other hand holding out a small box. He sighed, took it, extracted two paracetamols. She nodded to the machine in front of him, brows raised.

Index finger poised, he said, '*Listen*. Say *nothing*.'

He activated the recording. The words of the ambulance call-taker came again, followed by those of the victim, weighted with fear and pain. He watched her face change as the recording ran on. It ended with a sharp click.

She looked up at him. 'Word upstairs is it's a carjacking turned bad.'

'That's one possible theory.'

'What are the others?'

'There aren't any yet.'

She pointed to the machine. 'More than one victim?'

'Yes. Her name's Molly Lawrence. The male in the car is her husband.'

'Where are they now?'

'Hospital.' He looked at her. 'You've attended some carjackings.' He nodded to the recording. 'What do you make of it?'

'From what I've seen, they vary, like the one that happened a day or so ago, or the drivers are dragged out of their cars and the vehicles taken, but this . . . It's way different.'

'It is. Both of them were shot.'

'*Shot?*' She stared at him. 'If I didn't know you, I'd say you were having me on.'

'Wish I was. Brophy wants the investigation kept non-emotive.'

'Yeah? I want to be five-eight. Something else that's not going to happen.'

'Here.' He pushed his written notes towards her, pointed. 'That's everything I know so far from observing the scene, the actual vehicle and talking to SOCOs and the forensic team. Read it, ASAP.'

She took the notes. 'So, where's the scene, exactly?'

'Forge Street. On the fringes of the inner city, not far from the Bristol Road intersection. It's a scruffy brick-and-asphalt hellhole, part of the city the planners developed amnesia for over a lot of years.'

'Off the beaten track, then?'

'More a case of separated by neglect rather than distance. Jones, Kumar and I were there, first with paramedics, then with SOCOs and forensics.' He took a gulp of coffee. 'The good thing is there's a bullet, a bullet casing and a watch—'

'A watch?'

'The motive looks to be robbery. It probably belonged to one of the victims. It's all in what I just gave you, plus all other known details so far.'

She nodded, watched him stand, hitch his trousers. 'Where are you going?'

'Upstairs to have a word with Jones and Kumar who should be back from the scene by now, then to Brophy to make a few demands, none of which he'll like. After that, I'll be in the squad room to talk to officers up there, you included.'

* * *

TYDFIL PUBLIC LIBRARIES

Having gained nothing from Jones and Kumar which he didn't already know, Watts was now in Brophy's office being stared at across the desk.

'If you're planning to drop those six November carjackings I gave you, think again. They and the attack on this couple have "similar transaction" written all over them.'

'I see what—'

'I want your investigative plan.' Brophy sat, pen poised, eyes fixed on Watts.

Here goes, thought Watts. *Now for the fracas.* 'I want the Lawrence shootings designated a category-A inquiry.'

Brophy's eyes narrowed. 'Reason?'

'A double-shooting of two people, one of them male, moves the shooter straight to the high-risk category. My thinking is that he's an impulsive, antisocial type and he's out there, free to do it again. I want the squad room as the major incident room.'

Brophy nodded. 'If that's it—'

'No. We'll be using HOLMES so we need more terminals.' Seeing Brophy frown, he added, 'Home Office Large Major Enquiry Sys—'

'I *know* what it means.' Brophy drummed his fingers on his desk. 'Just a minute.' He opened a drawer, took out a file and rummaged through it. 'We sent half a dozen computers over to North Birmingham three months ago for use in that kidnap case which is now finished. I'll have them sent back immediately. How many can you get by on?'

Watts met Brophy's eyes. Having anticipated resistance to all he was now demanding, he realized how rattled Brophy was. 'Six, minimum, plus we'll need more space. I want the double doors to the room next door to the squad room opened up.'

Brophy's lips almost disappeared. '*That's* the formal function room!' Watts' eyes stayed on him. Brophy sighed. 'That it?'

'Going back to HOLMES, sir. I've asked Sergeant Miller to take a major role in its operation. She's agreed.'

'Is she any good?'

'Yes,' said Watts, swallowing his immediate response that Miller was bloody useless, which was why he'd selected her. Almost eighteen months since Brophy had arrived at headquarters and he knew the value of hardly any of the officers there. At least when Gander was the chief, he knew his personnel. 'Miller's got a mind like a steel trap for detail. PC Judd's got a nose for details linkage. I want both of them evaluating leads. The rest of the time, Judd will be with me as part of the direct investigation. I need every available officer on this.'

Brophy was looking increasingly harassed. 'My understanding is that the scene of the attack is small and contained.'

'Yes and no. The actual attack occurred in a small area but the scene itself extends once we factor in how the attacker arrived there.'

'A vehicle, is my guess.'

'No forensic indication of that so far. Unfortunately, there's no CCTV in the immediate area.'

Brophy sighed, shook his head. 'Anything else?'

'Yes. I want Judd to maintain the decision-making record for the investigation. She did it for the investigation last summer. Her memory is first class.'

The corners of Brophy's mouth headed south. 'Before we know it, PC Judd will be managing this whole investigation single-handed.' He looked across at Watts. 'I saw her earlier. She needs a tight rein. She needs to know her place.'

'Sir.'

If Watts knew of one attribute which Judd lacked, it was a sense of place. 'Finally, sir, I want four officers on Intelligence, looking for possible new avenues of inquiry as the investigation gets underway. I've given Jones and Kumar a heads-up on that.'

'Why four?'

'The other two officers will also be searching for potential angles via victimology re the Lawrences, their families, their social contacts.'

Brophy looked up at him. 'Why? These shootings are a clear case of attack by stranger.'

'Yes, but we need to start out flexible.'

Brophy tapped his notes. 'I'll be discussing this with the chief constable so I need to know what I'm talking about here.'

Fat chance, thought Watts. 'What I've seen so far suggests armed carjacking. I'll order an historical case search, which could turn up something, but we still keep the victimology angle in mind.'

Leaving Brophy's office, Watts went to the squad room. It was now crowded with officers, the talk full of the two shootings. It quietened as he came inside. He looked at each of them.

'We're getting all we need for a category A inquiry.'

Amid hoots, shoulder punches and high fives, he pointed across the room. 'Open those doors. Move six tables into that room. We're expecting more hardware.' He searched for Judd, almost missed her. The pink and blue had gone. Her hair looked damp. He raised his hand.

'With me.'

They went downstairs, passing a fresh-faced young constable on his way up. Watts turned to him. 'Got a job for you.'

The constable straightened, pushed back his shoulders.

'Easy lad. I want you to search all carjacking cases in this city which featured a gun during the last decade. Got that?'

'Sir!'

'Include replica weapons. Whatever you find, get down to the basement, pull out the files and take them to my office.'

'*Sir.*'

Watching the ramrod youth continue upwards, Watts was reminded of something he'd become increasingly aware of during recent months. Anybody under twenty-five made him feel tired. 'He's new. What's his name?'

'Reynolds.'

'I hope he's as keen as he looks.'

He detoured to the reception desk and the civilian worker in sole charge of it. 'Candy, I'm off out with Judd. If anybody rings, wanting to talk to me, let me know. You've got my number.' He tracked her gaze to where Judd was waiting. 'Unless it's the press. In which case, you know nothing. Got that?'

'Yes.' She turned away.

He headed from the building to his vehicle, Judd in tow. Inside, he started the engine, looked at the sheets of paper she was holding out to him, recognizing his own handwriting. His notes on the scene from the previous evening. He took them from her.

'That was quick reading.' He frowned, pointed to large capital letters across the top. 'What's "TLDR"?'

'Too long didn't read. Just tell me what you know, Sarge. If I've got questions, I can ask you.'

Face set, he reversed and headed from the car park, giving her an overview of what he had from the crime scene. He was also reviewing what he had just told his other investigative officers. In truth, he didn't yet have all that was needed for an upscale investigation. So far, Brophy had been unexpectedly amenable to his demands. Getting the one person he wanted onto this case could lead to a big fight.

10.10 a.m.

They were waiting close to the wide doors of the Intensive Care Unit, Watts having refused the family room, anticipating that members of the victims' families would be inside, full of questions to which he had no answers. One of the unit's doors opened. A nurse appeared. He and Judd stood.

'Detective Inspector Watts? Dr Harrison, the trauma surgeon, has a five-minute window. Follow me, please.'

They did, through the doors and across a quiet area to a small room off it. The woman inside it stood and offered her hand. Watts introduced himself and Judd.

'I'm the senior investigating officer for the investigation into the shootings. I was present at the scene when both victims were removed from their vehicle and brought here by ambulance.'

'Then you're already aware how serious their situation is.' Harrison glanced at her watch. 'I apologize for having to rush this, but family members of both victims are waiting for me. I can confirm the victims' names: Michael Lawrence and Molly Lawrence, a married couple. Mr Lawrence, twenty-seven years old, an interior designer; Molly Lawrence, twenty-three, a finance manager.'

'How are they generally? When do you think we'll be able to talk to them?'

Harrison gave Watts an evaluative look. 'You've just missed the neurosurgeon.' She paused, then lowered her voice. 'I regret to have to tell you that Mr Lawrence died thirty minutes ago. Mrs Lawrence remains sedated. She's suffered extreme trauma.' Watts stared at her, Molly Lawrence's terrified voice in the emergency call starting up inside his head. He took a card from his top pocket, handed it to her.

'When there's some news, I'd appreciate a call to either of those numbers.'

Harrison looked at it, then up at him. 'In case I wasn't clear when I referred to the trauma to Mrs Lawrence, in addition to being shot, there's another issue. She was four months pregnant.' She pointed to the door. 'Now, I need to talk to the relatives.'

Walking from the room with them, she kept her voice low. 'Mrs Lawrence was a patient of this hospital in regard to her pregnancy. It's my understanding that she attended here yesterday afternoon accompanied by her husband for a pre-natal check-up . . . She is, of course, no longer pregnant.'

They watched her divert to a room on the other side of the ICU, picking up muffled voices and sobs as she opened the door and went inside. Watts and Judd continued on in silence along several long, shiny corridors. At the end of one, she pointed to a sign indicating the way to the pre- and post-natal departments.

'Shall we talk to the people there about Mr and Mrs Lawrence?'

'Not now. I want to see whoever's in charge of security here to request CCTV footage from around the time of the Lawrences' appointment yesterday, which I'm hoping includes their arrival and or departure from this site.'

They headed to the ground floor. Watts went to the inquiry desk. After five minutes a security officer appeared, listened to Watts' request, made a note of it. He would have relevant footage located and delivered to headquarters as a matter of urgency.

They walked out into the damp December cold. 'Tragic, isn't it, Sarge?'

'It is.'

Gazing down from the hospital's high vantage point at heavy traffic, phone to his ear, he said, 'Adam, I'll be with you in fifteen minutes to have a look at the physical evidence you've got.'

Twenty minutes later, they approached headquarters. Judd pointed. 'Look!'

'*Sod* it!'

He glared at the half a dozen heavily-clad, loitering figures around the entrance. 'Zero eye contact, Judd.'

'I *know*.'

Barely slowing, he drove between the gates and parked close to the building's entrance, ignoring shouts of his name. They went inside. Brophy was in reception looking edgy, his eyes on the gathering outside.

'You've seen them?'

'Sir.'

'Get out there now and tell them you're SIO of the Lawrence investigation. Give them nothing else. *No* names. No details.'

'I'll be holding a press conference at some point, sir, but right now it might be best if you speak to them. Given the gravity of the case.' His eyes drifted over Brophy's uniform. 'They like a bit of brass.'

Having searched the words for slights and not locating any, Brophy tugged at his uniform jacket. 'You're right. I'll keep it to one brief announcement.' He eyed Watts. 'With more to come soon.'

Inside the forensics department on the third floor Watts and Judd pored over a report, Adam talking them through it.

'There were no useful fingerprints on the outside of the car. Same story for footprints. The ground around the car was too damp, too rough. No usable shoe prints inside, but a lot of fingerprints, as you might expect. They'll all be examined. It's likely that most belong to the victims, but we might get lucky.' He caught Watts' look. 'I know. Always a dream of mine at this stage of an investigation.'

'How often does your dream come true?'

'Not as often as I'd like.'

Adam reached his gloved hand inside a clear evidence bag, carefully removed the watch Watts had seen the previous night. He placed it on a small, round pad, where it sat, mired with dark red stains. 'Citizen. Not high-end, but a good make and worth taking. Or so the Lawrences' attacker must have thought, prior to dropping it and it landing just beneath the car. It belonged to the husband, Michael Lawrence.'

Judd was frowning at it. 'How can you be sure?'

Adam reached for it, turned it over.

She read aloud, '"*To our darling son. Happy 21st. Mum and Dad.*"'

'We got nothing useful from the smudged partial on the face but we're testing it for DNA. We don't know what went down during the shootings, but it's possible the gunman sustained an injury.' He reached inside a shallow plastic container, brought out a small, lozenge-shaped item, flattened at one end. 'The bullet recovered from the driver's sun visor. No prints. Having seen the vehicle, I'd say it was fired from the rear seat, but that needs verification. When Dr Chong is back, I'll be asking her to assist with that, just to be sure.' He reached for another container. 'This is the bullet casing found on the car's rear floor. Again, no prints. Whoever shot this couple has some basic savvy.'

Watts considered Adam's information alongside what he himself knew of young impulsive, antisocial types. Forethought rarely coexisted with impulsivity. He couldn't say never. 'Is the bullet telling us anything about the gun?'

'Not yet. We'll be taking expert advice on that. There's still a lot of work to do on the car, but that's all we have, so far.' He handed Watts a bulky manila envelope. 'Forensic report, plus copies of all scene photos.'

Back in Watts' office, Judd went directly to the Smartboard, powered it up, took a red pen and began listing the forensic detail supplied by Adam. 'When is Dr Chong back?'

'The weekend. She'll be in on Monday.'

She glanced back at him. 'Are you missing her, Sarge?'

In the process of clearing the table of everything except the six carjacking files and the case notes he'd made at the scene, he looked up at her.

'One more question like that and I'll personally see to it that you're back at Tally Ho for the next six months.'

She grinned. 'Got it. I went through a lot of carjacking files when I worked on some recent cases. I don't recall one which involved somebody being shot.'

'There's a first for everything.' He looked around, not finding what he was hoping for. 'That reminds me.'

He reached for the phone, rang the squad room. 'Is Reynolds there?' He waited. 'Anything on the search I requested, Reynolds?' He listened, nodded. 'Thanks.' He put down the phone. 'No carjackings involving a firearm or replica in the last decade. Depending on how desperate we get, I might tell him to go further back.'

He reached across for the envelope Adam had given him, opened it, slid out sharp-focused black and white images. Judd came to where he was standing. He scrutinized each one, passed it to her. Having looked at those of both victims, she laid them on the table, transferred her attention to others of the general scene.

'I see what you mean about the area. It's gone straight to the top of my avoid list.'

'Which is unfortunate, Judd, because that's where we're going now. To get a closer look while there's still some daylight.'

FIVE

His head full of the case, he watched Judd pick her way across the open area, avoiding holes and chunks of crumbling concrete. She looked up. 'This is grim! No houses, no apartments and you wouldn't want to live here anyway, because you'd probably be mugged or worse on your way—'

'Judd.'

'I know. Stop talking.'

Taking more careful steps, avoiding water-filled holes and scattered rubble, she came back to him. 'More to the point, how did a couple like the Lawrences end up here?'

'They would have hit all the traffic diversions and single-file access I did last night, similar to those we just came through. They must have taken a wrong turn. I know inner Birmingham, but it took me all my time to find my way. Even the ambulance had its work cut out getting here through the traffic.'

'Where were they going, the Lawrences?'

'Home to Moseley, according to Mike Lawrence's mother. She's confirmed the hospital appointment her son and his wife attended yesterday afternoon, after which they dropped in briefly for a family visit, then went to dinner at some place in Newhall Street.' He glanced down at her. 'If you like "salubrious", you'll approve of Newhall Street.' He took a few steps, nudged a chunk of concrete with his foot. 'They could have avoided the inner city when they drove home from that restaurant. I'm presuming they went in the wrong direction fairly early on.'

'You're always telling me that presuming is a bad idea.'

'It can be, but the indications are that that's what happened. It had been a workday for both of them, followed by the hospital appointment, the family visit, then dinner. They were probably tired, missed the road for home, hit the roadworks and ended up in this hellhole.'

He watched her mooch across the taped-off area, past SOCOs

and uniformed officers still searching for something, anything, no matter how small, and on to the abandoned petrol station. She was now heading back to him.

'How did he get here?'

'Who?'

'The gunman.'

'Like Adam said, there's no indication.'

'Got any investigative theories?'

Watts looked in the general direction of the Bristol Road intersection. 'This place is some distance from where the carjacking series occurred, but it's walkable. Right now, I'm not ruling out a link. Whoever did them might have decided to escalate his operation. If he's local he'd know about the road chaos, might have anticipated lost or confused drivers ending up here. That's what he would have wanted. Potential victims looking lost and confused.'

He took a folded sheet of paper from an inside pocket and handed it to her. She unfolded it. It was a map. He pointed out some of its features.

'We're here, and not too far in that direction is housing, just about visible, see? And beyond that the Bristol Road interchange.'

She looked up and nodded.

He continued, 'No need for a car. It's close enough to walk here without attracting any undue interest from other locals who might have been about, then get the hell out of here and he's home.'

'Sounds neat,' she said. 'You're ruling out that he drove here?'

'I'm ruling out nothing.'

'See that, Sarge?' He looked in the direction she was pointing. 'A convenience store.'

He narrowed his eyes through the growing murk at a lit sign, put on his glasses. 'Twenty-twenty wins every time. I know that place from way back. Its owner is an optimist or insured to the eyebrows. I want to talk to him.'

They quickly covered the distance and entered the small shop, sidling through aisles crammed with stock. One or two customers glanced at Watts, took in his height and casually left their baskets and the shop for urgent appointments they'd just thought of. A little man in a white, long-sleeved, Islamic shirt topped by a padded gilet suddenly appeared, both hands raised.

'*Mr* Watts, sir, what a long time it is I don't see you!'

'How's it going, Abdul?'

Abdul's face lost its pleased expression. 'You are here about that truly awful event which happened.' He raised his hands again. 'Who would do such a *terrible* thing?'

'This is my colleague, PC Judd. That's what we're here to find out.' His eyes drifted around the shop. 'Still in business, Abdul. Doing well?'

Abdul's face sobered. 'For now. My wife wants me to sell up. She says, too dangerous.'

'She might have a point.'

Abdul gave a quick headshake. 'No, no, Mr Watts. I have good clientele here. Good people. OK, one or two I don't like, but most others *very* good, *very* nice.'

Watts moved towards the door and peered out. 'Where do they come from?'

Abdul joined him, pointing. 'Over that way, mostly.'

Watts looked at distant housing, beyond it two blocks of medium-rise flats, like teeth jutting from otherwise empty gums. 'A lot of older people over there with no transport, Mr Watts. They need Abdul's mini-market.'

Watts turned back into the shop. 'Had any trouble here, recently?'

'Not in the last twelve months.' He turned, called towards the back of the shop. 'Nigel!'

The massive individual who appeared gave Watts that rare experience of looking up at another human being. Judd's mouth dropped open. He gave her a swift nudge. 'Afternoon, Mr . . .?'

The man stared down at him. 'Nigel will do,' he said, in a tone which sounded like an invitation to make something of it.

Abdul proudly eyed him. 'Nigel is in charge of security for Abdul's mini-market. Very good worker, *very* good.'

'You work here every day, Nigel?'

'Yes. Not to a fixed routine. I vary it, but mostly I'm here early and late.'

'Dark mornings, dark evenings, Mr Watts. No trouble since Nigel came.'

Aware that Nigel's eyes hadn't shifted from him, Watts reached inside his jacket for his notebook. 'We're interested in yesterday, Monday, the third. You were both here?'

'Yes.' Nigel's eyes were still fixed on him.

'You know what's happened in Forge Street?'

No response from Abdul nor his security operative.

'Did you see anything?'

'Nothing,' said Abdul. 'Too far away.'

Watts studied Nigel, waiting. 'How about you?'

Nigel shook his head.

Watts waited some more. 'Did you hear anything?'

Nigel and Abdul exchanged looks. Abdul nodded to Nigel, who said, 'What sounded like two shots at around nine twenty, nine thirty.'

Watts wrote down the time, then frowned at it. 'You sure about that?'

'Thereabouts, give or take.'

'Neither of you looked out? Went out?'

'Do we look like fools?'

Watts thought he had a point. He took out a card, handed it to Abdul. 'If you think of anything else, hear anything from the locals, give me a ring.' Abdul looked at the card, nodded.

Watts gave Nigel an appraising look. 'You work out?'

'Yeah.'

'Where?'

'Sidney's Place. My dad owns it.'

Now seeing the family resemblance, Watts' face cleared. 'How is your dad?'

'Like a butcher's dog.'

'Tell him DI Watts sends his regards, and that I might be seeing him.'

He and Judd left the shop and walked back to the Forge Street scene, which was still showing signs of forensic activity.

'That's a useful fix on the time of the shooting, Sarge.'

'You might think so, Judd.'

She frowned up at him. 'You don't?'

'The two shots they heard seem too early to me.'

Judd was silent, then said, 'How many shots are fired in the city per night, do you think?'

'My optimistic side says very few. It's possible they heard a car backfire. Or fireworks.' He took out his phone. She listened. He was onto Jonesy in the incident room.

'Request city centre CCTV footage as a matter of urgency. *All* possible vehicle routes from Newhall Street into the inner city and the Forge Street area.' He ended the call. 'Let's hope that turns up something.' He looked at his watch. 'Almost four thirty. We've got somewhere else to be, Judd. The home of Christy Williams, the sixth victim of the Bristol Road interchange carjacking series on Friday the thirtieth of November. She's expecting us.'

'Why her?'

'Because she was physically injured, but more to the point, she claims she saw a gun during the attack on her. Even more to the point, the Lawrences were shot just three days later.'

She studied him as he reversed the BMW. 'You stressed, Sarge?'

He was thinking about a criminologist and academic he knew and how he might approach this investigation.

'No. Just considering all possible angles.'

4.50 p.m.

They stepped inside the overheated Kings Heath terraced house, Ms Williams' partner leading the way along the hall, his voice low.

'I need to warn you, she's still a bit rocky, not dealing very well with sudden, unexpected movement, particularly on her left side.' He stopped, slowly opened a door. 'Christy? It's Detective Inspector Watts and a colleague.' He stood to one side. 'I'll leave you to it,' he said quietly.

Going inside the room they were hit by a wall of heat, a gas fire blazing. Watts introduced himself and Judd to the thirty-year-old woman with long blonde hair wearing a heavy red sweater.

She looked up at them. 'Sorry, I know it's hot in here, but I can't seem to keep warm.'

'It's not a problem.' Watts glanced at her heavily bandaged left hand propped up on a cushion.

She gave him a shaky smile. 'I never realized how inconvenient it is having only one usable hand.'

He took out his notebook. Judd did the same. He kept it simple. 'We need your account of what happened, Ms Williams.'

She nodded. 'I reported it to the local police when I got home. They rang this morning to tell me you'd want me to go through it at some time.' She took a deep breath. 'I left my office which is just beyond the mosque on Friday afternoon. It was raining. Getting dark. I put my briefcase on the passenger seat . . . I don't usually do that. I won't do it again, ever. I joined the dual carriageway, turned right at the traffic island and followed it down to the Bristol Road. I was preoccupied about some work I had to do at the weekend.' She gazed at the fire. 'The traffic was bad. Really heavy. As I reached the lights, they changed to red. I pulled up close behind the car in front of me.' She looked at Judd. 'After I reported it, two officers came here. I was advised not to pull too close in future . . .' She paused. 'So, there's room for manoeuvre if needed.'

She looked down at her bandaged hand. 'I was just sitting there, waiting for the lights, when I sensed something, a movement close to the passenger window, a dark shape. That's when the side of my car sort of exploded.' She took a couple of breaths. 'Glass flying everywhere, hitting my hair, wind and rain coming inside the car onto my face and . . . suddenly, an arm appeared.' She looked across at Watts. 'Crazy, I know, but without thinking, I reached out, grabbed my briefcase.' She took another deep breath. 'It was really nice. Mulberry.'

'What happened then?' asked Watts.

'I gripped the briefcase, felt him pull at it. That's when I saw it. The gun. At least, I think it was a gun.'

Watts sent Judd a quick look. She sat forward, keeping her voice low. 'Christy, how sure were you at the time that it was a gun?'

'I don't know . . . eighty per cent? He was holding *something*. He used it on my hand. Something heavy, like metal. The next thing, my hand felt like it was on fire. He shouted at me and then . . . he was gone, just disappeared.'

'He shouted. Can you tell us about that?'

'He said something like, "That's one easy way to get yourself killed, lady." I think that's what convinced me it was a gun.' She looked up. 'I keep going over and over the whole thing. I'm sorry. I can't be one hundred per cent it was a gun, but it's what I thought at the time.'

Watts allowed a short pause. 'In your witness statement taken shortly afterwards, you said you believed he was armed.'

'That's right. I actually thought that he had shot me in the hand. The whole incident lasted seconds but . . . I didn't hear anything like a shot.' She looked at her hand. 'At the hospital I was told that he had struck my hand very hard with something heavy. They were worried that there might be some long-term damage but I can move my fingers a little now, see? I'm hoping that it'll be all right.'

'Can you tell us anything else about this man that isn't in your statement?'

'I've thought about it. I didn't see his face but I can tell you that he was strong. My briefcase was crammed full, really heavy, but he pulled it through the car window as if it was nothing. He sounded confident when he spoke. I watched him run. He was agile. He moved like a young person.'

Inside the BMW, Watts looked down at his notes. 'The picture I'm getting of the person she described is confident.' He looked across at Judd. 'And confidence suggests what?'

'He's done it before.'

'Five previous times would do it, wouldn't you say?' He started the engine. 'The question now is who is he, closely followed by, did he have anything to do with what happened to the Lawrences?'

SIX

Wednesday 5 December. 10.15 a.m.

Hit by a combination of heat, sweat and testosterone, Watts came inside the gym and found himself surrounded by machines, weights and rippling muscles. Tensing his own abs, he waited for the short, muscular man heading towards him.

'*Allo,* Mr Watts. Here for our special offer, an introductory try-out?' He gave Watts a once-over. 'Have to say, you're looking a lot trimmer, a lot fitter than when I saw you twelve months back. Come on. I'll give you the tour.'

'Thanks, Sidney, another time. I'm here about the incident in Forge Street on Monday night.'

'Guessed it. Our Nigel told me he'd seen you.'

'Got anything for me? Anything that might involve carjacking?' Watts followed him to a table heaped with towels, then waited as he started folding them.

'Might have. Somebody from five or so years back. Young fella. Used to come in here, regular, and then he didn't.' He glanced up at Watts. 'Carjacking is what he was sent down for. Don't ask me for an address. I don't know any details.'

'I'll settle for a name.'

'Jonah Budd.'

* * *

As Watts left the gym his phone rang. It was the hospital, informing him that Molly Lawrence had regained consciousness an hour ago. 'Thanks. Somebody will be there in fifteen minutes.' He phoned Judd.

'Molly Lawrence is conscious. Go to the hospital. Have a word with the staff. Ask if she's well enough for you to see her. If she is, introduce yourself to her. I'll be there as soon as I can.' He made a second call, this time to the scene, spoke to one of the officers there.

'Any progress?'

'No, Sarge. We're still searching but this whole area is a mess of rubble, holes—'

'Keep at it.'

He got another call, this one from Jones to tell him that the major incident room in its basic form was up and running.

'Good. Tell everybody that the first formal briefing is this afternoon at two.'

Wednesday 5 December. 11 a.m.

'Mrs Lawrence is conscious but she's still heavily medicated,' said the doctor, 'so it's very possible she'll drift off again.'

'I won't stay long,' said Judd. 'I'll introduce myself and let her know that we've begun our investigation into what happened to her and her husband.'

The doctor nodded. 'Knowing that something is being done has to be good for her.' He beckoned to a colleague who approached them. 'This is one of the nursing team caring for Mrs Lawrence.' And to the nurse, he said, 'PC Judd is part of the police investigation. She'd like to see Molly and offer her some reassurance that the police are doing all they can.'

Judd followed her. 'Is Mrs Lawrence aware of what's happened to her husband and herself?'

The nurse stopped at a door, lowered her voice. 'Her mother was here for most of yesterday. Earlier this morning she told Molly that they had been shot, that her husband had been very badly wounded, but not that he had died. She did tell her that her pregnancy had ended. She did it as well as anyone might, given the circumstances.' She shook her head. 'I've worked in this ICU for eight years and I can't recall a case that's had such an impact on staff here.'

Her hand on the door handle, she looked directly at Judd, her voice now a whisper. 'I haven't seen any real indication that she's absorbed what her mother told her. She hasn't spoken about it to any of us caring for her. We were anticipating she would ask questions but she hasn't. Not even when her mother-in-law came in to see her very briefly.' She sighed. 'It's terrible, what's happened to them, but of course she's not even begun to process it. My impression is that she thinks her husband is going to walk in here to see her.'

'Were you on duty when they were brought in?'

'Yes. That's when I was assigned to Molly's care team.'

'Has she asked you about her own injuries?'

'No. That's another of our concerns. She knows she's injured but she doesn't seem to be making a connection between that, her pregnancy and what's happened to her husband. We feel desperately sorry for her. She's been quite agitated since she regained consciousness, telling one of my colleagues that she had to leave, that she had a gynaecological appointment.' Seeing Judd's face, she added, 'Molly's in good hands here. We anticipate her being with us for a little while. We have a bereavement specialist on site. We'll involve her as soon as the time looks right.'

'Has she had any other visitors, apart from her mother and mother-in-law?'

'No. She wasn't well enough.' She pushed open the door.

Judd followed her inside, keeping her voice low. 'Detective Inspector Watts is on his way. He should be here soon.'

The nurse nodded, went across the room to the bed, leant over its occupant and returned to Judd, whispering, 'She's asleep. I'll inform the desk where you are. I'll be back in a couple of minutes.'

She left the room. Judd felt suddenly vulnerable, out of her depth. She went quietly to the bed, the woman lying there barely making a shape under the covers, her eyes closed.

'Mrs Lawrence . . .? Molly?'

Getting no response, she turned away, went to the window and looked out, willing Watts to arrive soon. She turned as the door opened. The nurse was back.

'Any luck?'

Judd shook her head. 'She's sleeping.'

The nurse leant over the bed, lightly pressed the slim hand lying on the covers. 'Molly?' she said softly. 'Molly, there's a very nice young police officer here to see you. Her name's . . .?' She looked at Judd.

'Chloe Judd.'

'Did you hear that, Molly? Her name's Chloe. That's nice, isn't it?'

Judd slowly approached the bed, looked down at wavering blue eyes fringed with dark lashes. 'Hello, Mrs Lawrence,' she whispered.

The woman looked up, eyes drifting to the nurse who quickly moved over to her.

'I'm here, Molly. I'll help you up.'

The nurse reached for a keypad. Judd watched as Molly Lawrence's upper body was slowly raised a few centimetres. Sending Judd an encouraging look, saying that she would be close by if needed, she left the room.

Judd was again at a loss. 'Mrs Lawrence? . . . I'm here to let you know that we, the police, are doing all we can in respect of . . . what's happened.'

'What happened?'

Wrong-footed by the two words, searching for a fitting response but not finding one, Judd went with: 'It would be a big help if you feel able to talk to me.'

She waited, her eyes fixed on the small dual fans of dark lashes. When no response came, she quietly walked away, had reached the door when the voice came again.

'I remember . . . him.'

Judd was back, keeping her voice low. 'Who, Molly? Who do you remember?'

'The man . . . He said, "Don't look at me".'

She saw Molly's eyes squeeze closed, watched her chest rise and fall. *Come on, Sarge, come on*, a voice pleaded inside her head.

'Did he say anything else?'

'He said, "Hand me your valuables. Put them . . . inside your bag. Give it to me".'

'He gave you a bag?'

'No. My handbag.' She gave a long, wavering sigh. '"Now pass me the bag . . . nice and slow".' She squeezed closed her eyes, agitation rising in her voice. 'He was angry. "Where's the other phone?"' Judd felt another surge of unease, willing the nurse back here. Molly Lawrence was now staring up at Judd.

'I gave him Mike's phone. Told him I didn't have mine . . . I had to keep that phone . . . to ring . . . for help. I had to.' Her voice almost disappeared. '*Had* to. But I couldn't move . . . hurt so much . . . took ages to make the call . . . too long . . .' Tears sprang from her eyes, her hand tugging at the drip fixed to the back of her other hand, pushing at the covers.

Shocked by the suddenness of it, Judd tried to calm her. 'Mrs Lawrence? *Mrs Lawrence.* You need to lie *still*!'

On a quick surge of relief, Judd saw the nurse coming inside. Quickly approaching the bed, her hand moved to an array of lit buttons above it, then onto the drip. She laid her hand on Molly's shoulder.

'Easy, Molly, easy.'

'His *voice* . . . Something about his voice when he said some words . . .' Her breathing was rapid now. 'He said, "Watches". He didn't say it properly.' Her eyes huge, she gazed up at Judd, at the nurse now pressing a red call button. 'He . . . he had . . . a . . . lisp.'

Judd just caught the final word.

Seemingly oblivious to the nurse's hand on her shoulder, Molly Lawrence struggled upwards, grimacing, her hand against her side. 'His . . . coat. Thick. Big star on . . . back.'

The doctor Judd had met earlier was suddenly there. Molly Lawrence looking up at each of them, her face awash with tears, her voice anguished. 'It took him . . . just seconds to . . . ruin my life . . .'

The nurse held her hand, looked across at Judd, her eyes moving in the direction of the door. Judd took the hint, fled to it.

Watts was pacing outside the room. He looked up at her. 'What's happened? I was told not to go in. What's going on in there?'

Judd leant against the wall, running her hands through her hair. '*That* was the most useless I've felt in my *whole* life. She just started talking, then without warning she got really upset.' Judd leant forward, hands on her knees, taking deep breaths. 'It was the sudden-ness of it.'

'What did she say?'

'She described the man who shot her and her husband. Something about a bag she had to put some things into, like their watches, and that he got angry about a phone. She says he was wearing a thick coat with a star pattern on the back. She also said she couldn't move after he shot her – it took a while for her to call for an ambulance . . . too long, she said.'

'You didn't write all this down?'

Judd gave him a sharp look. 'What do *you* think!'

'Sounds like she was trying to describe one of those Puffa-type jackets the kids are all wearing. Did she say anything else about him?'

'Yes.' Judd straightened, some of her colour coming back. 'She said he had a lisp.'

The nurse came out of the room. Watts went to her. 'Any chance we can talk to Mrs Lawrence later today?'

'Sorry. We've had to sedate her. You need to leave it a day or so. I'll keep you informed as to how she is in the meantime.'

They left the hospital, Judd looking out of the BMW's passenger window. 'She never mentioned the gun. She never mentioned it firing or anything.'

'Have I mentioned a forensic psychologist mate of mine, Kate Hanson, who used to work with me in the Unsolved Crime Unit?'

Judd looked away. 'You mean, *Dr* Hanson who knew everything, had nerves of steel and never got anything wrong. You're on about *that* Hanson?'

'What's eating you?' He glanced down at her, the effects of what had just happened inside the hospital still evident on the young face. 'I was about to say that Hanson told me a thing or two about memory. About how it acts to protect people from trauma. It sounds like what you just saw was Molly Lawrence starting to join the dots, which was tough on you, tough for her, but it's what the investigation needs. Did she mention any direct violence?'

She shook her head. 'No.'

'Cheer up. You can report it to the first formal briefing at two o'clock.'

She looked out of the window. 'We're already half an hour late.'

2.45 p.m.

The incident room was filled with officers and technology, the double doors into the next room standing open. Watts was picking up that unmistakeable mix of edginess and mounting excitement that came with the start of a major investigation.

'Welcome to the first formal briefing of the Lawrence investigation. Judd and I have come straight from the hospital. Mrs Lawrence managed to say a few words, which Judd will tell you about.' The door opened and Brophy came inside.

Watts looked at the waiting faces. 'Anything yet on CCTV from the possible routes taken by the Lawrences that night?'

'Requested, sir.' Miller pointed at the terminal in front of her. 'There are two potential routes from the Newhall Street restaurant to Forge Street. There would have been more but for diversions and road closures.'

'I want that information. At this early stage, I'm not ruling out that what happened to the Lawrences was the result of an incident of road rage. When it arrives, we'll examine it for visuals of the Lawrences' Toyota obviously, but more than that, we'll be looking for indications of them being followed, any sign of a possible incident involving the Lawrences' vehicle and any other. I've already requested CCTV of the specific area where they had dinner. I want Automated Number Plate Recognition checks on any vehicles of interest.'

'On to it, Sarge,' said Jones, turning to a computer. Watts looked from him to young Reynolds and an older officer, Gillespie, drafted in from the inner city. 'How's the victimology going?'

Gillespie's eyes were fixed on the screen in front of him. 'We've been on to the employers of Mr and Mrs Lawrence, who've provided names of colleagues, plus others known to be friends of theirs.' He looked up at Watts. 'You want them contacted?'

'Hang on to the details for now. There's more urgent inquiries I want done first.'

Watts' eyes settled on Reynolds. He was looking stressed. A situation like this had to be a challenge for somebody hardly out of training. His attention moved to somebody else not that much further along. She looked as though she'd recovered from her experience at the hospital.

'Judd's going to give you the information she got from Mrs Lawrence.' He sat on the edge of a table, arms folded, as Judd stood, eyes fixed on her colleagues.

'Mrs Lawrence is still very unwell but she managed to provide some detail.' They listened as she read from notes she'd made on the way back to headquarters. 'She's confirmed that their attacker stole their valuables. You know that forensics have a watch which was recovered at the scene. Mike Lawrence's phone was also taken. I've had a quick word with forensics, who already have the number. They tried ringing it, but it was switched off within the inner city at nine p.m. on the evening of the attack. As you know, Mrs Lawrence managed to make the emergency call. She's described their attacker's voice and appearance to me, that he spoke with a lisp and was wearing a thick jacket with some kind of star pattern on the back.' Fellow officers exchanged looks as Judd continued, 'DI Watts has information relating to one of the victims of the Bristol Road carjacking series.' She passed her notes to Miller as Watts stood.

'We can't rule out a connection to the Lawrence attack, so those six November cases remain ours. The sixth victim sustained a serious injury to her hand. She believes she saw a gun during the attack on her. She's described her attacker as young, agile and confident. This investigation will focus on both the carjackings and the shootings. An inner-city gym owner has suggested a name for the carjackings: Jonah Budd. Budd already has form for it.'

He looked around the room. 'Kumar? I want Budd's full conviction record and social reports, plus his contact details, soon as.' His eyes moved over all of them. 'This major investigation has to stay aware of the possibility that somewhere in this city there's a young, armed offender who is prepared to use violence in the commission of theft. You all know the inner city, the Bristol Road interchange which was the scene of those six attacks, and Forge Street where the Lawrences were attacked. They're geographically close. The carjack victims lost personal stuff: handbags, briefcases. We've got few details as yet of what was taken from them, but as soon as we get them, I'll let you know, although theft appears to be the motive because Mr Lawrence's watch was found just beneath the car where it was dropped.' The room was silent, all eyes on him. 'Whoever shot Mr and Mrs Lawrence appears to place a low value on human life. Our prime concern has to be that he could do it again.'

He pointed at several officers. 'I want the five of you out there, meeting and talking to local residents, keeping it low-key, with your listening heads on.' He gave all of them a direct look. 'It'll come as no surprise that Mrs Lawrence is very unwell. The hospital has asked that we wait to talk to her again.' He watched facial expressions change. 'I know. It's frustrating but that's how it is. They'll keep us updated as to her progress over the next few days. That's it for today. Carry on.' He hooked a finger at Judd.

With a glance outside at the press which looked to have increased three-fold, they went downstairs to Watts' office.

'Blinds, Judd.'

He listened to them swish closed, his own words about the low value placed on the Lawrences' lives reverberating inside his head. He unlocked a cabinet, took out a file. Time to get moving on what he wanted. Bringing it to the table, he opened it, located what he was looking for, turned to the CV's last two pages, Judd's voice coming at him, as he looked down the long list of professional expertise, two items in particular snagging his attention.

Geographical Profiling. Trauma.

'. . . And you had them keen as anything up there, Sarge . . . What's up?'

'I've been wondering how long I dare leave it before getting in some help. Now I know. I've got a phone call to make.'

'To somebody with some particular savvy?'

He frowned. 'Where'd you get that from?'

'Just sensed it.'

He pointed his index finger. 'Then, sense *this*: keep it to yourself until I've made the call and had a chance to square it with Brophy or you'll be at Tally Ho till you're thirty.'

He took out his phone, tapped the number. His call was answered. His brows shot up at the female voice. 'This is Detective Inspector Watts. I need to speak to Dr Will Traynor as a matter of urgency.'

'Hold on, please . . . *Dad*!'

Watts' fingers drummed the table. They stopped as Traynor's deep, pleasant voice sounded in his ear.

'Hello, Bernard.' Watts noted the lack of surprise. Maybe Judd wasn't the only one with a sixth sense. 'Your current investigation is all over the media.'

'It's why I'm ringing. I could do with your help on it. All I've got so far is a likely connection between a series of carjackings at the Bristol Road interchange and the Lawrence shootings in a hell-hole otherwise known as Forge Street.'

'Is this call at Chief Inspector Brophy's instigation?'

'No, mine. Can you be here at seven thirty tomorrow morning?'

'Yes. I'll need to leave no later than ten.'

'Thanks for coming on board, Will.'

'Send me all the data you have.'

Watts glanced at Judd. 'On its way in the next two minutes.'

He eyed his phone, the connection already broken. Where Traynor was concerned, 'cool' didn't cover it. Judd was looking at him, waiting.

'Traynor's in.'

She raised both fists high. '*Yes.*'

'Email him copies of all we've got, while I think how best to persuade Brophy that we need him.'

SEVEN

Thursday 6 December. 7.25 a.m.

Desk phone clamped to his ear, Watts eyed the clock, listening to Brophy's summation of Will Traynor's contribution to the murder investigation back in the summer. 'I grant you he's got specialist skills and he's good at what he does' – Watts waited for the kicker – 'but during a lot of it he was an emotional mess.'

'He had problems, sir, but he also brought his professional expertise, insight and investigative experience to that case which did a lot to crack it for us. Officers here rate him. I've seen him a couple of times since and my take on him is that—'

'You're talking socially, not work-wise?'

'He's really together now.' He listened to Brophy's demands for further reassurance. 'Yes, I do think he's got a lot to offer the investigation, or I wouldn't be suggesting it.' He looked up as the door opened and grinned. 'Sir, I think you've made a wise decision.'

He replaced the phone as the tall, fair-haired, smiling man in the grey suit came inside.

'Hello, Bernard. Have your powers of persuasion worked?'

Watts went to him, his hand outstretched. 'Good to see you again, Will. Your arrival's well-timed. You're officially in.'

Seeing him again, Watts reflected that in terms of looks and build, Traynor had pulled all the aces. Watts' own inheritance included height from his father, plus a downside: his mother's heavy facial features. 'You look well. Been on holiday?'

'Ten days in the sun with my daughter which is now a distant memory. I've read all that you sent me. Any big developments?'

'I wish. I'm directing this investigation on the basis of a potential link between an inner-city carjacking series in November and the Lawrence shootings. Beyond that, I know nothing.'

Traynor grinned. 'According to a famous philosopher that probably makes you one of the wisest among us.'

'In that case, Lord help us.' He paused. 'Thanks for agreeing to work with us again. You've been following the news of the double-shooting?'

'It's hard to miss, although it's light on detail. I also heard members of the press outside complaining about a lack of a press conference.'

Watts shrugged. 'That's the second most frequent gripe in this game, the first being police failure to produce results. If we do share information with them, they inflate it beyond all recognition and create a frenzy of fear in the local populace which is then on the phone to us, clamouring for action. If we don't give them anything, they accuse us of a control-freak culture. Either way we lose. They'll have guessed you're on board so I'd better get out there. Give them a short statement. Want to be part of it?'

'I'd prefer to keep a low profile.'

Watts glanced at the clock. 'I'll be five minutes at most.' He pointed at the sheets on the table. 'You're welcome to read my latest notes.'

Watts faced several reporters, their breath in clouds on air turned icy as they recorded his words on phones or in notebooks. 'This is very early in a homicide investigation. You already know the names of the two victims, which I can confirm to be Michael Lawrence and Molly Lawrence, a married couple, residents of Birmingham. They were in the city centre that evening when their vehicle was attacked by an armed individual. The attack appears to have been motivated by theft. Mr Lawrence has died of his injuries. Mrs Lawrence remains in hospital. This is an appeal to all residents of this city to stay vigilant when out and about, particularly in the evenings. If anybody has information about, or merely a suspicion of, the likely identity of this attacker, please ring headquarters as a matter of urgency. Officers working on the investigation are available to take calls. There'll be a press conference at some stage but for now, that's all.'

He turned, walked away, exasperated voices following him, one or two pointing to the Aston Martin parked nearby. 'What about the criminologist, Will Traynor? Is he now part of your investigation? Sarge?'

'Come *on*, DI Watts, we're starving here—'

'Got any actual leads?'

'Any names in the frame . . .?'

Back inside his office he found Traynor still reading. 'Have you got anything you'd like to talk about to the investigative team, or do you prefer to listen for now?'

'I think, some of both.' He paused. 'Bernard, I've got one or two theories of my own which I want to share with you prior to this meeting.'

Watts looked at his watch, then shook his head. 'They're waiting for us. My main concern now is Molly Lawrence as witness. You've got expertise in talking to traumatized individuals and that's going to be your priority as soon as she's up to it. Are you OK with that?'

'I shall be when the hospital confirms that she is sufficiently recovered.'

They left the office and took the stairs to the incident room. As they came inside, Watts picked up smiles, nods, hands raised to Traynor, who acknowledged their greetings by raising the slim folder he was holding then standing to one side. Watts faced his team.

'I've just delivered a very brief statement to the press. Brief, because there's not much to tell them. As soon as we know that Molly Lawrence's release from hospital is imminent, she'll have round-the-clock protection at her home.' That got frowns from several officers. Nobody welcomed that kind of assignment. Tough. It had to be done.

'No forensic results yet. The poor-quality partial print on the watch that was dropped at the scene, property of Michael Lawrence, looks to be of questionable usefulness, but the watch itself will be tested for DNA which as always is going to take a while. So far, nothing to report on the weapon and bullets used. As we're beyond the first forty-eight hours with no identified suspect, the glass fragments from the Lawrences' car window are looking increasingly irrelevant for matching purposes. Two shots were heard at around nine twenty, nine thirty p.m. by the owner and his security worker inside a nearby convenience store. Given the ten thirty-five p.m. emergency call you've all listened to, that timing looks to be a bit early, but we'll bear it in mind. Molly did tell Judd that she couldn't move, and so it took her a long time to make the call.' He checked his notes. 'An inner-city gym owner has given a possible name for the carjacking series: Jonah Budd. Budd has done time for similar. I'll be chasing him up.'

He glanced to his right. 'As you see, Dr Will Traynor is with us again.' He paused for the flurry of low comments, nods and grins to subside, including an intent, lingering gaze from Josie Miller directed at Traynor. 'I've given Will a quick overview of the carjacking series and the Lawrence shootings.' He turned to him. 'Anything you'd like to say at this stage, Will?'

All eyes were on Traynor as he removed two large sheets from his file, calmly unfolded them, took them to the whiteboard and fixed them to it. Two maps. Watts felt a rush of adrenalin. A criminological evaluation of the two inner-city crimes and their scenes was exactly what was needed. Traynor pointed to the map on the left.

'I understand there's consideration being given to a link between the six carjackings close to the Bristol Road intersection here, and' – he pointed to the map on the right – 'the shooting of Michael and Molly Lawrence in this area of the inner city, specifically Forge Street. It appears to be a reasonable line of inquiry at this early stage, given the relative proximity of the two scenes and the fact that the first victim believes she saw a gun.' He paused. His audience waited.

'I've read all the available information on the interchange attacks and the shootings of Mr and Mrs Lawrence. They tell us something about offender thinking and action, plus the significance of "place" for both offences which I'd like to share with you.'

He came towards them, his face relaxed. 'What I've done is use the admittedly small amount of available information to analyse both of the crimes and the specific geographical areas in which they occurred.' He pointed back to the maps.

'Given the nature of the November carjackings, their location and timing in fading afternoon light, I would anticipate that there were two offenders involved, one acting as lookout at the traffic island.' He pointed. 'Up here to a confederate further down the dual carriageway.'

Watts' optimism rose.

'That whole series was ultra-smooth, with minimal engagement between the offender and five of the six victims.'

Watts nodded again.

'The geographical and temporal awareness shown by that attacker is reflected in his post-offence behaviour as described by victims: his leaving the immediate location in failing light and at speed, quickly disappearing into the urban landscape. It tells us something about him. He's likely to be of average intelligence, a planner, someone who is into criminal activity which is quick, low risk and involves minimal contact between himself and his victims. Descriptions of him from victim-witnesses fit with my expectations of him as strong, athletic, fast-moving.'

Traynor returned to the left-hand map. 'He's young. Between say sixteen and twenty-five. He knows that area intimately.' He looked back at them. 'It's where he lives.'

Brophy came into the incident room as Traynor placed both hands against the map, emphasizing each word. '*Smash. Grab. Run.* That's his MO. Straightforward. Efficient.' All eyes followed as he moved to the right-hand map and the Lawrence attack.

'Question: what does Forge Street and its surrounding area have to tell us about the individual who attacked and shot Mr and Mrs Lawrence?' The silence in the room was palpable. 'Based on what we know so far, he appears to have acted alone. In terms of his behaviour, the degree of violence exhibited was extreme. One of the victims was killed, the other very fortunate not to have been.' He gave them a direct look. '*All* offenders gain confidence via experience. Are the Lawrence shootings an example of a young, athletic carjacker, emboldened by a series of six successful attacks now intent on upping his game? To answer that question, we need to consider further the relevance of *place*.' He pointed to the Forge Street map.

'Some of you have been to that area as part of the investigation. I was there at six thirty this morning. I experienced a high volume of traffic as I approached it but very little the closer I got. In the forty-five minutes I was in that street, I logged just two vehicles enter and pass quickly along it without stopping.' He moved his hand slowly over the area of the Lawrence crime scene. 'Why would an experienced carjacker choose *this* as a place to commit further attacks? Of equal relevance, how did he plan to stop any vehicle of interest?'

'I was going to raise that with you,' said Watts. 'I'm thinking he used some kind of ruse to slow down or stop the Lawrences' car.'

Traynor returned to the map again. 'Let's consider that. The immediate area around Forge Street has a lot to tell us.' They watched his index finger move over it. 'Despite it being part of the inner city and relatively close to its constant traffic flow and activity, Forge Street is economically deprived, offers little to no business activity or employment. Housing is some way off. It's a neglected, forgotten place.' He turned to Watts. 'You've checked it out in terms of its history of criminal behaviour?'

Any optimism Watts had felt was draining away. 'Nothing in the last decade beyond minor vandalism.'

Traynor moved to the table, selected one of a number of photographs of the Lawrences' vehicle at the scene, the victims visible inside it. He raised it high. 'Murder, the ultimate crime, occurred in that location, late that evening. The exact timing is unknown but possibly sometime around ten, ten thirty p.m., given the timing of the emergency call made by one of the victims. I agree with Detective Inspector Watts that the shots heard at around nine thirty appear to be a little early. One possibility is that the attacker followed the Lawrences to that location, although it's also possible that he was waiting somewhere in the vicinity of Forge Street. Leaving aside for now how he got them to stop, at some point he gained access to the inside of their vehicle. Which raises a big question. Why place himself in such close proximity to his two victims? He had a gun. He could have remained outside the vehicle and threatened them' – he looked at Watts – 'which would be reminiscent of the carjackings. He chose to get inside. Why? From the information I've read, he already had the victims' valuables in his possession when he shot them. Why would he do that?' He indicated the left-hand map.

'I see a stark inconsistency between the carjacking series and the attack on the Lawrences. There's a lack of caution, smoothness and efficiency in the shootings. If one man is responsible for the carjackings and the Lawrence shootings, he changed his MO in Forge Street. Why would he do that? I don't have an answer but the question needs asking.'

Jones raised his hand. 'Are you saying we should be ruling out the carjacker for the Lawrence shootings? If it was the same offender, isn't it possible he and his mate know Forge Street, checked it out and saw its isolation as a big plus for extending the offence area? DI Watts mentioned the possibility of a ruse being used to stop the Lawrences' car. If that's what happened, he was probably confident that, whatever happened after that car stopped, nobody would come along, stop and intervene. Plus, he's already had one of his carjacking victims try to hold on to her property, so he's equipped with a gun and ready to use it, with enough confidence to handle any confrontation.'

'Those are all reasonable suppositions.' Traynor nodded. 'But step back a little. What's the attraction of Forge Street for an experienced carjacker?'

In the following seconds of silence, Jones frowned. 'Given what you've said about lack of through traffic, there doesn't seem to be any.'

Watts looked from him to Traynor. 'Are you saying that there's no connection between the carjackings and the attack on the Lawrences? How sure are you, Will?'

Traynor gave a wry smile. 'I understand why you're asking the question, but we both know that there are rarely absolutes in our line of work, particularly at this early stage.'

He returned to the two maps and placed his hand against one then the other. 'What I'm suggesting is that you *visualize* each of these areas, *compare* them, then ask yourselves the key question: how *likely* it is that the slick, youthful, six-times carjacker who lives close to his attacks, knows that area intimately, whose plan is minimal contact with his victims, and the individual who chose Forge Street in which to attack the Lawrences, rob them, kill one of them and almost kill the other, are one and the same?'

The silence was broken only by the door opening and Brophy exiting the room. A hum of voices started up, officers discussing what they had just heard.

Watts headed to Traynor. 'I was hoping for something different, but being an optimistic type, as and when the CCTV data arrives, it might give us some clarification—'

'Sarge, it's here!'

They headed for Kumar and gathered around the large screen filled with four stills of traffic scenes. He started the recordings and pointed to the one at top left. 'See that? Six twenty-nine, and that's the Lawrences' Toyota close to Mike Lawrence's parents' home in Handsworth Wood.'

They watched jerky footage of the car making a left turn. Kumar pointed again, this time at a road name. 'His parents' address.' They waited, their attention fixed on one or other of the on-screen scenes, searching for the Toyota. Seconds passed. 'Here it is again! It's now heading away from the parents' place.' They watched the Toyota move slowly, hemmed in by heavy traffic, time: seven sixteen p.m.

Watts pointed. 'That's Symphony Hall on the left. They're heading into town, to the restaurant in Newhall Street.' All eyes were fixed on the four-part screen, the Toyota no longer visible. 'I phoned the restaurant. It was busy that night. A member of staff thought they arrived at around seven thirty but couldn't confirm what time they left. The Lawrences' bill was handwritten, no time included. Mr Lawrence left cash on the table, alerted a waiter to it and they went. Run it forward a bit.' Kumar did, the four-part screen now filled with heavy evening traffic. They searched it. No Toyota Previa.

'Come on!' murmured Watts, frustrated. 'Where are you!'

Kumar pointed. '*That's* them, heading further into the inner city.'

'Stop it there.'

Watts stared at the scene, then up at the on-screen time: 20.50 hours. 'Run it on.' The footage continued. 'There's already a high volume of traffic. It looks to me like they're heading home, via the inner city.' The Toyota disappeared on a screen change. 'If their car is picked up again, we're looking for something, *anything* which might seem untoward. Anything which suggests somebody was taking an interest in the Lawrences' car, maybe following it, getting too close, tailgating, flashing his lights.' He pointed to the top-right scene. '*Here* it is at 20.58.' Officers leant forward, shoulders hunched, eyes fixed on the dark-coloured Toyota moving slowly, making a right-hand turn.

Watts pointed again. 'They're heading in the general direction of Snow Hill and a traffic island which would lead them in the direction of Moseley and home.'

The Lawrences' car disappeared from the screen. They waited. It reappeared at 21.04. Watts jabbed at the screen. 'See that? They've taken the wrong exit from the island, now going in the wrong direction.' They scoured the quartered screen. No Toyota. 'Run it on, Kumar. See if it reappears.'

It didn't.

Watts straightened. Officers flexed their shoulders. He stared at the now blank screen. 'They were heading straight for the roadworks and Forge Street. Like you said, the nine thirty shots do seem a little early to be connected to the Lawrence shootings. The emergency call was received at ten thirty-five p.m.' He moved to the front of the room. 'Did anybody see anything remotely interesting involving the Lawrences' vehicle and any other?'

Judd broke the silence. 'Something could have occurred once they were no longer within CCTV range. Perhaps somebody thought the Lawrences' car did something, like cutting them up, got really annoyed and followed them.'

'True. I contacted Traffic but they couldn't help. Their interest is in specific accidents, and there was no damage to the Lawrences' car when it was found, except for the smashed window which we know happened at Forge Street.'

Traynor paced. 'Shots heard at around nine thirty p.m., emergency call logged at ten thirty-five.' He turned to Watts. 'You were at the scene soon after.'

'Yes. I saw both victims before they were removed. It was Mrs Lawrence who made the call, but by the time I got there both of them were unconscious. I didn't know it, but Mike Lawrence was dying.'

He turned to the head of forensics who had come into the room a couple of minutes earlier. 'Adam, can you confirm the road worthiness of the Lawrences' Toyota?'

'Our examination showed the bodywork to be well-maintained with no indication of damage. The fingerprint examination of it yielded only the Lawrences' own.' Officers stretched, sighed, some looking dispirited.

'It's early days,' advised Watts. 'Save the morose looks.'

'Given Mrs Lawrence's situation, I'm assuming that she hasn't been spoken to yet,' said Traynor.

'Judd spoke to her very briefly earlier today and she's got a written record of what was said. It isn't much.' He reached for the sheet Judd was holding out to him, passed it to Traynor. 'I'm in daily contact with the hospital as to her progress. As soon as there's an indication that she's improving I'll be asking you to intro yourself to her.'

'Let me know when.'

Watts looked at each of his officers. 'We know the difficulties we're facing here. I'll be issuing specific assignments. Meanwhile, get really familiar with the facts. If anybody comes up with an idea, a theory, you know where I am.'

Traynor raised his hand to all in the room and headed to the door and out. Miller quickly followed. Watts tracked her, saw her look up at him, saw Traynor's face, pleasant in response as he turned and disappeared from view. He left the room, thinking back to when he and Traynor had worked together back in the summer. Despite all that had been said during the briefing, his spirits rose as he thought how focused Traynor was now, compared to back then.

He came into his office to find Judd already there. 'I'm parched. Stick the kettle on.' Getting no response, he looked at her. 'What's up?'

'It was really sad, watching them drive along, both totally unaware of what was going to happen.'

He went to the kettle, switched it on. 'A word of advice, Judd. Forget the emotional side. Stick to the facts. We've now got them on that journey. It's more than a lot of homicide investigations have at this stage.' He spooned coffee, then stared down at the two mugs. 'I've wondered myself how they felt during that drive lost through that traffic and the added chaos of the roadworks only to meet even worse chaos, more than they could ever have anticipated.'

Judd eyed him. 'Is that part of the "facts" you just told me to stick to?'

He poured boiling water. 'What's looking increasingly like fact to me is how the Lawrences probably appeared to an opportunistic type watching them from, say, the time they left that restaurant, who summed them up as affluent. If he followed them on their journey into the inner city, he might have observed a bit more about them: "affluent-plus-lost". If that's anything like what happened, he would have seen it as his Christmas arriving early.'

'Opportunistic and armed?'

'*Yes*, Judd. Watch the news on the box often enough and it'll seem like the world and his granny has a weapon. There's a lot of guns in every city. Birmingham's no exception.'

The door opened and Jones came inside. 'I've just sent you our notes on the victim interviews relating to the carjackings, Sarge.' Seeing Watts turn to the computer, he said, 'Nothing of interest, apart from the one you and Judd visited.' He grinned across at her. She ignored him. 'None of the other five could describe their attacker, or referred to seeing any kind of weapon.'

'No reference to a lisp?'

'No.'

Watts thought about it. 'A male with any kind of speech problem?'

'None of the five confirmed it.' Jones held out a sheet of A4. 'Kumar's sent the contact details you asked for.'

As Jones left, he skimmed them, recognizing a name. He reached for the phone, rang the probation office number and waited.

'Hello, Leila. Bernard Watts. I'm interested in one of your clientele.' He picked up the smile in her voice.

'*Really?* Which one would that be, from a case load stretching from here to forever?'

'Jonah Budd.'

'Oh? Why the interest in Jonah?'

'His name has cropped up. Is he seeing you regularly?'

'Like clockwork. Never late. I'm seeing him this afternoon, as a matter of fact.'

'Can I drop in and see you before he arrives?'

'No problem. His appointment is at three.'

'I'll be there at two thirty.'

EIGHT

Thursday 6 December. 2.35 p.m.

Leaving Judd mutinously gathering investigative data Brophy had demanded, Watts was facing Leila Kendal, absorbing her take on Jonah Budd.

'Jonah is a young man with a hell of a lot more going for him than most of my clients. He's intelligent, he attended college, completed a course in physical education and was a regular member at an inner-city gym. Until 2014, when he was arrested for a series of very well-planned carjackings about a mile or so from the Bristol Road interchange. Does any of that help?'

'It might. How about before or since?'

'Nothing known before. Since then, he's stolen cash from some of the casual jobs he's had, which is why he's still on my list.'

'What's he up to now?'

'He's twenty-four, currently unemployed, although our records show him to be "actively seeking employment".' She studied Watts. 'You're interested in him because of last month's carjackings plus a double shooting?' She opened the file in front of her. 'Jonah is all that I've said.'

'I'm hearing a "but".'

'You are. He's also weak, over-indulged, the youngest by miles of four brothers. The wider family dotes on him and his mother is more than ready to spoil him even further at every opportunity. As a consequence, Jonah continues to lack the impetus to act responsibly. He knows he has a safety net. That his family will support him, no matter what he does. What else can I tell you? His family doesn't approve of his lawbreaking but the way they deal with him is probably a strong signal to him that, where they're concerned, he can get away with anything. Like I said, over-indulged.' She turned a few pages. 'His sentence for the carjackings was twelve months in Young Offenders. On his release, he looked me straight in the eye and swore he wouldn't reoffend. Which is always nice to hear, even for a case-hardened realist like me. I've already mentioned his subsequent thefts.'

'Tell me about the carjackings he committed.'

'There were four' – she met Watts' eyes – 'as far as we know. During the second attack, he struck the female driver on the shoulder with the hammer he'd used to smash her window. He still emphatically denies hitting her, by the way.'

Watts' interest grew at this confirmation of Budd using a weapon during one of his offences. 'You've known him a while. What's the bottom line with him, as far as you're concerned?'

She shrugged. 'He keeps his appointments with me. He's always appropriately dressed. He says the right things.' She paused and looked directly at Watts. 'And all the time I'm wondering what's behind the face he's showing me.'

'Does he have a speech problem?' Seeing her surprise, he added, 'A lisp?'

'No.' She checked her watch. 'He's probably here now. Do you want to have a word with him?'

Watts stood. 'I might at some stage, but not today. I know you're

busy but if you think of anything else, learn anything about him
that you think we should know, would you email it to headquarters
for my attention?'

Reaching the building's entrance on his way out, Watts heard
the receptionist call, 'Mr Budd? You can go in now.'

He turned and watched a young, well-dressed male get up and
head for the room he himself had just left.

Watts jogged to the BMW in an icy downpour. Once inside, he read
the information the probation officer had given him on the four
carjackings committed by Budd. Seeing again the reference to
Budd's use of a hammer on one victim, he knew he couldn't discount
him for the November cases. Watching crystalized rain run down
the windscreen, he switched his thinking to the Lawrence shootings.
Shootings which had left a man dead, a woman injured, their child
lost. The stakes in this case were the highest. He had umpteen
official guidelines for the homicide investigation alone. Despite
Traynor's opinion of a lack of connection between the shootings
and the November carjackings, Budd's name was now tugging at
him as a possibility for both, and he wasn't about to be deflected
by a lack of lisp. Not yet, anyway. Watts' natural caution kicked
in. It was still early days for the Lawrence case. He thought back
to cases he knew of, in which senior officers got an early suspect
in their sights who seemed to fit so well that they ended up blinkered
to other possibilities. He wouldn't go down that road with Budd or
any other name that might crop up. But neither would he give up
on him until he was satisfied that Budd didn't figure in either the
carjackings or the shootings.

He reached down and pulled his homicide file from under his
seat. He created a file for every homicide case he headed, and this
one was maintained by Judd. He opened it and looked at the list of
every decision he'd made to date, plus copies of every document,
witness statement and evidence find and forensic result, including
the known CCTV timeline. None of it had so far provided a specific
lead. There was one person who could do that but right now she
was in no fit state to tell them anything.

He gazed across at the probation offices. Even though Traynor
wasn't seeing any connection between the November carjackings
and the Lawrence shootings, he knew that as a police officer he
daren't ignore even a remote possibility that they might be connected.

Ignoring possibilities was as bad as getting fixated. He rubbed his big hands over his face, blinked then shook his head. 'If anybody ever bothers to ask, I'll say it's *my* job that's the hardest.' Connie Chong's face came into his head. He started as his phone rang. It was Brophy.

'Sir.'

'I want an update on the progress of the Lawrence case by tomorrow.'

'I'll pull together what we've got so far, but—'

'My office, two o'clock.'

A second call made his scalp tighten. It was Judd. 'What?' he snapped.

'I've gone through the CCTV details again, Sarge, and found nothing. I've also searched the records Reynolds tracked down on dudes with rap sheets for carjacking over the last decade, plus an additional decade.'

He closed his eyes. Birmingham, UK and the Bronx remained interchangeable for Judd.

'There's nothing in any of them that remotely fits our case but they're in your office if you want to go through them.'

He ended the call and made another. There was something he had to sort out before this investigation got much older.

'Traynor.'

'Will, I wanted to say thanks for your views on the carjacking series and the attack on the Lawrences.'

'You're welcome, but you don't agree with them.'

'At this early stage, I can't dismiss any potential link. I'm glad you're working with us again because we need your expertise, but we, you and me, don't work under the same pressures. I can't reject the carjacking series as irrelevant this early in an investigation. One of those victims was subjected to violence, plus she believes she saw a gun. The young carjacker I mentioned in briefing, Joshua Budd, was armed with a hammer and used it on one of *his* victims. I can't ignore details like that, either. If I do and it turns out that they're relevant to my two cases, my future in the force, or what's left of it, could be behind me.' He paused. 'I'm continuing to investigate a potential link between the November series and the Lawrence shootings. I wanted you to know.'

'Thank you. I think it's a waste of resources but it's your investigation.'

NINE

Jones and Kumar were talking Watts through their follow-up of all six of the November carjacking victim-witnesses. Jones pointed to printed sheets. 'We went through each of their witness statements with them. We gave particular attention to the victim you spoke to recently, the one who said she saw a gun. She isn't one hundred per cent, Sarge, although she's adamant it was something metal. She said she saw streetlights glinting off it, but that's all we got from her.'

Sitting back in his chair, Watts looked lost in thought. 'What about the other five?'

'None of them had anything they wanted to add or change.'

The two young officers were startled by his sudden straightening, his eyes on them. 'In time, you'll both realize that witnesses who are one hundred per cent certain about what they saw are as rare as hen's teeth. Leave it a few days, then revisit them.'

They left and he stood, his eyes fixed on the folder containing what he had in terms of actual progress to offer Brophy. He pulled it towards him and hefted it in one hand. It looked and felt exactly what it was. Meagre.

Five minutes later, the folder was still closed and sitting between them. Brophy was looking irritated.

'Let me get this straight: you wanted Will Traynor on this case and now you're telling me you're already going against what he's advised?' Not waiting for a response, he rolled on. 'I heard what he said in the briefing. He sees *no* link between the carjackings and the Lawrence shootings. My question to you is why aren't you now focusing all of your attention and resources on it? That's what this category A inquiry was set up to do. *That's* the homicide. It's where the media pressure is.'

Watts was recalling Brophy's earlier insistence that he shouldn't drop the carjackings. This was typical straw-in-the-wind-Brophy. He knew that if he accepted what Brophy was saying, dropped the carjacking series and it eventually transpired that there *was* a link, Brophy would at best merge silently into the woodwork. At worst, he would be on to the chief constable, playing the blame game before Watts even had a chance to contemplate a quick retirement. Blame played a big part in internal policing. Not that Watts cared. He'd been in the job long enough to know that following his instincts, getting on with it, was his one option. Because it wasn't about internal politics. It was about the victims. All of them.

'I trust Traynor's expertise, sir, but as SIO of both cases, I have to continue investigating them until I'm satisfied there is no link.' His eyes were fixed on Brophy. 'Unless you're officially instructing me otherwise?' Brophy looked away. *No chance.* Watts took pages from the folder and pushed them in his direction.

'This is my overview of the intel we have so far, including forensic data, plus a summary of the CCTV evidence of the movements of Michael and Molly Lawrence prior to the shooting. The team is doing a thorough job with the technical equipment now at its disposal, but so far, there's no leads. I have a potential lead associated with past carjacking offences which I'll be following up.'

Brophy stared down at his desk. 'It was monumental bad luck that the Lawrences' path crossed that of somebody who values human life so little.' He sighed, then glanced towards the window. 'What happened to them is horrific, but Mrs Lawrence being pregnant makes it truly tragic.'

Watts saw a brooding expression on Brophy's face he hadn't seen before. As to luck, good or bad, Watts didn't subscribe to it, but he got what Brophy was saying.

'Yes, sir.'

'How is Mrs Lawrence?'

'Conscious, according to the hospital, but still very unwell. There's a record in the overview I've given you of PC Judd's talk with her two days ago. As of eight o'clock this morning, the word from the hospital is that her injuries aren't life-threatening, that she's medicated and resting. They'll let me know when they think she's up to being questioned.'

'Good, good . . . I take it no eyewitnesses have come forward?'

'No. The available CCTV information suggests that the two possible shots heard by workers at a local convenience store at around nine thirty are too early, although I'll keep them in mind.

Unfortunately, it looks like Mrs Lawrence is our sole witness, so we have to wait until she's fit enough to talk.' He picked up Brophy's muttered 'Wild West' and felt his eyes on him.

'What about carjackers convicted in the past? Any of those known to have used violence?'

'None of them known to "carry", sir.'

Brophy gave him an absent look.

'None of them known to go equipped—'

'I know what you meant.'

Brophy's odd mood was unsettling Watts, making him wish for his previous chief, Maurice Gander, with his direct approach and hands-off management style.

'The November carjacker had detailed knowledge of the area in which he and his accomplice were operating. As Traynor said, he probably lives close to where they were committed. The scene of the Lawrence shooting is no real distance from there.' He decided to give Brophy what he knew about Jonah Budd. 'There's somebody with a carjacking history named Jonah Budd who lives in the area and is known to have used a hammer on one of the female drivers he attacked.'

Brophy focused on him, eyes widening.

'He struck her on the shoulder. Got sent to Young Offenders. He's on probation for subsequent offences of theft. I'm planning to see him.'

'Good. What are your plans for interviewing Mrs Lawrence when she's fit enough?'

'Like I said, sir, we'll be guided by the hospital. Will Traynor will talk to her. He's got specialist skills in communicating with traumatized victims.' He paused, waited for Brophy to respond. He didn't. 'Given the importance to this investigation of getting all the information we can from Mrs Lawrence, we're lucky we've got his expertise. He's fully aware of the requirements of the PEACE framework.' He waited, then added a verbal nudge. 'You know, sir, planning and preparation beforehand, engagement with the witness, followed by obtaining an account, then clarification—'

'Do you have children, Bernard?'

Wondering where the conversation was going, Watts gave him a direct look, revising a past assumption that Brophy was younger than himself. 'One daughter, sir.'

'My wife and I don't have children.'

Watts made no response to this first personal comment Watts could ever recall from Brophy.

'Actually, that's not accurate. We had a son. Kieran. He was given the wrong blood in the hospital when he was born. We watched him die.'

Watts said nothing.

The wall clock ticked on. Brophy straightened. 'You're confident about your current investigative direction?'

'Yes, sir.'

'In that case, carry on. I'm anticipating that the local officers now seconded to the investigation will prove useful.'

'I'm sure they will, sir.'

Leaving Brophy, thinking that a couple of constables with a working knowledge of the inner city was better than nothing, he returned to his office.

Judd looked up. 'What did the Bro have to say?'

'Funny you should ask. It looked like Brophy. It almost sounded like Brophy. It wasn't. Watch yourself, Judd. There's body-snatchers in the building.'

'Wha'?'

He reached for his coat. 'The Lawrence family is expecting us.'

Watts slid into a space between vehicles parked outside several large semi-detached houses and pointed. 'The one with the dark blue front door is Mike Lawrence's parents' place.'

They got out into damp cold and headed for it. The door was opened before they reached it by a tall, dark-haired man so unexpectedly familiar to Watts that he was instantly back at the scene that night, looking at Mike Lawrence inside his car, already dying. This had to be the brother, unshaven, wasted-looking, his eyes shadowed. Watts took out ID.

'Mr Brendan Lawrence?'

Lawrence gave a brief nod. They went inside the house. It was full of people, the low, steady buzz of conversation dropping to almost nothing as Watts and Judd appeared. A man and a woman stood, came to them, looking shattered, the man speaking quietly.

'Detective Inspector.' He grasped Watts' hand. 'John Lawrence, Mike's father. This is my wife, Bernice, Brendan, you've just met and over there are our daughters, Rhoda and Oona and Oona's two little girls.' Unsmiling, the two young women acknowledged Watts.

Watts introduced Judd, catching sight of food and drink laid out on a nearby table. 'Our apologies for intruding, Mr Lawrence. I was hoping we could talk to you and your wife, but we can come back when it's more—'

'Please, stay. It's not a problem. You're welcome to have some food with us, maybe a drink?' Conversation in the room had resumed.

'Is there somewhere quiet we can talk, Mr Lawrence?'

'Believe me, this *is* quiet for this house.'

They followed the Lawrences through the press of people, Watts glimpsing a priest sitting on a sofa, cup and saucer in hand. Averting his eyes, Watts walked on and into a quiet, comfortably warm room. He closed the door.

'Mr and Mrs Lawrence, on behalf of West Midlands police and all at headquarters, please accept our condolences for what has happened to your son, Michael and your daughter-in-law, Molly.' Both murmured quiet thanks. Watts let a few seconds drift by.

'If you're able to talk to us about them, it could assist our investigation. We'd really appreciate it.'

The Lawrences exchanged glances. Mr Lawrence said, 'I don't think we can be of much help. Mike and Molly left here for dinner in town . . .' He paused. 'And that's the last we saw of them.'

'They didn't mention any other plans for that evening?'

'No. We assumed that after dinner they would be going directly home.'

'Any information you're able to provide about your son and daughter-in-law's lives could be useful to us.'

Another exchange of glances. Mrs Lawrence sent him a confused look. 'How might our talking about Mike and Molly help you find whoever did this? They wouldn't know anyone like that.'

'Any information you give us could add to the picture of what's happened, Mrs Lawrence. If you're able to help us with that we'd be very grateful.'

'Of course. I'm sorry. We're feeling stressed, in a bit of a turmoil . . .'

'We understand. Whatever you're able to share with us, we'd appreciate it.'

She looked at her husband. 'Mike was a good son, wasn't he, John? A friendly, helpful person. Popular. Eight GCSEs, two A levels. He went to art college. Goodness knows where he got that talent from. Not from me. Straight from college, he went to work for an interior design company, where he was still working when . . .' She took some seconds to regroup. 'Mike loved his work. He had a real flair for it, a nice manner with clients . . .' She looked away. There was another brief silence. 'He worked hard. He always wanted the best for Molly. He didn't earn a big salary and he was never particularly ambitious, was he, John? He chose to stay with the company and the work he loved.' Her voice wavered. 'Which pleased Sebastian, his boss . . .'

John Lawrence placed his hand on her arm and looked at Watts. 'What you've just heard is what our son was. A good man who did right by his family. Molly is like a daughter to us. She's a quiet person. I remember the first time she came here I was a little concerned that she'd find our family, this house, rather noisy. She has only her mother, you see, but she was always happy here. We're praying that she will be again. She believed in Mike. She encouraged him to set up his own design company. Mike preferred to stay where he was. He loved the work and clients sensed that. They liked him. He didn't get stressed by the high cost of some of the designs he brought to reality. He knew his clients could afford it which gave his talent free rein. That was the reward he got from the work.' His voice faded, replaced by a heavy silence. 'Sorry, I seem to be going on . . .'

Bernice Lawrence sat forward, looked Watts full in the face. 'You're making progress?'

'It's a major inquiry, Mrs Lawrence. We're doing everything possible. Having a sense of Mike and Molly as people is a big help to us.'

'Molly's a great girl. We love her. We can't believe what's happened.' She shook her head. 'How her mother is going to get through this, I just don't know. She's had some difficulties over the years, poor woman.' She paused. 'Molly was so thrilled to be pregnant, wasn't she, John?' She looked at Judd who was writing. 'As soon as they left here after telling us that the hospital had said everything was fine, we went online and ordered the *best* baby buggy . . .'

She stood, her face ashen. 'John, can you talk to them, please? I can't . . .'

She went quickly to the door and out. Biting her lip, Judd watched her go, then looked back to John Lawrence who was speaking.

'We're in touch with Molly's mother by phone on a regular basis because she's on her own. She's spending a lot of time at the hospital.

Bernice has seen Molly very briefly. She didn't want to impose on the time her mother has with her.'

'Did Molly say anything to your wife that might be relevant to our investigation?'

'No. Bernice told me she just held her hand.'

Watts took a map from his pocket, unfolded it and showed it to him. 'I need you to look at this, Mr Lawrence. It's a map of the area where the incident occurred.' Watts' thick forefinger moved over it. 'See this road? That's the route your son and daughter-in-law took from the restaurant and . . . this is Forge Street right here.'

John Lawrence studied the detail. 'We saw it on the news. It looked very rough. We can't understand why they were there. It's not the area they'd go through to get home from where they had dinner.'

'It looks like they got lost but are you able to confirm if either Mike or Molly ever mentioned Forge Street to anyone in the family?'

'Never, as far as I'm aware. Bernice and I had never heard of it before it was mentioned on the news.'

'As I said, we think that your son and his wife got lost during their journey from the restaurant.' Watts' finger moved over details on the map. 'They appear to have been heading in the direction of the town hall here, then home, but, in this area here there's multiple traffic diversions. It's really easy to take the wrong direction.'

Lawrence stared at the map, sighed, then shook his head. 'Mike mentioned that his satnav was playing up a couple of weeks back, but I don't know any more about that. If I'd asked him about it before this . . .'

'Mr Lawrence, I had trouble driving there even with a fully operational satnav.' He let a few seconds of silence go by. 'You're aware that the motive for what happened to your son and daughter-in-law appears to be robbery?'

Lawrence nodded, his colour heightening. 'Yes, and for *what*? Our son had to die for the sake of some jewellery?' He shook his head. 'What's this world coming to?'

'You know that we have your son's watch.'

Lawrence nodded again.

'We need to retain it for now but it will be returned to you as soon as possible.'

Lawrence shrugged his shoulders, looking suddenly exhausted. 'Sorry. I can't say any more about what's happened. It's all so bloody senseless.'

There was a soft tap on the door. It opened. One of the Lawrences' daughters looked inside.

'Father Mulvaney is leaving, Dad,' she said quietly.

He turned to Watts. 'If you'll excuse me, Oona will see you out.' He headed from the room.

Oona Lawrence looked at them. 'I just want you to know that Mike was liked, loved by everybody who knew him, his family, his friends, his colleagues. You have to find who did this.'

Avoiding words that might be construed as a promise, Watts went with: 'That's our aim. Do you know any of your brother's friends, his colleagues?'

She shook her head. 'Not directly.'

They followed her through the house.

'Mike loved his work. He and Molly loved each other, had made a life together. We just can't accept what's happened.'

They approached the front door. Mrs Lawrence was talking to Brendan a few feet away. Watts picked up her quiet words.

'All I'm saying is that you haven't visited her and I think you should.'

He turned to her, his face weary. 'Mom, you know how busy I am. I should be at work right now and from what you've told me, Molly's really bad and – yes, all *right*, I'll try and get there later.'

They left the house, Judd looking wiped out. Watts felt much the same. John Lawrence was right. It was senseless.

TEN

Saturday 8 December. 8.58 a.m.

His phone to his ear, Watts was relating to Traynor the little they had learned from the Lawrence family the previous day. He looked down at the memo he'd received five minutes before.

'It won't surprise you when I say that Brophy's agitating for progress. He's also anticipating that local residents will feel targeted by the investigation because of the use of a gun. I don't give a rat's backside how they might feel. This investigation will be as sensitive as possible but our priority is to find this shooter pronto.'

'I agree. Is there any news as to when Mrs Lawrence might be well enough to talk?'

'I phoned the hospital a few minutes ago. I'm waiting for a call back. I'll ring you when I know something.' He ended the call. The desk phone rang.

Judd reached for it. 'Hi, Adam . . . yes, he is. No!' She turned, looked at Watts. 'He's right here. OK, I'll tell him.' She replaced the phone. 'Ready for some *really* good news?'

'When am I not?'

'SOCOs have found the gun!' She watched his face register it. 'Correction. They've found *a* gun but I'm betting any money it's *the* one. It's being processed. Adam will let you know the results.'

'Where was it?'

'In a deep hole, a few metres from the Lawrences' car.'

The phone rang again. She reached for it, held it towards Watts. 'It's the hospital, for you.' He took it from her.

'DI Watts . . . Yes. I'll be there in ten minutes.' He replaced the phone and stood.

'How is she?' asked Judd.

'That wasn't about Molly Lawrence. It was the hospital letting me know that Mike Lawrence's post-mortem is in half an hour. As SIO, I have to be there.' He fetched his coat. 'Ever attended a hospital post-mortem, Judd?'

'No.'

'How'd you feel about seeing one done?'

She shrugged. 'I've been in the PM suite as Dr Chong showed us stuff. It won't bother me.'

He waited as she got her coat. He was thinking about confidence. He'd had plenty when he was Judd's age. Back then, life was simple. You hadn't yet developed that voice in your ear telling you to be careful, watch what you were doing. If you had, you ignored it. That voice had started to register with Watts when he hit forty, although its owner by then was long dead. It was the voice of somebody who had prized security above all else. His mother. His eyes moved over the multiple files on the table. Right now, the security that came with the job didn't seem to him to be that great a deal.

*   *   *

Forty-five minutes later, they were waiting, gowned and masked, inside one of the hospital's pathology suites. Watts gave the cold tiles and metal surfaces a quick once-over. It was much like the one Chong presided over at headquarters but on a larger scale. Hearing a security pass being keyed in and the door opening, he straightened, with a quick glance in Judd's direction. What he saw wasn't quite what he was expecting. Her face wasn't too dissimilar to the pale green scrubs they'd been given to wear. A guided tour of the aftermath of a headquarters' post-mortem with Connie in charge was one thing. Being here, inside this vast hospital complex with . . .?

'Detective Inspector Watts! Dr Wexler here.'

He watched the massive gowned figure approach them, a smaller man following, camera in hand. According to what they'd been told on arrival, Dr Anton Wexler, pathologist and specialist in head injuries, would be conducting the post-mortem on Michael Lawrence. Wexler beckoned them with a gloved hand to a series of light boxes. Taking an X-ray plate from the large envelope he was carrying, he pushed it upwards, did the same with a second. Watts and Judd stared up at them.

'I'll keep the technicalities to a minimum.' Wexler turned to another gowned figure which had just appeared. 'Take Mr Lawrence from storage, please. Place him on table C.' Wexler gave Watts a wink. 'Don't want to keep him waiting, so shall we begin?' He pointed at one of the X-rays.

'Can you make out the track of the bullet which entered Mr Lawrence's head close to his chin?' He indicated the other X-ray. 'It's probably easier to discern on this one.'

Watts stared at what looked to him like a narrow, worm-like area in the midst of not much else. 'This will be a full post-mortem. If I find no other injuries to Mr Lawrence's body, I'll focus on the excision of the bullet, which I'm assuming to be of significant interest to you, Detective Inspector.'

He pulled the X-rays free. They followed him to a distant table, its occupant covered by a thin green sheet, surrounded on three sides by centimetres-high glazed panels. Wexler glanced up at the wall clock, pulled a microphone close to his face, intoned his and their names and titles. 'My colleague John Haynes is responsible for post-mortem photography. It is now nine thirty-eight a.m. on the eighth of December. We'll begin.'

Watts and Judd watching, pens and notebooks in hand, Wexler

neatly folded away the sheet. Mike Lawrence was now as exposed as he had been the day he was born. Wexler reached up to a vacant screen suspended above the post-mortem table. It filled immediately with a partial image of Mike Lawrence's body, a portion of Wexler's enormous girth, Watts' head and shoulders, the camera poised in Haynes' hands, and very little of Judd. Watts took a slow, deep breath, and watched Wexler get to work.

The clock's hands moved steadily onwards. Forty-five minutes later, having found no evidence of injury to Mike Lawrence's body, Wexler was now giving his full attention to the head, his voice rolling steadily on.

'The first shot to Mr Lawrence grazed his left cheek. More of that later.' He manipulated Mike Lawrence's head. 'See? This second shot was the cause of death. It inflicted a particularly devastating injury to Mr Lawrence's brain as you saw from the X-rays. Let's have a look at it, shall we?'

They watched Wexler deftly apply the scalpel, starting from behind Mike Lawrence's left ear, continuing upwards, across his scalp, down the other side and behind his right ear. Watts kept his eyes on what was happening, his thinking on hold.

'You're in luck, Detective Inspector. There's only minor bullet fragmentation and, right here' – he pointed – 'is the tissue disruption and destruction caused as it progressed through his skull, do you see?'

Watts nodded, wishing he didn't. The camera whirred and clicked. Wexler continued, his eyes on the screen. 'Now, here we have the cavitation in detail: the effect of the bullet's passage through the soft tissue.'

Watts and Judd stood, mute, as Wexler continued his verbal description, pointing a gloved finger at destruction beneath one side of the jaw.

'One entrance point here . . . and also stippling which indicates that whoever fired this shot was probably within say a metre of the victim. Which may be of no surprise, given media reports suggesting that he was shot inside his car . . .' His facial expression focused, he applied the scalpel to the exit wound. 'Not that the press has any idea what it's talking about most of the time.'

Watts made brief notes, looked up to see Wexler grinning widely, the slim metal tool in his massive hand gripping a small object. 'This is it, Detective Inspector! The object what *done* it.' He shook his head. 'Which is not accurate, is it? The individual who set it on its course *did* it and I'm more than happy to leave that with you.' He moved the bullet towards a small metal dish, let it fall. It landed with a tinny sound.

'That minor abrasion you can see to Mr Lawrence's left cheek was caused by the first bullet, possibly a practice shot, which skimmed his cheek then travelled onwards and struck a sun visor. I understand that bullet is already in the possession of the police.'

He stepped away from the table. 'You'll have my report, plus the bullet I've recovered, within the next twenty-four hours. Give my regards to Dr Connie Chong, if you would, please and also to another of your colleagues, Adam . . . now, what *is* his surname?'

Despite his experience of post-mortems over the years, Watts still felt the effects of them and, right now, looking at what was in front of him, his mind was a desert. For the life of him, he couldn't supply it. He glanced at Judd. Her face told a similar story.

They left the hospital, Watts on his phone to Traynor. 'What's the soonest you can be in? Right. See you then.' He ended the call. 'He'll be with us early Monday morning.'

They drove the rest of the way to headquarters in silence, broken by Watts as they entered the car park. 'How many shots were fired at the Lawrences, Judd?'

'Two to Mike Lawrence and . . .' She stared at him. 'Three.'

'Looks like we can't rely on the locals when it comes to identifying gunfire.'

Back in his office, Watts photocopied his and Judd's notes. 'Unless you've got anything you want to add, I'll email these to Adam's team.' Not getting a response, he gave her a close look. 'You all right?'

She looked up at him. 'No, I'm not. I'm furious. Whoever did that to Mike Lawrence, then turned the gun on his wife, should be forced to watch what we've just seen.'

He thought she had a point.

8.10 p.m.

During the dinner he had made, Watts told Chong all he knew of the Lawrence case. It didn't take long. Aware of the opportunistic cat circling his ankles, he looked across the table at her, thinking how empty this house had felt during the last ten days or so. Ditto, his life, despite all that had been happening at headquarters.

'The good news – well, two pieces of good news: SOCOs have found a gun which you probably know about already, and Will Traynor is on board.' He gave her a quick glance, thinking that she must be tired after her flight, hoping that she wasn't.

'Glad to hear about Will. Yes, Adam told me about the gun.' She sat back. 'That was a really lovely dinner.'

'So are you. Lovely, I mean.'

She grinned. 'I was at headquarters this afternoon, getting my brain moving. Sorry I didn't have time to come and say "Hello". How is Will?'

'He's looking good and there's none of that edginess he had back in the summer. He's sold his house and he's living about three miles from here with his daughter, although she's dividing her time between his place and the university.' He stood, reached for their plates. 'I attended the Lawrence post-mortem at the hospital this afternoon.'

Carrying other items from the table, she followed him to the kitchen. 'What did you learn?'

'Stripping away the technicalities, basically what we already knew: Mike Lawrence shot at fairly close range, the first shot skimming his cheek, the second entering to the side of his chin and making a right mess of the inside of his skull.' He shook his head. 'I was surprised at how I felt, watching the post.'

She raised her brows. 'Hearing that, so am I. You've seen enough of them. How was it different?'

He rinsed plates and glasses, then put them inside the shiny metal dishwasher. 'Not sure. Maybe something to do with the brutality of this case. Possibly, because we know what happened to Mrs Lawrence. Do you know that she was pregnant?'

'Yes. Who was with you at the hospital?'

'Judd.'

'How did she cope?'

'Really well. A bit spacey afterwards.'

'Who did the post-mortem?'

'Big bloke. Wexler. He sends his regards.'

Chong grinned. 'He's a character. We trained together. Did he get you chatting during it?'

'He did the chatting. Towards the end, I couldn't remember Adam's surname when he asked for it and I'm not so sure I knew my own by the time we left.' He shrugged. 'I think I was distracted because of Judd being there and how she was doing.' He gazed down at Connie. 'I've put your bag in the spare room.'

She went to the door and turned, giving him a steady look. 'Bernard, I've just spent several days with my mother who is eighty-one years old, frail, not very well, but when I left she was making plans for a holiday with my brother and contemplating spending some of it, if not hiking, then on her feet.' She waited. 'Do you get what I'm saying?' She watched his eyes move from side to side. Shaking her head, she left the kitchen.

He gave it a quick once-over. Getting on for twenty-five years married until his wife died, and now a year-long relationship with Connie Chong hadn't made his understanding of women's thinking any swifter. He listened to the new dishwasher going through its paces. He patted it. One thing he did know: women had most of the good ideas.

'Bernard?'

'Coming.' He headed for the hall and stairs. 'How about I make mugs of hot—?'

He gazed upwards at small feet, their neat nails a deep rose colour and on, over honeyed skin, the dark triangle, the neat curves and swells and on to the pixie haircut and her face smiling down at him. 'My bag is in the main bedroom where it belongs.' The hall clock ticked its way to eight forty-five.

'You're not tired from your flight?'

She regarded him, one hand on her hip. 'Clearly, my reference to my mother was overly oblique, so try this. I'm fifty years old and my job, which I'll be resuming some time tomorrow and which I love, is also a constant reminder that life can be unpredictable, at times brutal and also unexpectedly short.' She turned, gazed over one shoulder at him. '*Now*, do you get it?'

Hearing his quick footfalls on the stairs, she laughed.

ELEVEN

Monday 10 December. 7.50 a.m.

The carjacking files were spread on the table close to the still-slim one relating to the Lawrence case, the Smartboard waiting to receive any information additional to that yielded by the post-mortem.

'What time is Will due in?' asked Judd.

'Knowing how prompt he is, in eight point five minutes.'

'When are we going to see Dr Chong?'

'About the same.'

She was silent, then: 'There's loads of guns in Birmingham, Sarge.'

'And I need reminding because?'

'Just saying. The one that's been found might not be—'

The door opened and Brophy came in. 'When Dr Traynor arrives, ensure that he knows that I expect, make that *demand*, due care be taken by all working with this force when interacting with various inner-city residents.'

'He knows that that's general policy,' responded Watts, wondering why Brophy was acting like his pants were on fire. 'Plus Traynor is sensitive to people's feelings—'

'I've just had one of the inner-city community leaders on the phone to tell me that concerns are already being raised by residents feeling targeted due to the high police presence in the area.'

Watts was unimpressed. 'We've hardly started and we're already taking due care but those kinds of concerns come second to my investigation.'

Brophy frowned. 'The situation *still* needs careful handling.'

Jonah Budd's name nudged inside Watts' head. 'Whatever leads we get, we follow them, regardless of ethnicity, and whatever we do will be appropriate and subtle. This isn't the seventies.' He watched Brophy swivel and disappear.

'How many days have we been on this case and he's already getting on my—'

The phone rang as Traynor came inside. Judd reached for it, nodded.

'We'll be there.' She replaced it. 'Hi, Will.' To Watts: 'Dr Chong is ready.'

Inside the PM suite, they watched Chong place copies of the hospital post-mortem report on Mike Lawrence in front of them, plus accompanying photographs, followed by a shorter report relating to Molly Lawrence.

'Both are concise yet thorough. Details of the injuries to Michael Lawrence you already know.' She indicated the shorter item. 'This is the hospital's overview of Molly Lawrence's injuries, which basically indicates the bullet entered low on her right side, after which it travelled upwards and, exiting almost instantly, avoided major organs. I'm guessing here when I say that the assailant probably had some difficulty aiming the gun from the rear seat. Her injuries are currently incapacitating but fortunately not life-changing.' She waited. 'Any questions?'

'No,' said Watts.

Traynor shook his head.

She headed for the door. 'In which case, a physical demonstration of the shootings should be mere icing on the cake. What I'm about to show you is something Adam and I spent several hours assembling yesterday.'

They followed her from the PM suite, along the corridor, up a flight of stairs to the ground floor and along another corridor towards the rear of the building.

'Where are we going, Sarge?'

They stopped at a door marked *Forensic Test Area*. A triangular warning sign bearing a laser symbol was next to it. Chong entered a code into the keypad to one side and they followed her into a vast, light-filled, featureless space.

Judd took several steps inside, looking slowly up and around, her mouth a perfect 'O'. 'I've never been in here . . . It's . . . it's like Lidl, without the *stuff*.'

Chong smiled, pointing ahead. 'This is where specific types of mock-ups are created.'

They followed her across a wide expanse of pale floor to the Lawrences' dark Toyota Previa, its rear doors standing open, its front doors removed and lying on mats nearby. Both front seats were occupied by white, featureless mannequins. 'We reconstructed all of this from the crime scene photographs.'

They stood, eyes fixed on slender rods, some blue, others red, protruding from the mannequins. Chong pointed. 'They're made of aluminium. Hollow for lightness. The blue ones indicate the bullet trajectories for Michael Lawrence, the red for Molly. Come closer.'

They followed her to the rear of the car, where she indicated its dark, carpeted floor, one area marked by a bright yellow circle. 'That's where the recovered bullet casing was found, which suggests that the gunman wasn't too concerned about removing evidence. The bullet from the sun visor has been recovered.'

They followed her to the front seats of the car. She pointed to the impaled mannequins. 'You have the hospital's reports on the Lawrences' injuries. What we've set up here is a visual indication of what occurred inside this vehicle. Adam and I have checked the rods with an inclinometer, so we're satisfied with their accuracy.' They tracked her moving finger. 'If you look to the mannequin representing Mike Lawrence, you'll see a small black cross on the cheek, yes? That's where the first bullet grazed his face then continued on before embedding itself in the sun visor immediately above his head.'

She placed her hand beneath the blank oval of the face. 'You know from the post-mortem that the second bullet entered Mike Lawrence's lower jaw close to his chin, continuing upwards and into his skull.' They followed her to the car's passenger side.

'You'll see from the position of these rods that the damage to Molly Lawrence was different. One bullet only, which entered low on her right side before exiting quickly and somewhat higher, as you can see from the rod's rising trajectory. Forensics did a complete sweep of the car and also located that bullet.'

Traynor leaned forward, his eyes fixed on the inside of the car. He looked at its doors lying nearby. 'That window was shattered from the inside?'

'Yes. All the indications are that both victims were shot from the direction of the rear seat.' She looked at each of them. 'In case there are any doubts, I've attached a laser to each rod. Stand over there, please, while I activate them.' They moved away, waited, seeing nothing. Chong turned to them.

'This space is so useful for the kind of investigative work I'm showing you, but it's very light.' The door opened. 'Ah, just the person.' She grinned as Adam walked inside, one hand gripping an aerosol can.

'Canned smoke,' he said.

She took it from him and sprayed each of the rods. The laser beams lit up. She pointed to the centre of the rear seat. 'See? This is where the rods more or less converge, showing us the likely location of the gunman.' They stared down at it. 'The covering material has been removed from the seats. Indications are that they were subjected to minimal use prior to this incident, which raises the possibility of finding trace evidence such as hair. Unfortunately, nothing to report so far.'

Watts walked around the vehicle and lowered his head. He looked at the front and back seats. He straightened. 'I'm having trouble seeing Mike Lawrence just sitting there, his pregnant wife next to him when all of this kicked off.'

'We give you the science,' said Chong. 'I'm afraid that's an investigative question for you to answer.'

He looked at Adam. 'Anything to report on the gun?'

Adam shook his head. 'Not yet. We've requested specialist advice which we're expecting at any time.'

Traynor walked around the car, his eyes moving slowly over it. 'My reading of the situation is that Mike Lawrence remained in position as the gunman got inside the car.' He regarded it for several seconds. 'It's very possible he was fearful of doing anything which might excite or antagonize him and place his wife at increased danger.'

'Sounds plausible,' said Watts.

Back in the office, they looked at the photographs of the mock-up which Chong had provided. Watts reached for one of them, showing the Mike Lawrence mannequin in its seat.

'What you said downstairs, Traynor, about Mike Lawrence's lack of action. It sounds to me like he was doing exactly what he should have done in that high-risk situation. In which case, why did it end with both of them being shot?'

Traynor passed other photographs to him. 'A contained space. Stressed people. A gun. At this stage we can only speculate on what happened inside that car. The gunman might have anticipated a challenge from Lawrence, misconstrued a sudden movement or tone of voice from either of them and believed that *he* was under threat.'

'A nervy attacker.' Watts thought about it. 'Somebody unused to handling a gun?' He looked at Judd. 'Remember the victim of the last November carjacking? Maybe that was some kind of practice run to give her attacker an idea how to extend his repertoire.'

Traynor's brows rose. 'There's nothing in any of those victim-witness statements which categorically confirms the existence of a gun. You already know my doubts of a link between those attacks and what happened to the Lawrences.'

'There's also still a lot we don't know. When Molly Lawrence is ready to talk, hopefully she'll clarify exactly what did happen. We're clueless as to how their attacker got them to stop their car.' He looked up as Traynor stood. 'Any plans for the rest of the day?'

'I've a couple of lectures to deliver, following which I'll be giving some thought to the best way to approach my first meeting with Molly Lawrence to obtain maximum information about what happened to her and her husband. I also need to consider the forensic information now available from their car, including the absence of external damage.' He stood. 'I'll be here at eleven thirty tomorrow with my perceptions.'

Watts watched him go. *Here at . . . with my perceptions.* Socially, Traynor was great company. When it came to his work, he was a theorist. A cool thinker. Watts pushed his notes across the table to Judd.

'Put these in the homicide file while I get a grip on *my* perceptions.'

Five minutes later, the phone rang. He reached for it. 'Watts. Yeah?' He came upright. 'That was quick! We're on our way.'

He cut the call, reached for his own phone, tapped a number, under close scrutiny from Judd mouthing, *What?*

'Hope you haven't gone far, Traynor.' He nodded. 'Yes. Soon as you can.'

1.10 a.m.

On headquarters' forensic floor, Chong was standing beside a tall, dark-haired man and making introductions.

'This is Detective Inspector Bernard Watts, Senior Investigative Officer for the Lawrence homicide, Dr William Traynor, criminologist who is consulting on the case and police constable Chloe Judd.' To all three, she said, 'This is Dr Miles Mathison, ballistics expert.

He's going to tell us what he knows of the weapon recovered on Saturday morning, fairly close to the scene of the Lawrence shooting.'

'Whereabouts, exactly?' asked Watts.

'Adam has photographs for you, but it was a few metres away from the Lawrences' car, inside a deep hole,' said Chong.

'Dropped or concealed?'

'Both are possibilities. I'm favouring dropped in the act of a quick exit by the gunman.' She turned to the ballistics expert. 'All yours, Miles.'

Mathison inclined his head to them. 'Follow me, please.'

Watched by members of Adam's team, they followed him to a workbench. Sitting at its centre was a lidded plastic box, something dark and shadowy inside it. He removed the lid, causing a quick intake of breath from Judd. They looked down at the dense, black object. A handgun, its grip grainy, *Made in Russia* etched on its side. Pulling on soft, white gloves, Mathison reached for it.

'First, I'll run through a description and some brief history. This is a converted Baikal Model IZH 798. They were originally made to look like a Marakov, a Soviet side arm, but unlike the military version they were designed with a semi-obstructed barrel which prevented the discharge of bulleted cartridges but allowed the discharge of eight-millimetre Lachrymator cartridges.' He looked up at them. 'So-called tear-gas cartridges. They were intended for the civilian market as a non-lethal personal protection option. There's been a huge influx of these guns into the UK from Lithuania since the early 2000s, which is where they were illegally converted to discharge nine-millimetre short calibre cartridges.' He looked at Watts. 'You're familiar with such a weapon, Detective Inspector?'

Watts nodded. 'I've seen them over the years. Usually with a silencer and Russian or Czech ammunition, all wrapped up nice and neat in a happy bag.'

Judd frowned. 'Happy bag?'

'Con lingo for anything holding criminal tools of the trade.'

They watched as Mathison expertly handled the gun and demonstrated its loading mechanism. 'The UK has a huge converted gun problem. The Baikal has some aesthetic appeal: see how black, how compact it is? Since it flooded into the UK it's become a popular street gun, in fact, *the* street weapon of choice, favoured within British gang culture and also by gang bosses to enforce compliance.

It's also known as Hitman's Kit because it can be used at close range, victims rarely escaping with their lives.'

Mathison replaced the gun in its container, then removed the gloves. 'Are there any further questions?' No one spoke. 'In that case, if further queries should arise, Dr Chong has my contact details.'

'Thank you, Miles. We're very grateful for your expertise,' said Chong. 'I'll show you out.' She turned to Watts. 'I'll see you all at the Lawrence vehicle in five minutes.'

They were back inside the huge space, Chong carrying the plastic box. Placing it on a shelf, pulling on latex gloves, she removed the handgun. To Watts, it looked harsh and sinister in her slim brown hand. They followed her to the Lawrences' Toyota, its front seats still occupied by the mannequins. She got inside and slid along the rear seat to its midpoint, her colleagues watching.

'You know from earlier how the shots fired at Michael and Molly Lawrence started and ended their journeys, plus the trajectory of each bullet. I want to see how easy this gun is to manipulate in a confined space.'

She raised the muzzle of the gun towards the light-coloured upholstery high on the rear of the driver's seat, close to an ill-defined mark. 'See that? This gun was resting on the top of this seat when it was fired, which resulted in a discharge of hot gases and particulates. In Mike Lawrence's case it left the star-shaped pattern on the left side of his face and probably a similar configuration on his wife's clothing. The marks confirm that the muzzle of this gun was held very close to each of them when it was fired. In Molly Lawrence's case, the gun was fired from this position.' She sat forward, moved the gun between the two front seats. She frowned. 'It feels awkward but the gun is light and handles easily, even for someone of my small stature. The added advantage of being in the rear seat is that it put distance between him and both victims.'

Lowering the gun, she slid across the seat and out. She looked at each of them, her face and tone serious. 'It's your job to deduce motive and intent for these murders, but to me there's an element of cold-blooded execution about them.'

Back in the office several minutes later, Watts was staring down at the table, his arms folded.

'Execution means punishment or retribution as motive.' He looked up. 'Why would anybody have that kind of issue with an interior designer and a finance manager, which as far as I can make out is an accountant? Why would anybody want them dead?'

Judd's head was resting on her forearms. 'How about one of Mike Lawrence's clients hated the puce-and-acid-yellow scatter cushions? Or, maybe somebody got done big-time by the Inland Revenue because of a dodgy tax return Molly Lawrence filed.'

'Execution as motive raises some real possibilities,' said Traynor quietly. 'A professional attack by a single-minded, organized, professional criminal operating entirely for financial reward.'

'Traynor, these are two ordinary people we're talking about,' protested Watts. 'What could they have done that attracted the attention of a hitman?'

'I don't know. It's also possibly the work of an antisocial, highly aggressive individual with zero empathy who came upon them at the right time for him but the wrong time for them.'

'*That's* more like it. I've met a lot over the years who would fit that description, who'd sell their own mothers if the price was right.'

'Both require consideration,' said Traynor.

Watts shook his head. 'Not the executioner. My job is to be evidence-led not theory-driven. What else can you say about this other type?'

'Despite what I've suggested about his personality and attitudes to others, it's also very likely that even the Lawrences themselves were unaware of the threat he represented to them.' Seeing Watts' face, he said, 'It doesn't necessarily have to be a motive which is understandable to other people. Once I start working with Mrs Lawrence, I'll indirectly raise the possibility with her.'

Watts reached for an envelope lying on the table, opened it, read its contents, then passed the single sheet towards them. 'Have a look at this.'

Judd sat up as Traynor took it, read it aloud: 'Forensic examination of the Lawrences' car engine: a loose electrical connection which could have resulted in a minor, intermittent problem.'

'*That,*' said Watts, 'could explain why they came to a stop in Forge Street. To get away from the roadworks and heavy traffic.'

Traynor handed it to Judd, who quickly read it.

'Hey-hey, we're on the right track, Sarge. That whole attack was planned, start to finish. I think they were followed by somebody who knew them. Somebody who knew them well enough to be angry with them about something or be holding some kind of grudge. Someone who tampered with their car, say, in the hospital car park.'

'Those are suppositions,' said Traynor, 'but a gunman with a personal grudge better fits my thinking than an opportunist who shoots two people for a handful of jewellery.'

Watts eyed him. 'What I've learned from thirty years on this job is that antisocial types who don't give a damn for anybody will do all manner of violence to get their paws on stuff we wouldn't consider worth the effort, let alone killing for. Open a newspaper any day of the week. You'll see reports of muggings, hold-ups by types like that, grabbing people's stuff, injuring them, even stabbing them and ending up with a phone, a few quid, for which they've created victims and traumatized families because they don't give a damn about anybody or anything.'

Traynor was at the door. 'What I don't see is how an intermittent fault affecting the Lawrences' car would serve this gunman's plan or purpose. I'm going to the incident room to look at what I think is hampering our understanding of and progress on the shootings.'

TWELVE

Tuesday 11 December. 11.38 a.m.

Traynor came into Watts' office. Without speaking he placed the six carjacking files on the table in front of Watts. Watts looked at them, then up at Traynor, who pointed at them.

'My view at the outset was that these six carjackings have no relevance to the Lawrence shootings. That remains my view. They were quick attacks with zero contact between attacker and unknown victim. Whoever attacked Mike and Molly Lawrence got access to the inside of their car. He spent time in close proximity to them. He may even have talked to them. His attack is of a different order entirely. This investigation needs to focus solely on the Lawrence shootings.'

Watts looked at him, then down at the files. 'You're wrong about zero contact by the carjacker. Ask the woman who had her hand smashed. She'll tell you exactly how she felt about his "proximity".'

Traynor went to the Smartboard, pulled up a screen of details and began adding to them. 'Anybody intent on stopping the Lawrences' vehicle wouldn't have been helped by an intermittent fault. "Intermittent" means that the car could have stopped anywhere on its journey to Forge Street. It could even have restarted, enabling them to drive on.'

Judd's head dropped back. 'Every time we get what looks like a potential lead, there's an "Ah, but".' She raked her hair. 'The Lawrences didn't choose to stop in that godawful place. How about this: if whatever was done to the Toyota caused it to merely slow down at times, is it possible that somebody was waiting at Forge Street, blocking the road with his own vehicle, waiting for them? We might not have any evidence, but you can't say that's not possible.' She looked from Watts to Traynor. 'It *had* to be something like that. His only alternative would have been to force them to stop, which would have been chancy. Even more to the point, it would probably have left damage to their car, but there isn't any.'

'The flaw in what you've said, Judd, is that whoever he was, he could have been left waiting, because, like Will suggested, the intermittent fault might not have occurred and they would have continued home as normal. He also couldn't have assumed they'd get lost.'

Watts looked down at files and papers covering the table. 'He shot both of them. Guns give a shooter distance. Whatever the antecedents, once that Toyota was stationary, he could have threatened them through the window, reached inside, grabbed whatever he wanted. What makes no sense to me is that by getting inside he increased his personal risk by putting himself in close proximity to two frightened people.'

Judd's brows slid together. 'What if he didn't know they were both in the car? The Toyota's windows are tinted.'

'He would know if he followed them to and from the hospital or wherever else he first saw them.'

Traynor paced, eyes focused on the floor, his voice low. 'I'm also bothered by his placing himself inside that car in such close proximity to both victims. If he harboured an extreme resentment to one or both of the Lawrences, did he get inside the car because he wanted to talk to them? Lay out his grievance against them?'

'Whoever he is, he's risk-happy,' said Judd, '*and* he was tooled up, on what he regards as a job—'

Watts looked at her, exasperated. 'Forge Street's a *dump*. This city has no rep for execution-style shootings of your middle class.'

'It's no good obsessing about what he was thinking or why he did it, Sarge. We might never know until we catch him.'

'So, exactly how do you propose we do that?' He watched her frown deepen. 'Let me know once you've got an investigative plan.' He glanced at Traynor. 'Meanwhile, both the carjackings and the shootings remain part of this investigation for the simple reason that it makes sense to me until there's solid evidence which points to there being no connection.'

Traynor sat, his eyes on Watts. 'There had to be another car involved.'

Watts mustered patience. 'There's no forensic evidence to support the presence of another vehicle.'

'With all that rain,' said Judd, 'there's no proof there wasn't, but if you don't like that, how about another possibility?' She ignored his groan, his hands going to his head. 'The attacker saw their car approaching and he lay down on the road, pretending to be hurt.'

'You're still saying that this was somebody hanging around on the off-chance of them coming along! They were *lost*. They should never have come along Forge Street.' Silence settled on the office. 'Judd, I appreciate your keenness, but this is going nowhere.' To Traynor, Watts said, 'I hear what you're saying, Will, about the carjackings, but for me this is a young thug who's no stranger to that kind of urban crime, who's built up his confidence on five of those robberies, and prior to the sixth decided to up his game with a gun. What you said about the shooter being an antisocial type supports it. He might be a gang member, like that Mathison chap talked about. There's no CCTV evidence that Mike and Molly Lawrence were followed after they left the restaurant, or that they knew their attacker. If this young, armed thug was around Forge Street waiting for somebody, *anybody* to show up, it just happened to be the Lawrences' bad luck that it was them. My job is to thoroughly explore and exhaust the most obvious possibility before I look at anything else and that's what I'm doing.'

'The CCTV footage I've seen is no confirmation that they weren't followed,' said Traynor.

Watts gave his face a brisk rub. 'I'm not dismissing anybody's theories.' He watched Judd fold her arms. 'But so far as I can see, all they do is raise more questions. My theory is uncomplicated. It's possible he was just there, on the off-chance. OK, it's possible he saw them leave a pricey restaurant, gave them a quick once-over and said to himself, "Well-dressed couple, she's got an expensive handbag, they're driving a reasonable-looking car." He's not bothered that they're a couple. He doesn't care. He's got confidence from the gun. So, maybe he does follow them. As for how he got them to stop, we can speculate, try and predict his behaviour all we like, but we'll probably not know until he tells us if we catch him.' He jabbed the table with his index finger. 'Make that "*when*".'

'Molly Lawrence could have some answers,' said Traynor. 'How is she?'

'I checked earlier. She could be discharged at the end of the week, depending on what the doctors say. According to the nurse I spoke to, she's asking to go home.' Watts studied Traynor. 'How about you check with staff? Depending on what they say, go and see her at the hospital today. Introduce yourself.'

Traynor took out his phone. 'When she does talk, I want the essence of this gunman's character from his appearance, his verbal behaviour.'

Watts got up, went across the office and switched on the kettle. 'In the meantime, I can make some suggestions about his "essence": local to that area, eighteen to twenty-four years old, a previous record for violence, possible drug user, possible gang affiliation. If I'm right, by now he's spent most of the money he got from robbing the Lawrences on stuff that's gone up his nose or into his arms.'

He looked across at Traynor who was ending a call. 'What did they say?'

'That I should ring later.'

'I take it they know how urgent this is?'

Traynor nodded. 'I'm sure they do, but they've got their own concerns right now.' He paced. 'Ours is to learn what moves this individual, what motivates him, how he thinks. It will have been evident that night in what he said and what he did. Molly Lawrence heard his voice, his words. She saw him. She was in close proximity to him. She has a lot to give us.'

Judd looked across at him, chin on fist. 'When I saw her very recently, she couldn't give me even a basic idea of what happened to them. The nurse told me that she doubted Molly had faced up to the events of that night.'

'That's a realistic summation of someone who's been through such a degree of trauma as Molly Lawrence has.'

Judd and Watts exchanged quick glances. If anyone knew about trauma first-hand, it was Traynor.

'She's our sole source, our best hope for understanding him, what he did and how they responded inside that vehicle. It's those kinds of details that will help us create a picture of him.'

'It's possible there was no interaction,' said Watts. 'He's in their car, shoots them, takes their stuff and he's gone.'

'Shooting them is a form of interaction. Actions don't occur within a vacuum. The progression of events could tell us a lot about how he relates to others, whether he was confrontational.'

Watts stared at him across the table. 'He *shot* them both. How much more confrontational could he *get*?'

Judd's eyes widened as Traynor stood, his eyes fixed on Watts, who was also now on his feet. 'I'm talking antecedents to the actual shootings, Bernard. If shooting them wasn't part of his plan, there had to have been a causal event which led to it. We know nothing about his initial contact beyond his producing a gun to them. Depending on their personalities, such an action could have shocked them into submission *or* triggered panic. How did he intend to maintain control?'

Watts stared at him. 'It looks to me like it was with the *gun.*'

Traynor shook his head. 'No. Guns can be a very poor method for achieving control.'

'Which leads to exactly what we've got in this case: chaos, ending with Mike Lawrence dead, his wife as good as, for all this low-life knew or cared.'

The silence was broken by Traynor. 'He didn't kill her.'

They both stared at him. 'Meaning what?' asked Watts.

'He could have killed her with a shot to the head. He didn't.'

'So? If he's young, like I said, he was probably as shocked as they were at the madness of what was happening. He starts firing indiscriminately—'

'Molly might have pleaded with him,' said Judd. 'You know, "Please, don't hurt me, I'm pregnant." I think a woman would do that in her situation. If he was young, not some hardened thug, she might have thought she could appeal to him not to hurt her.'

Watts covered his face with his hands, then let them drop. 'Maybe she did and maybe she didn't – he still shot her.' He looked across at Traynor. 'If he's really young, say sixteen or so, the shootings probably frightened the life out of *him*.'

Traynor looked across at him. 'There might be something in what you said about his being very young.'

'It was a guess.'

'Guesses can be informed.'

'What else do you want from Molly Lawrence?' asked Watts.

'If we assume that he put both Lawrences in fear, I want to know if he attempted to form some kind of link, some sort of relationship with them, perhaps to calm them. Or did something occur inside that car which led to his complete loss of control?'

He stood and gazed out of the window. 'He's a shadow man and that's how he'll remain until Molly Lawrence talks and we see his essential character within her words.'

The phone rang. Watts reached for it and listened. 'You don't say!' He made quick, neat notes. 'Any news on Jonah Budd? Right, carry on with it.' He replaced the phone. 'I've got a couple of officers watching Budd but so far nothing to report on him. The big news is that Adam has examined the gun and found a link from it to a drug-related, inner-city shooting a decade ago. A bit of a turf-war warning. No fatality. One suspect was a Huey Whyte. I know Whyte. Back in the day, he was living in the inner-city area. For the last few years his offence profile has been zero. He needs finding.' He looked at Traynor. 'Avoid Brophy until you've had contact with Molly Lawrence. If he asks you about your plans, keep it vague, no details, because they'll turn him into a micro-managing nightmare.'

Traynor reached for his backpack. 'In which case, it's fortunate that he has no management role with me.'

Judd watched the door close on him. 'Will's straight to it, isn't he? All business, clear thinking, determined and not about to be ordered around by the Bro. Which is just as well, given the mess we're in—'

'Judd, put a lid on it!'

Brophy was eyeing Watts across his desk. 'Where's Dr Traynor? What's he doing?'

'On his way to his day job.'

Brophy's mouth set. 'When's he planning to see the woman who was shot?'

'Mrs Lawrence. Very soon, he told me.'

'I don't want any foot-dragging on this investigation. Why isn't he going to the hospital today to talk to her?'

Watts started a slow count inside his head. 'A couple of reasons, sir. One, she's gone through a massive trauma which has left her husband dead. Two, she's in the care of the hospital and they say when she's well enough to have visitors – oh, and as a bit of forward thinking, once we've identified whoever attacked her and killed her husband, she will be a witness in an ensuing court case and we don't want any lawyers for the gunman rubbishing whatever Will Traynor got from her, saying he obtained it under duress or at a time when she was in no fit state to give accurate information.'

Brophy gave a reluctant nod. 'He still needs to get moving on it.'

'He will. He's aiming for maximum information from her without upsetting her or contaminating her recall. One of his research areas is eyewitness identification, its inherent weaknesses and risks. He doesn't want to interfere with any information, any memories of the attack which she has. He's taking the long view.'

'Right now, I'd settle for something shorter.' Brophy glared across his desk. 'What I don't need on a high-profile case is people being overcautious and pussy-footing about. Make sure he knows that.'

'Yes, sir,' said Watts, with no intention of doing so. The chief constable was evidently leaning on Brophy. Which was Brophy's problem, not his or Traynor's.

Listening to the Aston Martin's soothing purr, Traynor was thinking about Molly Lawrence and trauma. He glanced at his own hands on the steering wheel. Both steady. In control. Some months ago, his psychiatrist had suggested he consider a new therapy which would require Traynor to 'revisit' what had happened to his family. The psychiatrist thought it might help his PTSD. Traynor's response had been direct: 'Ellis, if you had ever come home to find your kitchen an abattoir, your young daughter hysterical and your wife gone for ever, I might entertain the suggestion. As you haven't, I won't.'

He was fine. More than fine. He had found his own way of dealing with the triggers that caused flashbacks. Avoidance. Avoidance of thinking about the experience. Avoidance of feeling. Both were too costly. As was clinging to his wife's memory. He had accepted that he had to move on. He had done so, loneliness replacing the ache for her. He had mentioned all of it to Ellis. It had elicited a slow headshake and the psychiatrist's low opinion of avoidance as a solution. For Traynor, it was working. He felt like a different person, compared to four months ago when he'd last worked with Watts' team. He was a different person.

His eyes fixed on the damp road ahead. He thought about his planned work with Molly Lawrence and felt a sudden surge of sympathy for this woman he hadn't yet met. He took a deep breath then slowly released it. She had to be approached with considerable care . . .

His phone rang. It was Watts. Hospital staff had just confirmed that 'they anticipate Molly Lawrence being physically well enough to talk to Dr Traynor today, from two o'clock onwards.' Traynor thought through his university commitments for that afternoon, now requiring quick reorganization.

'I'll be there.'

THIRTEEN

Tuesday 11 December. 2.10 p.m.

Traynor followed the nurse into the hospital's family room. It was empty but for a woman standing at the window, staring out at a bleak vista of bare trees, shopping centre and teeming roads. She turned to him. He thought she looked unwell. The nurse spoke.

'Grace? This is Dr Traynor, the criminologist. He's here to talk to Molly.'

The woman approached him as the nurse left, held out her hand. 'Grace Monroe, Molly's mother. I told staff I wanted to talk to you before you saw her.'

'I understand. I'd like to add my condolences to those of my colleagues at headquarters.'

She turned from him, went and sat down. He sat opposite. This pleasant-looking woman had a lot on her mind.

'You're working with the police and you want Molly to tell you what happened to her and Mike. In my opinion, she's not ready.' She looked away, clearly agitated. 'What's happened to my daughter and her husband is unbelievably shocking and awful. No doubt you're good at what you do, but right now no amount of talking is going to help her.'

'My purpose in being here is not therapeutic, Mrs Monroe. Detective Inspector Watts, the senior investigative officer, and his whole team are very anxious to find the individual responsible for what has happened to your daughter and her husband. To do that, they need information only she has.'

'And you think you can get it from her?'

'I'll support Molly in whatever way I can to talk about it.'

She gave him a direct look. 'I'm fearful of her being put under pressure. I've looked you up online, Dr Traynor.'

He nodded, anticipating what was coming.

'I know you're very experienced, very good at what you do. I also know about your family's personal experience – your name is a little unusual. I feel I should apologize for that intrusion into your life, but this is my daughter we're talking about. I want to protect her. I want the best for her.'

'I understand.'

She looked away from him. 'Molly and I aren't strangers to shock and grief. I had another daughter, two years older than Molly. She died when Molly was twelve. My husband died four years later. He was very ill.' She looked down at her hands. 'I'm only telling you this so you know that Molly *knows* loss. What she has no experience of is something so . . . so indescribably violent as this.'

'I appreciate the information you've just given me.' He recognized the truth in what she had said. 'Unexpected or untimely death is a universal experience which can be understood over time. Violent death is different. It makes us question everything we believe. Everything we take for granted.'

'Exactly. We got through those experiences together. It wasn't easy, but we gradually adjusted. Molly's got a good job. She's highly valued by her employers. She was so thrilled that her pregnancy was going well but, so far, she hasn't even talked to me about what happened, and believe me, I've tried to get her to do that.'

'Perhaps now isn't the time for Molly to talk to you? She might find it easier to do so with someone she doesn't know, has no connection with.'

'Surely, she should be saying *something*?' She leaned towards him. 'When I try to encourage her to talk, she turns her face away. Not a word about what's happened. About Mike. About the baby . . .'

He waited as she tried to regain her control. 'I'm really worried about her, Dr Traynor. When I'm with her, I don't refer to the baby, but the way I see it, by not doing so I'm actually helping her to store up even more problems for herself.' Traynor waited as she searched for words. 'It's as though she's thinking that if she doesn't talk about it, it hasn't happened. She cried when she lost her sister and then her father, of course she did, but I've seen very few tears since this happened. It's like . . .' She paused. 'It's like she's a million miles away from me and I can't reach her.'

'From what you've told me, Mrs Monroe, I think you know a lot about the grieving process. That it isn't straightforward.'

She got to her feet. 'I'm just hoping that you've not had a wasted journey. I'll tell her you're here.'

He watched her go, looked down at a low table nearby, leant and straightened the magazines there. She was back.

'Shall I introduce you to Molly?'

'Yes. It might help her to relax.'

She looked at him. 'You're a kind, patient man, Dr Traynor.'

He followed her out of the room, across the open area to a door. She pushed it open and went inside, Traynor some distance behind her.

'Molly?' There was no response from the slight figure in the bed. 'Dr Traynor is here. He's hoping that you'll talk to him.'

She went closer, reached down, gently moved aside the curtain of dark hair half-covering her daughter's face.

'*Don't!*'

'Come on, Molly,' she said softly. 'I'll help you sit up.'

Not looking at him, Molly Lawrence raised herself, then winced as her mother fussed with pillows. She sank slowly back, her face tightening. 'Mom, just go and . . . have some coffee or something.'

Traynor kept his voice low. 'Mrs Lawrence, it's fine for your mother to stay for a few minutes.'

She shook her head. Mrs Monroe turned away and left the room. The room fell silent.

'You're not a police officer. What are you?'

He moved his chair a little closer to the bed. 'I'm a criminologist. I'm part of the police investigation.'

She didn't respond.

'I study crime of all kinds, develop theories to assist our understanding as to why it happens, increase our ability to solve it. Hopefully find ways to predict and prevent it.' He waited. 'Is there anything else I can tell you?'

Still no response. Her face almost matched the pillows for whiteness.

Finally, she made eye contact, her voice shaking. 'I know what you're thinking. That I wasn't very nice to my mother. Well, Dr Traynor, right now I don't feel very "nice". I feel angry. I can't hold what's happened in my head. Each time I wake up, and it's like, "What's happened? What am I doing here?" and it hits me *again* and I'm *drowning*.' She covered her face with her hands and sobbed.

Traynor knew all too well the emotions she was expressing. He waited for the sobs to subside. 'Everybody experiences grief in their own way, Mrs Lawrence. It changes over time, believe me. It doesn't get better, exactly. It gets different.'

Not looking at him, she pulled a wad of tissues from a box next to her, pressed it against her face, whispered, 'I'm sorry.'

'There's no need for an apology. My force colleagues and I are truly sympathetic to your situation. I'm here because we need to know as much about what happened as you are able to tell us. If you feel unable to do that today, I can come back. It's not a problem, Mrs Lawrence.'

'Stay, please. You have a job to do and I know I have to help you do it, but I'm really worried.' She looked up at him. Her eyes were reddened, the pupils themselves a deep azure blue. 'How can I help you and the police if I can't make sense of it in my own head?'

'Talking about it might give you that sense. Anything you are able to say to me has value.'

She looked down at her hands. 'I don't know where to start.'

'Start wherever you wish.'

She pushed her hair from her face, her voice low, hesitant. 'It, we . . . I had an appointment. Here at the hospital. Late afternoon, sometime, I can't remember exactly. Then, we went to see Mike's parents to tell them . . .' She closed her eyes. 'We left their house and went into town for dinner . . . to celebrate . . .'

Behind his neutral face, Traynor listened as she approached that part of the evening they needed to know about. He kept his voice low. 'And then?'

'We left the restaurant. Went to the car . . . Started our journey home.'

He wrote, sending her quick, monitoring glances, seeing changes to her face which had lost the small amount of colour it had gained in the previous minute or so and was now tight with tension. 'And then . . . then, we were . . . lost and heading along a road.' Her words and breathing quickened. 'A narrow road. We got stuck in a diversion and we didn't know what to do and we took a turning into a street and suddenly there were no lights, no people, no cars . . .' She looked up at him, her eyes wide.

He leant towards her. 'Mrs Lawrence? Mrs Lawrence, it's OK. You don't have to say any more.'

She slowly focused on him. 'I can't go any further.'

She saw Traynor close his notepad.

'It's no good. I can't give you what you need.'

'It's early days, Mrs Lawrence, and I think it might help you to know that my aim is to support you as you talk about what happened.'

She gave him a tired smile. 'I haven't been much help, have I?'

'You've made a start. Right now, your memory is protecting you, holding on to what it knows. That's not unusual following trauma. Things could well change.'

He stood as the nurse came into the room. 'I'll check on how you are tomorrow. There's no pressure,' he added, knowing for many at headquarters it wasn't true. 'I can come back whenever you wish.'

Getting no response, he walked to the door, acutely aware of the urgent need for whatever information was locked inside Molly Lawrence's memory, also knowing it had to be at her pace.

Mrs Monroe was waiting outside the room, looking anxious.

He nodded to her. 'Molly has made a start.'

FOURTEEN

One hand gripping his phone, Watts raised the other to Traynor as he came inside the office. 'Yeah, we appreciate it. You hear anything else, let me know.'

He ended the call, raised both arms, linking his fingers behind his head, his face creasing into a broad smile. 'Traynor, I can assure you that there *is* somebody up there looking down on this investigation.' Traynor grinned, glanced up at the ceiling and back at him. 'And you'll be saying the same when I tell you about the tip-off that's just come in.'

'From?'

'Nigel. He's in charge of security at the mini-market close to the scene. He knows the area well. According to him, a youngster by the name of Presley Henry has been bragging around the area about a family member being involved in the Lawrence shooting, saying that his uncle "did the Toyota job". If you want to know why that's got my interest, Presley's uncle is Huey Whyte, a suspect in a shooting ten years back. I've checked the records. Guess which gun we're talking about for that? It's the same as the one used on the Lawrences. I've had no direct contact with Whyte during the last three or so years, but I know young Henry's aunt so I'm going to see her.' He reached for his coat and keys. 'Did Mrs Lawrence talk?'

'Yes, but it was very slow going. Her mind is resistant, but she made a start, talked about their afternoon hospital appointment, the restaurant, the traffic diversions and their arrival in Forge Street—'

'She mentioned it by name?'

'No. When I say "talked", she gave very few actual details. I'm hoping to see her again soon. But before I do, I'll go through what she said for anything which looks useful to us.'

'"Useful" is what I'm after. You staying?'

'I'm going up to the incident room to give Officer Miller details of the visit for logging, then back to the university.' Watts was thinking that Officer Miller would be more than pleased to have anything Traynor was offering.

'Judd's up there. Tell her I'm off to follow up this kid, Presley Henry.'

After a journey that should have taken him fifteen minutes but took thirty-five due to heavy traffic, Watts parked and headed for a block of maisonettes close to the Bristol Road interchange. With a glance in the general direction of Forge Street, he located his destination on the ground floor and jabbed the doorbell. After some delay, the door was opened by a whippet-thin woman, black hair mixed with grey. She rolled her eyes, one hand on her hip.

'And what do *you* want?'

'Morning, Lettie.' He got another eye-roll.

'That's *Le-tishah* to you.' She sighed, stepped back. 'In! The last thing I need is you hanging about out here, gettin' my name dragged down.'

He went inside the spotless maisonette and on to the cramped lounge dominated by a massive wall-mounted television, a large sofa covered in plastic, and small tables supporting knick-knacks. He pointed at the television and its vividly coloured courtroom scene, the judge gesticulating at a hapless complainant, the studio audience grinning. 'Mind putting that off?'

She searched for, then aimed the remote. 'Like I said, what you wantin'?'

'Your nephew, Presley.'

'*Presley?* Why?'

'I need to talk to him.'

'About?'

'That's between me and young Presley.'

Her eyes narrowed. '*And* me, as his guardian. He's in the sixth form at his school and doing well so you've got no business with him. In fact, sod off now. I'm busy.'

'You and me both, Lettie. I'm here for information and my understanding is that Presley has some.'

She glared at him. 'Sounds like you got nothing better to do than listen to *damn* gossips round here.' She left the room. Past experience of Lettie prompted him to close his eyes. She shouted upstairs from the hallway, 'Pres-*ley* . . . Presley! You get down here, *now*.'

Watts picked up a distant, brief response. 'I said, *now.*' She came back inside the lounge, face averted from Watts.

'I thought you said he was at school?'

'If it's any of your business, he's got a late-morning start and whatever you've heard, it's *wrong.*'

Watts picked up footfalls on the stairs. The door opened and a tall, neatly dressed youth came inside.

'Hello, Presley.' The youth made no response, his eyes moving between Watts and his aunt. 'I'm here to check something I've heard which concerns you.'

'I don't have to talk to you.'

Watts regarded him. 'You're a bit misguided there, son but if you prefer, we can have a chat at headquarters. What's your choice?'

Lettie gave Watts a furious look. 'He's going nowhere!' She struck Presley on the shoulder with the back of her hand. '*Talk* to him and he'll be gone!'

'That's good advice your aunt's giving you,' said Watts.

Presley sent him a quick glance. 'How can I talk if I don't have a clue what this is about?'

'It's about a man and his wife who've been shot—'

'I *knew* it.' Lettie stared at Watts. 'As soon as I heard about it, I knew you lot would be crawling all over the neighbourhood, but you must be desperate to come here—'

'It's got nothing to do with me!' Presley's eyes darted from his aunt to Watts and back.

Watts shook his head. 'My information says otherwise. It suggests that you know something about that shooting.'

Presley took another hit to the shoulder.

'Word is, you've been spreading rumours that you know who did the "Toyota job". He saw Presley's eyes widen. 'And now you're going to tell me what you know.'

Getting a virulent look from his aunt, Presley gave Watts his full attention. 'I never started that rumour, honest! I heard it and repeated it. That's all I did.'

'In that case, it'll be dead easy to tell me exactly who and what this rumour was about.'

Presley's face slammed shut. 'I don't know anything. Like I said, all I did was repeat it . . . I don't even remember what it was about.'

Watts walked slowly towards him. 'Ah, Presley, lad. Let's keep it real, shall we? I want details. Now.'

Watts and Lettie fixed him with direct looks.

Presley's eyes darted away. 'It was about some bloke who knew the gun that was used to shoot that bloke and the woman.'

Watts' head tightened at Lettie's shriek. 'And?'

'And, nothing. That's all I remember. You asked. I've told you. That's it.'

Watts took a few paces from him, turned. 'Know what happens when rumours get listened to then passed on, Presley?' He waited out the short silence. 'No? Then, I'll tell you. They get *added* to. A word here. An action there.'

Light on his feet, he was across the room looking down at Presley, who wasn't happy with the proximity.

He gave his aunt a nervous glance. 'All I did was add a name then passed it on.'

'Look at me, lad!' Watts held the youth's gaze. 'Whose name did you add?'

'It was like, a joke, right? He didn't do it. He didn't do anything!'

'Problem is, Presley, I don't know that. *Name*.'

'My uncle. Huey Whyte.'

Watts got in front of Presley as Lettie flew at him, shrieking, 'You bloody *fool*!'

'Time you were at school, lad.'

He watched Presley disappear upstairs then turned his attention on Lettie. 'Where's Huey?'

'You can go—'

'*Tell* me and I'll see if I can make it go easy on your nephew if we find that your brother Huey's up to his neck in this shooting.'

She sent him a malevolent look, the fight suddenly leaving her. 'He stays here sometimes but I haven't seen him much lately. I know one place he sometimes stays.'

Watts left the building, Lettie's wrath still in his ears. He took out his phone, rang Brophy and told him about the visit. 'Huey Whyte had a bit of a rep for guns and drugs a decade or so back, so I'm leery of sending unarmed officers to search for him at the address his sister says he sometimes uses, but it needs checking. If Whyte is there, we'll need to consider an armed response—'

He moved the phone away from his ear as Brophy erupted.

*   *   *

Back at headquarters, he found Judd in his office. Taking out his notebook, he opened it and placed it next to her. She looked down at the neat writing, then grinned up at him.

'Finally! A lead.'

'Possibly . . .'

They looked up as the door opened and a tall, blond-haired, twenty-something male in a leather jacket, jeans and boots leant inside the room.

'Hi, Bernie. Or, should that be, 'Detective *Inspector* Ber-nard Watts?'

Judd watched as Watts slowly headed towards him, his arms stretched wide.

'I don't bloody *believe* it. Are you a sight for sore eyes!' He grasped the visitor's upper arms. 'Where'd you get these shoulders?'

The man laughed and clapped Watts on the back. 'It's great to see you, Bernie. How's things?'

'Good, good. Come on in, Jules.' He pointed across the room. 'This is PC Chloe Judd. Judd, this is' – he grinned – '*Doctor* Julian Devenish. We used to work together when this room was the Unsolved Crime Unit. He was a skinny student back then. One of Kate Hanson's.'

Judd watched the visitor remove his jacket, absorbing the lean, wiry physique, the attractive, open face, the white, even teeth, the curve of his mouth, the—

'Hi, Chloe. How's it going for you?'

'OK, thanks.'

'Take my word for it, Judd is usually your chatty type.' Watts pointed to a place high on one wall. 'Remember that from one of our earliest cold cases?'

Devenish looked to where he was pointing at black, scripted words and read them aloud,

'"Let justice roll down".' He shook his head and looked at Watts. 'I remember. I learned such a lot here. They were great days. I hear you're heading a major investigation as SIO. Congratulations.'

'They're all upstairs in the incident room, the squad room as was. We've got a double shooting. William Traynor the criminologist is working on it with us. You know him?'

Devenish nodded. 'By professional reputation, yes. He's very highly regarded.'

'I'll get some coffee going—'

'I'll do it!'

Judd was already halfway to the kettle, Devenish following. 'Can I give you a hand, Chloe?'

Surprised by Judd's keenness to get coffee going, Watts watched, picking up unexpected hints of shyness, very contrary to the confidence she routinely showed around the male officers here. They returned to the table with mugs of coffee. Watts reached for one, his attention on Devenish.

'Last I heard you were lecturing in Manchester and "helping police with their enquiries".'

Devenish's quick grin faded. 'For the last six months, I've been assisting the force there with a series of disappearances.' Seeing Watts waiting, he added, 'The so-called "Phantom".'

'Wow,' Judd breathed.

'The name comes courtesy of some tabloid hack, but it about sums up what he is.'

Judd gazed at him. 'I've seen it reported on the news. I can't believe you're actually part of that. What are you doing?'

'Chloe Judd is back in the room,' observed Watts.

Devenish swallowed some coffee. 'Evaluating witness statements, such as they are. Trying to construct a suspect profile from next to nothing.'

'It sounds dead exciting.'

With a glance at Watts, he smiled at her. 'I'm not so sure it feels like that, Chloe. The pressure's relentless. I'm here because I requested a few days' break. To get away from it.'

Watts was recalling the spindly eighteen-year-old cutting his forensic teeth on cases in this very room, now seeing how much that youngster and time had moved on. Devenish must be, what, twenty-five now? 'The investigation isn't progressing?'

Devenish shook his head. 'It's a huge, dedicated team but, just within these walls, it's overwhelmed by what's happening up there. Five disappearances during the last two years.'

'No leads?'

'Nothing. It took months for the police to decide they were even connected. Three of them were students, all females in their twenties. The media is going nuts, as is the general population and all we've got is a single, possible sighting of a dark-haired male moving along the same road as one of the victims. That's it. It's like being inside a pressure cooker, trying to make progress yet nothing solid to work with.'

Watts gave him a closer look, now seeing evidence of what he was hearing on the young face. 'How long are you here for?'

'Ten days, max, after which I'd like to just get back to my lecturing job, but that won't happen. My assisting the investigation brings the university's psychology department a lot of research kudos. So, I'll be back in the boiler room. At least, that's how it feels.' He raised his coffee mug to Watts. 'I was sorry to hear Maurice Gander died. He was a good guy.' He sipped. 'It's great being down here, touching base with everybody who's still around.'

'Make the most of your time here. Don't let Manchester work you into the ground.'

Devenish grinned across at him. 'Same old Bernard. You don't know how good it feels being here, even for a few days.'

'You're here to relax?'

'That was the plan, but I dropped into the university earlier and the head of psychology practically begged me to do some emergency lecturing to cover staff on sick leave. I said yes. It's just a few hours with the undergrads and a real déjà vu for me. I love Birmingham's campus. Manchester feels like it's under siege. The Ripper Inquiry still casts a shadow, all these years later.'

'I bet it does,' murmured Watts.

Judd's eyes were fixed on Devenish. 'No leads at all? No forensics?'

Watts sighed. 'Whatever he knows, he probably won't tell you.'

Judd gave him a look. 'This is *officer* to *officer*.'

She caught Devenish smiling at her. Her face heated up.

He was looking serious again. 'No witnesses to those five abductions. Nothing seen, beyond that one possible sighting. Nothing heard.'

'Sounds like a right headache,' said Watts. 'Any theories?'

'No.' He stood. 'Look, I know you've got problems of your own, so I'll leave you to it.'

'Keep in touch while you're down here,' said Watts. 'We can always use fresh ideas.'

'Thanks. Maybe.'

'Got somewhere to stay while you're here?'

'An apartment in Edgbaston which belongs to my dad.'

Judd watched as he stood and reached for his jacket.

'Thanks for the coffee.' He smiled, then raised his hand. 'Good to meet you, Chloe.' To Watts: 'Is Dr Chong in? I'd like to say a quick hello.'

'She is, and if you didn't, she wouldn't be too pleased.'

They watched him leave. Judd looked across at Watts. 'He's staying with his father?'

'No. Far as I know, his father lives in Canada. He owns property all over the—'

The phone rang. It was Brophy asking if Huey Whyte had been located. 'Not yet, sir. No sign of him.'

'As soon as he is, let me know. The firearms unit is on standby.'

Watts brought Judd up to speed on the details relating to Presley Henry and his customizing of an inner-city rumour about his uncle Huey Whyte being involved in the Lawrence shooting.

Judd nodded. 'I heard talk in the incident room about Whyte having form for guns in the past.'

'He was never specifically tied to any offence. He's too slippery. We won't know how useful the lead is till we find him.' He reached for the phone again. 'I've got Jones and a couple of officers who know the area out looking for him, talking to the locals. Just two things would improve my view of this investigation. One, finding Whyte in the next twenty-four, and two, Traynor getting information from Molly Lawrence which produces a real lead on who shot her and her husband. Is that too much to—?'

The phone rang again. He reached for it. 'Yeah? And?' He ended the call.

'No progress on Whyte. Whereabouts still unknown.'

8.30 p.m.

'Bye, Dad! See you later!'

The few words brought Traynor to his feet, took him to the window of his study as the front door banged shut. His breathing under control, he watched his daughter reverse her car out of the drive, saw her wave, tracked her car's rear lights as they disappeared from view, his hand still raised.

He returned to his desk. She had a right to a carefree life. Months ago, such an everyday occurrence would have sent his control plummeting, intrusive thoughts, flashbacks filling his head. Things were different now. He was in control. He had stopped taking his medication. He was going it alone; he had a new life, not one riven with fear and heartache. Whenever stressors arose, he closed down his thinking. It was working for him.

He refocused on the notes he had made during his first brief meeting with Molly Lawrence, heard her voice speak the words inside his head. Her demeanour had been much as he'd anticipated. A mix of shock and frozen disbelief. What he had also anticipated was some recall of what had occurred, brief, chaotic, yet containing details which could assist him and the investigation to construct an image of the male who had invaded their car and shot them in cold blood. Within a minute of meeting her he had known it was too much to hope for. He read for the sixth time what she'd told him, her fear evident in every word. She had closed right down as soon as she got to the point where she and her husband entered Forge Street. There was so much detail he didn't have. What had led to them stopping in that place? What had their attacker looked like? Sounded like? Had he coldly shot them? Or, was it precipitated by some word, some action? And finally, was it possible that they knew him?

In the pool of light from the desk lamp, he tracked her few words. There was no reference to the actual shooting. Traynor suspected it was Mike Lawrence who was shot first: he would have been viewed by their attacker as the source of most potential threat. The emergency recording indicated that Molly Lawrence had seen her husband mortally wounded. If that was the sequence, the gunman had then turned his gun on her. She had survived. A witness. He adjusted the files on his desk, squared his notes with its edge. He needed to know more not only about this man who had fired those shots, but also the Lawrences. And right there was a problem. He had no knowledge at all of the people Mike and Molly Lawrence were, prior to this event. He knew nothing of their personalities, how they might respond under duress. She was now the key witness in this homicide. Except for the killer, she was the sole witness as far as they knew. He had to talk to her again as soon as it could be arranged. Until then, whoever had shot them would remain a shadow man.

His eyes fixed on his notes and he asked himself what conclusion he might have come to on motive if neither of the Lawrences had survived. The single word surfaced. One he had first heard from Dr Chong when they were inside the Forensic Test Area. *Execution.*

He had expressed his view on it and another possible motive for the shootings. Watts had rejected both. Now, more personality and behavioural descriptors relating to an individual likely to commit such an act flooded Traynor's head, beginning with behavioural problems in early childhood, a history of irritability and aggression expressed via physical assaults on others. Antisocial. Remorseless. Exploitative. He looked across to the detailed notes he'd made of the November carjacking cases, pulled them towards him, read the brief descriptions provided by the victims of that quick-moving, athletic, confident attacker who had spoken to his one unanticipated male victim: *'You're asking to get robbed, you twat!'* Local accent. Young voice. A *dude,* according to that victim.

He returned to his notes on the Lawrence shootings. Assisting police investigations was a key part of his professional life. It was demanding work over which he took significant pains for two reasons. One, he was expected to provide sound psychological theory as a guide for investigative officers, and two, he never wanted to be the criminologist whose theory later proved to be wrong and sent an investigation off track. When he saw Molly Lawrence again, he wanted more detail from her. He also needed to know about her as a person. He emailed his brief report of the meeting to Watts. Reaching for the desk lamp, he switched it off, anticipating he would wake as he usually did at around four thirty, five a.m.

He needed sleep.

9 p.m.

Watts thrust his hands inside his coat pockets, feeling the urgency in the scene he was watching, wishing it was happening much later tonight. Later increased the surprise factor, the likelihood of a sleep-fuddled suspect. He watched officers move soundlessly towards the house, their vehicles parked many metres away. Intelligence said Huey Whyte was inside. Stealth was all. He watched two officers silently take up position either side of the front door. Nobody moved. Beside the door, one of them raised his hand, pointed at the officer holding a metal ram and shouted.

'*Police!* Come to your door, Mr Whyte, *now*!'

After several seconds an upstairs window opened, a head appeared, then as quickly disappeared.

'Huey Whyte!'

A voice drifted down to them. 'What's going on?'

'Come to your front door, *now*!'

'You fuck off, *now*!'

A hand appeared. The window slammed shut.

Watts saw a nod pass between the officers at the door, watched as he marked passing seconds on his fingers, three-two-one.

The ram struck the door.

They were inside, feet pounding over fragmented wood, Watts hearing repeated shouts of, '*Show yourself!*' followed by '*Clear!*' as they went from room to room and upstairs. He held his breath.

'*On-the-floor-on-the-floor, now!*'

Watts breathed again, watching officers reappear, step through the wreckage of Whyte's front door, two of them holding his arms, his wrists cuffed, his head held down.

'What's this about? I haven't done nothing! And who's gonna pay for this fucking mess!'

FIFTEEN

Thursday 13 December. 7 a.m.

Brophy was pacing Watts' office. 'I assume your eyes are on the clock? Why hasn't he been interviewed yet?'

'When he was brought in, Mr Whyte complained of stress and chest pains. I got a medic to examine him. Whyte's brief then demanded he be given some rest time. His interview is scheduled for seven fifteen.'

'Any evidential link to the Lawrence case? Any guns in his house?'

'Zero weapons. Some cannabis. That's it.'

Brophy frowned at the clock again. 'This is Whyte manoeuvring a delay. He knows how long we can keep him here.' He looked at Watts. 'Is the cannabis any help?'

'Doubt it. Personal use quantity.'

The phone rang. Watts reached for it, listened. 'Has he been fed and watered? Has his brief come back?' He nodded. 'I'm coming down.' He looked at Brophy. 'He's ready.'

Brophy headed for the door. 'Is Judd in? Have her on the interview with you. I've got Tally Ho's report on her. She's impressed the instructors and since her involvement in the case in the summer, the chief constable knows her name.'

Huey Whyte was sitting on his lower spine, arms folded, his eyes intermittently on Watts. To Watts, he looked relaxed. Too relaxed. Ditto, his legal representative.

'I'll ask you again. Do you own a gun?'

Whyte smirked. 'No.'

'Intel says you had one.'

'*Did* I?'

Watts glanced at Judd. She opened the plastic box sitting on the table, removed the lid, tilted the box towards Whyte. Watts' eyes fixed on him. 'Now showing Mr Whyte a Baikal Model IZH 798 which is known to have been linked to him in the past. What do you say, Mr Whyte?'

Whyte shrugged. 'Never laid eyes on it before.'

'It was used in a 2007 drugs-related incident involving the wounding of one of your associates.'

'Got some proof of that? Or that it was even mine?'

'Use drugs back then, did you, Huey?'

Whyte grinned, unperturbed. 'Do ducks swim?'

'What about now?'

Humming to himself, Whyte slowly, casually, removed his jacket, revealing a short-sleeved T-shirt. He raised both arms, linked his hands behind his head. 'What do *you* think?'

Watts gave the arms scant attention. 'That proves nothing.'

Whyte flashed Judd a wide grin. 'Far as I'm going with a lady present.' She glared at him. He let his arms drop. 'Look, apart from a bit of weed which you know about, I don't do anything else. Haven't for years. It's a mug's game.' His brief scribbled words.

'You deny all knowledge of this gun?'

'I do.'

'Rumour has it that you're responsible for the recent shooting of two people.' More scribbling.

Whyte stared at him. 'Yeah? Says who?'

'Like I said, a rumour, which is going a long way to convincing us you were involved.' Watts' eyes were fixed on Whyte. Getting nothing, he went further. 'This rumour was added to by somebody who knows you.' Watts waited, guessing at the thinking now starting up behind Whyte's eyes. 'Got a name yet, Huey?'

'As soon as I get out of here, I'll make it my business to find one.' He looked up at Watts, grinned at his brief. 'I might even give it to you.'

'Very generous, but we've got it already.'

Whyte stared at him. 'Who?'

Watts sat back, his eyes on Whyte's face. 'A young chap who says he didn't start the rumour. That it was on the street and he just repeated it, customized it with *your* name.'

'*Who?*'

Watts leant towards Whyte, his eyes fixed on his face. 'The thing is, Huey, we'd be reluctant to divulge the name if we thought there was any risk of . . . let's say, repercussions.' He paused. 'Family important to you, Huey?'

At the change of direction, Whyte's eyes flicked from Watts to Judd and back. 'What you talkin' 'bout, man? Nobody in my family would rumour me. We're tight.' He raised his hand, made a fist. 'Like this.'

Watts sent him a mild look. 'That's the impression I got from Lettie.'

Whyte's eyes fixed on Watts who was seeing light dawn. 'You saying that little bastard, Presley, dropped me in it? Wait till I get hold of the little fucker, I'll—'

'You do,' said Watts, pointing at his face, 'and I'll be back for *you.*' He gazed at him. 'Plus, you'd have to get past Lettie first. Fancy your chances, do you?'

Whyte shrugged. 'I've got an idea how this rumouring come about. Presley's father is long gone. Presley plays up the family link to me. He hears about that shooting, right? You know the area. It's one big rumour mill. He thinks he'll make what he's heard his own, by adding *my* name.' He sat forward. 'I'll tell you about our Presley. He fancies he's a dude but the bottom line is, he's a sixth form kid with a future if he sticks at his books.' He eyed Watts. 'Don't fuck it up for him,' He glanced at Judd. 'Excuse me.' To Watts, he added, 'He's a young idiot who'd like to have a rep, some cred. In reality, he doesn't do nothing but his college stuff.' He glared at Watts. 'You *hearing* me?'

'The gun, Huey.'

'I know nothing about any gun. Got enough to charge me?'

*   *   *

Whyte had been released. Watts and Judd went to the observation room where Traynor and Brophy were watching the recorded interview, Brophy fuming.

'*There*.' He pointed at Whyte's grinning face. 'See that? See how laid back he is? He knows his way around a police interview. His dismissive attitude is telling me we can't rule him out of involvement in the Lawrence shooting. As far as I'm concerned, the least of his involvement is supplying that gun.'

'He could be laid back because he knows he has nothing to worry about,' said Traynor. 'Because he had no direct involvement.'

Watts stared at the screen. 'Whyte's got a lifetime of evading us. What we need is something specific about the Lawrence shootings which points directly to him. Which we haven't got.' He turned away, went to the door, tracked by Brophy.

'Where are you going?' Brophy asked.

'To see some people I know around that neighbourhood.'

SIXTEEN

Friday 14 December. 12 p.m.

Seeing Traynor heading into headquarters, Watts caught up with him. 'Morning, Traynor. Made any plans to see Molly Lawrence again?'

'I'm in regular contact with hospital staff. They know I want to see her again as soon as possible, but their priority right now is her physical recovery.' They came into the office.

'I'll get on to them,' said Watts. 'They need to know that there's other priorities to think about.'

'Hello, Chloe.' Judd sent Traynor a wide grin, eyeing Watts who was looking riled.

'I get that it can't be rushed, Traynor, but it needs to happen soon.'

'I'm aware of that. I hear you made an arrest.'

Watts shrugged. 'Huey Whyte. A lot of good it did us. We couldn't hold him on what we've got and after hours of me yacking around the area where he lives, I've got nothing that points to him as the shooter. But I'm not giving up on him. Judd's emailed you the details.'

Traynor took out his phone, read it.

Watts continued, 'One of my contacts very reluctantly confirmed hearing the rumour about Whyte and also identified Whyte's nephew Presley as the one who dropped Whyte's name into it. Apart from that, nobody's keen to talk because it's about guns. By the way, Julian Devenish, forensic psychologist and ex-colleague of mine, is back in Birmingham for a few days and he might be willing to make a contribution to the Lawrence investigation. You OK with that, Traynor?'

'Not a problem. We could use the help.'

'Good. Two more "psychological" eyes on this case has to be a plus. Getting back to Molly Lawrence, I understand your concerns about her, but I'm now in that very rare position of agreeing with Brophy on this one. We need her talking, *now*.'

'It has to come from Mrs Lawrence herself. It could be counter-productive, and potentially bad for her, to push for information.'

Watts held up his homicide file. 'See how thin this is? It represents what we've got from this full-scale investigation to date. I hear what you're saying and I'm sympathetic towards her for what she's suffered, *is* suffering, but I'm not allowing anything to go on hold in this investigation. We have to have what she knows.'

Traynor calmly regarded him. 'In which case, I leave it to you to take responsibility for talking to her at a time of your choosing.'

Judd turned to Watts. 'That's an idea, Sarge! When you do, I want to be there—'

'Zip it!' He stared at Traynor. 'You're the one with the expertise. If she's as emotionally dodgy as you say, it has to be you.'

The phone rang. He snatched it up. '*Yes?*' He listened, eyeing Traynor across the table. 'Thanks for letting us know.' He put down the phone. 'That was the hospital. Molly Lawrence discharged herself at eleven this morning and her mother took her home. As SIO, I'm saying it's over to you.'

As Traynor, then Watts, left, Judd reached for the homicide file. Sarge was right. It was thin. Most of it made up of questions with very few answers.

'Hi, Chloe. You look engrossed.' She looked up.

'Hi, Dr Devenish.'

He came and leant against the table next to where she was sitting, smiled down at her. 'You know, whenever I'm addressed like that, which is rare, by the way, I tend to think that the person saying it isn't too keen on me.'

She looked away, flustered. 'No, no, it isn't, I don't—'

He grinned. 'I'm joking. I've just been in the incident room. It's full of long faces. I'm guessing there's still a lack of progress.'

She pointed to the file in front of her. 'Sarge is trying to pressure Dr Traynor into speeding up his interviewing of Molly Lawrence. Will is more or less refusing.'

He shrugged. 'I'm with Will on that. It's often what happens in large investigations: two professionals go head-to-head, each with his own perspective.'

She watched as he stood, the words out of her mouth almost before she heard them. 'How about some coffee? Or juice? . . . Sorry, there isn't any juice . . . Coffee?'

'I'd love some, but Brophy is expecting me. He's going to instruct me on any role I might have here over the next few days' – he grinned – 'to which I shall listen with close attention while thinking about when I can next take you up on that offer of coffee.' He raised his hand. 'See you soon, Chloe.'

Fixing her attention on the file, hearing the door close, she cursed herself, unable to recall anyone, any man, with Julian Devenish's ability to turn her into a stuttering idiot.

On his journey to the Lawrence house, following a brief telephone conversation with Mrs Monroe, Traynor's thoughts were on the next hour. Watts was right from his police perspective: they needed all the information Molly Lawrence had to offer. Traynor's job was to assist her to do that but without causing her further emotional damage.

Parking his car, he approached the house, acknowledging the chilled-looking police officer standing next to the front door. It was opened by Mrs Monroe. She led him to a sitting room with offers of tea or coffee. 'I'm making one for the officer outside.'

'Thank you, no. We're very grateful to Molly for her willingness to talk again.'

'I wanted her to stay in the hospital. They were so good to her there, but she insisted on being allowed home and they gave into her. From the little she's said to me, I think she trusts you, Dr Traynor.'

'Since I saw her, has she spoken to you at all about what happened?'

'Not a word. I'm hoping that now she's home she'll feel more relaxed.' She looked around the pleasant, well-furnished room. 'The problem I see is that this was their home, hers and Mike's. How she feels being back here, I don't know. She hasn't said.' She pointed to a photograph on a nearby table. 'That's them on their wedding day. I want to put it away but I know I can't do that.'

Traynor went to it. 'May I?'

She nodded.

He reached for it, absorbing Mike Lawrence's dark good looks, Molly in her white, low-cut dress, a mist of fine veiling around her shoulders, her face open, smiling.

'Hello, Dr Traynor.'

Carefully setting down the photograph, he looked up at her. She was dressed in a soft pink sweater and jeans, looking somewhat thinner than when he last saw her.

'Hello, Mrs Lawrence. Thank you for agreeing to talk to me again.'

'Please, it's Molly. Have a seat.' To her mother, she said, 'I'll be fine.'

Mrs Monroe left the room. Traynor's optimism rose slightly. She looked frail, yet the few words and her general demeanour suggested an assurance he hadn't observed in the distressed woman he'd met at the hospital. Her next words confirmed his thinking.

'I'm glad you're here. Glad for another opportunity to talk.' Her deep blue eyes regarded him. 'I have to face up to what's happened. Talk about it. Help the police. I won't allow whoever did this to us to cause me to sink into . . .' She looked away. 'I have to get a grip, move on with my life. I owe it to Mike.' She looked down at her clasped hands. 'Ask me whatever questions you like. I'll do my best to answer them.'

'How about you tell me whatever you recall?'

She stared at him for several seconds. 'I don't know what to say. I mean . . . I don't know where to start.' She looked away to the window. 'I told you that Mike and I went to the hospital . . . and from there we visited his parents . . . left there, drove into the city, had dinner . . .' Her gaze was fixed straight ahead. 'The traffic was really heavy. Lots of road closures. We got lost. Mike was getting angry. Not angry. He was concerned for me. I was tired and he wanted to get me home as soon as he could and . . .' She stopped, drew breath. 'Everything changed. Everything got . . . difficult.' She pressed her hand to her mouth.

'There's no rush, Molly,' said Traynor quietly. 'Tell me how things got difficult.'

She squeezed closed her eyes. 'We didn't know where we were and suddenly there was a sign, an arrow. Mike followed it. To get away from the traffic, get us home . . . And then, we were in this horrible place. A street.' Her eyes moved to Traynor. 'We must have taken a wrong turn. It was so dark. No lights. I said to Mike to drive, get us away. He didn't.'

Traynor asked quietly, 'Why didn't he drive away, Molly?'

'There was something not right with the car. When we got into it after leaving the restaurant, I noticed that the interior light wasn't working. As we drove, the engine sounded . . . odd. I asked Mike what was wrong. I'd driven it the day before without any problem.' She looked up at Traynor. 'Have you seen that place? The place where it happened?'

'Yes.'

She gripped her upper arms. 'We were halfway along it when Mike pulled over and stopped the car.' She hung her head. There was another lengthy pause. 'Mike started revving the engine. It sounded OK, but then . . .' The knuckles of her hands showed white. 'There was a movement outside the car. A shadow. At Mike's window. Before we had a chance to think, to do anything, it moved to my side. One of the rear doors opened.' Her eyes were stark now in her pale face.

'You're in control here, Molly. You can stop whenever you wish.'

'He had a gun,' she whispered. 'I'd never seen a real gun. He pointed it at Mike.' She stared ahead, transfixed.

'Why did he point the gun at Mike?'

She turned to him. 'Mike put his hands up.' She slowly raised both her hands. 'Like this.'

'What happened next?'

There was a brief silence, then: 'He said something to Mike. Ordered him to "sit tight", or words like that. He said not to look at him, then pointed the gun at me. "Hand me your valuables. Put them inside your bag. Give it to me.".'

'Where was your handbag, Molly?'

'By my feet.'

'Then what happened?'

'I did as he said. Mike passed his phone, watch and wedding ring to me and I put them in the bag with my jewellery, then passed it to him, "nice and slow", as he asked.' Her voice dropped. Her eyes were fixed somewhere beyond Traynor. 'We both had platinum wedding rings. My engagement ring was also platinum with a single square-cut diamond, one carat. My earrings matched it. It all went into the handbag. It was Gucci, blue, black, not new, but . . . I loved it.'

'Can you say anything about the man?'

'I don't . . . It's all confused. Big. Heavy build . . .' Her voice rose. 'I *can't* remember any more . . . except that the next thing that happened is I came to and . . . realized I was hurt.'

'It's OK, Molly,' said Traynor, his voice low.

He put his notes to one side, glanced at the information he had brought with him, the list of items stolen from her and her husband, wanting something fact-based to ask her. 'Were you wearing a watch?'

She nodded. 'I don't know what happened to it. It was a present from Mike. I slipped it off into my coat pocket. I haven't seen it since. I was really frightened when the man got inside the car but suddenly, I was really angry as well. Mike and I worked hard for everything we had. The watch was the last thing I took off. I decided that I wasn't going to let him have it, nor my phone. It was like a silent protest. I told him I didn't have a watch or a phone. He was really edgy.' Tears spilled from her eyes. 'And now I know how *stupid* I was to say it. I hadn't realized what he was capable of doing.' Her head dipped. 'It makes no difference now, does it?'

'Did he touch your watch?'

'What? No, no. He didn't even see me slip it off and put it in my pocket where my phone was. My coat has really long sleeves. I was just praying it didn't ring.'

'You've described this man as big with a heavy build. Can you say anything more about him?' Seeing her uncertainty, he added, 'His appearance? His voice? His accent? Whether you detected any kind of scent about him?'

'I . . . his voice was deep. Rough-sounding . . . I smelled body odour . . . and most of his face was covered.'

'How?'

'I don't know.'

'Was there anything about him, anything at all, no matter how small or insignificant, that reminded you of someone you had seen before?'

She stared at him. 'You mean . . . someone we recognized? No. It's not possible. I can't answer for Mike, but . . . Dr Traynor, I don't feel very well.'

He stood. 'Can I get you anything. Let your mother know?'

'No, I don't want her worried any more than she is.' She stood, a little unsteady.

He offered his arm to her, aware that he had pushed the questioning further than he had intended. She took it, held on to it, walked with him to the door. 'I hope I haven't disappointed you again?'

'This isn't to do with how I receive what you tell me, Molly. My aim is simple: to hear whatever you recall.'

Traynor drove to his university in the middle of the city, into the secure parking and took the lift to one of the lecture rooms. He found his students waiting for him. Apologizing for his lateness, he began his two-hour lecture.

It was late by the time he came into his office and took out the notes he had made during his second meeting with Molly Lawrence. Reading through them, he saw how much more information she had provided than previously. They now had the reason why the Lawrences had stopped in Forge Street: the Toyota's intermittent fault. They also now had a more detailed picture of their attacker: a large male, much of his face concealed, a deep, rough voice, poor personal hygiene. He read the words Molly had used to describe how she hid her watch and phone. Given the situation she and her husband were in at the time, it suggested Molly Lawrence to be a woman of considerable spirit. It could have gotten her killed. He hoped that that spirit was about to reassert itself and help them find the man who attacked them. He reached for the crime scene photographs, his eyes moving slowly over the Toyota's interior. He looked up, his eyes fixed straight head. He was recalling a specific quality of her delivery, a certain hesitancy. A carefulness. Whether his impression was founded or not, Watts needed to know.

SEVENTEEN

Friday 14 December. 5.30 p.m.

They were seated around the table, Judd next to Julian, their attention fixed on Traynor.

'How did she do, this time?' asked Watts.

'Her defence mechanism is still distancing her from a lot of what happened that night, and she began with the same progression of events she'd indicated previously.' He pointed to the information he had added to the Smartboard. 'But now we know how the gunman happened to see their car. They had stopped because of car trouble.'

Julian looked at him. 'Is it possible he saw it parked while they were having dinner?'

Judd searched papers, located a CCTV image, held it up. 'This is the on-road parking where they left it but theirs wasn't captured.'

Julian took the image from her. 'It's possible somebody tampered with it while they were inside the restaurant. If that's what happened, it probably wouldn't have attracted undue attention, given the darkness and the heavy city traffic. When they leave, he follows.'

Watts left the table and returned with the half-full cafetiere, his eyes on Traynor. 'Molly Lawrence told you that when Mike Lawrence saw the gun, he raised his hands. That could have made the shooter jittery.'

'That's Molly's perception of the situation,' said Traynor. 'It may not be a full or even an accurate explanation although, as you can see, she was very accurate in her description of the items stolen from them.'

'She didn't give any detail of the actual attack on her and her husband,' said Julian.

'No.' Traynor paused again. 'But you need to know that I noted a hesitant quality within her recall which makes me think she is purposefully avoiding certain aspects of the attack.'

Watts looked at him. 'Meaning what, exactly?'

'My impression is that she was relatively willing to talk about parts of it, but not others. All I can say right now is that what happened to them that night was as terrifying as it was tragic. To have their safe space invaded in that place, in darkness, would have been shocking and intimidating.'

'Where does that leave you? Us?'

'Offering her more opportunity to talk about it.'

Judd frowned at her notes. 'What she's said confirms that they did what they were told. They handed over their stuff.'

'Mike Lawrence's watch, yes, but Molly didn't give hers to their attacker. She slipped it off into the pocket of her coat, along with her phone – the phone she used to make the emergency call. She hasn't seen the watch since.'

Judd raised her fist into the air. 'Atta-girl. Let's hear it for strong females.' She turned to Julian. 'You haven't seen Molly Lawrence but she's really small.'

He looked at her. 'Small doesn't preclude strong, Chloe.'

'She said she hid it because she was angry as well as frightened,' said Traynor. 'People can react unexpectedly and with spirit in such situations.'

'In my experience, usually the ones who wind up dead,' said Watts. 'By doing what she did, she increased the danger to herself and her husband in an already high-risk situation.'

Traynor looked at the remainder of his notes. 'We still have no details about the actual shootings.'

'Did she say anything else about the shooter?'

'Nothing beyond what I've already reported. I'll arrange to see her again.'

'Was she very reluctant to give what she did?' asked Julian.

'Not particularly, beyond the reticence I mentioned, although she still hasn't referred directly to her husband's death or the ending of the pregnancy.'

Watts frowned across the table. 'What shall I say to Brophy when he starts complaining about delay?'

'That he has to live with it if he wants detailed information without jeopardizing Molly Lawrence's well-being.'

Julian stood. 'In your position, I'd be taking the same approach.' He reached down for his backpack and opened it. 'Chloe? I've brought some textbooks in. I thought you might find one or two of them useful.'

She gazed at the books, then up at him. 'For me?'

'If you want them. Dr Traynor knows his theory, Bernard has his years of experience . . . I thought you might get something from these. They focus on different kinds of crime and the theories relating to them.' His brow creased. 'I hope you're not offended by my offering them?'

She quickly reached for the books. 'No way. *Thanks.*'

He lifted his backpack, then looked across at Watts. 'I've got a couple of late lectures to give so I'll see you tomorrow.' And to Judd: 'A few of us from upstairs are having a Christmas night out on Saturday. Come with us, Chloe. Jonesy has the details.'

She watched him leave, giving her a friendly wave.

Traynor stood. 'I have post-grad tutorials in an hour.' He gathered his notes together. 'When I see Molly again, I'll aim to clarify if her reticence is an indication that she's holding something back.'

'You've got no ideas on what it might be?' asked Watts.

'None.'

'I need to see Molly Lawrence in the next few days. I still haven't introduced myself to her as SIO.'

Having given the indexes of Julian's textbooks a thorough check, Judd slipped them into her bag, then looked up. 'Julian's left his jacket.'

Watts glanced at her, then at the leather jacket hanging on the back of a chair. He shook his head. 'He probably won't miss it. Far as I can see, everybody under thirty goes around with next to nothing on. I'll drop it off—'

'*No*, I'll take it on my way home.'

He watched her grab her bag and coat, plus the jacket and head for the door and out. He shook his head. Since when was Judd's bedsit between here and Edgbaston?

Peering through darkness, Judd turned into the wide entrance and drove inside. She stopped the car and gazed at the building ahead. Clearly, it had once been some kind of country house, back when Edgbaston was countryside. Her gaze dropped to the wide entrance. All she had was this address. No way of getting inside. She shoved the car into gear, ready to go home. She would take the jacket back to headquarters in the morning and . . .

She turned at sudden headlights, watched the car come into the parking area, recognizing Julian's small Fiat. Getting out of her car, his jacket in her arms, she walked slowly towards him.

'Chloe, hi!' He grinned. He pointed at the jacket she was holding. 'Oh, thanks for bringing it, but you shouldn't have. I've got another.'

She nodded. Of course, he had.

'That's OK. I didn't know where to leave it.'

'Come on.'

She hesitated, followed him to the entrance and inside the wide hallway. He turned to her. 'As and when you come again, Charlie here takes deliveries, buzzes visitors upstairs.' She looked at Charlie smiling behind his desk, then followed Julian to the shiny metal doors of the lift. As and when.

The doors opened on the second floor. Everything she had seen so far breathed money. Julian unlocked his door. She followed him inside. What she saw was further evidence of it, the layout, the furnishing of the apartment, like nothing she had ever seen outside of a magazine.

'Coffee, tea or something to take the edge off?' Julian grinned at her. 'Seriously, how about some tea?'

She walked across to the wide windows, looked out at an expanse of trees. 'Your dad doesn't actually live here?'

'No. He just owns it. Plus, two or three others in the same building.'

There was nothing in his tone which suggested either pride or complacency. She turned from the view, thinking of her bedsit. She shouldn't have come here. 'I just remembered. I can't stay, I need to go, get home. There's things I have to do.'

He looked at her, surprised. 'No tea? OK, that's one cup of coffee and now one tea we have to catch up on. I'll walk you to your car.'

She got into it, Julian's 'See you tomorrow night!' in her ears and drove away, reminding herself that she was a professional person. Somebody with a future.

All she felt was poor.

9.30 p.m.

Traynor was in his office at home, darkness excluded by a lowered blind. Hearing movement elsewhere in the house, he got up and headed for the kitchen. His daughter was there, her eyes fixed on her phone.

'Would you like a drink?' he asked.

'Please. Small juice for me.'

He poured it, placed it in front of her, took a mug from a wall cabinet and spooned instant coffee, aware that he was under surveillance.

'*Dad.*'

'I know it's late, but I've got work to do, and my understanding of our situation here is that I'm the car-*er*, you are the cared-*for.*'

She grinned. 'That's one way of looking at it.' She reached for her glass, went to him, kissed his cheek, briefly laid her head against his shoulder. 'Not too late, OK?'

He followed her down the wide hallway, detoured to his office, closing the door, his priority always that she should never see the detail of what he brought here from his work. It took him several minutes to read through all he had from his two meetings with Molly Lawrence. He sat back, looked at his notes with a strong sense of dissatisfaction.

He reached for his phone and rang Watts. 'Does Molly Lawrence know that the gun has been recovered?'

'*Evening*, Traynor,' said Watts. 'No. That's still under wraps. I've arranged to see her on Monday to introduce myself. Want to be there?'

Traynor neatened his papers and files. 'It's best we keep our roles separate. If you tell me how she is when you do see her, I'll confirm a date to see her again.'

EIGHTEEN

Sunday 16 December. 12.05 a.m.

Judd eyed the crowd of 'Christmas-Works-Do' revellers, feeling tired, wanting to leave the club. She wasn't having a good time. Having earlier managed to shake off one of the male civilian workers who worked reception at the office, she had joined a group which included Julian. He had bought her a drink and they had chatted. He'd done most of the talking. She had felt inhibited. He had talked a bit about his lecturing job in Manchester and touched on the inquiry he was assisting up there. She'd listened avidly to what he'd had to say about it but had felt insecure without the trappings of headquarters around them. He'd asked her to dance. She'd refused, not knowing why. Except that she was an idiot.

'Another of those?'

She glanced up at the bartender and away. 'No, thanks.'

Looking across the crowd, she caught sight of Julian on the other side of the dance floor, laughing with Candace Jackson, another of the civilian workers from headquarters who earlier had edged between her and Julian. Jackson was shapely and styled herself 'Candy'. Which told Judd all she needed to know about her. Judd reached for her glass, gazed over it to Candy squirming around Julian, who looked to be enjoying himself. She rolled her eyes. She had to be thirty. At least. She looked away from them, her attention caught by Reynolds' overenthusiastic antics.

'Hey, Chlo. Fancy a dance?' She looked up at Jonesy, then away. 'Not in the mood.'

He looked from her to Julian and back. 'Come *on*. We've all been working flat out. It's time for a little R and R.'

'I said no. I'm tired.' She looked at her watch. 'I'm going home soon.'

He studied her. 'OK. If you want a lift home, come and find me.'

As he walked away her focus returned to Julian, now laughing with three officers. And Candy. She sighed, took a gulp of her drink.

'Excuse me?'

She looked up, expecting to see someone she knew. It wasn't, although she vaguely recalled seeing him during the evening. 'I'm not dancing, thanks.'

He took a drink from the bartender and handed over money. 'Good. Neither am I. I'd rather talk. I'm Sean.'

She told him her name, half-listened as he described his work for a computer company. Without disclosing the true nature of her own work, the talk between them began to flow. She was surprised when she next looked at her watch and saw that it was well after one a.m. She finished her drink, got down off the barstool, sending a glance across the club, not locating either Julian or Candy.

'Thanks for the drink. I'm going.'

'Where to?'

She turned to him, her eyes slowly catching up with her head. 'Look, it was nice chatting, but I'm getting a taxi.'

'Are you OK?'

'I'm tired and it hasn't been the greatest night.'

He gently touched her arm. 'I like strong coffee after a couple of drinks. Stay with me and we'll both have some.'

She hesitated. 'If it's quick.'

He ordered the coffee and they talked some more. She watched him walk to the other end of the bar and return with two cups. 'Here you go.'

They sat and drank it, Judd anticipating he would start with the chat. He didn't.

'How's that? Feeling better?'

'Yes, thanks. I was fine anyway, but—'

'I've ordered a taxi. You're welcome to share it with me, but we'll need to get out there and claim it before somebody else does.'

About to refuse, she had second thoughts. Sean continued making light conversation. She laughed several times.

'That's nice to hear,' he said. 'You looked unhappy.'

She shrugged. 'Just pissed off with one or two people.'

'Not me, I hope?'

She looked at him and saw that he was smiling. A nice smile. 'One or two people I work with.'

'Ignore them is my advice. My team at work is ninety-nine per cent tosser.'

She grinned. 'And you're the one per cent good guy.'

'Exactly.' His phone rang. 'The taxi's outside. We'd better go.'

Collecting their coats, they left the club and quickly located the idling taxi. They got inside and Judd gave the driver her address, after which they sat in easy silence for forty minutes, much of it filled with the driver's complaints about the volume of traffic and the time of year. They looked at each other and grinned.

Judd sat forward as the taxi slowed and double-parked. 'This is me.' She reached inside her bag. Sean stopped her hand.

'Forget the money. I'll pay him when I get to my place.'

She looked towards the building and her darkened bedsit window. The evening had been a total downer. All that was waiting for her now was a cold, empty room. He was looking at her, his face concerned.

'Are you sure you're OK?'

She looked at him. 'Do you fancy more coffee?'

Carefully exiting the taxi, she waited as Sean paid and the taxi drove away. They stood on the pavement. She pointed. 'I'm over here.'

They walked in silence to the main door. She entered the code. It opened on the third try. They stepped into the hall. He followed her to her door. She unlocked it. They went inside. He looked around, smiled at her.

'This is really nice. Homely.'

She knelt unsteadily in front of the gas fire, switched it on and stood. He was standing close to her. She laid her face against his chest, listening to his heartbeat, feeling his warmth. During her first ten years, Judd hadn't known warmth. She didn't dwell on it. Just accepted that that was how it was. Not for her brothers and sisters. Just her. Until she'd been sent to live somewhere else. And now, she had a life. A proper life. Colleagues she liked who valued her, a job she loved which paid for the bedsit and the car she'd bought a month before. Beyond tired, she let go of the image of Julian's smiling face.

Sunday 16 December. 6.50 a.m.

Eyes squeezed closed, head full of cotton, Judd felt for her phone. Not finding it, she looked at the small travel clock.

'Holy *shit*!'

She leapt out of bed, headed for the bathroom. 'Sean? *Sean?*'

The bathroom was empty. She ran her hands through her hair. Sarge had asked her to be at headquarters early this morning and she'd agreed. She looked around, frowned, searched every surface, went to her bag, upended it, watching its contents fall onto the bed. She stared down at them. No phone. No purse. No keys.

Breath catching in her throat, she ran to the window, dragged open the curtains, looked outside, searching the line of parked cars.

'*No!*'

Watts was inside the incident room waiting for results from several officers occupied with calls to a tip-line set up on Friday. One or two looked up at him, shook their heads. Distracted, he headed for Jones whose eyes were fixed on the screen in front of him. He lowered his voice.

'When did you last see Judd?'

Jones glanced up at him. 'Around twelve thirty early this morning. Why?'

'She hasn't arrived and her phone's switched off. Get over to her flat.' He turned away, then back to Jones. 'No need to say anything to anybody else.'

More than an hour later, Watts was looking at her. She hadn't spoken since Jones brought her in.

'What happened?'

She didn't look at him. 'That's my business.'

'It's mine because when I couldn't reach you, I had to send Jones to fetch you, plus, I want to know how you've ended up with no phone, no keys and no car.' He watched her put her fingers to her lips to steady them. 'I've sent officers I can't spare to your place to organize a change of lock, and I've got Jones and Reynolds out looking around your area for your car. Come on!'

'Did I ask you to involve *them* in my private life?' She turned her face from him.

Her last few words caused Watts a rush of impatience. 'Idiot celebs rant on about "private lives". What *you* are is a cop who looks to me like she's been conned.'

She still wasn't meeting his eyes, looked like she hadn't slept in a week. When asked, Jones had given him a brief account of the previous evening, including Judd sitting at the bar talking to an unknown male.

'I know you left that club with a—'

'I'm *not* talking about it!'

'Jones has.'

She stared at him, flared, 'He had no *right*!'

'He had *every* right as a responsible colleague.' His phone rang. He snatched it up. 'Where?' He nodded, his eyes on Judd. 'Bring it here. Careful how you handle it.' He ended the call.

'They've found your car three streets from your place, keys inside.'

She covered her face with her hands.

'What were you thinking, to get yourself in a fix like this?'

Not expecting a response, he headed for the kettle and busied himself. This was way beyond his job description and his personal experience. Things had changed since his daughter was Judd's age and what he knew of his daughter's escapades had probably been sanitized for his benefit by her mother. He poured boiling water on to coffee, added three spoons of sugar and brought it back to the table. Placing it next to her, he saw the smallness of her. He reached out and let his hand drop. 'Drink.'

'My head's splitting.'

He went to his side of the table, moved files around, found what he was looking for. 'Here.' She reached for the paracetamols. 'As soon as they get back with your car, I'll ask Adam to give it a good going over for prints.'

She looked away. '*Another* person who's going to know all about it.'

'No. You're the only one who knows all the details. I'm not asking and neither should they. You're sure you don't want to report it?'

'I told you already, no.'

'Stay there. Drink your coffee. When your car's been fully processed and you've got your new key, take the rest of the day off.'

Not seeing a scrap of colour in her face, he reached into his pocket and pulled out a packet of chocolate biscuits. 'You don't feel sick?'

She shook her head.

'Eat these. You look as though you could do with something quick.'

She took them. 'Everybody's going to know about it,' she whispered.

'They'll know about your stuff being stolen. That's all.'

He watched her open the packet and bite off a small piece of the biscuit. 'In case it's slipped your mind, we've got a job to do. I want you back here tomorrow morning at ten.'

He still had questions but he knew he wouldn't get any answers from Judd. No matter. He knew of another possible source of information which might provide them.

NINETEEN

Monday 17 December. 9.50 a.m.

Watts looked up as his office door opened. It was Adam. Like everybody else here, he looked tired. 'All right?'

'I've done a thorough check of Chloe's car for prints.

No hits.' He sat on the edge of the table. 'On the Lawrence investigation, remember I said I'd test the gun for prints?'

'Yes, and?'

'Not good news. Only one that's incomplete and unclear, which doesn't give us much to work with. I'll ask Dr Chong if she thinks Supergluing it might help. I'll also test the gun for DNA. Keep you posted.'

He walked to the door, passing Judd on the way inside.

Watts tracked her, thinking she looked better than she had the previous day. Not bad at all, in fact. He still felt the need for some testing of the waters.

'How's things?'

She tugged smartly at the bottom edge of her jacket. 'Fine. A new day, and all that crap.' She glanced at her watch. 'Traffic's bad. We need to get going.'

They were waiting in silence inside Molly Lawrence's sitting room. They stood as she came in and closed the door, Judd's silent appraisal echoing what Traynor had told them: she had lost weight. She sat opposite them, violet shadows beneath her eyes.

'My mother is in the kitchen,' she said quietly. 'I don't want her hearing what's said. I don't know what I'd do without her here, but we're so busy looking after each other it's exhausting both of us.'

Watts said, 'You've already met PC Chloe Judd.'

Molly gave a faint smile. 'Yes. I remember.'

'I'm Detective Inspector Bernard Watts and I'm in charge of the investigation.' She gazed at him in silence. 'How are you feeling, generally?'

'I'm getting there. You have some news?'

'Yes. We've recovered the gun.'

She half-stood, her eyes starting to roll. On his feet, he took her by her upper arms and lowered her to the sofa, thinking how light she was. She took a couple of breaths.

'I'm OK . . . really, I'm all right.'

'Shall I get your mother?' he asked.

'No.' She took a deep breath. 'Where was it? The gun?'

'That's something I can't divulge, just now.'

She hung her head, the heavy curtain of hair falling around her face. 'I just can't . . . it's so senseless. I, Mike . . . we never hurt anybody.'

Watts waited, seeing anxiety on Judd's face. He took a card from his jacket pocket, held it out. 'Mrs Lawrence, I understand this is a difficult time but I want you to know that we really appreciate you talking to Dr Traynor, but if anything at all occurs to you in the meantime, no matter how small or insignificant it might seem, call me on one of those numbers.'

She looked at the card then up at Watts. 'You're hoping I'll suddenly come up with something which explains the inexplic-able?' She shook her head. 'I'll *never* make sense of what's happened.' She took a breath. 'And, if I did, what would change for me? I'd still be here, alone, frightened. The whole thing is just . . . senseless.'

Watts glanced at Judd. She sat forward. 'Molly, everyone on this investigation is committed to finding whoever did this, but we need information to do it.'

'I know, and I trust Dr Traynor. I want to see him again, although he seemed very disappointed after his last visit.'

Watts was surprised. In his experience, the Mona Lisa and the sphynx were an easier read than Traynor. 'I'll let him know you want to see him. If you'd prefer, you can meet at headquarters.'

She looked away. 'I'm . . . Sorry, but I'm not up to going out.'

'We'll provide transportation if it makes it easier for you?'

He watched tears start to flow.

'I can't,' she whispered.

Judd reached out, put her hand on her arm. 'Can I get you something?'

She looked at Judd, as if remembering that she was there. 'There's some medication the hospital gave me . . . It's upstairs in the bath-room. Second door on the right.'

Leaving the room, Judd went quickly upstairs, past the open door of the first room on the right. A quick glance inside the otherwise bare room halted her. A single item was standing in one corner covered by a delicately crocheted pink-and-blue blanket.

Continuing on to the bathroom, she located the medication, came downstairs and headed to the kitchen. It was warm. Smelled of baking. Molly Lawrence's mother was at the sink. She turned as Judd came inside.

'I'm sorry to disturb you, but Molly needs a glass of water.'

The woman quickly filled a glass, brought it to Judd. 'Is she all right? Is she feeling unwell again?'

Judd held up the pack of pills. 'She asked me to get these for her. We're almost finished.' Judd took the glass and returned to the sitting room, hearing Molly's low voice.

'The hospital has been wonderful. They've offered to hold a little service.' She took the water and medication from Judd. 'Mike and I hadn't discussed names.' She looked up, eyes huge in her pale face. 'I don't know what to do. If I agree to a service, I think I might have to provide a name but I can't do that. I don't even know if I could be part of any of it.' She looked close to exhaustion.

Watts stood. 'Molly, it's not my place to advise you on that, except that maybe your mother has a view on it.'

She got to her feet. 'Tell Dr Traynor that I know I have to talk. That you need help to . . . sort this out.'

They came out of the room, Judd quietly closing the door. Molly's mother was waiting in the hallway, her voice low.

'Did she mention the baby at all?'

'Yes,' said Watts.

'She *did*? That's the first time. I can't get her to talk to me. I think she's trying to protect me and I'm doing the same with her so it's a bit hopeless between us at the moment.'

'What about Mr Lawrence's family?' Judd asked. 'Might they help?'

'They've invited us to their house. They're nice people. There's a lot of them so it feels a bit full on for us, if you know what I mean, but we've said we'll go. I think it's better we go there. That way, if Molly finds it too upsetting, we can leave.'

She opened the door and they stepped outside into frigid December air. 'I asked Molly if she'd like me to phone one or two of her work colleagues and invite them to come here, but she said no. There's another worry. She's very reluctant to leave the house.'

Watts drove, picking up muted sounds from the passenger seat. He opened the glove compartment and handed Judd a pack of tissues. 'You can't do this, you know.'

'What?'

'Let a case get to you.'

'I was fine till I saw it.'

He gave her a quick glance. 'Saw what?'

'A baby buggy. In one of the upstairs rooms. Brand new. Labels still on it. Molly Lawrence is right. It's senseless.'

Watts understood what she was saying. He understood the emotion. After years in the job, some cases you didn't forget. The families. The victims. Some well-off. Others poor. Old. Young. Judd had had a rough couple of days, but he wasn't about to reinforce her feelings.

'What we provide in situations like this is sympathetic, calm efficiency. It's what victims and families need and expect. They need to see us as strong, determined. It's a big ask but it's not me doing the asking. It's what the job's about. Keep focused on your responsibilities as an officer.'

He pulled into headquarters' car park. 'Take an hour. Get yourself a coffee.'

He watched her go, the word 'senseless' echoing inside his head. He had hoped that by talking to Molly Lawrence he might get a sense of whatever it was that Traynor had said she might be holding back. He hadn't. Heading for the building, he recalled her asking where the gun had been found. 'If I had a pound for every unanticipated question asked by traumatized victim-witnesses . . .' He shook his head. It was Traynor's job to establish whether Molly Lawrence really was holding on to information. Right now, with Judd elsewhere, there was something Watts had to do.

He came inside, went directly to reception, eyeing the front counter staff. 'Candace Jackson.'

She stopped chatting, looked up at him, her smile fading.

'My office.'

She followed him as he headed to it and opened the door. Her face told him she had at least an idea what this was about. 'Sit.'

He took a seat on the other side of the table. 'What happened at the staff Christmas do?'

Her eyes drifted away from his. 'I don't know what you mean by what happened—?'

He pointed at her. 'You know what I'm talking about. *You* let your mouth rule your head and decided to tell somebody all about one of the officers here. One of mine!' He took a breath, reminded himself to watch his tone. 'A complete stranger by the name of "Sean". Unless he's somebody you know—'

'I don't!'

He stared at her. 'I can't decide whether that makes what you did worse, but right now I want to know what he said to you to set the ball rolling.' He waited. 'Come on!'

She bowed her head, shrugged. 'He just came up to me. Offered to buy me a drink. He told me he worked in a BMW showroom and we talked about that.'

'And?'

'He asked what I did, and I told him and . . . he seemed really interested.' Her head dipped further.

'So, you filled him in on your colleagues, including Chloe Judd. You know that's something we don't do.'

'Sarge.'

'So why did you do it?'

She gave him a look. He was taken aback by the sudden anger in it 'I'll tell you *why*. I'm thirty-three, feel like I'm forty, and I can't go swanning about like I'm on some professional fast-track!'

'You lost me when you said you're thirty-three.'

'I'm talking about Judd! She's, what, nineteen, twenty? She's got no ties, she's trappy, full of herself, been here no time and now she's part of your investigative team and earning more than I am!'

He absorbed her words. 'And that's why you gave a stranger confidential information about her?'

She gave him a defiant look. 'I work hard at my job here—'

'Which is what you're paid to do.'

'But all I hear is how well *she's* doing.' She pointed at herself. '*I'd* like a career but I've got two kids. I'm a single parent on less than half of what she's earning and that night out was the first I've had in eight months! Plus, she's after Dr Devenish because she knows his family is well off—'

'It sounds like Judd isn't the only one who knows that. It's still none of your business.' He waited for her to say something. She didn't. 'You resent Chloe Judd because she hasn't got your problems.'

She looked away, tears coursing down her cheeks. 'It wasn't something I set out to do. It just . . . happened.' She looked up at him. 'I heard she got robbed. I'm sorry.'

He sighed. 'You know this is a disciplinary—'

'No, *please*.' She stared at him and whispered, 'I need this job.'

He stood. 'I don't want to hear another word about bad feelings between you and Judd. Now, get back to work.' She got up, brushing her face with her hands and headed for the door. 'If anybody asks you what this discussion was about, have a quick and realistic response ready.'

He watched the door close on her. If he made this a disciplinary issue, Brophy would be all over it. Everyone here would know the full story or, more likely, stitch it together. He recalled something Judd had said a while ago about Jackson. Something critical, unflattering. They both seemed to have negative views of each other, but Judd was young. He might have expected more insight from Jackson. He shook his head. As an officer, he knew what was expected of him, but officially reprimanding Jackson was similar to pursuing and identifying 'Sean', the posh car salesman, or whatever else he was. How would that benefit either Judd or Jackson?

3.30 p.m.

Watts came inside the incident room and headed for Miller. 'Anything I should know?'

She rolled down her screen and pointed. 'Jones and Kumar have met with community leaders to discuss and reassure re the current number of feet on the street. For the last two hours they and the other officers you sent have been talking to residents but so far nothing of interest to report, Sarge.'

Traynor was searching the Smartboard screens. 'How did Mrs Lawrence respond to news of the gun?'

'Knocked sideways, but she more or less managed to hold it together.'

'Did she say anything about that?'

'Only to ask where it was found. She says she wants to talk to you again. Do you still think she's withholding?'

'It's a strong possibility.'

Watts studied him. 'Are you disappointed at the way it's going with her?'

Traynor looked up. 'Disappointment doesn't enter into it. This is Molly Lawrence's tragedy. My role is to assist her to move from a fragmented account to one which is sufficiently coherent to assist this investigation. It could also help her to move on with her life. Why do you ask about my disappointment?'

'Just saying,' he said, thinking that Judd's way of talking was infectious.

'How was she?' asked Traynor.

'Probably much the same as when you saw her.'

Traynor reached for his phone and scrolled through it. 'I'll see her at her home again. Unless she suggests otherwise.'

'Home still seems to be her preference. Make it pronto. Brophy's leash is at breaking point. He wants action.'

'You're planning to talk to people who know her and knew Michael?'

'Yes.' Watts waited. 'Something on your mind?'

Traynor looked at him. 'There is. I'm a hundred per cent sure that whoever shot the Lawrences has zero connection to the November carjackings.'

Watts dropped his coat on the back of his chair, sensing something unsaid. 'Come on, Will. Drop the other shoe.'

'You need to send officers to question everybody they find within a one-mile radius of the Lawrence crime scene.'

Watts stared up at him. 'That would take them to the inner city and the Bristol Road. More feet on the street and Brophy's demanding a softly-softly approach so as not to rile the locals. Give me a reason to do that.'

Silence built between them, broken by Traynor. 'Motive is key for any investigation. I can't recall a case in which there's been such confusion, such delay in identifying it.' He sat, his eyes intent on Watts. 'This was no carjacking gone wrong. My analysis of the gunman's behaviour says not. I've re-evaluated the "execution" theory. Yes, it has one or two associated features: Mike Lawrence killed at close range, shot in the head, which suggests that he was the planned target, but execution-style killings usually occur when the victim is alone. And why Mike Lawrence? I've heard nothing about him which indicates that he caused big problems for anybody. Not sufficiently big to have him killed.'

He stopped and looked across at Watts. 'Here's a key question: why wasn't Molly Lawrence shot in the head?'

'I don't get—?'

'It would make more sense. She would have died. As it is, he left her as a witness. Why would he do that?'

'You tell me.'

Traynor stood, paced, came back to the table and leant on it, his eyes on Watts' face. 'The working theory of this investigation was initially homicide-by-stranger. I've just given you my views on execution as motive.'

'So, where does it leave us and why the extended search of the area?'

Traynor sat, his face intent. 'That area is the one incontrovertible "known" we have. It was chosen by the gunman. I suspect he either knew one or both of the Lawrences or he knew of them. We look for evidence of him in the area where he shot them. Tell officers to ask all residents specific, targeted questions: do they recall seeing anyone close to the time of the shootings who looked out of place? Anyone who, for whatever reason, didn't appear to fit the area. They need to be asked similar questions about any vehicles seen. Their task is to focus residents' attention on any anomalies of the kind I've described.'

'You'll provide the questions?'

'I trust you to outline what I've said. Impress on them to keep it short. Specific.'

Watts stood. 'I'll send more officers to the Lawrence scene with an order to work towards the Bristol Road interchange, and I'll have Julian evaluate whatever information they get as it comes in.'

Checking his watch, he left the office and went up to the incident room, finding Jones and Kumar there.

'Any news for me?'

They looked at him, dispirited. Jones shook his head. 'No, Sarge, but the three community leaders we talked to were receptive, once we outlined why we've got such a presence there. The residents we met at the community centre didn't have anything to tell us but they've got our contact details and they seemed keen to assist if they do hear anything.'

Watts headed for the whiteboard, looked at the two maps, one showing the cluster of carjackings close to the Bristol Road, the other the Lawrence shooting. The distance between the two scenes still looked small to him.

He turned to other officers sitting nearby. 'I want you four with Jones and Kumar. You start at Forge Street and work outwards in the direction of the intersection. You talk to everybody—'

Jones looked at his colleagues, back to Watts. 'We have, Sarge. Nobody knows anything.'

'This is different. I want you asking a couple of specific questions of everybody you see: residents, shopkeepers, the homeless, *Big Issue* sellers, people in workplaces, anywhere else where there's people. You ask every single one of them to think back to a couple of days either side of the Lawrence shooting. Do they recall seeing anybody around that time who looked like he didn't belong, whose face didn't fit for whatever reason. Ditto, for any car seen passing through or parked.'

Jones and Kumar exchanged glances. 'You want us asking the same of everybody in that whole area, Sarge?' asked Jones.

'You've got it. You and these four know it well by now. This is a new phase of the inquiry. It's *targeted*. Keep your questions brief. You're not after anyone's life story. You don't need more than two or three direct questions. You ask them, you record the responses, you move on.' He paused, aware that what he was about to say wasn't part of Traynor's view of this phase. 'While you're at it, ask another, general question. What do they know about street crime such as attempted carjackings around the area? Plus, anybody who might have started carrying a weapon. *Any* sort of weapon.'

They quickly wrote, Jones looking at Watts.

'From what Will Traynor said, I thought the idea of a connection to the carjackings had been knocked on the head.'

Watts eyed him. 'Who's SIO of this investigation?'

'You are, Sarge.'

'Glad we got that sorted. We've got no motive for the Lawrence shootings so I'm ruling nothing out.'

'There's a lot of weapons about, Sarge,' said Kumar. 'People around there will be leery of volunteering anything for fear of reprisals. They stick together in those sorts of areas.'

Watts slow-walked to him. 'How long is it since you started here, Kumar?'

'Ten months, Sarge, straight from training.'

'How much inner-city investigative work have you done?'

'Not much.'

'Then you're in for a surprise, lad. That area is close-knit. The people who live and work there are no different from people in any other area. Yes, some might not give a toss about what's going on around them, but there's plenty of others that do. They've got homes there that they value, kids they need to protect, they're as sick of crime as anybody else and a lot of them are public-spirited. Get an early start tomorrow morning on what I've just said. Your focus is the Lawrence shootings, but keep alert for anything which might relate to the carjackings. If there's any problem talking to the Asian population, you lead on it, Kumar.'

Kumar stared up at him. '*Me*? Why me? I know my way around a takeaway menu but that's about it. Like my mom and dad, I was born in West Brom.'

Watts sighed, rubbed his eyes. 'Right. Take interpreters with you. Our area of inquiry is now extended to people living and/or working between the Lawrence scene and the Bristol Road.'

Watts came into his office to find Traynor sitting at his desk, long legs stretched, arms folded, looking like he had a lot on his mind. 'Officers will be out early, speaking to residents like you suggested.' He paused, then looked across at the maps. 'It's not a big area but there's a lot of people. It'll take more than six.'

Traynor stood. 'It could be a good return in terms of the data they collect. When Julian has analysed it, it might throw up motives we haven't yet considered.'

Watts was reviewing what he'd just told his officers, the order he'd given them to ask questions about carjackings. He had wanted Traynor on this investigation because he was good – he knew what he was doing. Which didn't mean that Watts would be swayed from the direction he believed it had to go, in the absence of a convincing reason why it shouldn't. He looked at him. It was time for straight talking. And Traynor wasn't going to like it.

'You and me are from different worlds, Will, and very occasionally I get a sharp reminder of it. You can take your time, choose your theories, work to prove or disprove them. It's all the same to you because everything you come up with *might* be of interest, might be relevant. That doesn't work for me. I don't have the luxury of time to chase whatever appeals, the "what-ifs". My job is about getting evidence, following it, identifying potential suspects, making a *case,* and while I'm doing that, the clock is ticking. In the absence of specific evidence to the contrary, I'm continuing to run the carjacking cases alongside the Lawrence investigation.'

Getting no response, he said, 'And while we're discussing it, what the Lawrence shootings are *still* telling me is that whichever cretin is responsible, he did it for one simple reason: the Lawrences were *there*, they looked well-off, he wanted their stuff and the situation turned lethal. It's a tragic but common enough story.'

'What's needed for both of us to be on the same page with this investigation?' asked Traynor.

'Evidence. Something concrete that tells me the Lawrence

shootings aren't what I think they are: mindless acts of physical destruction motivated by greed.' Watts watched Traynor head for the door. 'Let me have the date you agree to see Molly Lawrence again. Make it soon, yeah?'

TWENTY

Monday 17 December. 8.45 p.m.

Traynor was at his university window, looking at the inner city far below shrouded in mist, watching ghost vehicles surge, stop, surge again along tangled ribbons of roads. To him, it reflected the progress of the Lawrence case. He had called Molly Lawrence at her home earlier. Her mother had answered, told him that Molly was unwell, that today had been a bad day. He had given Mrs Monroe two possible dates on which he could see Molly again. She had agreed to give them to her. He had rung Watts with his doubts that Molly Lawrence would be a quickly available source of information. Watts hadn't taken it well.

He looked out at the darkened city, at arterial streets studded with lights. Somewhere in this diverse, brash, urban sprawl was an individual with a reason to destroy Mike and Molly Lawrence. He turned away. There was something he had to do. Something he should have done days ago.

He headed to the large worktable with its neat piles of textbooks and a large bundle of photographs. Sharing his thinking with Watts about motive in this case had not helped. Watts was right. Their roles were too different. The approach he was now taking was one he hoped might draw out, give shape to, the shadow man. Offender profiling per se was not an option. The attack on the Lawrences was a single event. There were no behavioural patterns to search for. But might the basic principles of profiling still be of use?

He reached for the data Molly had provided of the attack on that dark night in Forge Street. He went through it, read her descriptions of the attacker's appearance, the limited actions she had described, adding the few facts the police had in relating to the stationary Toyota, and finally, the man with the gun leaving the scene, Michael

Lawrence mortally wounded, Molly seriously injured, their blood seeping on to the Toyota's seats and forming deep pools. A merciless attack. In cold blood.

He reached for the transcript of Molly Lawrence's call to the emergency services, read again her fear-laden words, severely limited by pain and shock. Within the desk lamp's pool of light, he examined again the limited detail she had given him of their attacker. The few sounds inside the almost deserted building faded. He gazed down at the list he had constructed of the specific actions and physical details she had described, including some small additions she had recalled: the sudden movement at Michael Lawrence's car door. Reappearing on the other side. Opening rear door. Getting inside. Waving gun. Demanding valuables. Molly Lawrence's confidence that he never saw her hide her watch. Just as well he hadn't. This big, heavy-looking man with body odour and large staring eyes might well have killed her if he had. This man who told them to do as he said.

'And we did.'

And he shot them both. Because he could. Their car was not locked.

Traynor paused, reached for his notes on her recall of the attacker's words and actions, searching for the man within them. A man willing to commit two homicides to get his hands on the Lawrences' valuables. He scanned Molly Lawrence's words again, seeing little in the way of interaction prior to the shooting. His eyes stopped at three sentences: *Hand me your valuables. Put them inside your bag. Give it to me.*

Traynor's head rose. He gazed into darkness beyond the desk lamp's reach. Shadow man had issued three cool, discrete orders in a situation filled with risk to himself and fear for his two victims. Was this a man used to giving orders? A man with experience as an authority figure? Had he a job which required him to be authoritative? Traynor reached for his pen, wrote: *health worker, rescue worker. health and safety officer.* He paused, then added, *police officer.* If the big man with the staring eyes was any of those or similar, he wasn't young. He had sufficient intellect to participate in the required training. The commitment to see it through. The ability to remain cool under pressure, competent, in control. Traynor read what he'd just written. If all of that were true of him, why had he found it necessary to shoot the Lawrences?

He returned to Molly Lawrence's limited physical description of their assailant, his imposing build. Was his ability to impose his will on the situation also an indication of a pathological need to control? Was domination a payoff here? He reached for a file, opened it, found Watts' notes of a visit to a shop near to the crime scene, read them once, and again, stared into the darkened room. 'Come on. Show yourself,' he whispered.

He stood, reached for the stack of black-and-white scene photographs, took them to the middle of the room and switched on a nearby lamp. Slowly, methodically, he held up each one, looked at it, let it go, watched it drift down and gently land face up in the pool of light on the wood floor, his eyes fixed on each of the thirty scene shots as it settled there: the Lawrences' Toyota, one rear door open, another with three of its doors open, a glisten of fine rain on the dark bodywork, the startled half-face of a hooded SOCO captured at the extreme edge of another showing the car's bloody interior, its front seats heavily mired. More photographs drifted from Traynor's hand to the floor, two of them taken by police officers who had arrived very soon after Watts, relatively lacking in definition, yet both victims easily identifiable inside the car: Mike Lawrence's face a rictus of pain, his wife slumped, her face obscured by her dark hair, her heavily stained hands lying loose in her lap—

A loud buzz sounded. Traynor reached for the phone. It was night security. 'That's fine. Send him up.'

Traynor returned his attention to the photographs, paced from side to side, eyes fixed on them. The door swung open.

'Looks like neither of us can leave it alone.' Watts came across the room and stared down at the photographs.

Traynor pointed at them. 'Shootings are mostly simple to understand. Retribution for encroachment on gang turf. A raid for significant financial gain. In the Lawrence case, such straightforward motives don't apply. I'm doing something I should have done days ago: walked in his shoes to understand the individual he is. What he did and how he did it are indicators of what he is. They tell us about his life.'

'If you're saying he's done this before, I've had two incident room officers do independent trawls of past city shootings. Nothing fits the Lawrence case.'

Traynor's eyes were still fixed on the photographs. 'That's not what I mean. What I'm saying is that unlike the gang member and the bank robber, what we have here in the behaviour he's showing us is not this offender's reason for being, his way of life.'

'Say again.'

Traynor crouched, reached for the photograph showing Michael and Molly Lawrence bleeding inside their car and held it up to him. 'This is what he did, but I think he has a whole other life which doesn't feature violence. He doesn't need it. His authority, his strength of character carries him through. I doubt he's in any records. From what we know of the attack, from what Molly has been able to tell us, he's somebody who is confident at directing and controlling other people. It may relate to the kind of work he does. It may be a reflection of his personality. He has a natural authority which he's able to exercise in order to take control of highly charged situations. I was wrong about his age. This is no "young dude".'

Watts stared down at the photograph. 'Degree of authority suggests certain types of work to me . . . and I don't like what I'm coming up with.'

'You will if it leads us to him.' He looked up at Watts. 'All lives have diverse aspects. Criminality doesn't feature in most. I don't believe it does in his.' Seeing Watts' disbelief, he said, 'You'll have known at least one killer whose homelife was a model of conventional living: a wife. two-point-four children, relatives, friends, colleagues, all of them shocked when he's arrested and a court finds him guilty of unspeakable violence.'

Watts watched Traynor move away, letting the last of the Lawrences' photographs drift to the floor where it settled in the midst of the others. 'So, how does that help us?'

'It shows us what he is.'

'That he's a regular type who got a gun, saw the Lawrences and used it on them? That sounds psychopathic to me.'

'You say that because we still don't know his motivation. This is no thug who can't control his fury. Neither is he a young, antisocial male, bigged-up by a weapon. He's like most people . . .' He paused. '*Except*, when he did this. There had to be something he *really* wanted. When we finally have his identity, we might be shocked.'

Watts waited. 'I'm already shocked at what you're telling me.'

Traynor pointed to a photograph of Forge Street. 'There's a question there I can't answer.'

'Only one? Lucky you.'

'I joined this investigation thinking that what happened to the

Lawrences was opportunistic. It wasn't. It was thoroughly planned—'

'Hang on!'

'The question is, why?' Traynor returned to the photographs and crouched over them, his face intent. 'Why did he choose *that* place?' He glanced up at Watts. 'Actually, that leads to more questions. How did he know of Forge Street? It's a forgotten place. If he's not local, did he regularly pass along it and consider it ideal for what he had planned?'

Watts looked down at the Forge Street photograph, shook his head. 'There's a problem with what you're saying. Everything we know points to the Lawrences arriving there *first.*'

Traynor straightened. 'In that case, "everything" has to be wrong. I suggest you get the security guard who works nearby into headquarters.'

Watts' head came up. 'Nigel? Why? Come on, Traynor. I've known his family for years. He's—'

'The single individual in this case so far who has work which gives him a degree of authority, plus the demeanour and physicality to support it.'

Watts' phone buzzed. 'Yeah?' He looked at Traynor. 'And? . . . I'll be there as soon as I can.'

He ended the call. 'Like to know something really interesting which I doubt even you were anticipating? SOCOs are at Westley Country Park. Do you know it, Traynor?' Getting a headshake, Watts enjoyed the moment. 'They're dragging a sizeable pool there, based on information they got from an angler. Care to make a bet on what they're searching for?'

'Molly Lawrence's handbag.'

Monday 17 December. 10.50 p.m.

Watts and Traynor moved over rough paths through heavy tree cover.

'I've shut this whole place down and officers are ready to secure it overnight. We'll have a quick look and get an early start here in the morning.'

They reached an area of open land dropping steeply to water, Jones heading towards them.

'We've got him, Sarge.'

Jones jabbed his thumb at a male a few metres away wearing a thick coat, waders and a knitted hat with pompom and ear flaps. 'We got a tip-off he's been fishing here and he shouldn't be. His line snagged something. Eventually, he recovered it.'

Watts looked at the darkened scene around them. 'How did he manage that?'

'This was earlier, about seven p.m., with a powerful torch, plus' – he pointed upwards – 'a goodish moon, before this cloud built up.'

'He took his time reporting it.'

Jones looked over his shoulder, lowering his voice. 'According to him, when he first saw the bag, he linked it straight away to what he'd heard on the news about the Lawrence shootings.'

'And then what did he do?'

'He threw it back.' Seeing Watts' face change, Jones hurried on. 'He knows he's not allowed to fish here, so he decided he wouldn't report it.'

'So, why's he still here?'

'According to him, he hopped it to a mate's house down the road, had a brandy, some second thoughts and came back. He tried hooking the bag again. When that failed, he called it in—'

'What's his name?'

'Wright, Sarge. Colin Wright. I've got all his details.'

They headed for Wright, Traynor murmuring, 'So far, Mr Wright sounds like one of your public-spirited "types".'

Seeing them, the man straightened, looking tense.

'You're welcome to vote your way, Traynor, but to me he looks and sounds iffy.'

He glanced around for Judd, realized she wasn't there. 'I need a scribe . . . Kumar! Over here.' As soon as Kumar arrived at his side, Watts gave the nocturnal angler his full attention.

'Evening, Mr Wright. Detective Inspector Watts. Tell us what happened here.'

Wright gave each of them a nervous glance. 'It started out as a nice dry evening—'

'Skip the weather report. I want to know when you arrived, how you arrived, what you did after that and how that's led to us being really interested in you.'

'I got here around seven p.m.' He pointed at a dark-coloured people carrier some distance away. 'That's my vehicle over there.'

Watts glanced at it, raised a hand to Reynolds and pointed,

watched him move like a greyhound towards it. He turned back to Wright who was now looking very apprehensive. 'It's taxed and MOT'd. I know I shouldn't fish here but where's the harm?'

'A magistrate will soon be explaining that to you. Carry on.'

'I'd just set up here, on my own.' He looked from Watts to Traynor. 'I like being on my own. I like fishing. For the solace.'

Watts' eyes narrowed.

'I've got four kids! I come here for some peace and quiet.'

'OK, Mr Wright. Get to the point.'

'I had my line fully out, and I was just sitting waiting and having a quiet smoke.' He eyed Watts. 'No, no. Nothing dodgy. I can't smoke at home. All our kids are asthmatic. Anyway, there I was, waiting and . . .' Seeing impatience, he hurried on: '*Suddenly*, the line went taut. Tight as you like. I grabbed up my rod. Gave it a pull. Nothing. Then another. *Still* nothing. Then, something sort of gave and I thought the line had broken but no, there was still the weight on it.' Wright was now looking animated. 'I reeled it in, careful-like, raised the rod which was bent right over and . . .' He looked at Watts and whispered, 'There it was. Swinging from the hook. Sodden. Dripping. The line wrapped around it; the hook caught in it. I pulled it in, reached for it. That's when I saw it.'

'Saw what?' snapped Watts.

'The pattern of letters on it. Little "G"s all over it. Like they said on the radio. Gucci.' He pronounced it 'Gooshey'.

'What did you do then?'

'I opened it up and . . . there was stuff inside.'

Watts stared at him, glanced at Traynor. What this man in his waders and comical hat had just given them was a direct link to the Lawrence shootings. 'Get the stuff out and have a look at it, did you?'

Wright's eyes widened. 'You're joking! I didn't want to get mixed up in any shootings. I closed the bag up, threw it back into the water and went off to see a friend of mine who lives down the road.'

Watts looked at the water then at Wright. 'Why?'

'I was on edge seeing that bag. I didn't want any part of it, but I'd *seen* it, hadn't I?'

'So, you came back.'

'Yes. I had a rethink. About what happened to that couple, so I phoned you lot.'

Watts turned on his heel. 'Be at police headquarters at nine a.m., Mr Wright, to give a statement. *Don't* be late.'

'But I've got the school run . . .'

Watts turned and gave him a look.

'I'll be there.'

Wright got into his vehicle and left. Watts watched him go. He started at Traynor's voice immediately behind him.

'This is an interesting development.'

An hour later they were still watching the search of the dark pool.

'If I believe Wright, he's turned this investigation on its head. If it ever was a robbery, it isn't now.' Watts checked his watch. It was well past midnight and he'd called a full briefing for nine thirty in the morning. 'It's too dark to find anything now, so I'll tell them to pack it in—'

A sudden shout brought them to the water's edge where two officers in waterproofs and watch caps were moving in unison, up to their chests, their arms beneath the icy water, one of which slowly broke the surface, rose into the air, the hand clutching something dark by a long, slender strap.

Watts and Traynor waited as two forensic officers spread white plastic sheeting, watched as one of the search team made it out of the water, a SOCO taking the bag from him in latex-covered hands. Watts and Traynor went to the sheeting. A video camera was raised. They watched another SOCO carefully open the bag and let its contents slide slowly out. The small items were carefully separated. Watts and Traynor got down for a closer look at jewellery, including rings, one with an impressive square stone, an earring which looked similar. What had been done to the Lawrences hadn't made a lot of sense. Knowing Molly Lawrence's bag with their valuables still inside had been jettisoned here made even less.

'Traynor, I'd like you to explain to me what sort of person arms himself, gets into a car, steals jewellery, shoots two people, leaving them for dead, then lobs what he got into a mucky pond.'

Traynor took a pen from his inside pocket, crouched close to the items and carefully repositioned them, absorbing their detail. 'I don't know. I'm guessing someone who wanted something else.' He looked up at Watts. 'One earring is missing.'

Watts eyed the jewellery. 'Have a look inside the bag.'

Traynor opened it, inverted it. Nothing fell from it. Watts

straightened. 'I can't see Wright taking it, leaving the rest, then coming back and phoning us. It looks to me like it got washed into the water. We'll never find it.' He looked at Traynor. 'What's up?'

'There's something here . . . something I'm missing.'

'You don't say. The longer I run this investigation, the more I learn, the less bloody sense it makes, and *that*, Traynor, is not good.' He looked at his watch. 'I'll shift tomorrow morning's briefing to the afternoon.' He looked around. 'Reynolds!' The young officer rushed to Watts' side. 'Got a job for you. Be at headquarters at nine a.m. to take Colin Wright's witness statement.'

'Sir!'

Watts closed his eyes, opened them. 'When you do, bear in mind that *you*, as an officer, have the authority in that situation and you use it where necessary. Don't take any flim-flam, got it?'

He turned to Jones and Kumar standing nearby. 'And you two Cheshire cats can make yourselves useful by letting the rest of the team know that tomorrow morning's briefing is delayed to three o'clock, then start talking to the locals back at the scene, like I've told you.' He went to Traynor. 'I want to talk to every-body who knew the Lawrences. In the morning, I'll start with Mike Lawrence's family members. Hopefully I'll be back at head-quarters around one o'clock. I'll see you then.'

Traynor was looking distracted. 'That, you will.'

TWENTY-ONE

Tuesday 18 December. 8.45 a.m.

Watts brought the BMW to a halt and looked through the open gates to his left. 'Let's hope Brendan Lawrence has got something useful to tell us.'

Judd was skimming her notes. 'You asked me to phone his sisters. I managed to contact Oona. She described Brendan and Mike Lawrence as very different personalities: Mike much quieter than his brother, Brendan a natural businessman.'

'Based on?'

'According to her, he always wanted to be his own boss and he works long hours. She wasn't sure but she thought Mike might have invested money in Brendan's business.'

'I've rung him four times, left messages and got no response. When I rang his father, he said Brendan is under a lot of work pressure.'

Judd pulled a face. 'Join the club.'

Watts released his seatbelt. 'Let's get it done.'

They headed for the entrance to the builders' compound, went inside, Watts pointing. 'Watch yourself on that pile of wood.'

They continued on to a large, brick-built office, its windows slick with condensation. Watts grasped the door handle, pushed open the door. The man sitting at a desk looked up. As before, the similarity between him and his younger brother was striking.

'What do you want? I'm busy.' Watts flipped his ID and Lawrence's face changed. 'Ah, I've been meaning to return your call—'

'That's all right, Mr Lawrence. Assuming you've got a few minutes to spare, we can talk now. This is PC Judd who's part of the investigation into your brother's murder.'

He stood, then came towards Watts, his hand outstretched. 'I do apologize for not getting back to you.' He smiled, took Judd's hand and held on to it. 'People assume that building companies are dormant in the winter. It isn't the case.' Watts' eyes drifted over him, a memory surfacing of Mike Lawrence sitting inside his car, quietly dying. They took the seats Lawrence was indicating.

'Mr Lawrence, we're doing all we can to investigate the shooting of your brother and his wife, which is why we're here.'

Lawrence gave them a startled look. 'I thought it was more or less sorted. That it was an attack on their car by some low-life that went wrong.'

'We're investigating a number of possibilities. We're talking to all family members, friends, colleagues and other associates of both your brother and sister-in-law to see if they can shed any light on it.'

'I don't have a clue what happened if it wasn't what we've read in the press.' He gave Judd a fleeting glance. 'I don't think I can be of much help.' Seeing a frown arriving on Watts' face, he said, 'I think I need to put you in the picture about Mike and me. We weren't close.' He hurried on. 'I'm as upset as everyone else about what's happened. What I mean is we were very different people.

Did you know he went to art college? I went straight into the building industry and when I decided I'd learned enough, I started up on my own.' He sat back, eyeing Watts. 'I employ fifteen full-time workers, plus seasonal help, all of it producing a healthy turnover.'

'A costly business,' observed Watts. 'Equipment doesn't come cheap.'

'You're right about that, but we're doing well.'

'Get some help from the family, did you?'

Lawrence frowned. 'Is that relevant to your investigation?' Watts waited. 'A few hundred from my dad to get me started but that was about it.'

Watts nodded. 'I know how it is, being born into a big family. Money's scarce.'

Lawrence's face was registering impatience. 'I understand you've got a job to do but so have I. As I've said, I doubt I can be of any—'

'Did your brother Mike invest in your company?'

Lawrence stared at him. 'Hardly. He was still at college when I set up this place.'

'How about later?'

Lawrence's eyes settled briefly on Watts, moved away. 'No.' He stood, pulled back his sleeve to expose a large wristwatch.

Watts ignored the hint. 'You're saying that your brother never invested in your business as a going concern, once it was established?' Watts watched a lot of thinking going on behind Lawrence's eyes.

'I don't see the relevance of your questions.'

'Don't let that worry you, Mr Lawrence, just give me an answer.'

'I approached Mike for a loan a couple of years back. The usual cashflow problem that besets building firms. I presented it as an investment. He refused, as was his right, of course. It didn't cause any friction between us, although I'd rather you didn't tell my parents or anybody else in the family about it. They've got enough to think about, right now, and anyway, it's all history. Mike and I are . . . were always civil to each other. It wasn't money, it was more to do with the difference in our personalities which created a distance between us.'

He gave a quick laugh. 'I'm the boss of a lot of hairy ar—' He glanced in Judd's direction. 'I chase profits, keep my lads in work. My brother spent his working hours drawing nice, coloured pictures of rooms for clients with money to burn.' His eyes went to his desk and a photograph of a blonde woman. He looked up. 'I'm explaining the differences between me and Mike. I'm not being critical.'

'I get it,' said Watts. 'What about Molly, your sister-in-law?'

'What about her?'

'How'd you get on with her?'

'Fine. She's a nice woman, although I haven't had that much to do with her since she married Mike.'

'Knew her before, did you?'

'What? No. I'm just saying that since she joined the family our paths haven't crossed that often.'

'Anything else you'd like to tell us about your brother? His friends? Associates?'

'I already told you, our lives were completely different. I never met any of his friends.'

'And he never mentioned them?'

'No.'

As Watts and then Judd stood, Lawrence went quickly to the door to show them out.

Back in the BMW, Watts asked, 'What do you make of him?'

She looked across at the office. 'He was happiest when we left.'

'My take on what we just heard is that he and his brother didn't get on and the relationship between them is unlikely to have improved when brother Mike wouldn't stump up the money he needed.' He started the engine. 'And I'm not too satisfied as to how he was able to start up a company like this in the first place.'

Judd studied her notes. 'Brendan Lawrence has a way of looking at a female without actually seeming to look, if you get my drift.'

He glanced across at her. 'I get it,' he said, thinking it was a pity her good judgement had let her down big-time a couple of nights back. 'It's time we got a different perspective on Brendan Lawrence and his brother Mike.'

A half hour's drive brought them outside a large, white Georgian-style house behind decorative yet sturdy metal gates. Watts nodded towards it. 'On the face of it, it looks like Mike Lawrence missed a good business opportunity.'

He got out his phone, tapped a number, waited. 'Mrs Brendan

Lawrence? This is Detective Inspector Bernard Watts. I'm outside. I need to talk to you.'

He ended the call, watched the gates drift slowly, quietly open. 'It's time you worked for your keep, Judd.'

The woman who opened the door after a short delay looked similar to the one in the photograph on Brendan Lawrence's desk. Watts held up his ID. She scarcely looked at it.

'I was just finishing a swim. Come on in.'

Watts and Judd exchanged swift glances as she adjusted the silky robe fully closed, turned and walked barefoot across the wide hall. They followed her into a huge sitting room overlooking a rear garden.

'Have seats. How about a drink?'

She went to a low sideboard supporting enough bottles to host an impromptu party without disappointing anybody.

'Not for us, Mrs Lawrence.'

She turned to look at them. 'Of course. You're on duty. Well, I'm not, so I'll have one.'

She gave Judd a second glance. 'Are you on work experience?'

Notebook in hand, voice firm, Judd said, 'Your full name, please, Mrs Lawrence.'

'Gemma Lawrence. That's with a "G".'

Watts said, 'Mrs Lawrence, I'm in charge of the investigation into the murder of your brother-in-law and the attempted murder of his wife.'

She sat on the sofa next to him, the robe sliding open to show tanned, well-shaped legs. 'We're talking to all members of the family and—'

'Poor Mike.' She raised her glass, took a mouthful of brandy, swallowed. 'He had everything to live for. Has anybody told you she was pregnant?'

'We're aware of that,' said Judd. 'Tell us what you know about Mike and Molly Lawrence.'

She shrugged. 'We didn't see them that often. Brendan and Mike didn't have a lot in common and making small talk with an accountant and an interior decorator isn't my idea of a good time.' She gazed around the large, square room, at swag curtains, deep-buttoned chairs, pointed to a black leather and wood chair some distance away.

'See that? It's an Eames. You wouldn't believe what I paid for it. Mike's designs didn't do it for me.' She took another mouthful of brandy.

'Why didn't your husband and his brother get on?' asked Judd.

'What I actually said is that they didn't have much in common.' She shrugged. 'Money is the answer. Isn't it always, in families?' She gave Watts an evaluative look. 'I'm talking about *my* money. Whatever Brendan might have told you about his business, it's my money which got him started. My money which bought all of this. My dad owned a very successful recycling business. When he died, I got everything. No sisters or brothers, you see.' She grimaced. 'Not like the Lawrence tribe.'

She looked up at Watts. 'Brendan's got a good head for business, I'll give him that. He's pushy, doesn't give anybody a chance to take liberties but' – she inclined her head towards Watts, her tone conspiratorial – 'times change, situations change. Cashflow is what finishes off a lot of businesses like his, or to be exact, a lack of it. Recycling is the business to be in now. It's how I keep Brendan afloat.'

'What about Molly Lawrence?' asked Judd. She watched the face opposite harden.

'What about her? Has somebody been talking?' They waited. She shrugged. 'If I describe my husband as an "alpha male", you'll know where I'm coming from. When Mike first introduced Molly to the family, I could see Brendan was taken with her. I can always tell, you see.'

She turned to look at Watts, the robe sliding further. 'Have you met her? She's small and dark with these great, big, pansy eyes. I told him, "*One* more time, Brendan, just one more, and I phone Richard". That's all it takes, you see. Richard is my lawyer and whatever else Brendan is, he's no fool, so that put an end to whatever he might have been up to. Or thinking of getting up to.'

Judd asked, 'Mrs Lawrence, are you saying that there was a relationship between your husband and Molly Lawrence?'

Gemma Lawrence started laughing, tears flooding her eyes. Watts doubted the drink she was nursing was her first of the day. 'That's not what I'm saying! Molly was too into Mike to notice Brendan, and even if she had, she wouldn't have been interested.' She took more brandy on board. 'He dresses well, my husband, but scratch the surface and he's a yob and an idiot where women are concerned.' She glanced at Judd. 'Did he come on to you?'

Judd said nothing.

'If that's a "no", he must be slipping.'

'Mrs Lawrence, what's your understanding of what happened to your brother-in-law and his wife?'

She stared at Judd. 'What's there to understand? It's obvious. They were somewhere they shouldn't have been. Some rundown, scruffy area, by all accounts, although what they were doing there . . .?' She shrugged, took another mouthful of brandy. 'I didn't get on that well with them, but I'm sorry about what happened . . . and the baby, of course.' Her lower lip quivered.

Following a further ten minutes, during which Gemma Lawrence wept, told Watts about her dislike of her in-laws and her regret that she hadn't had children, but nothing which moved the investigation on, they were back inside the BMW and in a line of slow traffic.

'Takes all sorts, Judd.'

'I think Mrs Gemma "with-a-G" Lawrence is keen on you, Sarge.'

He shuddered. 'Behave. What did you make of her and what she said?'

'She's confirmed that the two brothers had little in common. She comes across as a hard case and she's no fool. Brendan Lawrence has an eye for women but he's in no rush to lose what he's got, so he toes the line.'

'A cynical summation from somebody still on work experience.'

She laughed – the first he'd heard from her in the last day or two. 'It's families, Sarge. People doing or going after what they want, while avoiding losing out to anybody else.'

Watts stopped behind a dithering Fiat, craning his head to see what was slowing down the traffic three cars ahead. 'If that's how it works, I was lucky.'

He glanced at her. She was staring out of the window. Given what he knew of her background, which wasn't a lot, and none of it good, he decided that she probably knew more than he did about families and their goings-on. 'What do you think about what she said about Brendan Lawrence having an eye for his sister-in-law, Molly?'

'I believe it, if that's what you're asking. Sounds like Gemma landed like a ton of builders' bricks on him because she wasn't the first he'd used his eye on. That needs exploring directly with Molly, Sarge.'

He shook his head. 'I can't see Will doing that with her in her current state, and right now his brief is specific: get an account from her of the attack that night.'

'How about I leave it a while then talk to her?'

'We haven't got a while.'

The nervous Fiat owner turned left. Watts picked up speed. 'My picture of Brendan Lawrence, alpha male, is that he's a main-chancer who drives his employees hard and gets what he wants without losing sleep over how.' He drove on.

'And he had no time for brother Mike.'

TWENTY-TWO

Tuesday 18 December. 2.30 p.m.

Judd was typing up the visits to Brendan Lawrence and his wife. She finished, her eyes fixed on the lines of text, searching for errors before she emailed it upstairs, hearing the door open.

'Hello, Chloe. You look busy.'

She looked up at Julian. 'Hi. Just finishing something.'

'How about that coffee you offered me?'

She hesitated, then grinned. 'OK.'

She sent the email, got up from the table, her foot striking one of its legs. Peripheral attention on him, her mind on coffee, she absently patted the table with a whispered, 'Sorry,' and headed for the kettle.

'I don't think I've ever heard someone apologize to furniture.'

Reaching for the coffee jar, she looked back at him and saw that he was smiling. She gave the coffee her full attention. 'I don't know why I said it. It's just a thing. From when I was little.' She tensed, hearing him coming closer.

'It's OK. We all have quirky stuff.'

She looked up at him then quickly away, feeling that his eyes were looking into her soul.

'It just says to me that you were a kind kid. Maybe a little vulnerable.'

She forced a laugh. 'Thanks for the psychological opinion. How much do I owe you?'

He came closer and reached for one of the filled mugs. 'Just this.'

The door opened and Watts came in, followed by Traynor. 'When did you pull all of this together?'

'Late last night,' said Traynor. 'It was too late to ring you.'

'How sure are you?'

'Come *on*, Bernard. How sure were you about the carjack-homicide approach?'

'Ninety per cent, as it happens.'

Watts went to the table, looked down at Colin Wright's single-page statement, searched the words, getting nothing from it that they hadn't already heard from Wright himself. He checked his watch. 'Judd and I saw Brendan Lawrence and his wife earlier. There's no love lost between the brothers, plus Brendan's got an eye for other women which, according to his wife, occasionally wandered in Molly Lawrence's direction.'

Traynor looked up at him. 'That's interesting.'

'I want verification of it from another source.' He reached for his papers, seeing that Judd and Julian had already left. 'Ready to share what you've said with the investigation?'

'Yes.'

'Got some notes on your theory?'

'No.'

'Impressive. I need notes for meetings.'

The incident room fell silent as they came inside. Watts put down his papers. 'What have we got on Huey Whyte?'

One of the officers working the inner-city inquiries raised a hand. 'I talked to his immediate neighbours. A couple of them confirmed seeing him in their local bar on the night of the Lawrence shootings. That he was there from around nine p.m. to closing time. CCTV inside the bar bears it out.'

Watts grunted. 'So much for Whyte. No wonder he was so chipper during his interview.' He looked around. 'Anything else?'

'An email from Jonah Budd's probation officer.' Miller pointed at her screen. 'She's done some checking. On the day of the Lawrence shootings, Budd was attending a Young Offenders' course in Nottingham which started at four p.m. and finished at nine thirty.'

'She's got verification of his attendance?'

'She's following it up.'

'Let me know as soon as you get her response.' He looked around the packed room. 'Anybody get anything on sightings of unfamiliar or out-of-place persons and/or vehicles?'

Julian held up several sheets. 'I've already got a hundred-plus responses from officers who started on it yesterday. I've analysed three quarters of them but so far there's zero confirmation of anything of interest. I'll continue with what I've got, plus those still to come. If there is anything which looks interesting, I'll let you know.'

'Thanks.'

His eyes moved over them, picking up tiredness on most of the faces and disengagement from Jones. He had his back half-turned to Julian, who was sitting next to Judd. 'The thinking behind that line of questioning was Will's. The recovery of Molly Lawrence's handbag plus valuables has strengthened his view that this investigation needs to reconsider motive.' He paused, seeing heads turn, some of the facial expressions increasingly downbeat. 'He's now going to tell you why.'

Traynor came and sat on the edge of a nearby table, looking directly at each of them.

'The finding of the Lawrence valuables indicates that the shooting of Mr and Mrs Lawrence was not motivated by theft. The taking of their belongings was intended to confuse and conceal the true intent.' He paused. 'I think this gunman was well known to one if not both of the Lawrences.'

The impact on the room was immediate. He waited for the tumult to settle. 'Which means that the search for sightings of people and vehicles unfamiliar to the area round Forge Street and beyond remains very relevant. Whoever he is, he does not belong to the Bristol Road–Forge Street area, either as a resident or a worker. We need to look closer at the Lawrences' family and friends, colleagues and associates of Molly and Mike Lawrence. As Detective Inspector Watts said at another briefing, a number of them have already been spoken to. What has been learned about Brendan Lawrence suggests he needs to be considered a person of interest.' He glanced at Watts. 'You'll want to come in here?'

Watts nodded. 'I want intel to compile a list of names and contact details for all of the people Will has just mentioned. I'll put together a rota of who goes where. It won't be a case of talking just to the names on that list. It's about talking to people *they* name, no matter how incidental they might seem.'

Jones' hand shot up. 'It might help if we have an idea of the type of individual we're looking for.'

Watts looked to Traynor. 'Will's got a profile.'

'It's based on limited available indicators,' said Traynor, 'but it suggests that he's a confident individual who's comfortable managing and directing people, including those under duress. It also tells us what he isn't: a young, urban offender. I would re-estimate his age range to be twenty-five to forty, probably the higher end. That profile fits a security guard who has already featured in the investigation. He fits the personality, attitude and age criteria I've described and he works and lives in the area. He's a person of interest. He will be spoken to very soon.'

Watts stood. 'As already said, those of you who are out there talking to people in the extended area need to keep at it. Whoever this individual is, it's highly likely he was in that inner-city area prior to the shootings, checking it out. I want to know ASAP if any of you get so much as a hint from anybody who remembers an individual or a vehicle that caught their attention for whatever reason.'

'Sarge?' Jones stood. 'All we've got from the people Kumar and I spoke to is that they're shocked at the attack on the Lawrences and fearful that some nutter is on the loose.' He glanced quickly around the room, getting confirmatory nods along with dispirited looks. 'Some of you will soon be talking to friends, colleagues and so on of the Lawrences,' said Watts. 'Judd and I will be doing some of it. I haven't got time to feel tired or fed up. Neither have you.'

He and Traynor exited from the room, Traynor on his phone. As he ended the call, Watts asked, 'When are you seeing Molly Lawrence again?'

'I've just agreed it for this afternoon.'

They walked into Watts' office. 'How optimistic are you?'

'Given the picture her mother just gave me, I'm not, but I'll see how it goes.'

Watts handed him the details of what they had from Gemma Lawrence. 'I'll leave you to phrase it, but if she's up to it, ask her about her brother-in-law, Brendan.' He frowned. 'Where's Judd got to?'

'She was in the incident room just now.'

'So I saw. If you get anything from Molly about Brendan

Lawrence, phone me.' He sat and looked at the sea of paper on the table. 'You do know that Miller's waiting for you to show up with your shorts over your trousers and the solution to this whole mess? She's probably not the only one.'

He looked up. Traynor was gazing at him with a look of utter incomprehension.

'Forget it. I'm expecting our person of interest in ten minutes. If it produces anything, I'll phone you.'

Coming into the busy reception area, immediately seeing who he was looking for, Watts raised his hand and pointed to a small room nearby. The big man got up and followed him to it. 'Thanks for coming in. Have a seat.'

The chair creaked as Nigel settled himself on to it. 'What's this about?'

'The shooting of two people, close to where you work.'

Nigel shrugged, his gaze drifting away. 'I already told you all I know.'

Watts sat back, tapping his pen on his notebook, eyes fixed on Nigel's face. 'This game makes most of us good judges of people. Tell me what else happened.'

Nigel shifted, causing more creaks. 'Like I told you . . .'

Watts sat forward. 'I've been in this job more years than I like to count. It's told me a lot about people and how they are, what they are, how they might respond to things that happen around them.' He paused. 'You said you heard two gunshots at around nine twenty or nine thirty that night. You're a security operative. You know that area well. Know what I'd have done in your place, in that situation?' He did a slow count to ten. 'I'd have taken my dog and I'd have gone for a short walk, to see what I could see.'

The small room was silent. Nigel eyed him, looked away, then back. 'If you spotted me, you should have said.'

'I didn't. Now you're going to tell me all about it.'

Traynor brought the Aston Martin to a stop and looked at the house. What was waiting for him was a make-or-break situation. Molly Lawrence's wellbeing was paramount and he would do nothing to jeopardize it, but if there was something related to the investigation which she hadn't disclosed, he needed it. Today.

Mrs Monroe opened the door to him. 'Hello, Dr Traynor. I'm so glad you're here. Please, come in.'

'How is Molly?'

She led him inside the warm kitchen full of the smell of baking. 'She's drying her hair. The good news is that she's had her first shower since she came home. She won't be long. The downside is she's now refusing to leave the house. I've told her she can't go on like this. Her response was that she doesn't want to go on. I rang the hospital yesterday without telling her. Now she's discharged, they're suggesting she goes to her doctor to get help.' She looked at him, indicating a large sponge cake. He shook his head. She brought coffee to the table, sat opposite him. 'Tell me what to do, Dr Traynor.'

Recalling his own feelings of helplessness after his wife's death, his inability to do anything constructive for months, he felt quick sympathy. 'Your being here has to be a great support. Yes, she needs help. She also needs time.' The door opened. Traynor stood.

'Hello, Will.'

'Hello, Mrs Lawrence.'

Her mother went to the cupboard for another cup. 'Sit down, Molly, and I'll pour you some coffee. How about a small slice—?'

'Nothing for me.' She looked at Traynor. 'I'm ready.'

He followed her to the sitting room, waited as she sat down. He sat opposite. 'How are you?'

She pushed her hands through her hair. 'I want to say that I'm OK. I'm not. For the first time, I'm seeing the world how it actually is: full of risk and violence and people out to do others harm.' She looked up at him. 'Would you believe, we're getting calls from newspapers offering obscene amounts of money for me to talk to them? It's madness.'

None of what she was saying was unexpected. Last time he was here, he had recognized her omission of the shots fired at her husband and herself, plus much else, as a form of denial. It seemed to him that that denial was beginning to erode. Now, he had something to tell her, before she learned it from the media.

'I have some news. The police have recovered your handbag.' Her head came up, her eyes widening with shock.

'*What?*'

'It was in a lake at Westley Country Park. Do you know it?' She shook her head.

He waited for her next question. It didn't come. 'Most of your property was still inside it, though one of your earrings is missing.'

'I don't understand. Why would somebody steal from us then . . . throw it all away?'

He looked down at the questions he had brought with him. 'How do you feel, knowing that, Molly?'

'Confused.'

'I want you to talk some more about what happened.'

'Yes.'

The directness of the single word response took him by surprise. 'You told me last time how events led to you and your husband being in that street and about the man who got into the car.'

'Yes.'

'From what you said, this man appears to have been very much in control of the situation, yet he still used the gun. I'm trying to understand that.'

She stared at him, saying nothing.

'Did something happen which led him to do that?'

'You're saying that we caused him to shoot us?'

'No. One person is entirely responsible for what happened that night, the man with the gun, but the police need to understand how and why events occurred in the way they did.' He waited for a response.

'You know, don't you?'

'What do I know, Molly?'

'You know it was my fault.'

'No—'

'It *was*, Will.' She clasped her hands at her mouth, her eyes fixed on his. 'He . . . he did something . . . the man.'

'What did he do?'

She looked away from him. 'He told me to open my coat. Unbutton my shirt.'

Traynor's thinking was in freefall. The investigation was now pursuing the possibility that the attacker was known to one or other of the Lawrences. Now, here, was a further dimension they knew nothing about. One which was giving Traynor a clear message. It wasn't appropriate for him to pursue it.

'Molly, do you recall Police Constable Chloe Judd who came to see you at the hospital?'

She didn't respond.

'How do you feel about seeing her again, talking to her about what you've just said to me—?'

'He *touched* me.' Her breathing quickened. 'He leant over me, put his face against . . . me, his mouth on my neck, my chest. *That's* when Mike lost it. That's when he shot us.'

Traynor waited out the silence. 'Is there anything else you want to say about it?'

She shook her head.

Traynor had carried within him for a decade the certainty that his wife had been attacked sexually by whoever had killed her and taken her away. He looked down at his hands, saw the tremor in his fingers, closed down the line of thinking. There was another question he had to ask.

'This man. Was there a physical characteristic, something in the way he moved, his voice or tone, the way he phrased what he said that led you to think he was at all familiar?'

Watts' eyes were fixed on Nigel's face, intent on what Nigel was telling him.

'I've done years of security work. I'm no overweight bladder of lard who rocks up to a building site or whatever, does one turn around it in an eight-hour shift then hangs around the office drinking coffee, or sods off home. I take pride in what I do. The shots we told you about. The ones Abdul and me heard that night. You were right when you said they would have got my interest. I usually take the dog for a walk when Abdul starts closing up at ten. I decided I'd go in the direction of the shots.' He saw Watts' face change. 'In the direction I *thought* they came from.'

'What time was this, again?'

'I'd say around ten fifteen.'

'Go on.'

'I walked over to Forge Street. There was a car there.'

Watts' head came up. 'Describe it.'

He shrugged. 'I can't say much about it. Dark-coloured. That whole lousy street was dark and it was raining.'

'And?'

'And, what? It was there. The car. In the dark.'

'Was one of its rear doors open?'

Nigel frowned. 'No, it wasn't. All the doors were closed and all was quiet. No lights. Nothing.'

Watts absorbed this. Nigel had either got the time wrong or he hadn't noticed the small detail in the dark. 'Did you see or hear anything else that night?'

'No.'

'Did you see any movement inside the car?'

'No. It had dark windows.'

Windows, thought Watts. 'Did you see any damage to them?'

'I didn't approach it, but not from where I was standing.'

'How close did you get to it?'

'I was on the other side of the road.'

Watts sighed, gave him a disgruntled look. 'You should have told me all this before now.'

'Told you what? That I saw a car?'

'You're sure you didn't pass anybody on foot or in a vehicle as you walked over to Forge Street?'

'No, nobody.'

Watts glared at him. 'I said, *think*. Think about your walk there. *See* it inside your head.'

'If you'd been there, seen how dark it was—'

'I *was* there. I know what you're saying.' He watched the big face opposite, saw it crease into a frown.

'Sorry, Mr Watts. It's all . . . The more I try to think, the less I remember.' Watts was on his feet.

'Stay here.'

Something he recalled Hanson his years-ago psychologist colleague saying about witness recall was inside his head. He opened the door, walked the corridor, saw Reynolds. 'Get a witness statement form. Bring it here.'

He came back to Nigel. 'After you've given a statement about what you've told me and anything else that occurs to you, I want you to go home, put it out of your head. All of it. Don't think about it.'

'I thought I'd do some brain-racking later—'

'No. Leave it alone. Relax. Watch the box. Do whatever you usually do. You've got my number if anything does occur to you, but what I'm saying is, don't push it.' Reynolds arrived with a statement form.

'Sorry I'm no help, Mr Watts. I'll do what you've said.'

Glancing outside, seeing the Aston Martin, Watts left Reynolds to take the security guard's statement and headed for his office. He found Traynor inside. He went directly to the Smartboard, started writing, talking over his shoulder to him.

'The security guard has just decided to tell me that he was walking his dog in Forge Street after hearing the nine thirty shots. He's not sure of the time but he thinks he was there around ten, possibly ten fifteen. He saw the Lawrences' car parked there.' He stopped writing, looked over his shoulder. 'One thing doesn't add up. He said all the doors were closed . . . What's up?'

'Molly Lawrence has told me that they were shot because Mike Lawrence lost control.'

Watts turned to him as Judd came inside. 'He lost control because the gunman sexually assaulted her.'

'You *said* she was holding back. What else did she say?'

'That he unbuttoned her shirt, put his mouth against her neck, her chest, that there was nothing about him that appeared familiar to her. She said he was a stranger.' He looked up at Watts. 'As a male, I'm not the appropriate person to talk to Molly about that.'

Watts looked across at Judd. 'Can you do it?'

'Yes, and I'll also pull all the jackets on sex offenders known for armed vehicle invasion.' She frowned. 'Hang on. How many days is it since the shooting? If we'd known about this sooner, we might have got DNA.'

Watts eyed Traynor. 'DNA might still be there.'

Traynor took out his phone. 'This morning, Molly Lawrence took her first shower since leaving hospital.'

Judd raked at her hair. 'Didn't it occur to her to tell us that any sexually motivated contact is something she should have told us about immediately?'

'I want to know what happened to her and her husband's clothes after they were admitted to hospital.' He reached for his phone. 'Mrs Monroe? Will Traynor. Do you have the clothes Molly was wearing on the night of the shooting?' He glanced at Watts. 'Yes. We'll ring them, thank you.' He ended the call. 'As far as she's aware, the hospital still has them. Molly was asked if she wanted them. She said no.'

Watts snatched up the desk phone. 'You said it, Judd. If we'd known about a sexual element sooner, we might have him by now. Molly Lawrence must know about DNA. Didn't she think?'

'I'm guessing that all of her thinking, her critical faculties, were fully taken up with the aftermath of being shot,' said Traynor.

Watts eyed him. 'Is that sarcasm I'm hearing?'

'No. Realism.'

Watts was talking into the phone. Judd looked across at Traynor. 'He's going to be mega pissed off if he doesn't get those clothes. Yes, I'll talk to Molly.'

Watts put down the phone. 'Can't fault the hospital's organization. They parcelled the clothes up for Mrs Lawrence to take home and when she refused them, they put them in store. They're sending them over now. I've requested Mike Lawrence's clothes as well. I'd better alert Brophy.'

Judd looked at him. '*Don't*, Sarge. Don't tell him you've only just requested them. He'll go on about why we didn't check them out before.'

'I've said it before, Judd, I like the simple world you live in. Unfortunately, I live and work in *this* one. You know that as soon as those clothes arrive here, they'll be logged into incident room records, logged again by forensics. Brophy's strength, if one exists, is that he likes facts, records. He'll know about it.' He headed for the door. 'That's the least of my concerns. Tomorrow, we start talking to the people who knew the Lawrences.'

Judd watched him go. 'The trouble with Sarge is he takes everything personally.'

Traynor looked up. 'Probably because his is the name heading the investigation.'

'That wouldn't get me in a state when I'm in that position.' She reached for the phone. 'Want me to ring Molly Lawrence to say I'm available to talk to her whenever it suits her? Will?'

'Leave it with me for now. There are some things I have to think about.'

TWENTY-THREE

Wednesday 19 December. 10.10 a.m.

Chong's gloved hands deftly unsealed the grey plastic bag and removed several others of brown paper from inside it. Watts watched, impatience climbing as she opened the largest of them, reached inside and pulled out a heavy coat. She carefully unfolded it on to the sheet of thick white paper covering the examination table.

'One black winter coat, property of Molly Lawrence.'

Her hands moved over it, patting its surface, stopping when they reached the pockets. She reached inside one – 'Left pocket void' – and reached into the other. 'Right pocket contains . . .' She drew out a dull looking object, laid it on the paper. They both looked at it.

'Her watch,' said Watts, seeing the thick layer of dried blood covering it.

'It's probably a nice one if we could see it properly.' She called to her PM suite assistant. 'Igor? Camera, please.'

He arrived with a nod for Watts, stood close to the table, angled the camera downwards and fired off several shots of the watch. She lifted it carefully, peered at it, took a lens Igor was offering, looked again. 'I can see one fingerprint in the blood . . . possibly a second.' She looked up at Watts, his eyes fixed on the watch. 'I can see that you're stunned by my expertise.'

'Molly Lawrence said she hid her watch in her pocket so that the shooter wouldn't get it. I should have been on to it before now.'

She reached for it and placed it carefully inside an evidence bag. 'I recall you telling me how heavily stained her hands were at the scene. She probably handled it after she and her husband were shot, maybe to check it was still safe inside her pocket.' She walked from the table and returned with a small, handheld device. 'Before I send it and the rest of the clothing upstairs, I'll vacuum the coat, including the pockets.'

'And once Adam has it all, he'll do the same.'

'Yup. That's because we're anal-retentive, science-y types.' She looked up at him. 'I phoned the hospital about Mike Lawrence's clothing when it didn't arrive and was informed that it had already been disposed of. Incinerated.' She watched his colour build.

'They *knew* he was a homicide victim!'

'I'm merely delivering the news that the disposal is a done deal,' she said, evenly. 'Like you, the hospital staff were under pressure that night. It's just another thing to let go of, Bernard.'

'I'll check is what I'll do.'

'Thought you might. Being a compulsive police-y type.'

Consulting the label on the next bag, she removed its contents.

'One expensive-looking cream silk shirt, property of Mrs Molly Lawrence.'

Gently unfolding it, she placed it flat on the paper-covered surface. It was stiff with dried blood on its right side, all of it now a dull rust. A picture of Molly Lawrence slumped against the front passenger door rushed into his head, a detail getting his attention: a small, round hole low on the right side of the shirt, another close to it.

'Entry and exit bullet holes,' said Chong, carefully folding it and placing it to one side, reaching for another item. 'Black wool trousers.' She turned them around to him. 'Extensive blood-run over the upper back portion from the waistband downwards.'

'I overlooked the possibility of DNA and I should have got on to the hospital and requested these clothes days ago. It's basic training-manual stuff.'

'They're here now and they'll all be thoroughly tested. We might get something.'

She folded the trousers, returned them to the bag, opened another and removed an item of pale pink underwear. She held up the delicate lace pants, also heavily bloodstained, reached for the matching bra. 'Molly Lawrence has a subtly expensive taste in clothes,' she murmured. 'And you were straight into a high-pressure murder case with all the markers of a non-contact shooting motivated by theft. There was no reason to consider the possibility of sexual contact.'

'You know what I'm saying. I'm losing my edge.'

He watched her return each item to its relevant bag, hand them to Igor, then methodically fold the thick white paper covering the table onto itself several times, before placing it inside a plastic bag and adding details to its label.

'That's my job done. I'll take it all to Adam so he can do his thing with any hairs, fibres and whatever else there might be.' She regarded him for several seconds. 'Bernard, his team might find somebody else's DNA, they might not. I know it's frustrating but try to lose the "bulldog-with-toothache" look. It doesn't become you.'

She shook her head as he headed for the door and out. Removing latex gloves, she rang the hospital and was informed that if an inventory of the Lawrences' clothes had been taken, its whereabouts was now unknown. Years ago, Chong had worked in an emergency hospital department. People did their best in life-and-death situations. Things got overlooked. It happened to all workers involved in those kinds of situations.

Going to her desk she consulted her copy of the Lawrence case file, found the home telephone number of the husband's family. A woman answered.

'Mrs Lawrence? This is Dr Chong, the pathologist at headquarters, Rose Road. I apologize for intruding at this time but I understand that your son and daughter-in-law visited you earlier that evening of the incident? Is there any chance that you recall in detail what your daughter-in-law was wearing?'

She listened, wrote down details, thanked the woman and put down the phone. From what she had just been told, they had all of the clothes Molly Lawrence was wearing on the evening she and her husband were shot.

12.10 p.m.

Mrs Monroe was looking agitated. 'I had to ring you, Dr Traynor. I'm so worried. She'll probably tell you she's feeling much better. She isn't. She sits upstairs or in here, staring straight ahead. No television. No books. She refuses to talk to her work colleagues when they ring, including this really nice woman who's her assistant. She doesn't go out. To be honest, I'm glad about that because if she did, I'd be worried sick about where she was and what she was doing or might do.' She looked across at Traynor. 'Tell me what to do and I'll do it.'

'Has Molly seen her GP?'

'She refused to go.'

'Then, I'm sorry to say, I don't think there's much you can do, Mrs Monroe.' He guessed that she was not yet aware of what Molly had told him about the sexual assault.

'Can you do anything, Dr Traynor?'

'My work with her is very specific to the police investigation.'

'I understand the police need answers and it must be very frustrating that she's so reluctant to talk, but . . .' She shook her head. 'There's just no end to this nightmare.'

The door drifted open. Traynor stood as Molly came into the room, with a glance for her mother.

'Are you telling Dr Traynor what a lost cause I am?'

'Molly, please—'

'I wasn't expecting you, Will, but it's not a problem.'

Mrs Monroe left the room. He watched Molly move slowly to the sofa and sit. To Traynor, she looked deathly pale. 'How are you?'

'Getting there. Shall we start?'

He kept his voice and tone low-key. 'The last time I saw you, you told me about something else that happened to you that night.'

'I remember.'

'Have you thought about speaking about it to one of my police colleagues, the young woman I mentioned whom you've met before?'

She looked up at him, a trace of a smile on her face. 'The young officer with the spikey blonde hair who came to the hospital? She was nice, really supportive, but . . .' She shook her head. 'I just can't talk about it.'

Traynor carefully framed his response. 'Given the nature of what the man did, if you reconsider, would you ring Detective Inspector Watts?'

'I don't want more people, police, in my life. I want everything just . . . normal.' She glanced in the direction of the front door. 'How could I be so *stupid*?' she whispered. 'Those two officers who stand outside. I didn't question why. They're here to protect me and my mother, aren't they?'

Traynor's response was non-specific. 'It's routine in a lot of situations. By the way, your watch.' She looked up at him, her face expressionless. 'It's safe. My police colleagues have it. They're examining it and it will be released to you as soon as possible.'

She rubbed her arms as though cold. 'I'm not sure I want it back.' She gave him a direct look. 'I remember afterwards . . . when he'd gone . . . I felt for it in my pocket and . . . it got sticky. From my hand.'

He made a quick note. 'Is there anything else you want to say about what happened that night?'

He wrote the now-familiar words she had used before when describing the progression of events that night. He could not recall anyone he had worked with who had had such rigidly fixed recall. Focused on his note-taking, he allowed no hint of frustration on to his face. Reaching the point where their belongings had been taken, her voice slowed, then stopped. She added none of the detail she had divulged previously. He looked up at her. She looked away, towards the window.

'I'm sorry, Will, but I just can't go there again. We need to finish this. I'm wasting your time.'

Traynor was now certain that he would not gain any additional information from her within a timescale useful to his colleagues, yet he had a professional responsibility towards her.

'How do you feel about talking to someone who has nothing to do with the police investigation? Someone to help you make sense of what's happened.'

She looked at him. 'Who?'

'The person I have in mind specializes in working with people who have experienced trauma, to help them adjust, to face the future.'

'Who?' she repeated.

'She's a forensic psychiatrist—'

'*No!*'

Her vehemence was unexpected. 'That's OK, Molly. It's your choice. If you change your mind, let me know—'

'I won't.'

He looked at her, wondering what might be behind her refusal to cause such a stark response. She turned away from him. 'I don't want to do that. I had a friend, years ago. She saw a psychiatrist. She told me it was horrendous. I can't do it, Will. I've been through enough.' She stood. 'I'm tired.'

He walked with her to the hall, watched as she slowly climbed the stairs. Mrs Monroe appeared from the kitchen. He had no reassuring words for this woman.

'I'll phone you in a couple of days, just to see how she is.'

He drove away from the house, preoccupied with the whole case.

5 p.m.

Inside the incident room all eyes were on Kumar writing up the details Jones was relating. 'We've talked to some of the close relatives, friends and associates of Mr and Mrs Lawrence, specifically to Mike Lawrence's parents, his brother and his two sisters to try and establish if it's possible that whoever attacked them knew them. They were really upset by the idea. None of them said anything which suggested to us that Mike Lawrence and his wife were shot by someone they knew.' He waited for Kumar to catch up.

'Where did you see Brendan Lawrence?' asked Watts.

'His business premises. He said you'd been there, Sarge. We know he's a person of interest but he didn't say anything to us that sounded useful. He didn't look well and he mentioned he was planning to take a few days off. Do you want us to see him again? Maybe at his home?'

'No.' Watts looked around the room. 'Anything else on the Lawrences' relatives, friends and associates?'

'Reynolds has made contact with two of his friends, Sarge. A Simon Williams and a Matthew Barnes.'

Reynolds stood, one hand raised, a leftover from the sixth former he'd been in the not-so-distant past. 'Simon Williams told me that Mrs Lawrence has very few close relatives. Mr Lawrence is from a large family. He said he met Mike Lawrence at college, but contact between them was very limited since Lawrence got married.'

Watts eyed him. 'You asked why?'

The young officer shook his head.

'Got any theory on it, Reynolds?'

'I was thinking that being married and all that, they had other things to do . . .' Hearing several low laughs, he looked flustered.

'What else did you get from this Williams?'

'He works from home. He's some sort of designer for a toy company. He lives about four miles from the Lawrences' house. He doesn't know Molly Lawrence that well. He said he has no idea why anyone would do either of them harm. He also said that Mike Lawrence had told him that his wife was pregnant.' He looked up at Watts. 'He did give me the name of one person Mike Lawrence didn't get along with: Damien Alphon.'

'Who's he?'

'He said he was one of Mike Lawrence's work colleagues.'

'And?' He waited. 'What about this other friend, Matthew Barnes?'

Reynolds quickly turned a page, his eyes searching the detail. 'Matthew Barnes and Mike Lawrence were friends for years, a similar story to the one I got from Williams.' He gave Watts a quick look. 'He told me he dated Mrs Lawrence very briefly before she met Mike Lawrence.'

'And you asked him about that and how he felt about what's happened to her?'

'No, sir. It seemed a bit . . . personal.'

Ignoring more grins and eye-rolls, Watts regarded the young officer, now a beacon of discomfort. 'You need to start asking the next question. Make it *soon* because I'm getting older by the minute.' Some officers were sending sympathetic looks to the hapless Reynolds. 'Anything else?' He waited out more page-searching.

'Yes, sir. I went to Mike Lawrence's place of work. It's an interior design company. I asked to see the boss there, a Sebastian Engar, but he wasn't there. I tried asking a few of the other employees what they knew about Mike Lawrence. They said Mr Engar had told them not to discuss it. That he would provide the police with "all relevant information" at a later time.'

Watts took the notes from Reynolds and looked at them. 'Very neat, Reynolds. Very clear. Just bear in mind the next time you're on a visit that *you* are the police and *they* give you whatever you ask for.'

'Sir.' Reynolds quickly sat.

'I'll be seeing Williams, Alphon and Engar.' Watts searched for Judd. 'You'll be on the visits with me—'

'Sir?' Reynolds half-rose. 'Mr Engar's on holiday.'

'Nice to know you're on the ball, Reynolds.' He picked up a note. 'A forensic update: still awaiting fingerprint and DNA testing of the gun, DNA testing of Molly Lawrence's clothing, plus fingerprint analysis of her watch. Needless to say, if any DNA was transferred from her upper body on to her clothes, it'll be our silver bullet. Not the best analogy in the circumstances, but accurate.' He paused, glanced at Traynor.

'Will has an update.'

Traynor stood. 'I spoke with Molly Lawrence for the third time, earlier today. It's extremely unlikely that she will be able to supply this investigation with a more detailed account of the attack on her and her husband. She has also declined to speak with PC Judd about the sexual aspect of it. I'm considering a possible change of approach with her. If I decide there's a chance it could assist this case, I'll discuss it with Detective Inspector Watts.'

Amid a low buzz of talk, Watts reached for his file. 'That's it for now.'

He headed for the door looking irritated, hooking a finger at

Jones. Outside the incident room, he turned to him, forefinger raised.

'You *don't* send somebody who's got about as much nous as a nun at a swingers' party to do visits *you* should be doing *with* him. How else is he going to learn?'

'Sorry, Sarge. We're up to here with investigative visits, paper-work, and I thought Reynolds—'

'Who isn't "up to here"? What you do is your *job*, part of which is to have Reynolds with you on visits so he can see *how* you do it!' He turned and headed downstairs, Jones following him.

'There's another mate of Mike Lawrence's I haven't managed to make contact with so far, Sarge. Benedict Sill.'

'Leave it with me.'

Back in his office, Watts was feeling rattled. Traynor's admission of what amounted to defeat with Molly Lawrence wasn't what he'd wanted to hear. He looked at the board, his eyes drifting over what was up there. Brendan Lawrence's name got his attention. Except for the extra weight, he could almost be a twin of his dead brother. Was this case one of mistaken identity? Were the shootings motivated by a business-related grudge against Brendan, and brother Mike died as a result? In Watts' experience, builders overcharged, disre-garded completion dates and were a pain in the tail. To his knowledge nobody had ever killed one because of it.

He ran his hands through his hair, reached for the desk phone, dialled the number for Sebastian Engar, Mike Lawrence's boss. After a brief exchange, during which he learned that Engar would be in his office at the end of the week, he said, 'Please inform Mr Engar that I'll see him at his office on Friday. I'll see Damien Alphon at the same time.' He ended the call as Judd came in.

'I want you in here at eight in the morning. Thanks to Reynolds' non-attention to detail, we'll be seeing Simon Williams and Matthew Barnes, the two mates of Mike Lawrence's. On Friday we visit Sebastian Engar at his business address where we'll also see Damien Alphon.'

She was looking keen. 'How about I go and see Williams and Barnes and you see Engar and Alphon on Friday? *Or* the other way around. Whatever you want . . . OK, I'll be here at eight.'

Within twenty minutes of Judd leaving, Watts had tracked down a phone number for Benedict Sill.

TWENTY-FOUR

A youngish man with a wispy beard opened the door in response to Watts' ring. He and Judd absorbed the baggy jeans, flip-flops and ratty-looking sweatshirt.

'Mr Williams? Detective Inspector Watts and Police Constable Judd. I phoned you.'

Williams stepped back. They walked inside. The place was a muddle, but warm and clean-looking. Williams went ahead of them, moving what looked to be laundry in need of an iron from a couple of chairs. 'Sorry for the mess, but I'm working to a deadline. Sit down.'

Judd took out her notebook. Watts evaluated Williams. On first examination he looked to be a gangling youth, although he had to be in his early thirties if he was a contemporary of Mike Lawrence. 'You've already had a visit so you know why we're here, Mr Williams. To talk about Michael and Molly Lawrence.'

'Yes. Sorry, hang on.'

He disappeared through a door. They waited, picking up a smell of burning, heard a muttered expletive and the sound of a toaster ejecting something. Judd jabbed her pen at a nearby worktable. Watts eyed the large-screen computer, surrounded by what looked to be bits of plastic of various shapes and colours.

Williams was back, grinning. 'Breakfast beyond saving. It can wait.' He dropped on to a nearby chair, his face serious. 'I just can't get my head around what's happened to Mike and his wife.' He shook his head. 'What a tragedy.'

'Tell us all you know about them, Mr Williams.'

'Mike has been on my mind since I first read about it. He was a mild, cool kind of guy, you know? We were students at the same college but following different courses. Mike was into art and design. I was on the digital arts course but we hung around together when we weren't in lectures.' He nodded to the table. 'I design activities.'

Watts glanced at it. 'You mean for kids?'

'They're not toys. They're constructional. The people who buy my stuff are all ages, from eight to eighty.'

'I've seen them in shops,' said Judd. 'Somebody I know who's into that kind of construction says they're great.'

Watts asked, 'You knew Mike Lawrence for quite a while?'

'It was an on-off friendship, but yes.'

'Start by telling us about the off part of it.'

Williams looked nonplussed. 'No, no. I didn't mean that the way it might have come across. We got on well as students.' He grinned. 'Both interested in the pub, women, you know.' Seeing Watts waiting, he carried on. 'As I said, we just hung around together. After we finished our degrees, our paths diverged.' He shrugged. 'It happens. We still met up occasionally. When Mike got married, that got less, of course, but when we did see each other, it was always a good catch-up.'

'What about Mrs Lawrence?'

'What about her?'

'How much contact did you have with her, Mr Williams?'

He frowned. 'What do you mean, "contact"?'

Watts sent him a direct look. 'How often did you see her, where did you see her, who was there, who's idea was it—'

'I get it. There's not much to tell. I met her two or three times, always with Mike, so I didn't know her that well. Actually, she wasn't at all what I expected.'

'Say again?'

'I knew some of the women Mike had dated. They were' – he shrugged – 'straightforward, I suppose. Molly struck me as very serious. Not somebody given to small talk.'

'And you didn't see much of her.'

'I didn't see that much of either of them once they were married. Mike phoned me a few weeks back to say that Molly was pregnant. He sounded really chuffed. I decided to cool it a bit. They had enough to do and think about.'

'When was the last time you had direct contact with either of them?'

They waited as Williams appeared to think about it.

'It had to be shortly after he phoned me. I dropped in at their place one day when I was passing and saw Mike's car outside. It was the first time I'd been there. It was really nice. All the expensive mod cons.' He grinned, looked around. 'No living like a student any more for Mike. Molly was at work. Mike showed me the room they were going to make into the nursery. He had colour charts and stuff . . .' Williams looked at the floor. 'When I heard what happened to them, like I said, I couldn't believe it. It sounds like they were in the wrong place at the wrong time.'

'What makes you say that?'

'Because of what it said on the news. About the area.'

'Know it, do you?'

'What? No. I hardly ever go into the city.' He indicated the room. 'This is where I spend most of my work time.'

'What about when you're not working?'

'I tend to stay local. See a few mates.'

'Are you married, Mr Williams?'

He frowned. 'No. Not that that's relev—'

'Did you and Mike Lawrence have friends in common?'

'A couple, yes. Matthew Barnes. Benedict Sill.'

Watts' eyes fastened on Williams. 'Has there been any contact between you and either of those two individuals recently?'

Williams' eyes went from him to Judd and back. 'No, none.'

Watts slow-nodded. 'Work gets in the way of life, right?'

Williams didn't reply. His legs jiggled.

'This Benedict Sill. Where's he?'

'I've no idea. I can't provide any details for Matt either. In the past, when I met up with them it would be Mike who arranged it.'

'Is there anybody else you know who was a friend of Mike Lawrence?' He watched Williams choose his words.

'Not a friend, exactly. Sebastian Engar was Mike's employer. Seb has to be in his fifties but from what Mike told me I got the impression that Seb thought highly of him. So highly, according to Mike, he was planning to hand over the daily running of the company to him when he retired.'

Watts gazed at him. 'Was he, now? Very generous.'

Williams shrugged. 'I'm not so sure about that. Mike would have had all the work and you can bet that Seb would have kept his eyes on everything he did. The way I see it, you can't beat being your own boss.'

'Mike wasn't that keen on what his boss was proposing?'

'I can't really say, although I told him what I thought about it. Molly was probably keen, but I don't know that for sure.'

'Why would Mrs Lawrence have been keen?'

'Mike told me she wanted him to strike out on his own.' He shrugged again. 'Mike was much too cautious for that. It sounded to me like taking over the running of the company from Seb might have appealed to both of them as an ideal compromise, but like I said, I can't be sure of that.'

'You know this Mr Engar?'

'Only from what Mike said. He showed me a couple of photos of the people he worked with and Seb was in one of them.'

'Anybody else you want to tell us about?' Watts waited. 'You're looking uneasy, Mr Williams.'

'Of course I am. You're the police and it feels odd to give people's names to you, even if they're people I barely know.' He looked up to find Watts waiting, his eyes fixed on him. 'There is somebody else. My impression was that Mike was dubious about him, but I never actually met him. One of Mike's colleagues. All I know is that Mike didn't like him. There was some sort of issue between them. From the little Mike said, it could have been jealousy because Seb favoured Mike.'

'Got a name?'

'Damien Alphon.'

During a brief face-to-face conversation with Matthew Barnes at the clothes shop he owned, Barnes had supplied Watts with information about Mike Lawrence in terms similar to those provided by Williams. He confirmed some indirect awareness of Mike's work colleagues, specifically that there was friction between Mike and a co-worker named Damien Alphon. Questions asked about Molly Lawrence hadn't produced anything informative beyond Barnes' confirmation that yes, he had very briefly dated Molly Lawrence some twelve months prior to her marrying Mike, and that neither of them had regarded the brief courtship as important.

'A couple of dates for drinks, another for a meal and that was it. She was really good looking, you know, but not my type.' Asked by Watts what his 'type' was, Barnes had grinned, eyeing Judd.

'Oh, you know, somebody who's up for some fun, who likes a good time. Molly struck me as way too serious.' He grinned. 'The old "ball-and-chain" type, but Mike seemed happy enough with it.'

By the time they left the shop, Watts' head was pulsing from what passed for music playing non-stop inside it.

They were now in a coffee shop, Watts bringing drinks to the table. He sat heavily. 'We're risking pneumonia in this bloody weather. One caramel latte with marshmallows.'

He passed it to Judd, sat, took a quick gulp of his black Americano and glanced at the steamed-up windows, thinking that England was a great place between July and September. He looked back to Judd who was attacking the marshmallows and whipped cream.

'Remind me what we've got.'

'Hang on . . .' Licking her spoon, she tracked her notes. 'Simon Williams knew Mike Lawrence for several years, got on fine with him. Hardly knows Molly Lawrence. Doesn't know current whereabouts of Benedict Sill. Mike was a valued employee of his boss, this Engar bloke. Bit of a "blue-eyes" by the sound of it, Sarge.' She turned a page. 'Matthew Barnes confirmed he dated Molly Lawrence before she married Mike. No surprise he didn't get far with her, on account of his being a tosser.'

'Judd—'

'Trust me. According to Barnes, Sill is backpacking in Thailand.' She let the pages fall back. 'Both Williams and Barnes mentioned Damien Alphon, this work colleague of Lawrence's. According to Barnes, there was friction between Lawrence and Alphon but he wasn't specific.'

They sat in silence. Watts glanced at windows running with condensation as Judd finished the last of her drink.

'Mmmm . . .' She licked her lips. 'What's up, Sarge?'

'Nothing.'

'You've been a bit narky since yesterday. If it's Reynolds that's still annoying you—'

'Forget Reynolds.' He sipped his coffee, gazed out of the window. 'I hate winter.'

'Right. You're not that keen on summer, either, nor spr—'

'Ever heard of SAD, Judd?'

'No. What is it? A club for miserable gits?'

He got to his feet. 'Let's go.'

'Where?'

'To Mike Lawrence's design company to see his boss, Sebastian Engar.'

'I thought that was tomorrow?'

'We're going there now. I'm not warming to Engar and his

"providing the police with all relevant information in due course", or whatever he said.'

Watts brought the BMW to a halt. They looked across at the large, turn-of-the-century house now converted into business premises. They got out into icy bluster and headed across the parking area to the building. Watts spoke into the grille next to the front door and they were buzzed inside. He held up identification to the woman who approached them. 'Detective Inspector Watts, PC Judd, police headquarters. We're here to see Sebastian Engar.'

The woman gave him an all-business smile. 'About?'

'Tell Mr Engar we're here, please.'

The woman's face changed. 'Mr Engar is just back from leave. He isn't officially here—'

'But we are. Tell Mr Engar we'd like a chat with him.' They watched her hesitate, walk away. After several seconds, she reappeared, hand raised.

'This way, please.'

She showed them into an ultra-modern office. A man who looked to be in his mid-fifties, silver-haired, with a neat grey beard was standing behind the glass and metal desk. He came to Watts, hand extended. Watts noted the subtle tan.

'Detective Inspector.' He did the same to Judd, his blue eyes crinkling. 'What a charming hairstyle. Please, have seats.'

Watts gave him another once-over. No glasses. Contacts, probably. 'Mr Engar, we appreciate your time. Tell us all you know about Michael Lawrence.'

Engar's face became suitably downbeat. 'I understand why you're here. This whole company is bereft at what has happened. Michael was a very highly valued member of our staff.'

'So highly valued that you were considering handing over your company to him?'

If Engar was surprised, he wasn't showing it. 'Not *quite* accurate, Detective Inspector.' He glanced down at his hands. Watts eyed them, seeing glossy, manicured nails. 'Michael was excellent at his job. Extremely talented. He also had an easy manner with clients. He listened to their needs. Gave them what they wanted' – he looked up, smiled – 'or subtly persuaded them to accept what he judged to be a more suitable alternative. So subtle that they hardly noticed. That's a great skill, you know.' He gave Watts a direct look.

'I was not handing over this company to Michael on my retirement, just the day-to-day running of it. I would, of course, have retained control.'

Watts nodded, thinking that whatever else Engar was, he was no pushover.

'Mr Lawrence was pleased about your plan?'

'He was giving it consideration.'

Aware of Judd's interest spiking along with his own, Watts said, 'That doesn't sound like the keenness I was anticipating.'

Engar gazed out of the window at greyness. 'Michael loved his work. The design aspect. He knew that if he accepted my offer, he would be much more involved with the daily aspects of the business, although he would continue to do some design.'

'And that wasn't to his liking?'

Engar looked back at him. 'Michael wasn't a particularly ambitious person. As I said, he loved the work he did and he was finding it difficult to contemplate the change involved in what I was suggesting.'

'Given what you've said about Mr Lawrence's strengths, I'm struggling to see why you'd want him to change to what sounds like a management role.'

'One offers one's employees opportunities for personal growth, Detective Inspector.'

'Did Mrs Lawrence have a view on it?' asked Judd.

'That, I don't know.'

'Do you know her well?'

'I wouldn't say well, but on the odd occasions when we met, I found her to be very pleasant.'

'We'd like to talk to your staff about Mike Lawrence, Mr Engar,' said Watts. 'They may have information about him which could help our inquiries.'

'Of course. We're a relatively small set up. Five design staff. Four admin workers.'

'Was Mike Lawrence particularly friendly with any of them?'

'I don't believe so, although Michael was a very sociable kind of person. He got on well with all of his colleagues, but his focus was the work.' He reached for the phone. 'I'll inform my PA that you need to see each of them.'

'Before you do, is Damien Alphon available?'

'He's not here right now, but he will be this afternoon.'

'What can you tell us about Mr Lawrence and Mr Alphon as colleagues?'

Engar studied him. 'You've made some inquiries already, Detective Inspector.'

'It tends to save time.'

'When Michael joined the company, Damien was already here. He's good at his job but he doesn't have the flair that Michael had. Fortunately for the firm, they were able to put their differences to one side and work cooperatively.'

'What differences?'

Engar gave a cool smile. 'I'm assuming all police officers have a *forensic* style of conversation. Is it innate, or the result of training?'

Watts waited.

'The differences to which I referred were around one issue to which I've already alluded. Damien had anticipated that when I retired, he would take over the running of the company. He was disappointed at my plan to ask Michael.' He stood. 'I'll show you to my PA's office. She can introduce you to the staff you wish to speak to.'

An hour later they were alone inside a formal meeting room dominated by a large table. 'Want a rundown of what we got, Sarge?'

'Is it worth it?'

She shrugged. 'Probably not. James Tanner, accountant, said he liked Mike Lawrence but they didn't socialize outside of work. Described him as always prompt with his expenses, very organized. The other three admin staff have worked here for less than two years and, according to each of them, they didn't know Lawrence that well but found him likeable and helpful. The gist of what we got from the other designers, Dominic Ames, Charlotte Benner and Ross Davies was that they didn't socialize with Mike Lawrence either but regarded him as excellent at his job and a good colleague. Hard working but good for a laugh.' Watts looked up at her. 'I'm paraphrasing, using my own words, Sarge.'

'Don't.'

The door swung open. Engar's PA came into the room carrying a large tray. Watts stood.

'Sit down, Detective Inspector. Mr Engar thought you might like some lunch. We're expecting Mr Alphon in about forty-five minutes.'

She put down the tray and left the room, quietly closing the door.

Their eyes moved over the sandwiches, crusty bread, olives and the cups of coffee she had delivered.

'Look at this!' said Judd. 'I wish this happened every day, *and* I've still got my lunch back at headquarters.' She reached for a hefty slice of bread, a sandwich, some olives.

Watts selected a sandwich, opened it, peered inside. 'Knowing you, you'll eat it when we get back.'

'I might leave it in the fridge for tomorrow.'

One of the things he knew about Judd was that she watched her finances like a hawk with a rabbit. Small wonder she was upset when her car disappeared. Chong was right. He wouldn't get on to her about what had happened, nor push her to officially report the thefts, although it went right against all he stood for. Nor would he get on Julian's case for not keeping an eye on Judd. She wasn't his responsibility. What he'd learned in the last few days was that she was resilient. She had to make her own decisions. Hopefully, learn from them. He looked up to find her studying him.

'What's up?'

'None of my business, Sarge, but if I were you, I'd give up on that SAD group you were on about earlier.'

'When *I* was twenty, Judd, everything looked simple—'

'I'm twenty-one.'

He looked at her. 'You never said.'

'Like, I'd come into headquarters, going, "Hi, guys, it's my birthday!" You're unreal sometimes, Sarge.'

'When was it?'

She shrugged. 'Last week some time.' They ate in silence for several minutes. 'Got any more ideas on the Lawrence case?'

Watts swallowed, took a gulp of coffee, shook his head. 'Nothing that explains how he came to be gunned down and his pregnant wife half-killed, but I'm definitely considering moving the focus of the investigation from stranger-attack to it being the work of somebody who knew one or other of the Lawrences.' He glanced at Judd. 'And, no, I don't have an idea who that might be.'

'But, like me, you're interested in this Alphon—?'

The door swung open. It was Engar's PA again. 'More coffee?'

'We're fine, thanks.'

'In that case, Mr Alphon has arrived and he'll see you now.'

*   *   *

Watts gave Alphon an evaluative look as they were shown inside the office, picking up on the confidence, the smile, plus something else: an air of entitlement. Alphon extended his hand and waved them to chairs. 'Apologies for the wait. You want to talk to me about Mike Lawrence.'

'Yes, Mr Alphon.'

'All I can say is that it's tragic. If it hasn't already prompted West Midlands police to commit more officers to the inner city as a matter of routine, it needs to give the idea some serious consideration.'

'Know it well, do you, Mr Alphon?'

Alphon gave him a small smile. '*Hardly.*'

'We're following up all possible leads and your name has come up.'

'Oh?' He looked from Watts to Judd. 'In what context, exactly?'

'In the context of there being some sort of friction between you and Mike Lawrence.'

Alphon stared at him. His head fell back and he laughed. Watts and Judd glanced at each other.

'You think what I just said is amusing, Mr Alphon?'

'Yes. It is. Who's been talking to you?'

'That's irrelevant. The point is your boss here was planning to let this company pass into Mike Lawrence's hands after his retirement, but Lawrence was murdered before it could happen. Got any observations on that, Mr Alphon?'

Alphon sighed, then smoothed back his hair. 'What Seb has told you isn't entirely accurate. Yes, he had been considering Mike running the practice but he changed his mind some weeks ago. Mike was good at the design work, but from a business point of view he was a plodder and Seb knew it. Under Mike's management, this company would have ground to a halt. To run a company such as this requires other skills which Mike sorely lacked. I'm referring to the nurturing of existing clients, finding new ones, *active* promotion.' He fixed his eyes on Watts. 'Here's an example of Mike's commitment to promoting this business. Last year, Seb wanted him to go to a business fair in London. Mike's response? He refused, saying his wife needed him at home, that they were working on their house.'

'Which tells you what?'

Alphon adopted a patient air. 'Detective Inspector, as a public servant, you're probably unaware of it, but if you run a business, personal issues come second.'

Watts gazed at him, Judd's word 'tosser' coming into his head. 'When, exactly, did Mr Engar have this change of mind about Mike Lawrence?'

'I don't exactly recall.'

'Try this: when did you know that Mr Engar would pass the running of this company to you?'

Alphon grinned. 'Oh, I'd say around twenty or so years ago.'

'How's that?'

'Seb is my godfather.'

Leaving the building in heavy rain, they got into the BMW. Watts was seething. Any time you thought things were different, that times had changed, you got a smack around the face with the ripe kipper of class. *Privilege*. What they'd learned was a clear indication of Engar's manipulation of his employees, although where that took this investigation, he wasn't sure.

'That Alphon's a real piece of work, Sarge. Smooth as sno—'

'So is Engar. He uses employees, sets them in competition with each other as it suits him.'

Judd yanked at her seatbelt. 'I wouldn't trust him if he told me it was raining, unless I was outside.'

'That was a reality check. The old "who-you-know" ways are still alive and well. I'll ring Engar to check what Alphon just told us.'

4.15 p.m.

Traynor was in Watts' office when they returned. Watts went to the phone, his face set. Traynor raised his eyebrows at Judd.

She kept her voice low. 'We've been to the company Mike Lawrence worked for. His boss is a right git. He'd got Lawrence and another employee named Damien Alphon who, by the way, is his godson and also a git, each expecting to take over the running of the company when he retired. That's why Sarge is on the phone. He's checking it out.'

'Mike Lawrence's boss sounds like a cynic with control issues.'

'Bang on. People have probably resorted to violence on finding out they were being used like that.' She started as phone met table.

'Afternoon, Traynor,' said Watts. He looked across to Judd. 'He's confirmed what Alphon told us. Alphon is taking over the running of the company on Engar's retirement, whenever that is. According to Engar, Mike Lawrence was aware of it and wasn't upset about it. My opinion? Engar and Alphon deserve each other.'

Judd was on her way to the door. 'That Alphon needs checking out—'

'Throttle it back while I tell you and Traynor the rest. It wasn't Alphon who was making that company toxic.'

'Engar?' said Judd.

'Exactly. He's your Machiavellian type. He as good as admitted it just now. He knew he had a couple of talents in the shape of Lawrence and Alphon. One creative, the other a main chancer *and* related. What better way from his point of view to keep both keen and productive than to create a bit of a competitive spirit between them, pit one against the other, keep both as keen as mustard.'

'The b—'

'As you almost said, Judd. I'll request checks on both but I can't see either of them shooting Mike and Molly Lawrence.'

'How about one of them paid somebody to do it?' asked Judd.

'Why? It was already resolved way before the Lawrences were shot. Mike Lawrence would stick to what he did best; in time Alphon would take over the daily running of the company and Engar the manipulator would have things exactly how he wanted them.' He looked at Traynor. 'When you talked to Molly, did either of their names come up?'

'Never.'

Watts shook his head. 'You don't shoot two people so you can run a design company. Engar wasn't offering either of them anything that was worth that.'

The room darkened on a distant rumble of thunder as Judd left the room. They sat in silence, Traynor looking lost in thought, Watts staring ahead at nothing. Judd was back.

'Nothing on Engar or Alphon. This investigation is well and truly stuffed, if you want my opinion—'

'I don't,' said Watts. 'Let me have a copy of that list of Molly Lawrence's friends and co-workers. We'll start seeing them tomorrow—'

'I have a way to move this investigation forward,' said Traynor.

TWENTY-FIVE

Thursday 20 December. 5.30 p.m.

Traynor was laying out his idea. 'We've got a lot of information already but it's not getting us anywhere. We need what only Molly Lawrence knows but it's not going to happen in the way we hoped.'

Judd looked at Watts, then back to Traynor. 'If we're talking *reconstruction*, that could have legs. Get it on to primetime news, say, and we'll get loads of leads.' To Watts, she added, 'Why didn't we think of that?'

'Because of the geography of Forge Street and the surrounding area. Scarcely any through-traffic, next to no footfall, so where exactly would these "loads of leads" come from? Brophy would demand justification for the cost, given this force, like most others, is close to a tipping point through cuts and more cuts. Before I even ask, I can tell you what his response would be.'

'A reconstruction is not what I'm suggesting,' said Traynor. 'What's needed is a *re-enactment*. A video-recorded account of the shootings with Molly Lawrence directing it.'

'She's having enough trouble talking one-on-one with you about what happened. What makes you think a re-enactment would be any better?'

'It requires an entirely different kind of engagement from her to what has been attempted, which so far has been Molly inside the house she shared with her husband, listening to her own voice recreate mayhem, knowing that her mother is just feet away and worried sick.'

'And you think a re-enactment might be different?'

'Yes. A change of surroundings, an opportunity for her to be in control of the situation. Plus, her focus would be on the factual aspects of what happened, which is likely to reduce her emotional engagement with the process.' He paused. 'We need to offer her a situation in which her practical brain function has free reign.'

Watts checked his watch, reached for the phone. 'How many

officers are in right now, Reynolds?' He nodded. 'Tell them to stay put. We're on our way up.' He replaced the phone. 'Most of them are here. I take it you're as confident about this re-enactment as you sound?'

'Sufficient to outline it as the way ahead.'

'In that case, they need to hear about it. I'll give Brophy a quick heads-up. He needs to know about it as well.'

Investigative officers were waiting as they walked inside the incident room. Judd headed for Julian, took the chair next to him. The door opened and Brophy appeared.

Traynor faced them, looking pensive. He had to provide an explanation which was sufficient for what he considered the only way forward, but no more.

'As a team we're aware that Molly Lawrence has provided some useful information about the attack on her and her husband. However, the trauma of that experience is blocking her efforts to tell us more.'

'Trauma, my—'

Seeing Brophy's lips thin, Watts said, 'Watch what you're saying, Judd.'

'Sarge, we're here every day, working long hours, chasing all possible leads, avoiding the press. She has to get a grip and start working with us.'

Watts pointed at her, keeping his voice low. '*You* were full of sympathy for her a day or so ago. Keep your gripes to yourself so Will can tell us how his idea can move this investigation forward.'

She flushed, ran her fingers through her hair, leaving it spikier than before. 'Sorry, Will, Sarge, but the hours we're all working with nothing coming of it, it's doing my head in.' Her words got several nods of agreement, plus an awed look from Reynolds.

'All yours, Will,' said Watts. They waited, Traynor choosing his words.

'Molly Lawrence continues to experience significant difficulty in providing details of the shootings. In her interests and those of this investigation, I'm considering a different approach which could help her verbalize the memories she does have. Re-enactment. It's our best hope.'

He tracked the various officers' responses, ranging from uncertainty to scepticism. 'I want to encourage her engagement with events of that night while reducing her emotional responses to them. I believe that inviting her to *show* us what occurred could give her a sense of control so that she is able to release the detail she has. She has managed to provide some of that detail during my three visits to her but not at the pace or to the degree needed by this investigation. She is frustrated by her own difficulty in giving more. I believe this behavioural approach is in her and our best interests.'

He looked around the room, still seeing uncertainty on some faces. 'When we put this into practice Molly needs to feel comfortable so I'm going to ask a small number of you to be directly involved. If what I'm suggesting sounds strange, once we start the planning process, I believe you'll appreciate what I've suggested. I want the following officers directly involved in the re-enactment: Jones and Kumar, Chloe Judd, DI Watts as SIO, Adam as head of forensics, plus two of his officers, and Dr Chong. There will be a meeting at six forty-five this evening for those named.'

He glanced around the room. 'I'm asking all of you to trust what I'm saying about this as the way forward.'

He stepped away. Watts stood. 'That meeting will be in my office.'

He and Traynor followed Brophy's stiff-backed figure from the incident room.

'I'd say four out of ten for enthusiasm,' observed Traynor quietly.

'They need some thinking time to get their heads around it,' said Watts. 'What matters is that you're fully committed to it as the only way Molly Lawrence is going to give us more information.'

'That's exactly what it is.'

They came into the office, Watts' eyes fixed on him. 'What would you say, Traynor, if I said that I've got a feeling that you're on to something in this case?'

'I'd say that all I have is a theory, and that theories have no value unless tested.'

'Come on, Will.' He watched Traynor shake his head and walk to the door.

'It might give us nothing.'

As Traynor left, he reached for the phone. Barely a minute later, Reynolds appeared, looking apprehensive. 'You want to see me, Sarge?'

'Yes. I've got a job for you.' He outlined what he wanted. 'When you've done what I've asked, I want a detailed account which shows me that what I said to you the other day about authority struck home.'

'Yes, sir!'

Scarcely a minute after Reynolds' departure, the door flew open and hit the wall. Judd came inside, dropped onto her chair, jumped up again. 'I've just been ranted at by Brophy, I've had enough. I'm going home!'

'You're still on duty and you will be for a while.'

'The way he went on at me! You should have heard it. He said—'

'That being bolshy wasn't your best bet for progressing in the force and phrases like "my arse" are inappropriate from an officer, particularly one who's female and young, such as yourself.'

She gave him a look. 'Sexism and ageism, is what *that* is!'

He had to tell her. She had to know that, whatever she'd learned from life so far, it didn't give her carte blanche to say what the hell she liked. Not in the force.

'You want to get on here?'

'You know I do. I *will*.'

He looked directly at her as the door opened and Chong came inside. 'Advice time, Judd.'

She rolled her eyes.

'Policing has moved on a lot in the last few years but you're missing a key point. It's got traditional values, conservativism with a small "c" running straight through the middle of it and it won't change, so it's you who has to.' He watched her swing her bag onto her shoulder and head for the door.

'Bloody old fashioned is what I think of it,' she snapped, walking past Chong and out.

Chong looked in the direction she'd gone, then back to Watts, brows raised. 'Anarchy in the ranks?' She came to him and put her hand on his arm. 'Hey.'

'I learned something today. She's just turned twenty-one.'

'Which seems to be adding to your mood, because?'

'I've seen too many cases involving kids growing up in situations which most people couldn't imagine and wouldn't believe. I doubt Judd ever had a birthday card or anything else to mark the day. I've checked. I suspect the date she uses for official forms is one her parents thought would do and stuck on her birth certificate when they could be bothered to get around to registering it. That's what years in this job tell me happened.'

He got to his feet. 'And now you've come to take me from this to something better?'

She put her arms around him, something she'd never done at work before. 'That's the general idea,' she whispered. 'Where do you fancy?'

'Anywhere you are, and close enough for us to be back in about an hour.'

7.15 p.m.

They were seated around the table, Traynor outlining his plan.

'The objective is to create a situation in which Molly Lawrence feels as relaxed as possible, able to tell us all she recalls of the attack on her husband and herself. As a victim-witness, she has information no one else can give us. Without that, we have nothing except the gun, a problematic fingerprint, the value of which is uncertain and circumstantial at best.'

He searched their faces. 'Witnesses to extreme violence invariably experience anxiety as a consequence. They often need considerable therapy to assist them to move beyond the experience to a point where they can talk about it. Unfortunately, we don't have that time. There's a violent individual out there who needs identifying. The re-enactment is our only chance of doing that.'

'You sound pretty sure, Will.'

'As sure as I can be, Adam. I provided Molly Lawrence with the freedom to say whatever she wished. It failed. There's too much we don't know. We need her focused on the practical side of her thinking. She's an accountant. That kind of thinking, that clarity is the norm for her.' He glanced around the table.

'I've agreed with Dr Chong and Adam that the Forensic Test Area is an ideal setting for a re-enactment. It's large, featureless, a space Molly has never seen and which has zero emotional significance for her. It is an ideal situation in which she can move around and guide us through her recall. We can't exclude emotional responses but the aim is to reduce them to a minimum as she physically guides us through the events of that night and shows us *what* happened, *where* it happened and *how*. I've used it on other cases in the past. It worked.' He paused. 'My next task is to present the plan to Molly. She may refuse. If she does, it looks increasingly likely that no one affected by those shootings will get justice. There's nothing harder to bear than that.'

Judd broke the silence. 'Forge Street, the actual scene, won't be part of this at all?'

'No. It's too emotive.' He turned to Adam. 'Can your department produce a replica of the Lawrences' Toyota?'

'You're talking life-size.'

'Yes, but featureless. A stand-in for the actual car which needs to be moved somewhere out of sight. Can you do that?'

'No problem.'

Traynor looked to Judd. 'Molly remembers you very positively from your visit to the hospital. If she agrees to this plan, you'll have a central role alongside her, prompting her with brief, non-emotive sentences such as "how did that happen?" and "what happened next?" It might sound simple but it takes a lot of concentration. I need you to tell me now if you're not comfortable with it, Chloe.'

'I'm in. I'll do it.'

'Thank you.' He turned his attention to Jones and Kumar. 'You were both at the scene as its aftermath was unfolding. I need your eyes and ears on every aspect of the re-enactment, checking and comparing all you see and hear with what you observed.'

Jones spoke for them both. 'No problem. Before we do it, we'll go through our own statements of that night.'

Traynor nodded, looked across to Watts. 'You have to be there as SIO, Bernard. If we get information which identifies this gunman, you'll have your day in court.' He looked along the table. 'Dr Chong has to be there to oversee Molly's physical and emotional responses, be ready to assist her if necessary.'

Chong nodded.

'And finally, we need two of your forensic team, Adam, each video-recording the whole process from two different vantage points. Go through your record of what you know happened that night. Molly might recall something small, incidental and easily-missed.'

'Any ideas as to what her response to your proposal might be?' Watts asked.

'None.'

Watts took out his phone. 'We need Brophy's approval.' Judd's fingers drummed the table, Traynor paced the room. Watts ended the call. 'He said yes.' They all breathed out.

Traynor lifted his phone. 'Now, I have a call to make.'

8.45 p.m.

'Hello, Molly.'

'Will?'

'I hope this call isn't too late for you?'

'No. I avoid sleep. I wake with all kinds of madness inside my head. Accidents involving aircraft, boats, people being blown up . . . I'm afraid of everything, Will. Being alone. Being with people. Going out, staying in.'

'They're all normal responses, Molly.'

'What about feeling guilty?'

'That too.'

'Why do I feel guilt, Will?'

'Because you're still here.'

'A lot of the time I feel nothing. But when I try to leave the house . . . the fear starts up and I can't do it.'

Traynor was now foreseeing a difficulty in what he was about to propose. He wanted her positive. 'It's possible to challenge those responses, Molly.'

'Is that what you did?' She waited. 'I searched your name online. Saw what happened to your family. You really do understand, Will.'

'Yes.'

'I know what you, the police need from me, but it's like there's a video running in my head and it's faulty. It keeps stopping. I don't know how to get it going again.'

What he was hearing was how most people viewed memory processes. In reality, it wasn't like that. 'Molly, I'm going to suggest a way which might encourage your recall.'

'How?'

'By giving you the chance to re-enact what happened to you and Mike but with all of the control in your hands.'

'I won't be hypnotized.'

He heard spiralling panic.

'I *can't* feel more out of control than I am already, I just can't.'

'It doesn't involve hypnosis. It's a practical way for you to revisit what happened.' He waited.

'What do you mean, "practical"?'

He briefly explained the plan to her, and where it would take place. 'Remember, you told me that you liked officer Chloe Judd? What she said about the big indoor space I've described when she first saw it was that it "looked like Lidl without any stuff".' He heard her quiet laugh and realized he had never heard it before.

'I have to think about it, Will. Can I phone you back?'

'Of course. You're entitled to refuse.' Traynor ended the call, looked at them.

'Now, we wait.'

They sat or paced, each preoccupied with what they wanted and what Molly Lawrence's response might be. Traynor's phone rang.

He reached for it and listened. 'Thank you, Molly,' and ended the call.

'She said yes.'

TWENTY-SIX

Friday 21 December. 8.30 a.m.

Constable Reynolds eyed himself in the headquarters' wash-room mirror, wishing he looked older. Wishing he had Chloe Judd's confidence. DI Watts' criticism of him for not using the authority of the job still rankled. He found Watts off-putting. Watching *The Apprentice* recently, he had realized why. It was the finger-jabbing. Plus, his height. And probably a bit more besides. And now Watts had given him an order. For the first time since joining the force via its degree apprenticeship scheme, he was wondering if he should have given his university philosophy-psychology degree course a bit longer than six months. When he told his father that he was applying to join, his mild response had been, 'Are they *very* short of officers in Birmingham?'

Reynolds smoothed down a bit of wilful hair. He was pleased to be working in the incident room, rather than on some mundane task of the kind he'd anticipated, but, surrounded by confident officers like Jones, he felt wary, out of his depth. Judd was friendly, but she could be a bit challenging when it suited her. He got out his own version of Watts' instruction and read it again: *Go to Molly Lawrence's office. Get information. Follow up other names suggested.* He folded it, slid it back inside his pocket. He had to get this right. He daren't mess up again. He thought of DI Watts' words about the authority he carried with him as a member of the force, looked directly at himself in the mirror. Confidence sliding, he checked his pockets for his ID.

Forty minutes later he was heading across thick carpeting to a glossy reception counter, a woman sitting there, her head bowed to something he couldn't see. He reached the desk. She didn't look up. He waited.

'Excuse me?'

Her head slowly rose. She made eye contact. 'Yes?'

'I'm here to see Stephen Wells.'

Her eyes drifted over him. 'And you are?'

'Reynolds.'

'First name?'

'Toby.'

'The only Reynolds on my list for today is a police officer.'

'That's me.'

She eyed him, looking unconvinced, waited with studied patience as he searched for, located and produced, his ID. She pointed to a corridor. 'Down there, second door on the right.' Reynolds headed for it, feeling her eyes skewering his back.

Reaching the door, he squared his shoulders, took a breath and pounded on it. The sound ricocheted up and down the entire corridor. Hearing a voice from inside, he went in, closed the door, walked to the fifty-ish man sitting there and thrust his ID in his eyeline. 'Police Constable Reynolds.' His words hit every hard surface in the room. Wells smiled, waved him to a chair.

'Non-uniform officer?'

'Yes, sir. I'm here to ask about an employee of yours, Molly Lawrence.'

'I assumed so. Would you like me to tell you about Molly or do you prefer to ask me questions?'

'I'd appreciate your observations. Once I have them, I'll ask any questions which I consider necessary.' Reynolds took out his notebook and waited, impressed with his own gravitas.

Wells sat back, looking troubled. 'Words are rather useless to describe how we're feeling about what's happened to Molly and her husband. A young couple with everything ahead of them.' He looked across at Reynolds. 'Molly has worked here for five years, possibly a little more. She's our financial analyst.'

Reynolds frowned in his note-taking. 'I understood she's an accountant.'

'Oh, Molly is much more than that. Insurance is a growth sector and this company is growing with it. If we become aware of a company which might fit our portfolio, Molly's job is to evaluate it. Her analytical skills and commercial acumen are second to none.'

'Right.' Reynolds' pen sped, some of the words making sense, others bypassing him. 'Are you able to say anything about her as a person?'

'Why do you ask?'

He stopped writing, his pulse-rate climbing. How to respond? That the police needed to know all that there was to know about anyone victimized by violent crime? That it was an important part of procedure to build a complete picture of all those involved, in whatever context? He looked up at Wells.

'I'd appreciate an answer to my question, sir.'

Another smile. 'Of course. Molly is honest, which hardly needs saying. She's a friendly co-worker. She works hard and she's reliable. I know that if I hand Molly a project, it will be done thoroughly and within any deadline required. You're welcome to talk to other employees whose work brings them into contact with her. It's a small circle. Molly has an assistant she works closely with and that's about it.'

'No one else?'

Wells shook his head. 'Not that I can think of. Sometimes when that assistant is ultra-busy, Molly takes any basic jobs she wants done to our general admin worker. Unfortunately, she left three months ago. We have a temporary worker who replaced her but I'm not sure how informative she might be given the relatively short time she's been here.'

Reynolds stood. 'I'll see Mrs Lawrence's assistant first and then the temp.'

Wells reached for his desk phone. 'I'll alert them. There's a vacant office next door. You're welcome to use it.'

Ten minutes later, Reynolds was sitting facing a weeping woman, trying to recall anything from his training which might move the situation on. Nothing was coming back to him.

'Mrs McBride, I'm sorry to have to ask you these questions, but we're all working very hard at headquarters to find whoever did this to Mrs Lawrence and her husband. This is the only way we have of getting information which might help us do that.' He searched for inspiration. 'How about I ask somebody to make you a drink?'

She shook her head, applied a tissue to her face. 'No, thanks. I'm sorry I'm wasting your time here.'

'No—'

'Molly wasn't only my immediate boss. She was my friend.' The tears continued.

Reynolds gave her an uncertain look. The crying was making him feel uncomfortable. Like, each time his mother watched *Sleepless in Seattle*. A life raft of words arrived in his head.

'Might it help if you talk about her as your friend?'

She sent him an unsteady smile. 'You're very kind, very astute for such a young officer.' She took a breath. 'When I say Molly is a friend, obviously I'm several years older and we don't socialize, beyond a glass of wine if it's been a particularly hard day, but I suppose I take a motherly interest in her, which she seems to like. Her job here is very demanding, you see. My job is to make her workload easier by providing whatever she needs. She doesn't have much opportunity to speak to her other colleagues but she does talk to me sometimes about herself . . . her life.'

Reynolds saw the woman's mouth tremble and silently willed her on.

'Molly and her husband were such a happy young couple. I'm not aware that they socialized much, probably because Mike, that was her husband . . . Oh, you know that, sorry. They were both so busy, with demanding careers.' She smiled. 'When I was doing up our house a couple of years back, Molly actually brought in some lovely sketches he'd done to give me ideas.' She smiled. 'Busy as he was, he'd actually done them for *me*. Wasn't that nice of him?'

Reynolds nodded, steeling himself for more emotional outpouring.

'You're aware that Mrs Lawrence was pregnant,' he said, his eyes fixed on his notes, listening to another emotional onslaught.

'Yes. She told me, of course, although she didn't say much about it. Well, you don't when you're only a few weeks along. All she did say was that they were both very pleased and, typical of Molly, she reassured me that she would be working from home as soon as she could after the baby was born . . . and be back in the office after her maternity leave.' She sighed. 'She told me about the date they had for the scan. She and Mike had agreed that they didn't want to be told the baby's sex.' She looked up at Reynolds. 'One of my hobbies is crocheting, so I made them a blue and pink baby blanket.'

'Is there anything else you'd like to say which you think might help me – the police?' McBride shook her head.

'Mr Wells mentioned a general admin worker who might help.'

'She left weeks ago.' She looked at Reynolds. 'There's a temp but I doubt you'll get anything useful from her. She's been here no time.' Seeing him waiting, she added, 'Her name is Eunice Sowden. Shall I send her to you?'

Chin propped on one hand, Reynolds was making quick notes from the stream of words coming from the woman sitting opposite him.

'And I can tell you that this isn't the friendliest of places to work. I'm not interested in office gossip, so I just get on with what they give me to do. Being a temp here, I feel like I'm invisible and—'

Reynolds looked up at the fast-moving mouth, searching for the words which would get him out of here and back to headquarters. 'Mrs Sowden—'

'*Ms.*'

'Sorry. You're saying that you're unable to say anything about Molly Lawrence and anyone else who works here—'

'Did I say that? You weren't listening.'

Reynolds frowned at her then at the words he had written.

'You just told me that this place isn't friendly, that you just do your work—'

'It sounds to me like you haven't had a lot of training.'

The words scythed through Reynolds' head. If Watts could hear this. He looked up at her, saw the contempt, suspecting that he was looking at what Judd referred to as 'bitchface'. And something else. Avidness.

'If you have information, Ms Sowden, you need to give it to me.'

Sowden leant on the desk towards him. 'The woman you're asking about, this Molly Lawrence, she's a bit of a looker, know what I mean? The clothes! I never saw anything like it. She comes in here looking like she's part of a fashion show or something, although a baby would have put a stop to—'

'You're saying that Mrs Lawrence was inappropriately dressed for work?'

'To my way of thinking. Too expensive. Me, I wear basics to come here.' Reynolds eyed the beige and black. 'If it's good enough for me, it's good enough for them, is my motto.' She pursed her lips. 'She's the sort who's all work. No time for basic pleasantries or a bit of a chat. In fact, at times I found her very off-hand.'

Recalling Watts' words, he said, 'I need you to be more specific, Ms Sowden.'

She gave him an irritable look. 'I'm telling you, she's very demanding. She wants everything the way *she* wants it, *when* she wants it. Everything has to be done just so. No doubt the others who work here will tell you how great she is. I believe in telling things like they are.'

'Isn't it a part of her job to make it clear how she wants things done and when?'

She stared at him. 'How would *you* know? I've worked for her. There's something else. You have to be careful around her. We had a big rush on a few weeks back. Roger Kemp, this other accountant, because that's what *she* is, despite the fancy title she's got, he was up to his ears in work and she did some bits and pieces for him and *then,* I overheard her telling Wells, the boss man here, that she'd done the lot!' She sat back, arms folded.

Reynolds was now avoiding looking at her. 'I'll speak to Mr Kemp.'

'You can't. He left soon after. I keep a low profile around her but once or twice when I took stuff to her office, I've heard her on the phone.'

'And?'

'She wasn't talking to her husband, if you get my drift.'

'No, I don't. What was she saying?'

She rolled her eyes. 'It wasn't *what* she was saying, it was *how.* The *tone.* The way she was whispering and smiling.'

'If you didn't hear any words, how can you be sure it wasn't her husband?'

'Because nobody I know talks to a husband like that!'

He closed his notebook, wanting rid of her. 'Ms Sowden, if you have something to say about Mrs Lawrence, something which doesn't come under the category of office gossip, I want to hear it.'

*   *   *

A few minutes later, the door opened. Wells leant into the room. 'Sorry for the interruption, PC Reynolds. Eunice, I'm still waiting for that report I gave you to type.'

She stood. 'I've been tied up here, talking to *him*.'

She marched past Wells and out. Wells watched her go, turned back to Reynolds. 'My advice is to be cautious about anything Eunice told you. Women such as Molly, attractive, well-dressed, with a good job, plus a husband, Eunice views as . . . well, I don't quite know how to phrase it—'

'Personal criticism?' said Reynolds.

He gave the young officer a surprised look. 'Exactly.'

Reynolds was back at headquarters, reading what he'd got from the visit on his screen. The conclusion section was incomplete. He'd brought back two conflicting pictures of Molly Lawrence, one of them positive, the other from a dark, acid place. He re-read both, then reached into his holdall for a book which had been part of his brief engagement with his university course. Consulting the index in a couple of places he flipped pages, wondering if he should add what he was reading. Why not? It chimed with what he was thinking.

Returning to the conclusion, his fingers flew over the keys. Ending it with a question mark, he pressed send.

He was reflecting on his interviews with Molly Lawrence's colleagues when Kumar came into the incident room. 'You're looking pleased with yourself, Tobes.'

'I am . . . I think.'

4.30 p.m.

Watts looked around the packed incident room. 'Now we've got Molly Lawrence's agreement, we can crack on with Will's plan.'

Chong said, 'The Lawrences' Toyota has been moved out of the Forensic Test Area and is completely covered. There's no chance she'll see it.'

'Adam?' said Traynor. 'How's it going with the stand-in for it?'

'We're working to the same dimensions and shape as the Toyota. How does a pale grey colour sound?'

'I'd say ideal for keeping emotional responses to a minimum.'

Watts looked around at his officers. 'Will says this is our best chance. To me, it looks like our only chance. Anything you want to add, Will?'

'Only that those of us directly involved in the re-enactment need to monitor our own facial expressions and body language. I'll introduce the scene to Mrs Lawrence because she knows me. We maintain an air of calm. If, say, a video camera malfunctions, we continue with the camera that is working. No drama. No stress. No fuss. If Mrs Lawrence exhibits signs of distress, we take our lead from her. If she wants to stop, we stop. It proceeds at her pace. If she is unable to take us through the whole event, we'll have recorded whatever she is able to give us, which could still move this investigation forward.' He looked around the room. 'Any questions?'

Jones raised his hand. 'What happens if Mrs Lawrence shows even small signs of being affected? Or Chloe, for that matter.'

'Just focus on yourself, Jonesy,' she snapped.

'Leave those concerns to me. I'll be monitoring her responses throughout,' said Traynor.

At the edge of the room, Reynolds raised his hand. 'Will it ever be shown on television?'

Watts mustered patience. 'No, Reynolds. No TV.' He looked away then back at the young officer. 'Did you do what I asked you?'

'Yes.'

'Email me your information.'

'Already done, Sarge.'

'Good. I'll read it when I get a chance.' Watts looked at each of them. 'Does everybody directly involved in this plan feel up to this, know what's expected? Good. Back here at seven a.m.'

TWENTY-SEVEN

Saturday 22 December. 8 a.m.

The huge Forensic Test Area was a scene of quiet, understated activity. Watts and Judd watched Traynor and Julian in deep discussion, one or other of them raising an arm, pointing, nodding. The Lawrences' Toyota had been replaced by a pale grey, to-scale, two-dimensional, featureless outline which Julian was manoeuvring into position. Checking it, he stood back, held up his hand, palm to Traynor. After a brief pause Traynor's palm made contact. He moved to the middle of the huge space.

'Officers Kumar and Miller are due to arrive with Mrs Lawrence in the next few minutes. She'll be otherwise unaccompanied.' They watched him scrutinize the space, raise his hand to Julian who moved the facsimile of the car forward a little and nodded. 'We'll begin with an initial walk-through by PC Judd with Mrs Lawrence. Once Molly is familiar with the set-up she will take control of the re-enactment, guiding us through what only she knows happened. If it becomes apparent that she's at a loss, PC Judd will prompt her, using agreed wording.' Judd gave a quick nod. 'If Mrs Lawrence does become distressed or appears unable to continue for any reason, we bring the re-enactment to an end without any physical or verbal indications of disappointment. Everyone clear?' Traynor's phone pinged. He looked at it.

'She's arrived.'

The door of the test area swung slowly open. Miller and Kumar appeared, followed by Molly Lawrence. Subtle glances showed how pale she was. Feeling guilty about her recent outburst of criticism against this woman, Judd watched her, now seeing what she hadn't fully realized at the hospital: Molly Lawrence was a beautiful woman. As Traynor went to her, Judd's eyes skimmed her dark navy coat with its narrow waist and full skirt, the dark tights, low-heeled suede shoes, and felt a quick rush of envy, followed by an even quicker surge of guilt. She listened to Traynor's words to Molly, saw him raise his arm and point.

'Those two officers over there have video cameras to record the action as you direct them.' She nodded. He indicated the grey outline of the car standing nearby. 'This is for you to refer to as you relate whatever you recall. Your sole task here is to show us what took place.'

The team watched her walk slowly forward, Judd thinking it was very possible that they could all be out of here within five minutes. Molly looked at the facsimile for a few seconds, turned to Traynor.

'Where's our car? I expected it to be here.'

'We thought a representation would be less distracting.'

'Yes. Of course.'

Judd headed slowly and quietly towards them, hearing him say,

'You can start your recall at any point which suits you, Molly. If you need to stop, that's fine.'

Seeing Judd approach, she smiled at her. With a nod to the grey outline, she asked Traynor, 'Could I just walk around it? Get used to it not being real?'

'Do whatever feels right for you, Molly.' The SOCOs' cameras were now running. 'Take a walk around the whole space, if you wish. As soon as you feel comfortable, tell me and I'll go—'

'You're not *leaving*?' She stared up at Traynor, her eyes huge.

'No. Nobody's leaving. PC Judd will be with you the whole time and I'll be over there with Detective Inspector Watts.'

She looked at Judd, at the 'car' outline, then up at Traynor. 'I'm fine. I can do it. I'm ready.' He moved away. Judd arrived at her side. Looking directly into one of the cameras, Molly took a deep breath. 'OK, this is just a model, but I'll use it to show you what happened.' She beckoned to the videoing officers to follow her.

'I'll start with the inside.' She went closer to the grey shape, pointed. 'Here is where the passenger seat was. Mike was in the driver's seat . . . and . . . there were movements around here.' She pointed to the area in which she was standing next to the driver's door 'And, a man, *the* man, shouted at the window, right here, but before anything else happened' – she pointed – 'he moved around to the other side. He moved really quickly.'

Peripheral gazes were on this small woman describing the catastrophic event which had left her bleeding and her husband dying. Traynor watched, his face devoid of expression.

'That's when the rear door of the car opened. He got inside and . . . a voice shouted for Mike to do something and . . . Mike turned to look at him . . . he had a gun.' She was silent for several seconds, her eyes fixed on the grey cut-out. 'There was a scream. Mike swore. He reached forward, turned the key in the ignition . . . he wasn't thinking straight. The man yelled at him to stop the engine.' She moved, raising her hand. 'He waved the gun.' She turned to the nearest video camera and gave a faint smile.

'Come closer.' She gestured to one of the officers with a camera. 'He's now sitting in the middle of the rear seat. Right about here' – she spoke over her shoulder, eyes fixed on the facsimile – 'and something was said. He said to be quiet. He demanded valuables; said he wanted my handbag by my feet on the floor of the car.'

Traynor was now listening intently.

'The valuables went inside it.' She looked straight to camera.

'All except my watch and phone. He took the bag and . . . then he . . . did something . . . to me and Mike got angry . . . and . . . that's when he shot Mike . . . He shot him again. The man leaned forward . . .' She lowered her head, lifted it again. 'There was a flash, a sudden, sharp impact, a burning sensation and . . . heat flowing down.'

Watts took a quick look around. The officers' faces were expressionless, most not looking directly at her.

'It gets hazy here . . . He had Mike's phone in his hand.' She shook her head. 'I don't know what happened next . . . but after a while . . . I managed to call to emergency services.' She stopped, looked to Traynor.

Judd asked, 'Is there anything else?'

She shook her head. 'He was there and then, gone. He ran. Very fast. Away from the car.' She frowned, her eyes fixed straight ahead.

'*Wait.*' She took a couple of steps forward, her eyes wide. Everyone was now looking at her. 'He was running . . .' She whispered, the video cameras quietly whirring. 'He ran . . . I don't know how far . . . and suddenly, from nowhere, there were some people there. Two, three of them. Younger than him. Much younger. He high-fived one. I watched, heard whoops and' – she shook her head, her voice barely a whisper – 'laughs. They were *laughing* as . . . my husband was . . . quietly drifting away from me . . .'

Traynor came to her, his voice soft. 'Molly?'

She looked up at him, dazed. 'I just remembered. I just remembered how they were. He had just shot both of us . . . and they were' – she shook her head – '*celebrating*. How could anybody do that?'

Judd reached out to her, held her arm. 'You did really well, Molly.'

Getting a nod from Traynor, Watts raised his hand to Miller.

Molly Lawrence looked up at him. 'I'd like to see the video sometime.' She turned and walked away with Miller.

They came into the office, each of them looking worn. 'It wasn't one person,' said Judd. 'Not a lone gunman. It was one man and probably some inner-city kids.'

Watts sat by Traynor. 'Before the records are searched and I send out all the officers I've got, can we trust her memory?'

Traynor was looking preoccupied. 'I need to view the video. I'm waiting for a phone call from forensics.'

'What's Molly like as a person, Will?' asked Julian. 'How certain do you think she is about what she's told us?'

'I've only seen her under extreme duress. I don't know.'

'When you worked with her, she wasn't confident like she mostly was just now?'

'No.'

The phone rang. Traynor took the call, ended it. 'We can look at the videos.'

On the forensic floor they watched in silence as first one then the other video, differing only in angle, played out on the huge, high definition screen, Molly Lawrence looking calm, her voice firm in the main, a little hesitant at times. The second video ran its course, Molly smiling and beckoning to its operator. The big screen darkened.

'She's given key information we didn't have,' said Watts.

Traynor gave an absent nod.

'What she's said changes everything,' said Judd. 'We need to move on it.' She stared at Watts. 'Sarge, we need every available officer in that area, shaking things up—'

'Let it rest for a bit.'

Frustrated, she leant on her forearms. 'I just noticed the way she talked about what happened. It sounded weird at times, like she was describing something that had happened to somebody else.'

'That's not unusual,' said Traynor. 'It probably helped her to stay distanced.'

Watts' eyes were still on the blank screen. He had to make a decision on when to flood the inner city with as many officers as he could spare to find the kids Molly Lawrence had described. He agreed with Judd that Molly Lawrence had sounded odd. He had a pretty good idea why.

'I've been involved in and seen a lot of reconstructions which I know are different to what we've done, but my point is I've watched witnesses do and say stuff you wouldn't believe. Some completely change the accounts they gave, others cry, crack jokes, laugh in odd places, even throw up in one or two cases.' Judd's nose wrinkled. 'You can never anticipate how a person might react, what they might say in that kind of situation, especially if they were both victim *and* witness. Whatever happened, whatever they saw, they're convinced that they stared death in the face. Molly Lawrence is your prime example. What do you say, Traynor?' They waited. 'Traynor?'

Julian stepped in. 'My reading of what we've just seen is that Molly Lawrence appears to be dissociating from the experience, right Will?'

Traynor nodded. 'When I saw her previously, she was blocking her recall as a means of self-preservation. Today, dissociation seems to have helped her get through the process by keeping her emotionally distanced from what she was recalling.'

'Like, she wasn't there. Wasn't part of it,' said Judd.

Watts stood. 'I have to decide what I do about these young types she described.'

The door opened. An officer came inside. 'Sarge? Manchester is on the line for Julian.' He turned to him. 'You've been recalled, Jules.'

Judd absorbed the four words, watched Julian head for the door.

At home, Traynor raised the remote a third time, skipped through Molly Lawrence's arrival, let it run on, watched her directing the officer with the video camera, holding herself together. What they had was brief but better than he had hoped for. The re-enactment had provided what he wanted. Back to the beginning again, he ran the video a fourth time and listened. '*I expected it to be here.*'

His computer bleeped. He looked at an email response to one he had sent earlier that day, a reply he hadn't anticipated this close to the holiday period. It was a coroner's report. He read it twice and activated the video again. Each time the same four words grabbed at him. *Handbag . . . on the floor.*

3.45 p.m.

Watts went down to reception, immediately seeing the person he was looking for. As always, he was hard to miss.

'Thanks for coming in on a Saturday.'

'No problem.'

Watts led him into the informal interview room. 'Have a seat.'

Watts sat opposite him. 'OK, Nigel. Let's talk some more about the shooting at Forge Street.'

Nigel shook his large head. 'Sorry, I did what you said, left it alone, but nothing's come back to me.'

Watts studied him. 'You walk that dog of yours regularly.'

'Three times a day.'

'What time's the last walk?'

Nigel shrugged. 'Ten thirty, give or take half an hour. All depends on Abdul and customer flow.'

'You were around Forge Street that night.'

'You know I was.'

Watts looked him in the eye. 'You told me you didn't recall seeing anything except a car with all its doors closed.'

'That's right.'

'How about another night since then? There hasn't been that many. Think about it,' he invited.

Elbows on the table, Nigel rubbed the stubble on his lower face. Watts saw something happening, deep in his eyes. 'Come on, Nige.'

'That place is always deserted, and for good reason. Anybody who goes down there's got a death wish – apologies to the woman whose husband got done there but that's a fact, Mr Watts.'

Watts lowered his voice. 'That's exactly what I think. I also think that the place is no problem for a big lad like you, *plus* dog.'

'Ha! It's a bloody shi'itzu!'

'You're getting my drift, Nige. Much as you don't like the place, it doesn't hold any fear for a big lad like you, who's light on his feet.'

Nigel nodded. 'You got that right.'

'I'll ask you again. What about the few nights since the shootings? You'll have been out in the area, following your usual routine, you and the dog, walking that street, looking, listening.' He waited. 'Come on! I'm turning myself inside out here building the picture, laying it out . . .'

'There was one time I did see somebody. Two people. But that was a couple of nights before the shootings.'

Watts stared at him, swallowing hard. 'Why didn't you bloody *tell* us? Tell me everything you remember, and I mean *everything*.'

Nigel shrugged. 'That's it. I couldn't see them that well because it was dark and with the street lights being out, it's black as the ace—'

'What time was this?'

Nigel puffed out his cheeks. 'Around nine-thirty-ish, near as I can recall. The shop was quiet. The dog spotted it first. Movement. Around that abandoned garage. It's a yappy little sod so I picked it up to quieten it. That's when I heard low voices. It sounded like a bloke and somebody younger-sounding, a kid, although they were too far away for me to hear what was said.'

Watts waited, gave him a direct look. 'What were they doing?'

'Nothing. Just walking slow-like, looking around.'

'Did you get a proper look at either of them?' Watts sat forward. 'Come on. I need your head on this, Nige. Start with the bloke. What did he look like?'

'Just a bloke. On the big-ish side, dark hair but that's just an impression. I wasn't taking much—'

'Did he look like anybody you'd seen before?' He waited. 'Did he move in a way that reminded you of somebody local?' He watched Nigel's forehead crease in concentration as he stared down at the table, giving it some thought. Finally, he looked up at Watts, who leant forward.

'No.'

Exasperated, Watts changed tack. 'OK, this kid, you mentioned. Did *he* look at all familiar to you? Was there anything about him that struck a chord?'

Nigel considered it. 'Like I said, they were a way off from me.' His face cleared. 'I've just remembered. He was wearing a baseball cap.'

Watts was thinking that as an identifier a baseball cap had serious limitations. But Molly Lawrence had described youngsters at the scene and Watts now had a particular individual in mind.

'You know a young kid from your area called Presley—?'

'It wasn't Presley.'

Watts stared at him. 'Hang *on*. How can you be so sure?'

'Huey brings him into Abdul's shop occasionally. It wasn't Presley. He's too tall. Too thin.'

Watts sighed. 'Carry on. Tell me what this pair were up to.'

'I've told you. We watched 'em, me and the dog. They were just wandering around, talking and *then*'– Watts sat forward, shoulders bunched – 'they took off.'

'Meaning?'

'They went.'

'Where?'

'How would I know?'

Watts sat back. 'Did you see or hear anything as they went?'

'Like what?'

He glared at Nigel. 'My hair has nearly reached my shoulders in the time we've been sat here! The sound of a vehicle! *Anything.*'

He looked at Watts. 'Now you mention it, I did hear something like that, but it was quiet, not much to speak of . . .' The big face split into a grin. 'Now, I'm thinking it might have been one of those electric jobs, or diesel, like a taxi? Like I said, they took off, the bloke first in the direction of a slip road that leads on to the main thoroughfare. The other one, the kid in the baseball cap, hung around a bit then took off in the same direction.'

Nigel had gone, Watts was heading for his office, Nigel's statement in his hand, his head full of one question.

If this wasn't robbery, why in God's name would *one* person and a kid, or any number of kids, set out to kill an interior designer and his accountant wife?

10.05 p.m.

Huey Whyte was relaxing, drink in one hand, roll-up in the other, eyes half-closed. Letisha lifted the remote to the television. 'Why'd you bother with that depressing crap?' he murmured.

'I like the news and, in case you've forgot, this happens to be *my* place.'

She sat up, raised her face to the ceiling. Huey pulled his woollen hat over his ears, hunched his shoulders. '*Presley!* You get out o' that bathroom *now,* and get to bed!' She shook her head. 'You need to talk to him. He spends too much time messin' about.' She pointed to the television screen. '*Look.* That murder is on the news again. The one where that couple got shot.' Huey's eyes were already on footage of church doors, people coming outside, a preacher-type shaking hands with them. Letisha pointed again. 'That could be the mother and father of one of them . . .'

'If you listened, you'd know.'

'I don't *need* no listenin'. See? It's obvious. Father, mother and . . . some other relatives . . .'

Huey was picking up the news voiceover. 'Earlier today, the Lawrence family attended a service for their murdered son at their local church: Mr Lawrence's parents, his two sisters and—'

Huey came upright, eyes riveted on the screen, ears closed to his sister's voice. The screen changed to another news item. He sat back unseeing. He'd already had one brush with DI Watts about that gun. Now he was anticipating a second. It would all come out. He would be in deep— He got a poke in the ribs.

'I *said,* do you fancy a taco, or some o' that chilli rice?' He was on his feet, reaching for his coat. 'Where you going?'

'Out!'

TWENTY-EIGHT

Sunday 23 December. 9.30 a.m.

R estlessness had brought Watts into headquarters. He needed to decide on the best way of responding to what Molly Lawrence had told them which didn't include going mob-handed into an already touchy area of the inner city. Going through message slips left for him, he stopped at one timed at 10.20 p.m. the previous evening, an unnamed caller wanting to speak to him. He rang the number. A cautious-sounding male voice responded.

'Yeah?'

'This is DI Watts. I'm looking at a message you left me last night.'

'About bloody time.'

Watts frowned. The voice was familiar. 'What's up, Huey?'

'I might have information for you.'

'About?'

'The shooting of that couple.'

Watts' eyes narrowed. 'You don't say. Is this the same Huey Whyte who denied knowing anything? Make it snappy. I've got things to do.'

'Before I give you what I'm ringing about, I want some guarantees.'

Watts laughed. 'Get real.'

'I'm *serious.* I've got life sorted, see. I don't do nothing, trouble-wise, you hear what I'm saying? I'm living mostly at my sister's. I help her with Presley. He's sharp, Mr Watts. He's got a future and I want—'

'We all have "wants", Huey. Mine right now is for you to tell me why you've phoned.' He waited out the long pause.

'I don't watch the box but my sister had it on last night. The news. About that shooting. I saw somebody. If I tell you, you'll know that that business with the gun you're interested in is nothing to do with me.'

'Is that a fact? Tell me what you've got.' He reached for messages he hadn't yet read, picked up one, read it, let it drop, reached for more.

'I recognized him.'

'Recognized who?'

'That Lawrence bloke. Not the one that got shot. His brother.'

Message slips fell from Watts' hand.

'He's a builder. He looks a bit older, a bit heavier than I remember, but it was him all right, you hear what I'm sayin'? I had a bit of business with him, nine, ten years back. His firm was doing a lot of refurbing in the area back then. He was looking for a plasterer.'

'And being a graduate of HMP The Green in just that subject, you said, "I'll do it, Gov". So what?'

'*So,* he needed something else. He must have asked around. He comes to me. Says he needs to make a purchase. A shooter.'

Watts' head was racing. 'Say that again, and slow.'

'He asked me to get him a gun.'

'And?'

'You already know about that Russian piece. I *told* you I didn't have it no more. That's where it went. I sold it to him for five large.'

'You're telling me Brendan Lawrence paid you five hundred quid for that gun?' Huey didn't respond. 'Did he say why he wanted it?'

'Yeah. Security. Told me his house was secluded and his old lady nervous.' There was a pause. 'Look, I want to get off my phone and I don't want to see you hanging around my family, asking no more questions—'

'I want a statement from you.'

'No! You've got it all. That's it.'

Watts looked up as the door opened and Judd came in. 'Get *real,* Huey. You made an illegal gun sale. That gun has been used in a homicide and I don't care how long ago it was that you had your hands on it, I want everything you know about Brendan Lawrence and that gun.' He waited out a long pause, feeling Judd's eyes on him. 'Look at it this way. Kids like your Presley need stability. You cooperate on this and there's a possibility you'll be around to make sure he has some. Get yourself here. Somebody will be waiting to take that statement.'

Ending the call, he went to one of the filing cabinets, searched the files, dragged one of them out, found what he was looking for. He phoned the incident room. Kumar's voice sounded in his ear. 'I'm expecting Huey Whyte here to make a statement. Give it an hour. If he's a no-show, you and Jones get over to this address. It's another of Huey Whyte's occasional boltholes. He sold Brendan Lawrence the gun that was used on his brother and sister-in-law.'

'You want us to bring Whyte in, Sarge?'

'Not yet. Just don't let him out of your sight if he leaves that location.'

He ended the call, then looked at Judd who was waiting. 'There's somewhere you and me need to be.'

23 December. 1.15 p.m.

They drove between the familiar wrought-iron gates, along the curving drive and stopped near to several parked cars. 'Looks like a Sunday family gathering,' he said, recalling similar events in his own background, minus the ritzy backdrop.

They got out, walked towards the front door. It was opened by Brendan Lawrence. He was looking tense. 'DI Watts and PC Judd, Mr Lawrence. Apologies for dropping in on a weekend. We've met before, very briefly.'

Lawrence shook his head. 'Sorry, this isn't convenient. My family's been through the wringer during the last few days and my parents and my sisters are here for lunch. They don't need any more upset . . .'

'It's you we want to talk to, Mr Lawrence.'

'Me?'

'I'm guessing you'd prefer it to be in private.'

The colour leaving his face, Lawrence stepped back. They went inside. Gemma Lawrence appeared from one of the rooms off the hall, saw Watts and Judd.

'Brendan, what's going on?' And to Watts, she added, 'What do you want?'

'Get back to my folks, Gemma.'

'It's just a routine call, Mrs Lawrence. Apologies for interrupting your Sunday.' He glanced at Lawrence. 'It'll only take a minute or two.' Giving Brendan Lawrence a sharp look, she turned away, closing the door behind her.

'We need somewhere we can talk without being overheard, Mr Lawrence.'

'I don't have secrets from my family.'

'You might want to reconsider that statement when I tell you why we're here.'

They followed him to a door on the other side of the hall and into a large room expensively fitted out as a home office. Once they were inside, he closed the door. 'Whatever this is about—'

'Murder, Mr Laurence. A shooting, to be exact.'

Lawrence didn't respond.

'Own a gun, do you?' He saw the words strike home.

'No.'

'How about a few years back?'

Beads of sweat were now visible on Lawrence's upper lip. 'For security reasons only. There were burglaries all along this—'

'On a permit, was it?'

'No. I don't have it any more. It was stolen . . . in a burglary.'

Watts slow-nodded. 'And you with an eye for security. Just goes to show. Report the burglary and the theft of the gun, did you?'

Lawrence said nothing.

'That gun is putting you in a *really* awkward situation.'

Lawrence looked up at him. 'You seem to be implying something.'

'Implying's not my style, Mr Lawrence, but rather than disrupt your family time' – he turned towards the door, ignoring the frustration on Judd's face – 'it'll keep for an hour. Which is when I expect you at headquarters so we can discuss a gun you bought around a decade ago.'

Lawrence's face was now bloodless, mouth gaping. 'I'll bring my lawyer.'

'You do that. If you don't arrive, I'll be back here to talk to your family.'

Back at headquarters, Judd was still looking moody. 'If you've got reason to suspect that Brendan Lawrence shot his brother and sister-in-law, why didn't we bring him in?'

'Your tendency to want everybody who gets our attention banged up has its appeal. It also has its problems. Lawrence is a person of interest, but he might be moving shortly to suspect because of this.' Watts reached for a sheet of A4 lying on the table, re-read it, then passed it to her. 'Huey's statement about supplying a gun to Brendan Lawrence ten years ago is not proof of anything. We need more. Lawrence might tell us when he gets here.'

'Which should have been over half an hour ago.' The door opened and Traynor came inside. 'You've watched the re-enactment video?' asked Watts.

'Yes.'

'And?'

'I'm still considering it.'

'I've got information from Nigel, the security guard. Remember him? He was in Forge Street a couple of nights prior to the shootings and saw an adult male and a younger male. According to his description, the adult was big, well-built and had dark hair. That description says "Brendan Lawrence" to me.'

'I see.'

Judd looked up at him. 'There's been another development, Will. Huey Whyte sold *that* gun to Brendan Lawrence a decade ago.'

Traynor took Whyte's statement from her, read it. 'Have you spoken to Brendan Lawrence about this?'

'Briefly, when I confronted him earlier, he denied it, but he looked like somebody with a lot on his mind. I told him to come here to talk about it. So far, he hasn't arrived.' The phone rang. Watts reached for it. 'Yeah, Adam.' He listened, nodded, got to his feet. 'Thanks a lot.' He put down the phone.

'Remember Adam was trying to retrieve a useful print from the gun. It's still a non-starter but he's tested it for DNA. Care to guess the match he's come up with?'

'Brendan Lawrence.'

'One of these days, Traynor, I'll tell you something you don't know. It matched a sample taken from Lawrence following a drunk and disorderly incident back in 2006. Judd, you're with me.' He reached for the desk phone.

'Where to?' she asked.

'I'll tell you in a minute.' He tapped a number, then waited. 'Gemma? Bernard Watts here. Is Brendan with you?' Her voice drifted across the room.

'No. He took the dog and left straight after you did and we haven't seen him since. He's been acting weird for days. What's going on?'

'Any idea where he's gone?'

'As he's got the dog, my guess is he's where he usually walks it. Westley Park.'

Watts ended the call. 'He's heading to where Molly Lawrence's handbag was disposed of.' He reached for his keys, his eyes on Traynor. 'Why am I getting the idea that none of this is a big surprise to you?'

'The bits and pieces are beginning to slide together. I'll follow you.'

TWENTY-NINE

Sunday 23 December. 6.30 p.m.

Judd was on her phone alerting incident room officers as suburban landscape flashed past the BMW's window. They joined the darkened dual carriageway curving ahead. Seeing the road sign, Watts followed it, turned on to a narrow lane then into a large parking area, his headlights sweeping over a single vehicle. A black Range Rover, similar to one he'd seen parked outside the Lawrence house earlier in the day, registration letters, BNL.

They got out into silence and damp chill as Traynor's car purred to a halt. Watts raised his hand as he got out, his voice barely a whisper. 'Nice and easy.'

They followed the mud-covered path for several metres. Directly ahead was the pool from which Molly Lawrence's handbag was recovered. They skirted it, walked on, picking up subtle sounds within the undergrowth, then a sudden, high-pitched whine starting up from heavy tree cover to the right. A sudden rushing from within the trees, followed by a frenzy of barks, sent Watts grabbing for Judd's coat as the big dog bounded towards them. Judd grabbed Watts' arm as Traynor went forward, seized its collar, the dog jumping up, pounding its muddy paws on the ground and against Traynor's legs.

'Easy, boy. Easy,' he whispered to the big chocolate-coloured Lab. '*Shhh . . . good* boy.'

He looked up at his two colleagues, his hands either side of the dog's shoulders. 'He's not a threat. He's young and very upset about something.'

They moved forward, the dog now darting ahead of them, doubling back, running on again.

'I don't like the feel of this place,' whispered Judd. She pointed to where the dog was disappearing into some trees. 'And, what's wrong with him?'

They followed the muddied path through heavy trees and on to a small clearing. Brendan Lawrence was there, lying on cold, damp ground. The dog ran to him, moving to and fro, with more whines, more drumming of paws. Traynor went to it, held it by its collar, led it away and crouched beside it as Watts approached Lawrence, knelt and placed his fingers against Lawrence's neck.

'Is he dead?' whispered Judd.

Watts reached into his pocket for a disposable glove. 'Call an ambulance. One unconscious adult male in need of urgent assistance.' He carefully inserted his index finger inside the mouth of a half-empty brandy bottle lying nearby. 'Tell them the indication is that he's dead drunk.'

The ambulance arrived within fifteen minutes. Its crew walked to where Lawrence was lying. They checked him, removed him to their vehicle where they continued working on him. Watts waited with Judd, Traynor and the dog at the open doors. One of the paramedics jumped down to them, speaking quickly.

'Information provided by the family indicates that he's a regular drinker. Preliminary exam indicates no physical injuries but he's taken a lot of alcohol on board in a relatively short time. He was pale and unresponsive when we arrived, with a blood alcohol count of 0.39. Fortunately, no signs of other substance use. We've got him lying on his side and we're taking him to hospital. On the way he'll be given oxygen, intravenous fluids, probably glucose.'

Watts grimaced. 'When will he be in a fit state for us to talk to him?'

'Lap of the gods, sorry.'

They stood back, watched as the ambulance doors closed and it moved away.

Traynor looked down at the Labrador, gently rubbed the soft fur between its ears. 'What happens to you in the meantime, boy?'

The dog looked up at him and gave a quiet whine.

Watts pointed at it. 'Can you keep it overnight? The family will have enough to think about when they find out what's happened.'

Traynor stroked the dog. 'I need to call into the university. I'll take him with me, then pick up some food for him on the way home.'

12.05 a.m.

Traynor gazed down from his university window at relatively light, inner-city traffic, reviewing the latest developments in the case. Developments which had taken them from a double shooting, its solution rooted in the area he was looking down at, to a possible grudge-attack by someone who knew one or both of the Lawrences, and now to the victims' family. His phone rang. He reached for it.

'Yes?'

'Dad! It's *me*. Where are you?'

Hearing her anxiety, he looked at his watch, saw how late it was. 'I'm sorry. I should have phoned you. I got caught up with the investigation, then I had to come back to the university.'

'DI Watts rang to tell me what happened, that you might be late but there was no reply at the house.'

'I'm on my way home in the next ten minutes.' He frowned, picking up an insistent, rhythmic beat. 'Where are you?'

'I'm with Beth at her halls.'

'It's well past midnight.' Hearing her light laugh, he rubbed his eyes. 'As long as I know where you are.'

'I left pizza for you. Its looks might improve, once you heat it up.'

'No calls for me?' he asked, keeping the hope out of his voice.

'Nothing on the machine while I was home. See you!'

He glanced at the phone in his hand, then out of the window, feeling a familiar dull ache. He went to his desk, leafed through his office schedule, seeing entries made by students requesting his time, saw that it was Christmas Eve. Was it three days ago that he'd made the phone call? One he had never envisaged making? He located the number and tapped it, immediately halting the connection because of the lateness. It rang almost immediately.

It was Watts with news from the hospital. Brendan Lawrence's condition was stable. 'Depending on his progress during the next few hours, their plan is to discharge him. I've told them to inform me before they do. We're having too many late nights, you and me, Traynor. How's the dog?'

Traynor looked across his office to the sofa, the dog lying on one of Traynor's sweaters, saw the rhythmic rise and fall of soft fur.

'He's sleeping.'

'It's what we should all be doing.'

THIRTY

Monday 24 December. 8.45 a.m.

Traynor drove into headquarters and parked close to the building, well away from the press waiting around the entrance. Getting out of the Aston Martin, he pulled the seat forward and reached for the lead, whispered, 'Come on, boy.' He quickly reviewed the plan he had worked on until four that morning. It needed Watts' endorsement. His phone rang.

'Traynor.'

'Merry Christmas, Will Traynor. This is Jess Meredith, returning your call.'

Stopped by a dopamine surge of pure pleasure at the warm, low-pitched voice with its hint of laughter, he smiled. It was just as he remembered it from the investigation he had worked on with Watts back in the hot summer.

'Jess. I hope you didn't mind my calling you. When I didn't hear from you, I thought that was it. That you weren't . . . I rang again, just to be sure, but it was late, so I . . .' He closed his eyes. He sounded like a teenager on heat.

'Obviously I didn't mind, or I wouldn't be calling *you*. I've been away for a few days.' Traynor gave her words a quick evaluation. She has someone. Of course, she has . . .

'Will?'

'I'm at work, but can I ring you later?'

'Yes. You do that. Whatever the time.'

He came into headquarters, instantly picking up the tight atmosphere. The kind he had experienced on other cases. The feel of an investigation on the move. Watts was coming towards him, his eyes on the dog.

'Hello, mate.'

He ruffled the short fur on its head, gestured to the bored-looking young officer on the desk. 'Company for you, Reynolds.'

Brightening, Reynolds came and took charge of it. 'Have you read the email I sent you, Sarge?'

'When I have a minute, I'll get to it.'

Reynolds watched them go downstairs, the dog at his side whining, straining at its lead.

The custody sergeant looked up as they came into the suite. 'Whatever you two have been up to, to deserve being here today, I hope it was worth it.' He turned the screen towards them. They looked at the heavy, dark-haired male lying on a single bed.

'Following his arrival and pre-custody risk assessment, we put him in one of the holding rooms, rather than a cell. Want to see him?'

Watts studied Brendan Lawrence on screen. 'If he's up to it.'

'He discharged himself from the hospital very early this morning and one of our lads brought him in without any trouble. A medic who was in at seven thirty had a quick look at him and said he was OK.'

They followed the duty sergeant's broad back along the corridor, waited as he unlocked a door. 'Visitors for you, Mr Lawrence.'

Lawrence looked up from where he was lying. He looked awful, the smell of alcohol pungent and clinging.

'How are you feeling?' asked Watts.

'Like death . . . sick.' He put a hand to his mouth and paused. 'I don't want to go home. I can't face any of them but somebody needs to phone my parents.'

'All taken care of. The big question for us is are you up to being interviewed?'

He looked up at them. 'It wasn't meant to happen. It wasn't supposed to turn out like it did.'

Watts held up his hands. 'Save it for the interview, Mr Lawrence. Do you want legal representation?'

Lawrence slowly stood, somewhat unsteady on his feet. 'I have to tell you what I did. Until I do, I'll never be able to face my family.' He rubbed his eyes. 'I can't face them, full stop, because of what I did—'

'*Stop* right there, Mr Lawrence. This has to be done properly in interview with your legal representative present—'

'It was a simple idea. It was planned easy but it didn't work out like that.' He stared at them, wavering. 'I have to tell you. Put an end to it. I want to close my eyes without seeing my brother's head—'

'Sit down, Mr Lawrence.' He sat heavily. 'I want a doctor to see you. Only if he or she says it's OK will we interview you.'

Watts and Traynor stepped outside the room. Watts lowered his voice. 'I'm gagging to get it done, but the way he's looking, plus his refusal of representation, it has to wait.' They returned to the duty sergeant.

'Get another medic here pronto to have a look at him. I need to know when he might be fit for interview.' The duty sergeant wrote quickly in the daybook. 'Until the medic arrives, I want Lawrence checked every fifteen minutes.'

They left the duty sergeant and headed back upstairs. Watts asked, 'What did you make of what he said?'

'A non-specific admission,' said Traynor.

Watts gave him a frustrated glance. 'I rang his family to tell them he's here without giving details. Both his wife and his mother referred to him being in a volatile mood of late. There's a bottle of brandy missing from his house. As far as they're aware, he's being kept here for observation.' He looked at Traynor. 'Keep in phone contact, Will. As and when we interview him, I want you observing. I'm aiming to charge him with the murder of his brother and the attempted murder of his sister-in-law.'

Traynor left the building with the dog and got into his car. There was a lot on his mind. A lot to think about.

Walking into his house, he went straight to his study, sent an email, wanting a quick response but not anticipating one any time soon. Theories about crime-related trauma, emotional upset and resistance filled his head. He had all the textbooks. He didn't need them. The Lawrence case was running, like a video, inside his head, bringing with it a long series of clear images. He looked down at the mass of notes, the hundreds of words he'd heard, written and absorbed, during this investigation, the theories they had produced, words which had drawn him in. Stranger. Stranger in the dark. Handbag in the dark. Handbag filled with water. A stranger, morphing into someone who knew Mike and Molly Lawrence.

Traynor sat, his eyes fixed straight ahead, thinking of a type of crime which had featured in narratives since there were people to write them. Fratricide. An hour ago, Brendan Lawrence had been about to confess. Watts had stopped him because there were procedures which had to be followed, but now they knew from Brendan Lawrence that what had happened was planned. It had not surprised Traynor to hear it. His thinking over the last couple of days had gradually led him to really know the guilty actions and to understand the motive. Money.

Traynor drove with the dog along almost deserted roads. Nothing was about to happen with Brendan Lawrence for the next few hours and right now he was experiencing the rare, for him, pleasure of knowing that there was a woman waiting for him. Getting out of his car, he reached for the dog's lead and a plastic bag and walked with them towards the house, the tension inside his head soaring. The door opened and she was there, her curls a blonde-brown halo around her face. He recalled their first meeting in the hot summer when she had told him about a talented young reporter she had employed who had become a murder victim. So many sad stories. Too many.

'Hello, Jess.'

She held out her hand to him, drew him inside, took the plastic bag from him and looked down.

'I didn't come alone, sorry.'

'So, I see.'

'He's between families. I have temporary custody. I bathed him earlier. He was really muddy . . .'

'What's his name?'

'I don't know. I call him "boy".'

He followed her into the large, warm kitchen filled with good smells. She looked inside the plastic bag and lifted out the bottle. 'Mmm . . . Moet. How did you guess it's my favourite?'

She reached inside the bag again, took out a small soft item with dangling legs. 'What's this?'

The dog looked up at it and gave a low whine.

'It's a dog toy. It's actually a mouse but he'll probably think it's a dog. I thought he might get lonely at night.' He reached for it and pressed its middle. 'See? It's got a squeaker, but if it's too loud or he . . .' She put her hands around his, her voice soft.

'It's all right, Will. Everything's fine.'

He watched as she took a folded rug off the back of a sofa, opened it out, arranged it in one corner and patted it. The dog looked up at him, then went to her. She stroked its head. It jumped on to the sofa, turned twice and settled down, head on paws, its eyes fixed on Traynor. She placed the mouse beside its paws.

She looked up at Traynor, came to where he was standing, reached for him and gently drew his head down on to her shoulder. She held him, listening to the vast wave break inside his chest. They stood together, her arms around him.

'It's OK, Will. It's all OK.'

Tuesday 25 December, 6.30 a.m.

A long time later, he was lying beside her, at the point of falling asleep. His next conscious movement was sitting upright. He was used to sudden wakefulness. It still happened on occasions when sleep made him vulnerable to memory. Now it was memories of the case which were crowding into his head. Molly Lawrence had her own memories, as did her brother-in-law. He and Watts would be hearing them soon.

'Will?'

He turned to Jess, lowered his head to her face, her neck, exalting in the contact, the scent of her, the softness. Like a man long deprived of water, he pushed his face against her skin. 'Sorry, there's somewhere I have to be. For work.'

She looked up at him. 'Come back as soon as you can, Will.'

The Aston Martin hummed along the road as the pale sun rose. Traynor watched it, thinking about the power of trauma coming from nowhere, wrecking us physically, scrambling us emotionally, demanding we rethink all we ever believed about life, relationships, time. He wanted to hear again from Molly those she had experienced.

THIRTY-ONE

Tuesday 25 December. 9.15 a.m.

'It's going to hit the news today that Brendan Lawrence is here.' Watts looked at open files covering the table between them, then at the dog lying close to Traynor's feet. 'The update from the custody sergeant is that Lawrence is now loudly denying every word he said to us and demanding to be released. I'll interview him before he is. I want to know how he thinks he's going to get out of the fix he's in.'

Traynor reached for the phone, dialled the number and switched it to speaker. 'Hello, Molly.'

'Will? I wasn't expecting to hear from you.'

'There's been a development in the investigation and I wanted you to hear it from me.'

'What kind of development?'

'Brendan Lawrence has been arrested.' He waited out the long silence.

'I don't understand. What has he done?'

'He has told us that he was involved in the attack on you and your husband.' He waited. 'Molly?'

'I don't know what to . . . He must have been drinking. He drinks a lot.'

'I regret having to give you the news but you need to know. As and when we know any more, DI Watts or I will ring you.'

'Thank you. What happens now?'

He answered carefully. 'We're working on your sighting of the two or three young people in close proximity to the scene on the evening of the shootings. We're going there again later to look around.' He listened, hearing only her breathing.

'Thank you for letting me know.'

He ended the call. They looked up as Judd came into the office. Watts stood, then reached for his jacket and his homicide file. 'I was about to ring you. You're with me. I want more from Brendan Lawrence.'

With a glance at Traynor, she followed him out of the office. At reception, Watts said to Reynolds, 'Give Gemma Lawrence a call. Remind her that somebody needs to collect the dog.'

Reynolds reached for the phone. 'On to it, Sarge.'

They continued upstairs to one of the interview rooms. 'What's up with Will?' she asked.

'He's doing some heavy-duty thinking.' His phone buzzed. 'Yeah? Right.' He ended the call. 'Sod it.'

'What's up?'

'Lawrence's legal representation has shown up. It's Lang and Yeo.'

'And that's bad?'

'For us, it is. It's a firm which prides itself on getting its clients off, no matter that they were witnessed at a scene, bloodstained and wielding a chainsaw. Running legal rings around us is their forte.'

He pushed open the interview room door, dropped his files on the table, straightened his tie and reached for the phone. 'Let's see if we can run some rings of our own.'

Following a silent eight-minute wait, the door opened and an officer appeared, ushering Brendan Lawrence inside, followed by an austere, immaculately dressed man. He and Lawrence took seats side by side facing Watts and Judd.

Watts nodded. 'Mr Lawrence, you'll have brought Mr Lang up to speed on why you're here.' Seated next to the pristine Lang, Lawrence was a mess, his eyes red-rimmed and deeply shadowed, a sour odour coming from him. Watts reached out to the PACE machine.

'You've been arrested on suspicion of killing your brother, Michael Lawrence and wounding your sister-in-law, Molly Lawrence. I'll remind you that you're still under caution. Following your arrest, you made certain statements to me, which I'm going to read to you to refresh your memory and to which you are welcome to respond—'

Lang jumped in. 'My client is now retracting all that he said to you.'

Watts started reading them. '"It wasn't supposed to happen. It wasn't supposed to turn out like it did."'

'No comment,' muttered Lawrence.

'"I have to tell you what I did", plus—'

'No comment.'

Watts' eyes drilled into Lawrence's. 'At the time you made those admissions, Mr Lawrence, you said that you saw your brother's head. I believe that to be a reference to his injury which places you at the scene of your brother's murder.'

'*No* comment.'

Lang gave a wintry smile. 'Mr Lawrence is responding to your questions in the way I have advised.' He opened a slim file and took out a single sheet of A4. 'This is a medical report on my client, which indicates the time he arrived at hospital where he was treated for significant alcohol intake, plus the treatment he received. All other relevant times are included, plus a brief statement from the attending doctor.' Watts watched Lang slide it across the table. It was Lawrence's 'Get out of Jail' card. 'Our position is that when you spoke to Mr Lawrence he was still experiencing the effects of that intake. In consideration of those facts, firstly, I have advised my client that your speaking to him at that time was highly inappropriate and, secondly, if you are planning to bring a case against him, based on the utterances he made, our stance would be that he lacked sufficient cognitive ability at the time to fully participate in any discussion, that those utterances should be viewed as the ramblings of someone who was seriously impaired by gross substance abuses and that it was a serious professional error on your part to place him in that situation.'

Silence dropped like a blanket on the room as Lang and Watts sized each other up in a face-off. 'Is that sufficiently clear as to my client's position, Detective Inspector?'

'Crystal.'

'Good. I'd prefer to avoid lodging a professional complaint against you on his behalf.' Lang turned to Brendan Lawrence. They both stood. 'Good day to you, Detective Inspector.' They watched them go.

Judd stared at Watts. 'You're not letting him get away with that?'

'You heard what he said.'

Traynor looked up as they came into the office and saw their facial expressions. 'You haven't charged Brendan Lawrence.'

'He's walked, but I'm not done with him.' Watts sat, his eyes on Traynor. 'You've been doing a lot of thinking and not much saying over the last couple of days, Traynor. I want to know what's inside your head. *All* of it.'

They listened as he gave them the details.

'I don't believe . . .' Judd shook her head. 'What you're saying could get Brendan Lawrence *and*—'

'How sure are you?' asked Watts.

'Brendan Lawrence was *there*. You trust what I'm telling you, Bernard?'

'As always.'

'Good. Because we're facing a lot of waiting around in the cold, starting late this afternoon as the sun goes down.'

Wednesday 26 December. 3.55 p.m.

In fast failing light, they looked out at the scene, a sharp wind blowing through gaps in glass. 'Bloody *hell*,' whispered Watts. 'All three of us are risking pneumonia.'

Traynor consulted his phone. 'Sunset today is fifteen fifty-eight.'

'What if nothing happens?' asked Judd.

Watts folded his arms against his thick jacket, feeling cold air rising off the concrete floor. 'Traynor has already phoned to prime the trap. Let's hope it works.'

'Who else have we got, Sarge?'

He pointed. 'Jones over in that direction, Kumar on that side and Reynolds behind the petrol station.' Silence built, the vista quickly fading to blackness.

'The darker it gets, the better it looks,' she murmured.

Another fifteen minutes and Watts had lost all feeling in both feet. He moved to one side of the window, executing small, silent bounces.

'What's up?' she asked.

'Getting the blood moving. Something you'll know about in thirty or so years' time.'

'I'll hold a séance and let you know—'

'*Look.*'

They did, to where Traynor was pointing at a moving, bobbing light, a dark-clad figure in a baseball cap, moving slowly over the rough ground.

They silently walked out of the building, Traynor in one direction, Judd in another and Watts towards the intent figure oblivious to its surroundings. He continued on, stopped at the sound of a lone vehicle slowly approaching along the potholed street, headlights rising, dipping. The figure also stopped dead, looked up.

Seeing Watts, it turned and fled. He followed, hoping Jones was in position, seeing Reynolds speeding towards it. A split second of indecision on its part and Traynor hurtled past Watts and launched himself, arms outstretched. They closed on it. It resisted, flailing and kicking. He increased his hold on it, pushing its head low. As Watts arrived, the baseball cap hit the ground, long, dark hair swirling and swaying, the figure held captive in Traynor's arms.

'Hello, Molly,' he said.

She grew still. He slowly released his hold. 'Will? Thank *God* it's you! You have to help me.' She looked up at him, touched the long scratch. 'I'm so sorry, Will. I thought you were *him*.'

Thursday 27 December. 12.10 a.m.

'Tell us what you were doing at Forge Street,' said Watts.

She looked exhausted. 'Now you've arrested Brendan I can finally breathe properly, instead of jumping at every sound in case it's him.'

'We've released him,' said Watts.

She stared at him. 'Why? You said he confessed. He was *there*. He . . .' She lowered her head. 'I don't know why you did that, but you've put me in a really terrible situation. These last few days he's been threatening me, telling me not to talk to you about what happened. He said that if I did and he was arrested, he'd say I killed Mike.'

'Why would he think he could incriminate you?'

'You don't know Brendan. It all started ages ago, before Mike and I got married. Brendan was always hanging around, pestering me. I tried to discourage him. He wouldn't listen. I didn't want to say anything to Mike and cause problems within the family, although I think Gemma his wife picked up that something was happening. He just wouldn't be put off. If anything, he got more blatant. This was the family I was marrying into. I loved Mike and I really liked his family. Apart from *him*.' She sighed, put her hands against her eyes, let them drop. 'I felt sorry for Gemma. How could I tell her? I didn't know her that well and I was really worried that Mike's parents would realize something was wrong.'

She looked across to Traynor. 'I apologize for not being honest with you, Will. I think you guessed that there was something stopping me from talking. Remember me telling you how Mike pulled the car over when we got to that awful street? That he told me something was wrong with it?' She took a breath. It sounded like a sob. 'I had no idea what was going on. I told him to just keep moving. Get us away. He wouldn't.' They waited; watched her struggle to hold herself together. 'That's when he told me.'

'Told you what?' prompted Watts.

'That he had agreed to help Brendan because Brendan owed a lot of money to some people who had sold him drugs. They were threatening him. His business was in difficulties. Mike said that Brendan was coming to stage a hold-up and take our valuables, that he would claim on our insurance and give the money to Brendan. He told me that he'd already given Brendan twenty thousand pounds but he needed more and there was nobody else he could go to for help.' She shook her head. 'That's one of the things I loved about Mike. He wasn't a worldly sort of person but he was very caring. I just couldn't understand his insistence earlier that evening that I wear my diamond earrings to go to dinner. I only ever wore them on special occasions, but I agreed because it seemed important to him. Whoever Brendan owed that money to, it must have been a huge amount.' She stared ahead. 'I trusted Mike. I thought we had a relationship that was open.'

She bowed her head. 'Brendan arrived. He got inside the car, took everything from us and . . . that's when it all changed and turned into a nightmare,' she whispered. 'I could see that Mike was uneasy. There was something about Brendan. The way he looked. His manner. He drinks a lot but I didn't smell any alcohol on him. It crossed my mind that he'd taken drugs. I turned to pass the handbag to him. He took it from me.' She looked up at Traynor. 'What I told you about the touching was the truth. It was like it was an afterthought on his part. Something he did because he thought he could . . . I told you about it because I just couldn't keep it to myself any longer. Brendan has no morals. Like I said, he was always hanging around, sly with his hands. I should have said something. Made a fuss. I didn't . . . because it was really nice to feel part of a large family. But I swear I knew nothing about it until that evening when Mike told me.' She looked up at them. 'After the touching, that's when he fired the gun. At Mike. The sound of it, the smell . . . and then he leant forward, pointed it at me. I just . . . sat there. Waiting. Listening to Mike moaning. Knowing it was my turn.'

Despite her ravaged face, Watts wanted more. 'Why were you at Forge Street earlier this evening?'

She looked at him, tears flowing unchecked. 'Brendan phoned me when I was in the hospital – told me he'd taken one of the earrings from my bag and left it somewhere at that place for you to find. That it would incriminate me. I asked him how that was possible. I hadn't done anything wrong. I was so worried. You don't know Brendan. He's a liar and a horrible, evil person. I wanted to go to the place and look for it but I knew the police were there, and I wasn't well enough. When I began to feel a bit better, I was too frightened to leave the house. I told myself that Brendan was lying, like he always does, but when Will told me that one of the earrings *was* missing, I knew I had to find it. I couldn't stand the stress of waiting, worrying that it had been found, wondering what Brendan had planned, how he was going to make things bad for me. I was desperate. He said that that earring could send me to prison for killing Mike.'

Watts got to his feet. 'I want you to wait here, Mrs Lawrence.'

They left her with an officer and went to a nearby room. Watts closed the door, his voice low. 'We have to get this right, Traynor.'

'We will.'

'Your theory's holding up?'

'Yes.'

Watts paced, frowning. 'This is about money. Money and murder.' He looked up at Traynor. 'You know Molly Lawrence's mother pretty well?'

'I've met her, talked to her, so yes, I suppose I do.'

'I need you to phone her. Ask her about any life insurance that Mike and Molly Lawrence have.'

Traynor glanced up at the wall clock. 'It's very late. Or very early. I'll need to tell her who wants to know.'

'Do that. We need that information, soon as.'

Traynor got out his phone. The door opened.

'Sir?' Watts' phone rang. He reached for it and listened, then looked up at Reynolds. 'Mr Lawrence is back here. Is there anybody with him?'

'No.'

'Put him in interview room one. *Don't* let him leave.'

THIRTY-TWO

Thursday 27 December. 6.30 a.m.

Watts entered the interview room where Lawrence was pacing. He'd looked bad before. Now, he was haggard, looking years older and pounds lighter than when Watts had first seen him. 'You've come alone, Mr Lawrence.'

'Yes. I want to talk.'

'That's good. It's still my duty to advise that you need—'

'I want to talk and I don't want anybody putting obstacles in the way of me doing it.'

Looking at him, Watts could see that he was at the end of his rope. 'You're still under caution. It has to be formal.'

'I understand.'

'Wait here.' Watts left the interview room, posted an officer inside the room, and came into his office. 'Lawrence is refusing representation. He says he wants to talk. We've been down that road with him already. This time we do it right.

'Judd, go up to forensics. Tell Adam what's happening. He'll give you what we need. Bring it to interview room one. After I finish with Lawrence, I'll have another job for you.'

Lawrence's head was resting on his forearms. He didn't stir as Watts came inside and sat opposite. The wall clock ticked. Judd arrived, placed what she was carrying on to the table and sat next to Watts.

'Mr Lawrence?'

Lawrence raised his head, blinked at them.

'This is my colleague, PC Chloe Judd, whom you've met.' He reached out to the PACE machine, gave the date, time and details of the room's occupants, indicating the cameras trained on them from its two corners, then asked Lawrence to confirm his details and waited.

'You're still under arrest, Mr Lawrence.' Watts waited. 'You need to confirm what I just said.'

'Oh, sorry. Yes, that's correct.'

'You attended a second time with your legal representative, during which you responded, "No comment", to all questions put to you. That interview was halted. On arrival here today you have indicated that you wish to proceed with this interview without benefit of legal representation. Is that correct?'

'Yes. All correct.'

'Are you able to confirm that you are not under the influence of alcohol or any other substance?'

'Yes.'

'I am now advising you again, that it is in your interests to have such representation. Do you wish to have it?'

'No. I don't.' He clasped his hands either side of his head. 'It's all in here, you see. Playing on my mind. I can't cope with it anymore.'

'Are you now wishing to make changes to what you told me previously?'

'I want to tell you all of it.'

Watts glanced at Judd. 'First, Mr Lawrence, I want you to look at an exhibit.'

Judd removed the lid from the box on the table, slid it towards Lawrence. He got to his feet, his eyes fixed on the gun inside it.

'Sit down, please, Mr Lawrence.'

He sat, averting his eyes.

'This is the gun which was used to shoot your brother and sister-in-law. We know it was in your possession for several years prior to those shootings. What do you have to say about it?'

'I admit it. I was there.'

Watts fixed him with a direct look. 'Mr Lawrence, are you now admitting that you were at the Forge Street scene when your brother and sister-in-law were shot?'

Lawrence lowered his head. 'Yes.'

'On that occasion, did you handle this gun directly?'

'Yes.'

'What I want now is a straightforward account of what happened at the time your brother and sister-in-law were shot.'

Lawrence's hands were clasped to his head. 'It was about money. I was in deep trouble. My wife was refusing to help. I didn't know where to turn and suddenly I had a proposition put to me. I agreed to it. All I had to do was go to Mike's car, remove a couple of items and go.' He looked up. 'That was it. End of story.

Except that it wasn't. When I got there, I could tell something was wrong. As soon as I opened the car door, it was obvious something wasn't right with Mike. I grabbed what I'd come for and got out as fast as I could.' He sat back, looking exhausted. 'I was in a real panic. When I heard the news about the shootings, I couldn't believe it. That wasn't part of the plan. I got rid of the bag and the valuables. It was supposed to be an insurance scam involving the jewellery but by then I wanted nothing to do with it.'

Watts' phone lit up. A text from Traynor. He read it, read it again, then looked up at Lawrence.

'It *was* a scam,' said Watts, 'but not to do with any jewellery. Your brother and his wife had some really heavy-duty life insurance.'

Lawrence's head came up. 'What?'

Watts got to his feet. 'Mr Lawrence, I'm halting this interview temporarily. You'll remain here until I return. Do you understand?'

Lawrence looked spent. 'I've got nowhere else to go. I know everything at home is finished for me.'

'I'll arrange for coffee, tea, and anything else you need.'

He shook his head. 'Don't bother.'

'In that case, this interview is temporarily halted at . . .' Watts added date and time and deactivated the PACE machine.

Leaving Brendan Lawrence under the gaze of an officer, Watts and Judd headed downstairs. He gave her a sideways look. 'I want you to lead on the next interview with Molly Lawrence.'

She stared at him. 'This case is massive. It's—'

'You've got some doubts that you're up to it?'

'No.'

Seen in a different context, she might be taken for a sixth-former, yet he knew she was far sharper than her years, that her irreverent attitude hid a keen awareness of legal procedure. 'Our approach with Molly Lawrence remains that she is a victim-witness. We'll use an interview room down here, away from Brendan Lawrence. Don't forget. Accuracy. Reliability.'

'Where's Will?'

'He's following up some information.'

Reaching into his pockets, he called to Jones walking ahead of them.

Jones turned and took the small plastic bag Watts was holding out to him.

'Check Sebastian Engar's home contact details. Go and see him and ask him what he knows about this item of jewellery. If he recognizes it, I want whatever paperwork he's got for it. Quick as you can.'

Jones took it, headed for the door. 'On my way.'

They walked on. 'Let's see what Molly Lawrence has to tell us,' Watts said.

Traynor had received a phone call forty-five minutes ago. He was now inside Molly Lawrence's mother's house, waiting. She looked to be in torment.

'It was bad enough when I got your call about the life insurance. I knew then that Molly was in real trouble.'

'If you know anything else which you think might have some bearing on the shooting of your daughter and son-in-law, you need to tell me.'

'You don't know what you're asking of me. Of any mother,' she whispered, reaching for a folded piece of paper lying on the low table in front of her. Her hands shaking, she opened it and held it out to him. 'You need to read this.'

Traynor took it from her and looked at the heading in bold black letters. A coroner's report. His eyes moved slowly over the concise words to the end and a decision in more bold letters: *Verdict: Open.*

'I can imagine what it's taken for you to make this available to us.'

'I don't have a choice.' She glanced at the report still in his hand. 'I know what Molly said happened that day.' She looked away from Traynor to the window. 'I always had my doubts. Can you begin to imagine how that felt?'

He was at a loss to find words to convey his sympathy and understanding of her situation. 'Yes. I can.'

She nodded and gazed out at trees being whipped by a cold wind. 'It's not easy raising children and I'm thinking that I've made a mess of it.'

Traynor's natural response was to reassure but he said nothing.

'What does one do, Will, when two children are so . . . *different*, one outgoing, the other . . .? All young children are self-centred to a degree.' She paused. 'But it never changed. There were always the lies, the indifference to other people's feelings and . . . using people, relationships, sex as a means to an end. Some of those things, the selfishness, became less obvious, but *I* knew they were always there. I tried to be a good mother, to guide, believe me. Our house was always full of children, playmates . . . but not one of them was like *her*.'

She looked up at Traynor. 'If I'd said something, done something . . . would her sister and Mike be alive today?'

Traynor folded the report and returned it to his pocket. 'I appreciate how hard this was for you. It was the right thing to do.'

Watts looked at a text which had just arrived from Traynor. He turned his phone to Judd, who read it.

She looked up at him and whispered, 'What the *hell*?'

'Are you still happy to lead?'

'Yes.'

They entered the room. Molly Lawrence stood, her face deathly pale.

'Mrs Lawrence,' said Judd, 'before you are interviewed under caution, do you wish to have legal representation?'

'Under . . .?' She looked at Watts. 'What's going on? I want to go home.'

Judd reached for the PACE machine and cautioned her. Molly Lawrence's blue eyes were still fixed on Watts.

'I don't understand. I've been honest with you, Detective Inspector. I've told you all I know.'

'Mrs Lawrence,' said Judd. 'I'm leading this interview. You're under caution because we believe that you are withholding information from this investigation into the shooting of your husband and yourself.'

As if Judd had not spoken, Lawrence's eyes remained fixed on him. 'I've *told* you I was under duress from Brendan. I need protection from him!'

'Because we believe you are continuing to withhold information,' said Judd, 'the purpose of this interview is to give you every opportunity to add to or amend what you've told us so far, and also the information you have given to Dr William Traynor. Do you understand?'

She stared at Judd. 'Why aren't you listening to me? I couldn't be open. I was afraid for my *life*!'

'Mrs Lawrence, you've acknowledged some involvement in your husband's death.'

'If you mean I was there, then, yes.'

'We have reason to believe it was far more than that. Do you now wish to add to or amend what you said earlier?'

'No. I don't.' She pushed her hair behind her ears, her eyes fixed on Judd. 'If you're suggesting that I had anything to do with what happened to Mike, you're wrong. That is monstrous. I'm as much a victim of Brendan Lawrence as Mike was. I lost the baby I wanted.' She gave Judd a direct look, her chest rising and falling. 'Until that night, I knew nothing of what was about to happen.'

'Brendan denies shooting you and your husband.'

'Ha! Brendan is a liar. Whatever he's told you is lies. Like I said, when we approached that place, Mike suddenly stopped the car.'

Judd was recalling Nigel's description of the stationary Toyota, all of its doors closed.

'What time was that, Mrs Lawrence?'

'I'm not sure. All I remember is Mike telling me what he and Brendan had planned. I was terrified. We started arguing. I was almost hysterical, asking him how he could have agreed to do what Brendan was suggesting, knowing the situation we were in with the baby. He told me Brendan needed money, that he had to pay off a massive drug debt, that he'd promised he would help him. You know all of this. I threatened to get out of the car.' She looked at Watts. 'But if I had, where would I have gone? I didn't have a clue where I was.' She brushed tears from her face. Her voice dropped. 'Brendan arrived.' Her eyes widened. 'When I saw the gun, I couldn't believe it. I fell apart, crying, shouting at Mike, at both of them, to stop.'

She covered her face with her hands. 'That's when Mike slapped me. Hard. He'd *never* done anything like that before. I was in shock. I just sat as they talked. Brendan asked for Mike's watch and phone, my jewellery and my handbag. I just did what I was told.'

'Mrs Lawrence—'

'And then . . . Brendan shot both of us. Mike sort of jolted on his seat. I felt pain on one side and' – she shook her head, looked away – 'he left us there. I was bleeding. Mike was just sitting there, his eyes closed, not speaking, not moving and . . .' She closed her eyes. 'I need some water.'

With a glance at Watts, Judd stood. 'I'll have some brought to you, Mrs Lawrence. We'll take a short break.'

They went out of the room and looked at each other. 'No reference to any sexual aspect,' said Watts.

'No. She's making it up as she goes along.'

Watts went down to the post-mortem suite where Chong was standing before a microwave oven, fumes spiralling inside it. She looked up as he came inside. 'How are the interviews going?'

'What looks like truths from one and lies from the other. Got anything for me?'

She nodded at the microwave. 'Soon, I hope.'

Leaving her to it, he went to his office where Judd and Traynor were sitting in silence.

'Before Judd and I continue the interviews, you queried how Molly Lawrence was shot. Tell me again.'

'It didn't seem plausible that, having shot Mike Lawrence in the head, the gunman wouldn't do the same to her. Why leave her as a potential live witness? The progression of events appeared to be that the gunman took their belongings and *then* he shot them. That made no sense either. As for the work I did with her, in that kind of situation I proceed with an open mind. It's part of the job. But, if each account of a situation starts from the beginning, if the responses themselves are lacking in detail, if it is repeated in similar limited detail, over time I consider I'm being lied to. That the person giving the information is being very economical in order to keep the story straight.'

Watts sat on the edge of the table, his arms folded. 'Brendan and Molly have both given false information during their interviews. Question is, which one do I most believe? I'm hoping for something else from Chong that will clinch it.'

They waited in silence for a further ten minutes. 'Science is taking its time.'

'What if it doesn't arrive?' asked Judd.

'Let's hope it does, and soon. Ready?'

'Sarge.'

Molly Lawrence stood as they came into the room. 'I don't like being made to wait. It's extremely stressful.'

Judd switched on the recording equipment. 'Sit down, Mrs Lawrence. You're still under caution. This interview is being recorded as before, so we'll continue. Tell me why you were at Forge Street late yesterday.'

Lawrence looked from her to Watts. 'You already know why. Brendan told me that he'd left one of my earrings there and that it might incriminate me, and Will confirmed an earring was missing. I thought, if I found it, it might somehow incriminate *him*.'

'Why didn't you simply come to headquarters and tell us about it?'

Lawrence sighed, closed her eyes. 'I've *told* you. I was under duress. Under threat.'

At a quiet knock, Watts stood, went to the door, returning with two A4 sheets which he glanced at then passed to Judd. She read them, looked up. 'Mrs Lawrence, can you confirm whether at any time you had physical contact with the gun during the attack on you and your husband?'

She looked up. 'Of course not. No.'

'Are you also able to confirm that you had no direct contact with that gun at any time prior to that attack?'

'How could I? I didn't even know of its existence.' Aware of Judd's eyes still on her, she sighed. 'No. I didn't.'

'For the benefit of the recording, I'm now showing Mrs Lawrence the results of an analysis of a partial fingerprint taken from the gun which was used to kill Michael Lawrence.' She slid one of the A4 sheets towards her. 'This partial print has been matched to ones left by you on the car belonging to you and your husband.'

Lawrence stared at the sheet.

'Do you want to comment on that, Mrs Lawrence?'

'Yes, I do. It's either a mistake or you're lying.'

Judd slid the second A4 sheet towards her. 'I'm now showing Mrs Lawrence a forensic report on a watch, plus samples of the lining of a coat, both of which were worn by her on the night Michael Lawrence was attacked, which—'

'What are you saying? *I* was shot. *I* was robbed!'

'Confirms the presence of significant gunpowder residue on both watch and lining.' Judd paused and looked directly at her. The atmosphere in the room tightened. 'The presence of that residue indicates that your hand was in extremely close proximity to that gun when it was fired. What do you say to that?'

She stared at Judd. 'I say it's ridiculous. I'm beginning to question the expertise of everyone working here.'

'There's no doubting the results, Mrs Lawrence.' She pointed. 'Scanning Electron Microscopy was used to test samples from your

watch and your coat lining.' Judd looked at her. 'You described the
sleeves of that coat as very long. The right sleeve was tested and
gave the same result.'

Judd took back the A4s. 'We have other information which
strengthens our suspicions that you shot and killed your husband
and then shot yourself. Evidence is fast accumulating against you,
Mrs Lawrence. This is your opportunity to respond.'

She gazed back at Judd, arms folded, lips pressed together.

A further knock took Watts to the door. He returned with information which he handed to Judd.

'Here's something else for you to consider, Mrs Lawrence.' Judd
pushed the two stapled sheets across the table. 'For the recording,
I'm now showing Mrs Lawrence a statement by Sebastian Engar,
employer of Michael Lawrence, which states that he has been shown
a diamond earring, property of Molly Lawrence, and has confirmed
he bought a pair identical to it.'

Judd looked up at her. 'We're now saying that those were the
earrings you were wearing on the night of the shootings. Do you
wish to comment on that?'

Lawrence gazed coldly at her. 'Seb is a dear friend of mine
and Mike's. He's fairly elderly, a very kind man, also, a very
lonely one. He gave me those earrings as a wedding present. They
belonged to his wife who died several years ago.' She straightened.
'I want those earrings back. In fact, you can fetch all of my
property right now because I'm leaving.' She stood. Watts did the
same.

Judd looked up at her. 'Sit down, Mrs Lawrence. This interview
hasn't finished.'

After a tense few seconds, she sat. Judd reached out, turned over
the first sheet, pointed, then pointed to the second. 'This is a copy
of a receipt dated January last year, bearing a description of those
earrings and that Mr Engar paid for them with his credit card. He
has confirmed that you and he began an intimate relationship very
shortly after, that you wanted to end your marriage and were pressing
him to make the relationship formal between the two of you, which
he declined to do.'

They watched Lawrence's eyes move over the printed words,
watched their relevance sink in. She pushed the sheets away. 'What's
written here is what *he* was hoping for. What *he* wanted. Why would
I want a man in his fifties when I had Mike?' She reached for the

sheets, crumpled them in both hands, threw them to the floor. 'It's ridiculous. As ridiculous as me supposedly shooting myself.'

'Our in-house pathologist, Dr Chong, has revised her opinion on your injuries.'

'Oh, *really*?'

'And the hospital pathologist has re-evaluated them, particularly the close proximity of the entry and exit wounds and the angle of the bullet. He agrees with Dr Chong. He is willing to state that your injuries could have been self-inflicted.'

Lawrence gave a mocking smile. '"*Could* have". Any lawyer would drive a tank through that kind of prevarication.'

'Mrs Lawrence, I have one last matter which I need to raise with you. It is not connected to your husband's murder, but this investigation is now regarding it as of interest and likely to form part of the case against you. This is a copy of the coroner's report on the death of your sister ten years ago' – Lawrence's eyes darkened – 'which gives an "open" verdict.' Judd slid it across the table. 'You're welcome to read it. You'll see that it's very clear that foul play could not be ruled out. Do you have a response?'

'No. I'm just enjoying this farce! Seeing how far you're willing to go.'

'Mrs Lawrence, we've examined the timing of events of the evening your husband was shot. We've spoken to residents local to where it occurred.' Judd sat forward. 'According to our information, those shots were fired prior to ten p.m. At around nine thirty, to be exact.' She paused. 'You delayed your emergency call until ten thirty-five so that *you* could be as certain as possible that your husband was at the very least incapable of communicating with any help that would arrive. You need to properly engage with the information I've shown you, rather than dismissing it.' She instinctively sat back as Molly Lawrence's face came towards hers.

'Why should I care what you have?' Her eyes slid over Judd. 'You, with your boring suit and your ghastly hair. I'm not interested in anything you've got to say.' She sat back and folded her arms, her eyes fixed on Watts. 'I don't care for the way I'm being questioned, nor your colleague's accusatory attitude towards me. She's taking so-called evidence at face value, believing what other people say. She's not listening to me. I demand legal representation. Get it for me, *now*.'

'It's going to take a while.'

'So? Arrange it!'

Getting an almost imperceptible nod from Watts, Judd reached for the recording machine. 'This interview is concluded at . . .' She added the time.

They both stood and went to the door. Watts signalled to an officer who came inside and led Molly Lawrence from the room.

They walked into the observation room where Traynor was waiting. Watts headed to the water cooler, filled a paper cup and drank. It was a while before he broke the heavy silence. 'She knows all we've got on her, she's got no plausible explanation for any of it and now she's decided she wants representation.' He dropped the cup into the waste basket. 'Mad as it sounds, I think she's actually enjoying the attention.'

'She is,' said Traynor. 'Just as she enjoyed the attention of the re-enactment. She also loves the game playing involved. And she'll want something from you.'

Watts looked across at Traynor. 'Like, what?'

'She'll want to make some kind of deal.'

'A *deal*?' They both stared at him, Watts searching for words. '*We* know what she's done. *She* knows we know!' To Judd, he said, 'As soon as the duty solicitor arrives, we're in there to formally arrest her.'

'You need to understand that Molly Lawrence is her own creation. She doesn't reflect on her actions. Pushed into a corner, she merely blames others.'

Watts huffed. 'She's facing a long prison sentence, which will give her plenty of time to "reflect".'

Traynor shook his head. 'She will never accept personal responsibility for what she's done.'

'She's got no option,' snapped Watts.

'She thinks she has. Everything is possible as far as she is concerned. When her representation arrives, she'll tell him or her what it is that she wants.'

'Which is what, exactly?'

'An admission of guilt in exchange for a special hospital sentence.'

Judd's mouth fell open. Watts stared at him. 'In her *dreams*. That's a court decision.' He paused. 'What's the payoff of special hospital for her?'

'An opportunity to manipulate everybody, including staff, maybe get out.'

'Wherever she serves her sentence, that won't happen for years and I'll be at every parole hearing to make sure she stays put.'

'I doubt her plans involve legitimate release.'

'You're saying she's an escape risk?'

'She's devious, highly manipulative, so, yes.'

Their heads came up at raised voices coming from nearby. Watts headed for the door, opened it, the voices growing louder.

Jones was there, pointing upstairs to the interview room. 'Duty solicitor has arrived, Sarge.'

'So, I hear.' He looked at Judd. 'Do you want me to take over?'

'No.'

They came into the room where the duty solicitor was sitting, face flushed, his eyes fixed on Lawrence. He looked up at them. 'Beyond informing me that she might consider an admission of guilt in exchange for a specific disposal of her case, Mrs Lawrence is refusing to talk to me—'

'*Don't* speak about me as if I'm not here!' she snapped. 'Who the hell do you think you are!'

Judd placed papers on the desk and reached for the recording machine. She and Watts sat. 'That isn't how the system works, Mrs Lawrence. It's for the court to recommend disposition. You can't just demand it.'

The solicitor sent Judd a weary look. 'I've already *told* her.'

Lawrence turned her blue eyes onto Watts. 'Tell them both to leave. I want to talk to you.'

Judd placed her hand on the papers. 'Mrs Lawrence, I'm leading this interview. The evidence we have here indicates that you murdered your husband.'

Lawrence's eyes remained on Watts as Judd continued.

'What you're saying is that you want control over the outcome of the case against you. That's not going to happen.' She paused. 'But some indication of a willingness to cooperate with this process *might* help you in the long term.' She watched Lawrence's face break into a smile, her eyes still on Watts.

'She thinks she's good, that she's got this case by the tail.' She turned her face to Judd, the smile switching off. 'But not good enough.' She sighed then shook her head, her attention diverting to her cuticles.

'Mrs Lawrence, you can't dismiss evidence . . .'

Lawrence yawned. 'Yes, I can. I was there. It was Brendan who killed Mike and shot me. There's nothing else to say.'

Judd glanced at Watts, then: 'We know about the life insurance on you and your husband.'

'So what? Most professional people have life insurance.'

'Not for almost a million pounds.' Judd looked at her. 'One of the worst aspects of what happened that night in Forge Street is that your husband believed he was there solely to help his brother out of a financial problem. He had no idea that *he* was about to become a victim. *Your* victim.'

The blue eyes settled on Judd's face. Lawrence yawned widely and blinked, her mouth set.

'You're being uncooperative, Mrs Lawrence. Let's move to a different issue. Tell me about your sister.' Judd hadn't anticipated a reaction from the woman sitting opposite her. She didn't get one. '*You* were there when *she* died. What happened?'

'I don't want to talk about that.'

Judd stared across at her, weighing up what she was about to say. 'It might eventually get you what you want.'

The cuticles were now getting more attention. 'How do you know about that?'

'What happened?' repeated Judd.

'We went swimming. In the sea.'

'A risky place for two young girls. Whose idea was that?'

'My sister was a strong swimmer.' She shrugged. 'I don't remember.'

'What happened?'

'She got into difficulties. I tried to save her.'

Judd slow-nodded, willing to bet that, while she could feel her own heart thudding, the same wasn't happening inside the woman sitting opposite. 'Did you get on with your sister?'

Lawrence looked at her and laughed. '*You* are so transparent. She was a pain in the bum, if you want to know, but that was OK because she was leaving to go down to London to stay with one of our aunts so she could go to ballet school.' Judd heard the exaggerated delivery of 'bal-*leigh*'.

'Envious, were you?'

'Oh, please. I was *glad.* At least, with her out of the way, I didn't have to listen to the bloody music, watch her prancing around, listen to Mum and Dad going on about how talented she was.' She looked directly at Judd and grinned. 'I meant "out of the way", as in *London*.'

'According to the coroner's report, your sister had a deep gash on her head.'

'So?'

'How did she get that?'

The blue eyes widened. 'How am I supposed to answer that? Maybe she struck her head on something as she sank slowly beneath the waves.' A pin dropping to the floor would have been louder than the silence in the room. The duty solicitor was staring at her, his mouth open.

Judd said, 'Going back to the murder of your husband—'

Lawrence raised both arms and stretched. Folding them, she gazed ahead, unblinking. 'I'm *bored*. I've had enough of all this talking. I did it. So what?'

Watts' pen stilled. Judd stared at her, momentarily outflanked. 'When you say that you did it—'

'For Christ's sake, what's the matter with you people! Do you want me to spell it out?'

'Yes. Are you admitting that you shot your husband, or that you killed your sister? Or both?'

'My husband. That's it. End of topic.'

'It isn't. You need to tell us why you shot him.'

Lawrence's half-closed eyes slid over Judd's face. 'What do *you* know about anything?' She sighed, tilted back her head, then gazed at the ceiling. 'Mike was boring. No drive, you see. No ambition. Happy to just go along, doing whatever he had to do at work, then come home to paint the house, plan the nursery, talk non-stop about the baby, going on and on and bloody *on*.' She took a deep breath. 'It wasn't what *I* wanted.'

'And the only way out that you could see was to kill him and claim the life insurance.'

The blue eyes were back on Judd. 'You're making some big drama out of this. I wanted out. Out of the marriage, out of being a mother, but I wasn't leaving good old, sensible, responsible Mike empty-handed. I wanted that pay-out.' She laughed. 'In fact, the only interesting thing he ever did was agree to help Brendan out of his financial hole!' She shook her head.

'I went online, got the facts on shooting at the right angle to avoid seriously damaging myself, but hopefully ending the pregnancy. I told Mike that something was wrong with the car and sat in the back with the gun. I knew Brendan would arrive shortly.'

The duty solicitor was now looking as though he needed some air.

She looked from Judd to Watts and back. 'You two need to lighten up. It added realism to Mike's shooting and put me in the clear as a second victim. It almost worked.'

'And your sister? Did you kill her?'

She grinned. 'No comment.' Then she sat back. 'I've got nothing else to say.'

A couple of hours later, they were in Watts' office. 'How were you so sure she was after a special hospital place?' he asked.

Traynor shrugged. 'From experience. I've met individuals like her over the years, not all of them female. Her tragic situation when I first met her made me slower than I might have been to identify her extreme personality problems.'

'We all bought into it,' said Judd. 'Now we have her admission to killing her husband, plus the strong likelihood that she murdered her sister, it looks like she might get the sentence she wants.'

Watts shook his head 'What I want is her banged up in general population.' He looked at Traynor. 'What's your thinking?'

'It wouldn't surprise me if she has a 360-degree change of stance in the weeks to come and claims to having been coerced into confessing to Mike Lawrence's murder.'

Judd stared at him, looked at Watts. 'She *can't*. It's all recorded.'

'I'm merely flagging up her possible stance. People like Molly Lawrence view truth and rules as applying only to others.'

'If you want my opinion, she's ten stops past Barking—' The phone rang. Watts reached for it. 'Yeah?' He nodded. 'Thanks for chasing that down, Leila.' He ended the call. 'Jonah Budd's probation officer. He was arrested earlier today for the November carjacking series and possession of a replica gun.' He turned to Traynor who was lifting his backpack. 'Thanks, Will.'

'What for?'

'Your insights on this whole case, on Molly Lawrence. For helping us identify what she really is. We appreciate it.'

He and Traynor walked from the office together. Traynor continued downstairs, turned and raised his hand.

Judd was suddenly at Watts' side. 'Will, *wait*. I've just taken a call from Gemma Lawrence about the dog. She doesn't want him. She says to take him somewhere and get him rehomed. I told her to put it in writing.'

Traynor grinned up at them. 'Not a problem. He's been mine since the day we found him.'

They watched him go, then walked slowly down the stairs. 'I don't know about you, Judd, but I feel sorry for Mike Lawrence's family. And Mrs Monroe.'

'Families,' said Judd, with a quick headshake.

They walked on. She looked up at him. 'What's the smile for?'

'Seeing you in that interview room has reminded me of your first week here.'

She grinned. 'You told me to go and get details on a suspect called Robin Banks.'

'And you were back in less than ten seconds, saying you couldn't find anything but would a Robin Bastard help?' He stopped, looked down at her. 'You drive me nuts sometimes, but I've never doubted how sharp you are. The work you did today was faultless.' She glanced up at him, then away. They walked on.

'Well done, kid.'

She rolled her eyes. He nudged her. She tutted. He nudged her again. She looked up at him and smiled. Seeing the young officer on duty, he diverted to reception. 'Reynolds!'

Watching, Judd murmured, 'God, what's he done or not done, now?'

Watts reached the desk. 'Relax, son. I've been meaning to have a word with you about the information you got from your visit to Molly Lawrence's office.' He pointed his thick forefinger at him. 'It was first-rate. It's now part of the evidence we've got on her.'

'What did he get?' asked Judd as they walked away from a glowing Reynolds.

'Some very useful office tittle-tattle. Molly Lawrence was in the habit of receiving calls from what Reynold's informant there described as her "fancy man". It seems that informant took it on herself to check the phone number.' He nodded. 'That's right. Engar.'

A brief silence grew between them. Judd asked, 'Have you seen Julian?'

'At around seven this morning. He's probably back in Manchester by now. He left while we were tied up with the Lawrence interviews.'

Judd looked miffed. 'He just *went* while I was beating my brains out, doing my job?'

'Afraid so. All part of being a career woman—'

'*Careerist.*'

'He said to tell you that he'd ring you.'

'That's up to him.'

THIRTY-THREE

Mid-April

Watts had been up since six a.m., drafting a letter for Brophy. He was giving it a final read when his phone rang. It was Traynor. 'I rang headquarters and was told you're on leave.'

'Yes, working on my first step to getting a life away from the job.' There was a brief silence.

'I see. Have you seen the email from the Crown Prosecution Service?'

Watts' pen was tracking the draft. 'Which email is this?'

'Molly Lawrence is demanding a move.'

The pen stopped halfway through deleting a word. Details of the Lawrence trial weeks before flooded his head. Brendan Lawrence had offered a guilty plea to a charge of obstructing a police investigation, plus his part in the events which had led to his brother's death, for which he was eventually given five years. Against the advice of her defence lawyer, Molly Lawrence had given evidence, presenting herself in court as wronged, misjudged and badly used. In short, everybody's victim. The jury hadn't bought it. The judge had given her life in prison for the murder of Michael Lawrence and ruled that the death of her sister should remain open on the case file.

Watts recalled his heart sinking when he heard the judge's words. He'd been hoping for an indeterminate sentence. As the situation now stood, she could be out in fifteen years, depending on what a parole board was told about her, how slick she was at presenting herself and her case to them.

'No chance! She's only done a couple of months.'

'According to my contact at the CPS, she's requesting a move to a special hospital, "due to severe emotional deterioration".'

'She won't succeed by playing that card, not while I'm around. First thing I'll do when I'm at headquarters is give them my views on her as SIO of the Lawrence case.'

'What about the future you're planning away from it?'

He picked up the amusement in Traynor's voice. 'It'll be my finale to ensure that she stays wherever she is for as long as possible.' He paused. 'It's probably the single reason she admitted anything.'

'Molly Lawrence has the kind of personality which takes the long view. That, plus game playing and manipulation of those around her. It is far too soon for her to succeed in what she's requesting, but she'll keep on with it until she does, supported by people who either think they know her or who buy the façade she's showing them. We could both be involved in her future in some way for years to come, Bernard.'

'Not me.' Watts glanced at his draft letter, thinking that it wasn't only felons that the force held captive. He flexed his shoulders. 'I'm getting out. I've applied for an allotment I've seen. It's a wilderness, so it should keep me busy and non-contactable for the next decade.'

Traynor laughed. 'This doesn't sound like you.'

'This is the new "me" that's seeing Brophy to tell him I want early retirement.'

There was a short silence, broken by Traynor. 'I'm happy for you if it's what you want, Bernard, but I'm also sorry to hear it. Keep in touch. Say hello to Connie for me.'

'Will do.' He hesitated, then, 'Look after yourself, Traynor. Keep on with the fight.'

'The fight?'

'Yeah. The one that gets justice.'

ACKNOWLEDGEMENTS

As always, my sincere and grateful thanks go to my agent, Camilla Bolton at Darley Anderson and to all at Severn House Publishers.

I also want to acknowledge two people to whom I am eternally grateful for so generously sharing their time, professional knowledge and expertise:

Chief Inspector Keith Fackrell, West Midlands Police (Retired) who continues to respond patiently and tirelessly to my queries over several years.

Mark Mastaglio BSc (Hons) Forensic Scientist, Forensic Firearms Consultancy (FFC) Ltd. London who, without knowing me, willingly gave both his time and professional advice.

I am hugely grateful to both Keith and Mark for their help and what they have taught me. Any errors which may have occurred in the writing of this book are solely mine, due to my reluctance to reduce them to shadows of themselves with the hundreds of additional questions I might have asked.

Rule number one: value experts but *don't* wear them out.

Thank you, both.

Lightning Source UK Ltd.
Milton Keynes UK
UKHW011834010921
389863UK00001B/25